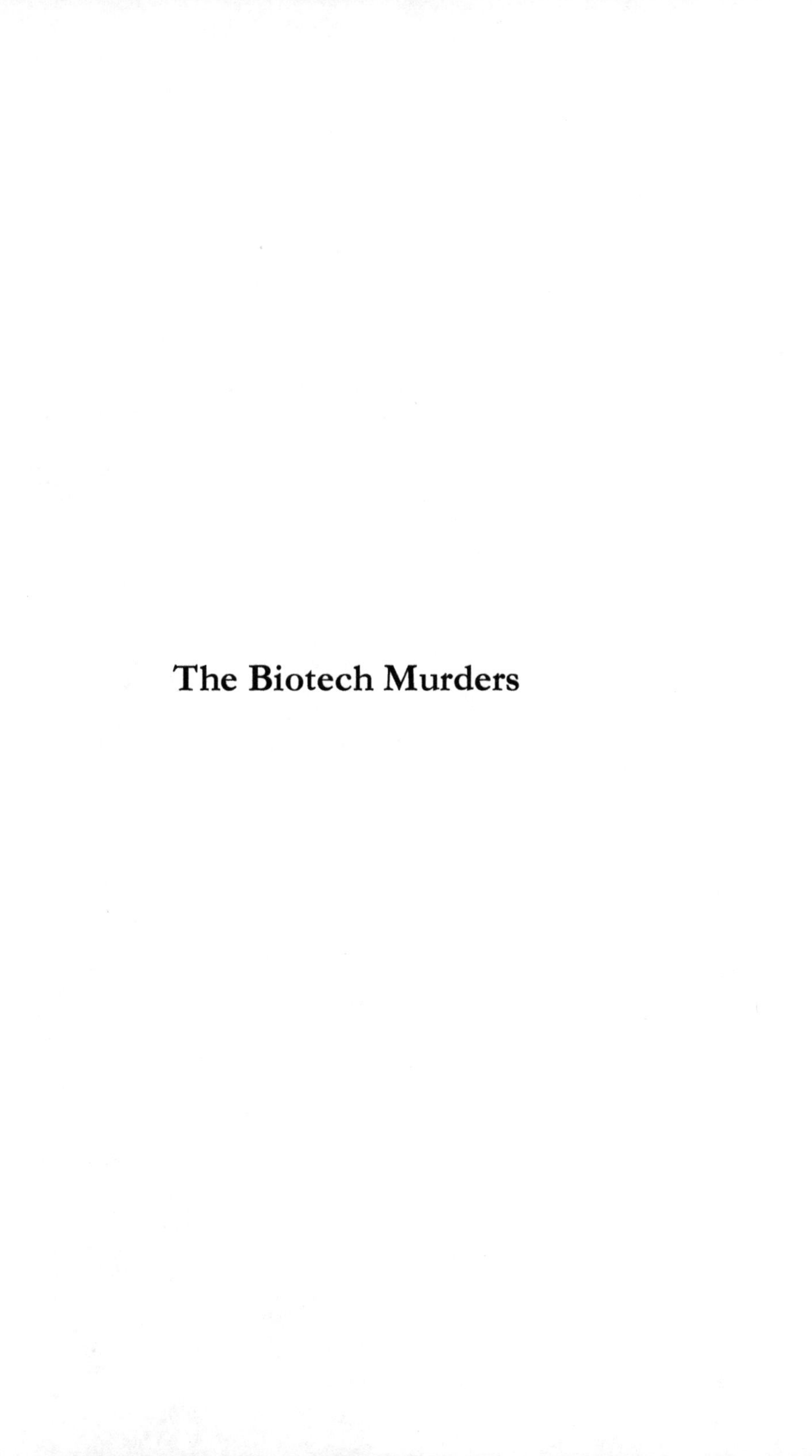

The Biotech Murders

The Biotech Murders

By Ronenn Roubenoff

Roubenoff Writing
Brookline, Massachusetts, USA
2026

Printed in the United States of America
ISBN: 979-8-9996619-2-0

Dedication

To Rebecca, for her determination
To Abby, for her love
To Barri, for her bravery
To Laura, for everything

Contents

Prologue

Biotech has changed all our lives. Starting with now seemingly primitive tools of molecular biology in the 1970's, through the Human Genome Project in the 1990's, and to gene editing in living people today, this industry has invented cures for diseases that were previously death sentences. If you know anyone with cancer, arthritis, psoriasis, obesity, or colitis, they're probably being treated with a biotech drug, and are better off for it. The RNA vaccines for Covid-19 saved millions of lives around the world and were invented, tested, and widely distributed in record time.

But like any human endeavor, biotech has good guys and bad ones. There is greed, jealousy, pettiness, and hatred, alongside brilliance and creativity. This story is fictional, but it is based on people I met and events I experienced during almost a quarter century in biotech. That was plenty of time to meet people one would like to knock off, but so far, no one has gotten away with murder. At least, as far as I know…

Chapter One, Tuesday Morning, May 23rd

Maggie Thompson was running late. Even doing the reverse commute up I-93 from Boston to Woburn would be slow today. There was an accident at the Medford exit, so it would be a good 45 minutes, plus the extra 10 minutes at Dunkin Donuts. As she did most mornings, Maggie used the time to catch up on voice mails and other bits of her life that threatened to slip out of control, much like her unruly brown hair. She had dealt with the hair by chopping it back to pixie length, which was also useful to avoid giving creeps a handhold.

I wish I could do that with other things, she thought, half-listening to another rambling voicemail from her mother in California, where she had decamped with her most recent boyfriend, some dimwit about Maggie's age who was supposed to be an actor. Or was it author? Artist? Starving one, whatever he was, relying on Jessica's life-insurance money, such as it was.

There was a reminder call from her doctor's office for her annual Pap smear (yuck), and three texts from her best friend Emily about dinner tomorrow night (not yuck), and how she was inviting a blind date for Maggie (well, probably yuck). In the moveable parking lot that was Interstate 93 North at 8:30 a.m. on a Tuesday, she angled the rear-view mirror to apply pale pink lipstick, one eye on the car ahead and telling herself that as a State Trooper she better not rear-end someone, or she'd never hear the end of it.

But it was the brown air, full of smoke, that really kept this from being a normal day, Maggie thought. A thousand miles away in Canada, a forest the size of West Virginia was going up in flames. The fires had sent a fug of toxic smoke southeast, covering the eastern United States with a brown haze that filled emergency rooms with respiratory cases, forced the cancelation of outdoor activities, and closed schools from Bangor to Baltimore. Radio and TV were full of dire warnings about health hazards that had people reaching for masks they had gratefully put away after the Covid-19 pandemic ended.

The hazy air, smelling like a day-after-party ashtray, must have made everyone crabby, and the Massholes were driving even worse than usual. She shrugged, eyeing herself in the mirror again – not bad for a 30-year-old single girl (her mother's voice in that thought). At 5'10" and 150 pounds, she was able to handle most perps without too much difficulty, thanks to 20 years of martial arts training and a naturally lithe and athletic body. Her somewhat severe face, punctuated by a pointed chin and nose that had been broken once too many times (meaning, once), was relieved by large, laughing eyes so light brown as to be almost lioness-tawny. Her dad used to say she had hazel eyes, just like his. They had lulled more than one suspect into talking a bit too much.

Half an hour later, she parked her blue Ford Explorer outside the bland fortress-like building in a Woburn industrial park that housed the Middlesex District Attorney's office. She made a face as the smoke-laden air hit her lungs, no longer protected by the car's air conditioning, and hurried inside, balancing a cardboard Dunkin Donuts tray with 4 large coffees in one hand; a bag of donuts, ID badge, and cell phone in the other; a backpack on one shoulder; and her Smith & Wesson M&P45 inside its holster under her blue blazer on the other shoulder.

Badging her way through the double bulletproof glass doors at the entrance, she nod-smiled to Sandra at the reception desk, noted it was 9:05 on the clock above Sandra's head, and went through to the Homicide & Unsolved Unit on the ground floor. She plopped the tray and donuts down on her desk and shrugged her backpack off her shoulder onto her chair.

"Hey, Sarge, thanks! You're a life saver," smiled Detective Eddie Bushell, putting down his cell phone with its perennially cracked screen and reaching across his desk for the donut bag. "And good timing – we can skip the morning conference today, we've got a body out at the Fells."

"Seriously? An outdoor scene with that crap in the air? The air is fucking *beige*, and it smells like one of L-T's cigars. Couldn't you arrange a nice, air-conditioned hotel room murder?" asked Maggie.

"Sorry, blame Jimmy. He caught the call." Jimmy O'Connor was the other detective trooper in Maggie's team, one of three State Police homicide detective teams in the Woburn office. In contrast to Eddie, who was small and dark, Jimmy was 6'4" of muscle, white-blond hair, and intense blue eyes. Now he separated the coffees from the tray, handing each out according to the hieroglyphics on the plastic covers, leaving one on the desk of their supervisor, Lieutenant Mike Davis.

"What do we know? Male or female?" asked Maggie.

"Yes," said Eddie, deadpan. "One of those".

"Hah hah. Did you need Chat GPT to figure that out?"

"Evidently they can't tell. They say the body is wrapped – like in cellophane or something."

"What?" Maggie shot him a look to see if he was making this up, but Eddie just raised his hands, as pure and innocent as can be. She shrugged. "I knew this was going to be a strange day, with that brown sky."

In Massachusetts the responsibility for investigating any unexplained death lay with the District Attorney for the county where the body was found. Each DA's office had a group of State Police detectives assigned to it. Only a few big cities – Boston, Cambridge, a few others – had enough resources (and enough murders) to have their own homicide detectives. Anywhere else in the state, it was up to the State Police. Middlesex County DA homicide teams covered 850 square miles and 1.6 million residents. The teams were not short of work.

Maggie Thompson had been with the State Police for nine years, undercover for two of them, and a death investigator with Middlesex DA for three. She had been promoted to sergeant and team leader a year earlier. Most days, she loved her job.

* * *

Jimmy pulled the unmarked Ford SUV into the parking lot of the Botume House Visitor Center, at the western edge of the Middlesex Fells Reservation. There were two marked State Police cruisers in the lot already, and one of the troopers was waiting there with a Ranger. The other, Maggie hoped, was securing the scene. As the sun rose higher and the air turned warmer, it made the air even hazier and more acrid than before.

Only 10 miles north of Boston, Middlesex Fells stretched over two thousand acres of wilderness spanning five towns, with lakes and ponds to fish, hills and trails to hike, and enough birds to keep birdwatchers busy year-round. Even though it is bisected by Interstate 93, the Reservation is big, beautiful, and many parts are surprisingly isolated for a place so close to a major city and surrounded by suburbs.

The Ranger's name was Chuck Angely, and it was he who had called in the cops. The Department of Conservation and Recreation had decided to close all parks until further notice due to the hazardous air. Chuck had been sent to walk through his section of the Middlesex Fells Reservation, clear out any hikers or fishermen, and lock the gates.

Introductions made, the group followed Chuck past a manicured lawn and onto a trail that led into the woods. Maggie absently noted the steady hum of insects and chittering of squirrels and chipmunks. A blue jay scolded them for interrupting its breakfast. Through gaps in the trees and tall grasses, they could see the blue water of the reservoir, now muted by the brown air, which smelled like a dying fire and tasted like burnt hot dog. Even though the trail was hard dirt and shale stones, Maggie made them walk single file to minimize their footsteps, as it wasn't clear yet what the crime scene boundaries would turn out to be. A cardinal flew by in a streak of red.

Four hundred yards down the trail Chuck led them toward the Tudor Barn, an abandoned stone building standing in a clearing off the trail. The Barn was a common meeting spot for hikers, and for less savory activities as well. Because of the latter, the windows had been nailed shut with red-painted plywood and the door padlocked.

The Barn, about twenty feet wide and ten deep, looked like a house drawn by a child, with grey granite walls, a sloping black shingle roof, a center double door surmounted by a square window, a larger rectangular window to the right of the center door, and a smaller single door to the left. The windows, instead of glass, were closed by vertical wooden planks painted a brownish red and fitting tightly into wooden frames. Everything was closed except the left side smaller door, now open, which was held in place by three foot-long iron strap hinges on the left jamb, with a padlock hanging from a loosely mounted hasp on the right one.

"That's what made me suspicious," Chuck said, pointing to the door. "It was shut tight last time I checked it, but somebody's been messing with the lock. This happens once in a while – usually kids looking for a place to get high."

"When did you last see it intact?" Maggie asked.

"I was off Sunday and Monday, so it must have been Saturday. Saturday afternoon, I would say."

Standing at the edge of the lawn between the trail and the house, Maggie paused and held the others back. Absently, she noted a hummingbird hovering in front of a foxglove plant, beak inside a purple flower. Slapping at an insect buzzing behind his ear, Eddie opened a black suitcase he'd been carrying and distributed booties and spacesuits, and Jimmy put a yellow numbered inverted-V shaped site tag down along on the grassy verge below the dangling hasp and padlock. A uniformed trooper was standing by the open door. Maggie noted he had already equipped himself with a clipboard and pen to record who was entering the crime scene, and though it wasn't yet bordered with black-and-yellow police tape, he had a roll of it under one arm. The perennial background music of the State Police dispatcher came too loudly from a two-way radio on his hip.

"Morning, Joe," Jimmy said to the uniformed trooper. "Anybody been around before we got here?"

"No," said Joe. "Nobody here but us field mice."

Once they had the white polypropylene suits and surgical masks on, making the warm day even hotter, and their shoes covered by white plastic booties, the team moved into the barn. Until Crime Scene Services showed up with lights and a portable generator, they would have to use their flashlights. That increased the risk of missing something, or worse, of contaminating or destroying evidence. They moved slowly and methodically, looking at their feet and flashing the lights just in front of each step before addressing the body on the floor.

It was almost pitch black inside the barn, with the only light coming from the open door, and from a few chinks in the wood of the windows. A shiny blue bundle lay on the floor in the middle of the room, wrapped in blue plastic film, just as Chuck had described it to the 9-1-1 operator. The left end of the bundle was darker than the rest, and the right side stuck up perpendicular to the floor. Maggie poked the film with a gloved finger, running her hand along the body, resisting the unbidden urge to call it Mummy Smurf.

"This is industrial film," she said. "I worked in a lab one summer, and we used this to wrap stuff before freezing it in minus 80 or liquid nitrogen."

"Can't be hard to get," offered Jimmy. "Doesn't help narrow things down much, does it? Anything else that could identify the vic in here?" He scanned his light along the perimeter of the room and up and down the walls.

"I don't see anything except a lot of cobwebs," said Eddie.

"Call OCME, Jimmy," said Maggie, referring to the state Office of the Chief Medical Examiner. "We need to open this up and take a look at the body, get some ID if we can."

* * *

They still didn't see anything two hours later, but now they could see it a lot better. Crime Scene Services had shown up with floodlights, cameras, and all the paraphernalia of modern crime scene processing. Two technicians, looking like astronauts on the moon, were slowly and meticulously documenting the scene. They had set up a scanner that used lasers and GPS to create a 3-dimensional digital map of the interior of the barn to a resolution of 6 millimeters. A laptop in a shockproof case sat on the ground, showing the data acquisition in progress.

The Medical Examiner on duty, Dr. Shirley Kung, came trudging up the path with two additional technicians in tow, who were guiding a bouncing gurney along the narrow, stony road. They had cases on the gurney as well as one the doctor carried, and they weren't looking too happy.

"So much for that 45-minute response time, huh Doc?" said Eddie with a smile.

"Tell me about it, Eddie. Another collision on I-93, right by TD Garden. I think this smoke has people hypoxic – their brains can't function right and they're driving even worse than usual." Shirley Kung was a petite Korean-American pathologist, usually vivacious and easygoing, but, Maggie knew, very sharp and observant.

After a cursory look around, Shirley knelt by the body, pulling a scalpel out of her black Haliburton case. "You all done?" she asked one of the crime scene techs, who nodded. "OK, let's go," she said, making an incision in the plastic wrap lengthwise from one end to the other. There was a sickly-sweet whiff of deco stench – decomposition of the body – that hit them immediately, but not as bad as it could be. The team gathered around anyway as she started describing her every move into a digital recorder.

"Asian female, appears about 50 years old, black hair, eyes closed. Lying supine, arms at sides, wearing light jogging clothes and running shoes. No obvious trauma from this angle. No blood. What's the ambient?"

"Seventy-seven now," replied one of the technicians.

"OK, thanks. Clearly there is rigor mortis. Liver temp…" she pushed an instant-read thermometer under the ribs on the right side of the body, "…is 84 degrees Fahrenheit. Mild corneal clouding. Livor mortis is present and looks fixed, but no obvious bloating. Not great dental work – could be foreign in origin." She looked up at Maggie. "We can turn her over now, unless you see anything else."

"Any ID in the pockets?" asked Maggie. Shirley patted the Lycra pants and matching Nike zippered jacket, which were in a bright fuchsia and purple, but oxymoronically in a camouflage pattern. She unzipped the jacket to reveal a sleeveless black mesh top.

"Nothing," she said. "No watch either."

Maggie nodded. With help from one of the technicians holding down the plastic wrap, Shirley gently turned the corpse on its side. "Looks like blunt trauma to the back of the head. Matted blood and hair at the occipital bone." She felt the head with one gloved hand. "Suggestion of bone crush and some crepitation in this area." She lowered the body gently onto its back.

Maggie raised an eyebrow. Shirley shrugged her shoulders and said, "I'm guessing now, but death probably occurred 12-18 hours ago. Rigor mortis is present, livor mortis and corneal clouding are present, but no abdominal bloating. Of course, this modern mummy wrapping is messing everything up – I could be off by a day or two. I'll know more after we do the full autopsy."

"I wonder if somebody knew that, about the wrapping messing things up," Maggie mused. "No ID, no keys, no watch or phone. Who goes running without their phone?" She looked down at the corpse. "Lady, who the hell are you, and how did you wind up here?"

No one answered, but one of the Crime Scene Service techs had brought a small black box with a glass top, about the size of a Rubik's cube, that he connected by a wire to the laptop. It was a biometric fingerprint scanner, and he proceeded to roll each finger slowly on the scanner to capture postmortem prints. If they were lucky, they had found the body early enough after death that these would still be readable. And if they were luckier, the victim had some interaction with the law that would have put her fingerprints into AFIS, the automated fingerprint identification system. Not necessarily as a criminal. People get fingerprinted for all sorts of reasons: for visas into the US if they are from abroad, or if they want to adopt a child, or get a Global Entry card, or a dozen other law-abiding reasons. And of course, for law-breaking reasons as well. It would take a few minutes for the Crime Scene tech to load the scans into the system and start running a match.

Shirley stood up and motioned to her two assistants, who brought the gurney into the room and started to move the body, first into a body bag and then onto the gurney for the journey back to the Medical Examiner's truck in the parking lot. Maggie, Eddie, and Jimmy stepped out into the bright sepia light outside, blinking even after the klieg lights of the Crime Scene Services setup inside.

"How did she get here?" Maggie asked. "Do we have video cameras at the Visitor's Center parking lot?"

Joe had left his post by the door and had the laptop open on a nearby boulder. He looked up. "Yes, and there's another parking lot just south of here, at the Flynn Rink. No ice skating or hockey now that the season's over, so it's pretty quiet there. I'll ask somebody to retrieve the tapes." He reached for the walkie-talkie on his belt. At that moment, the computer pinged.

"Looks like we have an ID," he said, as the detectives approached.

"Great! Who is she?" asked Maggie.

Joe was peering at the screen. "Ling Tzu Zhao, a.k.a. Lilly Zhao, age 51. Home address 75 Shore Drive, Somerville. That's like ten minutes from here. Married, one daughter, age 20. Naturalized US citizen. No Wants and Warrants. Not even a parking ticket. Employer is something called Quercus Therapeutics, however you say that, in Cambridge."

"Oh, shit," said Maggie. "That's my brother's company."

She couldn't see Eddie and Jimmy exchanging startled looks behind her, clearly shocked by her announcement.

*   *   *

This is not going to go down well, Benny Mason thought. He was sitting in what they called simply the "Large Conference Room" at Quercus Therapeutics, on Sidney Street in Cambridge. It was a little after 10 in the morning, and this meeting had been going on for over an hour. There were perhaps a dozen Quercus "associates", as Human Resources insisted they be called, sitting around a series of narrow white tables connected into a large U shape, facing two stadium-sized video screens. The room lights were reduced to movie theater dimness. One of the screens showed faces of additional colleagues who were dialing in by video call; the other showed a slide with graphs, histological sections, and immunohistochemistry pictures. It was the second screen that was making Benny groan, this time audibly.

"What's up?" asked Rob Handler, sitting next to Benny. They were on one corner of the U, sitting at 90 degrees to each other so they could speak quietly and without being overheard. Aside from Benny, Rob was the only physician in the company, and headed up the medical section in Benny's Clinical Development group. Actually, he was the entire medical section. Where Benny was small, dark-haired, forty-five, and a mixture of Asian and Caucasian backgrounds, Rob was all Northern European – red hair, freckles, blue eyes, fair skin. Ten years younger than Benny and new to biotech, Rob was learning fast. Because Quercus didn't have any drugs in the clinic yet, Rob didn't really have anything medical to do, so he was mostly shadowing Benny and planning for the upcoming studies.

"This is where Clinical makes enemies," Benny answered, *sotto voce*. More loudly he raised his hand and said "Lisa?"

Lisa Clark was presenting the data, standing in front of the table and to the side of the video screens. Late 30's, Yale PhD and Harvard post-doc, she had risen to be head of Research at Quercus quickly, but, it seemed to Benny, she sometimes got ahead of her data. In the world of biotech and pharma, that wasn't a compliment – like a skier getting ahead of their skis, it would lead to a fall. And while Benny thought Lisa was pretty good on biologics like their lead compound, QT-101, now she was trying to push a small molecule program into humans, ironically a much bigger challenge. Still, they were technically equals, both reporting to Jorge Perez, the head of R&D at Quercus. In Benny's opinion, Jorge was another kettle of fish altogether. Lisa nodded to Benny now to continue.

"So we would have some problems with taking this molecule into humans, if that kinase panel is right. We've got at least three major flags there. I don't think we can move this ahead to a development candidate if these problems also show up *in vivo*, in mice I mean. Sorry to be Debbie Downer here, but I think we need more time in lead op." Lead optimization is where the chemists played around with the structure of a potential drug to tweak out undesirable effects and tune in good ones. Medicinal chemistry had gotten so good, that if researchers could draw a molecule, they could usually make it. But it could take years. Quercus didn't have years.

The room was silent now, the video faces still and intent, not reading or writing emails for once. Since Benny was in essence Lisa's internal customer, he had the final word – if Clinical wouldn't accept it, Lisa's program would die on the vine. Next to Benny, Rob stirred uncomfortably in his seat, but Benny sat still patiently, a benign smile on his lips but his eyes boring into Lisa's unapologetically.

Jorge, sitting in the middle of the crossbar of the U-shaped table, broke the silence with a hearty "Well! Why don't we take a ten-minute bio-break? We can come back to this discussion after that." He stood up, not waiting for a response, pushing a button on the panel in front of him on the table that raised the room lights to full and another to mute the microphones, cutting off the people on video from hearing what was being said in the room. Chairs were pushed back, voices rose, people grabbed their mugs and headed for the hallway common area with its coffee and soda machines.

Benny turned to Rob with a smile and whispered, "Run! Save yourself! Bring me back a black coffee with one fake sugar." Rob nodded and ambled away.

Lisa advanced on Benny from the presenter side of the table, while Jorge came at his flank. They both looked down on the small, seated man, who seemed unfazed. Lisa was no taller than Benny, about 5'5", but Jorge was a lean six feet, with dark hair and the knotted muscles of a gym rat. Benny knew Jorge was a fitness fanatic. He lifted weights at a gym around the corner from Quercus at lunch every day. He cycled in from Wellesley to Cambridge every day, rain or shine, 15 miles round trip, a feat even more impressive considering the nonzero mortality risk that went with riding a bicycle through Boston traffic.

"Benny, I think you're being a little conservative here," Lisa said, clearly trying to stay calm and sounding a bit like a nanny reasoning with a recalcitrant four-year-old. "I'm sure we can work these issues out in parallel to the IND-enabling tox." The Food and Drug Administration, or FDA, requires that any drug going into humans be tested for toxicology, or tox, to show it was safe for the animals at doses 10-30 times higher than the dose expected to be used in humans. The drug would have to pass this test in two animal species before an Investigational New Drug, or IND, application could be approved to allow human testing. And these animal studies had to be meticulously documented with a continuous electronic audit trail, a process called Good Laboratory Practice, or GLP, which doubled the cost and time that the experiments would take. But without that, no drug candidate could go into patients. That process normally took six to 12 months and cost about a million dollars.

Benny shook his head. "I think the risk is too high, Lisa. It's more than likely we'll fail in GLP tox and have to start again. That's about a million bucks down the drain, that I don't have in the Development budget. Sorry."

Lisa opened her mouth to rebut this, but Jorge put a proprietary hand on her shoulder and said in a low but urgent tone, "Benny, I know approving a Development Candidate is your decision as head of Clinical, but we have to be practical. We're going public with an initial public offering next month, and if we don't have a new DC, we don't have an inflection point on which to pin it. It could cost us millions. With the DC, and the IPO, I'm sure we can cover the cost in your budget."

"And how will it look when it fails in tox, Jorge?" asked Benny. "You know, at Pfizer we'd never approve something like this."

"You're not *at* Pfizer anymore, Benny!" Jorge leaned over him. "You wanted to get away from Big Pharma and the bureaucracy and politics, didn't you? That's why you're here, right? Forty people instead of forty thousand, or whatever. Move fast and break things. Well, that's how we do things at Quercus. Look at the efficacy in the animal models – Lisa's got a really revolutionary drug here. There's nothing out there that has such strong effects in the mouse model, and you know it!"

Lisa nodded, but Benny sat still. "If only mice had insurance, we'd all be rich," he said calmly. "Look, this model has been used for years, and lots of drugs have worked in it but failed in humans. The tox is much more likely to translate into human injury than the model is into benefit. I'm sorry. Let's give it another couple of months and see if you can tweak out the kinase inhibition."

"You don't really know the tox will be an issue at this point, Benny," Lisa said.

"Oh, so our strategy is to get lucky, is that it?" he shot back.

"And the IPO?" asked Lisa. "We need the funding to keep going, Benny. You know that."

"OK," said Benny. "Shall we take this up with Thomas? I'm sure the CSO will have an opinion, don't you think?"

Jorge turned a shade pale, while Lisa stepped back and compressed her lips in a thin line.

"I'm sure we can settle this ourselves, Benny," Jorge said after a pause. "It's a research matter, really, not strategic at this point."

"Don't be so glum, guys," said Benny. "After all, this is a backup program. The lead is still good, right? I bet we can raise all the cash we need on the back of QT-101. That's the frontrunner anyway, and it's almost in the clinic, remember?" He stood up. "Sorry, I have another meeting to go to," he said, gathering his laptop and notebook. "See you later."

*　　　　*　　　　*

The house on Shore Drive was a modest three-story white clapboard building, with a one-car garage at the end of a short driveway at street level, a flight of white-painted stairs leading to the entrance on the first floor, and what looked like a couple of bedrooms above it. The garage door was white-painted wood, without windows. The driveway was empty.

A series of identical houses, differing only in color, lined the block, and it looked like a nice if not high-end neighborhood. Maggie noticed that the cars parked along the street were mostly late model, clean but not fancy – Toyotas, Hondas, and Fords, not Audis or BMW's. Jimmy had arranged for a Somerville Police cruiser to meet them there, in the interests of good interdepartmental relations, and a black-and-white was waiting at the curb when the detectives arrived.

Two uniformed cops stepped out of the cruiser and introduced themselves as Murphy and Gonzalez, and the state troopers explained their errand. It was warmer now, well over 80 degrees, but the sky was a darker brown, giving everything a darkness-at-noon, solar eclipse vibe. Murphy grimaced as he inhaled the acrid air and put on a black face mask. Maggie idly wondered if that would do any good at all against smoke and whatever nanoparticles came with it. He went around the back of the house while Gonzalez preceded the detectives up the steps. There was no response to the doorbell, nor to knocking. Looking through the glass part of the front door and the adjacent windows showed no lights on, and it sure seemed like nobody was home. Murphy came back and shook his head to say that there was no evidence of anyone home from that side either.

As they regrouped on the driveway, Maggie said, "OK, let's canvass the neighbors – if you guys can do that, along with Jimmy? Eddie, get hold of the ADA on duty for the search warrant team, and let's get permission to enter. I'm going to Cambridge to check on Lilly Zhao's work site. I'll take the car now, and come back here ASAP. Let me know when you have the SW, and unless one of the neighbors has a key we'll need a locksmith too."

It was only about 15 minutes by car from Shore Drive to Sidney Street in Cambridge. Nice commute, thought Maggie as she wandered through the back streets of Somerville and into the biotech hub behind MIT. She considered calling Benny first, but decided that a bit of surprise could be an advantage. After all, she hadn't seen or spoken to her brother – half-brother really – in three years. Since their father's funeral, as a matter of fact.

Chapter Two, Tuesday Afternoon, May 23rd

Quercus Therapeutics took up two stories of a research building on Sydney Street, all red brick and reflective green glass. The reception area was on the ground floor. A couple of video screens flanked a security counter, scrolling upbeat messages with smiling families extolling all the good that Quercus was doing, or planning to do, or that would just be nice if they happened. A smiling receptionist with multicolored dreadlocks welcomed Maggie and telephoned Benny for her, indicating she should wait in one of the Herman Miller chairs until he came down.

She was startled to see that Benny had grayed at the temples, and his face looked drawn. He wore silver wire-rim glasses. Maggie stood about six inches taller than her brother. Benny's mother had been Vietnamese, petite, and from the pictures Maggie had seen, very pretty. She had died 12 years before Maggie was born. Their father, Henry Mason, had been an Army captain during the Vietnam war, and had found himself in a very nasty place indeed, at the Battle of Fire Support Base Ripcord, in July 1972. Wounded, he was evacuated to Saigon, where he met a vivacious army nurse named Hue Bac Nguyen, who the GI's of course called Way Back When.

Unlike most GI romances, this one stuck. Henry brought Hue back home to Vermont, and they got married. Benny was born in 1978, but Hue developed lupus, and died of kidney and heart failure when Benny was six. Bereft, Henry doted on his son when he thought about it, but spent most of his time working a series of teaching jobs and writing science fiction stories that sometimes even got published in long-vanished magazines. Inevitably perhaps, after his mother died, Benny had been drawn to medicine. One day in 1993 Henry shocked Benny by announcing that he was going to marry Jessica Thompson, a fellow schoolteacher 23 years younger and already pregnant with Maggie. It wasn't an auspicious beginning to a brother-sister relationship.

He approached her now with a tight smile. "Maggie? What a surprise…I wasn't expecting…"

"No, I know you weren't. Is there somewhere we can talk privately? This is kind of a business call."

"Uh, sure. Come this way." He badged them in through a double glass door at the far end of the entrance foyer and up a curving staircase of blond wood, glass, and chrome that led up to the second and third floors. On the second floor, he ushered her into a small glass-walled conference room with four seats around a central table. He sat stiffly, looking a bit over Maggie's right ear.

"How long have you worked here, Benny?" Maggie asked.

"About nine months now. The company was moving into the clinic with our first drug candidate and they needed someone to lead clinical development. That means, pick what disease to try and treat, design the studies, write the phase 1 protocol, write the IND, line up the CRO's, et cetera. So I came up from Pfizer, hired a couple of people, and we're off to the races."

"I don't even know what any of that stuff is. Why is it called Quercus, anyway? What does that even mean?"

"It's the Latin name for oak. You know, from little acorns mighty oaks grow? Seems a little, um, aspirational. But it's gotten really hard to find names for biotechs, you know? All the easy ones are taken."

Maggie nodded. "Do you know someone here named Lilly Zhao?"

"Sure, she's our head of toxicology. Actually, she's kind of our entire safety department. I think she's on vacation this week. Why? I can't imagine she's in any trouble, is she?"

"She's missing. I'm looking for information on family, someone who might know where she might be. I can come back with a warrant, but it seemed easier to just come ask."

He looked directly at her now. "Missing? How can that be? Are you sure?" She didn't bother to answer that, knowing he would go on. The handiest tool in an interrogator's kit, she could hear her instructor at the Police Academy saying, is silence.

"I had lunch with her last week, on Monday, I think, and she was fine. Her husband is back in China, visiting his parents for like a month. He's a pretty well-known cancer researcher at Dana Farber, name's Vincent…Vincent Chen. They have one daughter, she's at Stanford, I think. Lilly was going to take time off at the end of the week to help her move back here for the summer. I bet that's where she is, in Palo Alto. Have you tried there?"

"I will, thanks. Do you happen to know the daughter's name? I guess her last name would be Chen, right?"

"I don't, but you know, Lilly has a newspaper clipping on her cubicle wall about her daughter being valedictorian of her high school. I've seen it there a hundred times. Let's go up and get it." He stood up, ready to walk out.

"Hang on a minute. Do you know why anyone would want to harm Lilly? Did she have enemies here? Did she mention anything about trouble at home? Neighbors? Stalkers?"

Benny looked shocked. "Wow, what a world you live in, Maggie. This is Cambridge. Biotech Central, you know? People here fight about budgets and data, but the worst harm is an anonymous post on the Café Pharma website."

She smiled. "Too much time hanging around with criminals – it's an occupational hazard."

She stood up and followed Benny out to the common area, which had open-space desks in clusters of four, separated by chest-high gray partitions. There were a few people around, but most of the desks seemed empty, at least at the moment. Benny led her to a corner of the second floor.

"That's Lilly 's desk there, in the back. She wanted as much quiet as you can get in an open-plan office. Here's the newspaper clipping I was telling you about. Her daughter is Stephanie. Stephanie Chen. Stanford class of 2026. Lilly is very proud."

Maggie nodded. The terrible damage caused by murder never ceased to disgust her: not just the victim who loses her future, but everyone close to her who must live with the results. This young woman she had never met would never be the same.

"Thanks, Benny," she said, copying the name into a small spiral notebook. "That's really helpful. I'll get after finding her. You said she's an only child?"

"Yes, as far as I know," Benny said. "Lilly talks about her a lot, but not about any other kids."

She looked into his eyes purposefully. "Well, we didn't talk to our friends about having a sibling when we were younger, did we? I don't think most of my friends after high school even know you exist. Do you tell anyone about me? I guess we're about as distant as siblings get, aren't we?"

Benny's face softened, though he didn't smile back. "Well, fifteen years age difference, right? Different mothers. Different last names, too – at your mother's insistence, as I recall. And I was out of the house by the time you were two or three – it's not like we grew up together. But still, family counts. I'm sorry I didn't get in touch when I came back to Boston. I…I wasn't sure you'd want me to."

I'm not sure either, Maggie thought. "Well, you kind of disappeared from my life on your first day of college," she said. "Yet, here we are."

"How about dinner? Maybe tonight? We can catch up," he waved a hand, "away from here."

Maggie nodded slowly. "I guess so. Dad's gone, my mom's in California ditzing around after some idiot boyfriend. I just broke up with mine a few months ago. It would be nice to get to know each other as grownups, you know?" Which was true, but didn't prevent her from lying – or at least not telling the whole truth – to her brother, or half-brother. And he's also a suspect, she thought, until proven otherwise.

* * *

By the time Maggie got back to Shore Drive, Eddie had obtained a search warrant and Jimmy had found a next-door neighbor who had the spare keys to Lilly's house. They were already inside when she arrived. The place was old, but well cared-for: the roof was new-looking, and the stairs, though a little saggy, had been painted recently. There was a three-year-old Honda Accord in the garage, locked and benign-looking. Inside, nothing looked disturbed, there were no turned-over lamps or ripped cushions, no smell of cooking nor of decomposition, either. It looked like the occupants were on vacation.

Jimmy turned to Maggie as she walked in, "Crime Scene Services are on their way. I figure we can fingerprint some high-likelihood areas and then get out."

Maggie nodded, looking around as she went upstairs, pulling on a pair of nitryl gloves she had fished out of her backpack as she went. She found a bedroom being used as an office and sat in a rolling chair, closing her eyes, and inhaling deeply. Cleansing breath, she thought as she opened her eyes.

There were two desks in the room, each with its own laptop docking station and monitor, a filing cabinet, a couple of Chinese prints of mountain scenes with a paragraph of Mandarin to one side. One of the desks had several piles of papers with Dana Farber Cancer Institute letterhead, along with DeVita's textbook of oncology and a precarious stack of medical journals. The docking station on this desk was empty – no computer. Assuming that was the husband's, and he'd taken his computer to China with him, she turned to the other desk.

This one was almost bare – a yellow notepad with some scribbled numbers, dates, and a few words she didn't understand; a block of sticky notes that was unmarked; a photo of a grinning young woman in a bright scarlet graduation cap and gown, and a laptop docking station, also empty. In the top drawer she found a lanyard with a Quercus Therapeutics ID with a smiling photo of Lilly. The side drawers were mostly stationary supplies above, and files with what looked like scientific manuscripts, correspondence, and miscellaneous papers below.

Nothing here of any use, Maggie thought, pulling off her gloves. That figures. It would be too easy if there was a big envelope labeled "Clue" in the drawer, wouldn't it? She stayed in Lilly's chair, putting her hands behind her head to avoid touching anything, pursing her lips and taking slow deep breaths, swinging the chair from side to side in an arc. Communing with the departed, her old boss used to say. Maggie smiled crookedly – no psychic messages here, she thought, getting up from the chair.

Downstairs she found Jimmy talking to the Crime Scene techs who had just arrived, arranging with them to fingerprint doorknobs and the office desks. Eddie came in from canvassing the neighbors as they were speaking.

"I found a couple of neighbors at home. Family here goes by Chen, not Zhao. Quiet, no trouble with neighbors, keep to themselves pretty much. Lady next door is the one I got the housekey from. She watches the place if they're away and vice versa. Says the husband is visiting family in China, and the daughter's in college in California. Doesn't know about the vic being away or anything. Last saw her a couple of days ago, thinks it was Monday, coming back from work around four in the afternoon."

"Okay, that fits with what I heard at her work," said Maggie, "though they said that she might be going to California this week to help move her daughter back at the end of term. If she was supposed to be on a flight to San Francisco already, the daughter may be frantic. We have to find a number for her, and for the husband."

"I didn't see any video cameras on the street," Eddie said. "This is a residential neighborhood, no businesses or parking lots. How about smart doorbells? I'll ask the Somerville guys to check the houses around us, see if anyone has video from the past 48 hours."

Maggie nodded, looking at her watch. "Good idea. Look, it's 3:30 now. Let's wrap up here and debrief back at the fort with L-T. I've got a dinner date later to learn more about her workplace." L-T was short for Lieutenant Mike Davis, head of their detective unit; the fort was the bunker-like office building in Woburn.

* * *

Jimmy drove them back, with Maggie riding shotgun and Eddie in the back seat. The air was still brown, and their eyes were tearing just from the walk to the car from Lilly's house.

"Air smells like ass," Jimmy said gruffly. "Like one of L-T's cigars."

They drove in silence for a few moments, letting the car's air conditioner filter out some of the pollution outside.

"So Sarge," Eddie piped up behind her. "We've been working together what, three plus years, right? And this is the first we hear that you have a brother? Seriously?"

Maggie groaned inwardly, but kept her composure. "Um, I guess it never came up, Eddie." After all, I try not to think about it myself.

"Well, you've met our families, right?" Eddie went on, while Jimmy nodded as he drove. "I don't think we've ever met yours, have we?"

"Well, you've met my best friend Emily, guys. She's really my closest family – sister by another mother, et cetera."

She knew that Jimmy and his wife Katherine had twin nine-year-old boys. She'd been to their home and seen Thing One and Thing Two – er, Coby and Jason – in action. And Eddie was divorced from she-who-must-not-be-named Shannon but they both tried hard to be civil when it came to raising their now-sixteen-year-old daughter. They were right, she realized. She had always compartmentalized them off from her family for a few reasons. First, since her father had died, she found mostly pain in dealing with her mother; she loved her father's brother, Uncle George, but only saw him sporadically, since he lived down on Cape Cod; and she had had no contact with her brother Benny since their father's funeral.

Second, there was her innate need for self-control, and control of her narrative. She knew it wasn't her best feature, but her instinctive reaction was to put up walls and let strangers in only after a thorough vetting. That certainly wasn't an issue with Jimmy and Eddie, though. They were her partners and teammates. It was just force of habit.

"You're right, you guys. My dad died before I was transferred to Woburn and started working with you, and I just kept that whole side of my life in a box. There's not much to know. My mother is in California with some younger dude. My brother Benny is actually my half-brother. He's 15 years older than me, and his mom died way before I was born. He left for college when I was about three, and I've barely seen him since."

They drove on in silence for a while, until Jimmy sighed. "Okay, Sarge, you get a pass for now. But you better show up at our Fourth of July picnic with either Emily or a date."

*   *   *

Mike Davis was a burly Black man in his early fifties with prematurely white hair, but smooth, unwrinkled skin, and deep-set eyes that betrayed nothing. He wasn't a good enough politician to be promoted to captain, but he was a damned good homicide detective, and his current job was all he wanted. He had three kids in college at the same time, and when he wasn't overseeing the detectives he was out doing extra details to pay for the kids' tuitions. As usual, he listened to the team's summary of the case without interruption, then asked, "So, what do you think?"

Maggie said, "Look, she was at the Fells, and in jogging clothes. Okay, so she's going jogging. Maybe she went to meet the killer, or maybe she was just out for a run. It's still light out, but not for much longer. It was raining lightly on Monday night, right? Under the trees it wouldn't be as wet, with the shelter from the leaves. But it's darker too. So he comes up behind her, hits her on the head, drags her into the barn. Can't have been many people there anyway, but in the barn he'd have privacy."

Jimmy nodded. "I think whoever killed her thought he was hiding the body for at least a few days. He wrapped her up so she wouldn't smell, and he left her where no one would be likely to go for a long time. If that Ranger hadn't been sent to close the park because of the smoke, she'd still be there."

"Yes, but why not dump her in the river, or bury her in the woods?"

"First, he'd have to drive to the river – it doesn't connect to the Fens. Second, the river is chancy, she could float downstream in a day or two and show up in somebody's back yard. It would be the Charles River, or the Mystic, but neither one is exactly the mighty Mississippi, you know?" Eddie answered. "If he weighs the body down, how does he get her out there without a boat? If he needs a boat, he's better off taking her out to sea. Go out a mile beyond the Boston Harbor Islands and you're in a hundred feet of water. Nobody is going to be finding her there. Maybe he didn't have time to bury her, or he couldn't get far enough out of town without rousing suspicion to do it where she wouldn't be found. Plus, you know how it is, digging a deep hole is hard work if you're alone and only have hand tools. Too shallow and the animals dig her up. Hundreds of people walk their dogs around there. If they're anything like my dog, they have their nose within 6 inches of the ground the whole time. Plus, putting her in the ground in the Fells would take hours, and it's too close to town to assume *nobody* would come by."

Davis grimaced. "He's a pretty cool customer, isn't he? Took her phone, maybe an Apple Watch if she had one. Car keys? How did the vic get there? Did she walk in? Bike? Drive?"

Eddie looked up from his notes. "There's a silver 2017 Toyota Camry registered to her. It wasn't at the house, or in either parking lot at the Fells. We've put out a BOLO for it."

Davis nodded. A BOLO – be on the lookout – would go to all police departments in the six New England states plus New York, for starters. "Good. Check with TSA about the husband. If he's in China, that takes out our automatic lead suspect, right? So what's that leave? Jilted lover? Drugs? Or work-related?"

Jimmy said, "Yeah, I've got the flight query on the list, but it'll have to wait until tomorrow first thing. Kinda hard to think a druggie could do the job Maggie says this lady had. It sounds like detailed and technical work."

Eddie stirred. "Could be some sort of serial killer, though. Could be his first time, and the wrap job is his weird sicko thing that he gets off on."

Maggie wiggled one hand in an equivocating gesture. "The way the body was wrapped doesn't make me think of a drug user, or an upset lover. Makes me think 'scientist', mostly. Serial killer is possible, but we all know they've become pretty rare since the 1990's. The wackos just shoot up schools now. Plus, you can't be a serial killer until you've killed more than one person, right?"

Eddie shrugged. "Gotta start somewhere."

Jimmy blew out a breath through puffed cheeks. "Well, if that's the case, we don't have any leads at all, do we?"

Davis nodded. "Agreed. We have to work the angles we can. If this is a serial killer, we'll find out about it the hard way, when he kills again. Do a computer search just to be sure there haven't been other bodies wrapped in plastic in the past year. Let's hope not."

He turned to Maggie. "So your brother works at this company, huh? Where does that put you?"

Maggie flushed. "Don't make me recuse on this, L-T. My brother – my half-brother actually – and I aren't close. Like I told Jimmy and Eddie, he's 15 years older than me, and I haven't spoken to him in at least three years. But I do know him well enough to be pretty sure he's not a suspect. He's such a boy scout, you know? Boring, really, and a little bit 'on the spectrum', you know what I mean?"

Eddie looked at her. "We all know some murderers like that, Maggie," he said gently.

Davis said, "Look, from what we've seen so far, the work angle looks the most, ah, promising. Maggie, I don't think you should recuse, though I'll talk to the Captain about it and put a note in the file. On the contrary, I think you're going undercover."

Maggie stared at the lieutenant, feeling herself breaking into a mild sweat. "What?"

Davis nodded. "You've done undercover work before, Maggie, as I recall."

She nodded, looking down at her hands. "Yes, two years with a vicious drug gang, remember?" It was not a pleasant memory.

"And you got a promotion and citation out of it, along with putting a bunch of them in prison for a long time. Well, this will be a lot easier. They're much more civilized in Cambridge."

Maggie shook her head to clear it. "Yeah, sure."

Davis smiled. "We'll look for her computer, look at her phone records. Eddie, you track down the husband and daughter. Dana Farber must have a number for him, and if we can get to him, we can find the daughter. Otherwise you can call Stanford directly, but that will probably leak to the press, and I'd rather not go there. But at the same time, we need to understand what's going on in that company. It seems like the most obvious connection to the murder, if we don't think she was involved in organized crime, her husband didn't kill her, and she wasn't just a random victim of some wacko who also happens to carry around a big roll of laboratory film. We'll have to go public with the murder as soon as we've contacted the daughter and husband. Maggie, your brother being there is an opportunity. Find out if he needs a secretary, or convince him that he does. I think you're about to start a new career."

* * *

Maggie's recollection of her father's funeral was a blur. She had seen the death certificate later. A DC form has 3 boxes for causes of death, arranged in a hierarchy, x due to y due to z. Henry Mason had died of a pulmonary embolism due to clotting diathesis due to acute myelogenous leukemia. She barely understood what the words meant, but she knew it meant that her father – the human being she had loved the most in the world – was gone.

The house – an old Cape in the West Roxbury section of Boston – was full of people after the burial. She barely knew most of them. Work associates, friends from the school where he taught, students from his decades as a teacher, neighbors who were friends of her parents and parents of her friends. Faces she knew floated in and out of focus – her mother Jessica; Maggie's best friend since childhood, Emily; Benny; her father's younger brother, Uncle George – voices distorted, speech going past her. She thought she answered people rationally, but it was hard to tell now, more than three years later.

Finally, people had left after many rounds of well wishes, hugs, and tears. The silence after an afternoon of tumultuous emotional pitch was both a relief and frightening. It seemed like the house would never hold happy people again.

The remaining family gathered in the family room. It had one wall of ceiling-high bookshelves, a nubbly old sofa, and a couple of saggy but comfortable armchairs. Just Maggie, Benny, Jessica, Uncle George – sort of a family, but it had been her father Henry who held them all together. And even then, not so much. Benny hadn't been back in that house in almost 20 years. Uncle George would only come at Thanksgiving. Jessica, lying dramatically across the sofa, was pretty hammered by that point. She had always been a maudlin drunk. Tonight was no exception.

"I'm so glad you guys are staying here tonight," Jessica said.

Nobody replied, so Maggie answered, "Sure, mom. We're here."

"How am I going to go on without your father?" Jessica's voice went up a register. "I can't believe this is happening. I'm, I'm all alone."

"Well, Jessica," said George, "that's not quite true. We're all here, and you have a lot of good friends who are here for you."

"Oh, it's not the same thing, you know. Henry was the center of our family. He loved you all so much."

Benny snorted. "Don't worry, Jessica. At least he had life insurance. I'm sure he left you well provided for. You'll have all the friends you need."

Jessica whirled around to face him, no mean feat given what Maggie thought her blood alcohol level had to be. "How would you know, Benny? You haven't seen him in twenty years. You cut yourself out of this family after high school."

Benny was pale, but his voice was steady. "More like you cut me out of it, Jessica. Isn't that right? I left, because it was what you wanted."

"How dare you?" Jessica shrieked. "I did everything I could to be a stepmother to you."

Benny raised an eyebrow. "Is that what you thought? I remember it differently. And anyway, I have seen Henry for lunch nearly every week for the past two years, since he got his cancer diagnosis.

I'd come up from Connecticut and we'd eat in town. And even before that, he was always there for me. He just kept you out of it."

It was Jessica who was pale now, and shaking. "You autistic little creep. Get out of my sight!"

Benny looked at her impassively. He nodded once, as if confirming an opinion. Then he pivoted and walked toward the front door. As he walked past her, Maggie thought she heard him mutter what sounded like, "Eff sixty point four." Maggie and George looked at each other in dismay, George shaking his head, Maggie burying hers in her hands. Behind them, Benny closed the front door with a firm snick of steel and oak.

Chapter Three, Tuesday Evening, May 23rd

Maggie walked into Area Four, a restaurant in Cambridge's Kendall Square neighborhood, at 7 p.m. that evening. The restaurant was on the ground floor of one of the many lab buildings in a quadrangle called Tech Square, the heart of the biotech industry in town, and in some ways, the world. It wasn't crowded on a Tuesday night – this was a place that was full of dealmakers and celebrating teams at lunch, but evenings were for post-meeting drinks and team-building dinners. She found Benny at a corner table by the bar, with a martini in front of him.

A collegiate-looking waiter came over. "What's that, gin or vodka?" she asked Benny.

"Vodka, actually. I'm allergic to gin."

She rolled her eyes. "Plymouth gin martini, please. Straight up, dry, two olives." The waiter nodded and left. On the way to the restaurant, Maggie had debated with herself how open to be with Benny, whether to trust him or not. But twist it one way or another, Maggie couldn't see how she could get Benny's cooperation on her undercover assignment without telling him something. How little could she get away with saying? She took a deep breath, a diver readying for the plunge.

"So I wasn't quite on the level with you before, Benny," she said, watching him carefully. "Lilly Zhao isn't missing. She's dead. We found her body up in the Middlesex Fells this morning."

Benny stopped raising his glass in mid-lift and put it down carefully. He looked right into her eyes this time. "Oh my God, that's awful. You're sure it's her, I guess?"

Maggie nodded. "So now back to my question this afternoon. She seems like a very law-abiding citizen. Is there anything she was doing at work that could have gotten someone pissed off enough to kill her? What exactly does she – did she – do at your company?"

He puffed out his cheeks. "You know anything about drug discovery? Or clinical development?"

She shook her head. "Nothing much, except what you hear about drugs costing too much."

It was Benny's turn to roll his eyes. "It takes about ten years to figure out if a drug works in people and is safe enough to approve, and it costs hundreds of millions of dollars to get through to final approval. Ninety percent of experimental drugs fail. The ones that succeed usually have about 8-10 years of patent life left." He shrugged. "The winners pay for the losers."

"So what's that got to do with Lilly?"

"You've heard of biotechs, right? Mostly small companies like Quercus, or Moderna, the guys that made one of the Covid vaccines? And then there are big pharmas, companies like Pfizer or Merck that have a whole bunch of drugs on the market. Well, biotechs mostly work on what we call biologics – drugs that are made from antibodies, or proteins, or RNA, or gene therapies. Pharmas, on the other hand, mostly work on pills, because those take a lot of chemistry, and pharmas have lots of chemists. So small companies work on big molecules, and big companies work on small molecules. Oh, and big companies also buy small companies. That's the dream for biotechs like Quercus – show a drug works and then get bought out so somebody else pays for the big expensive studies at the end to get approval."

"And you get the big payday sooner. But why aim to make these biologics? Are they better than pills?"

"No, not necessarily. It actually depends on what target you're trying to hit with the drug. If the target is inside the cell, you usually need a small molecule to get at it, but if the target is on the cell surface, antibodies are easier to make and usually have fewer side effects. But the biggest reason is that it takes about twice as many people on a team to make a pill as to make a biologic, and small companies are always short of money to pay for more scientists."

"OK, so where does Lilly fit in?"

"If you want to try an experimental drug in people, you have to get FDA approval to start clinical trials," he said. "To do that, you first have to show that the drug is safe in animals, usually in two species, like rats and dogs, or sometimes rats and monkeys. It's toxicologists like Lilly who design and run those studies – and we call them tox studies, of course. It makes us real popular with the animal rights people, but the idea is that patients matter more."

The waiter came with Maggie's martini and they ordered. Caesar salad with chicken for Benny; sausage and pickled pepper flatbread pizza for Maggie. After he left, Benny went on.

"And if we show safety, and also some evidence that the drug works in an animal model, we can still only treat patients for as long as we've treated animals. If you think it'll take six months or a year to show benefit in a disease like Alzheimer's or arthritis or emphysema, you have to treat animals for six or twelve months first. Those studies actually take almost twice as long to complete, because of all the analysis that has to be done after the treatment period, so you could be looking at a year or two years of tox before you can even try it in patients."

Benny paused as the waiter came back with bread, butter, and olive oil, and then resumed as he buttered a roll.

"So our first studies are usually pretty short, about a month, so they don't cost as much and use as few animals as possible. That gets us into healthy volunteers, which is called Phase One. We give healthy people a single low dose of the drug, and watch how they feel and how the drug works in their system. Then we slowly go up in dose, and then we give it more than just one time, watching every participant very closely. Maybe a third of drug candidates fail at this stage. Treating healthy people doesn't tell us if a drug works for a disease, of course, but if there's a problem with the drug, healthy people are better able to recover from it than sick people."

Maggie sipped her Martini, nodding in appreciation, more at the drink than at the crash course she was getting in drug development. Benny didn't seem to notice.

"Once we get through the Phase One stuff, we're ready to go into Phase Two, which is in patients. So while we're doing the Phase One, we also have to start the longer animal studies so we can treat patients for longer than a month. Not many diseases are helped by just a short treatment. And that's what Lilly was doing – running a longer term tox study in monkeys so we can start Phase Two for our lead drug next year."

"And what is this drug that you're all so excited about?" asked Maggie. "What disease are you even treating?"

"It's a whole new approach to treating ALS. Do you know what that is? It's also called Lou Gehrig's Disease, if you've heard of that."

Maggie nodded. She had heard of it, anyway.

"It's awful. Usually hits adults in their forties to sixties, and kills them in two to three years by breaking down their nerves and muscles. Most people die because they can't breathe. Sure, we can keep them alive with ventilators and tube feedings and move them around with mechanized wheelchairs, but that's just using technology to offset the lack of useful treatments. And the entire family is consumed with taking care of the patient, often someone has to quit their job to do that, and then figure out how to pay for it all."

"And you think you can fix that?" Maggie asked.

The waiter returned with their food. Maggie's pizza smelled great, and she dug in. Benny accepted black pepper for his salad and kept talking.

"We hope so. We have an RNA drug – like the Covid vaccine, kind of, but against a protein that is messed up in ALS – but packaged in a whole new way using special carriers called lipid nanoparticles so it can get into the brain without having to have a spinal tap every month. These nanoparticles are like microscopic soap bubbles that carry the RNA to the brain. We're going to start the Phase One study in healthy adults as soon as we have the money from the IPO, and when Lilly's data come through we'll be able to start treating patients. But her study isn't going to finish for a few more months."

"So why would anyone want to harm her?" Maggie frowned, chewing.

"I don't know. The whole company's only about forty people, and they're trying to do a second research program as a follow-up to the first one. That's okay as a way to diversify, hedge your bets, whatever, but it's a huge strain. And, it's not going so well, so there's a lot of stress right now. And top of that, we're about to go public, and hopefully raise enough money for the clinical program for QT-101. That's our lead program. The place is a pressure cooker."

"Was Lilly causing trouble? Did she disagree with what the plans are?"

He hesitated, pushing salad around with his fork. "Nooo, I don't think so. Not that I know of, anyway. She's really a very good worker bee, you know? She is…was…technically very good, and very diligent. I don't think she bothered much about the big picture strategy – she was all about perfect execution."

"Well, somebody executed her, Benny. And I'm going to find out who." Maggie leaned forward. "I need you to get me into Quercus Therapeutics, Benny. Undercover. I can be your new admin. Something's fishy there."

Benny sat back in his chair. "What? Are you kidding? I can't do that. I don't even *have* an admin. The last one quit a couple of weeks ago."

"That's perfect – I can be the new temp to support you. If I show up and you get me a badge, I bet no one will ask questions. It's not like you have to put me on the payroll. By the time anyone gets curious, I'll be gone." She smiled thinly. "Besides, the alternative is search warrants and blue lights and you all get shut down for a month."

"That's…that's blackmail!"

"Damn right, it is. But anyone at the company has to be considered a suspect for now. And that actually includes you, buster. Where were you on Monday afternoon, by the way?"

He sighed. "Okay, okay, fine. I'll get you a badge in the morning. Show up around ten. And as for Monday, I was at work until about 7 o'clock – I'm sure the computer can verify when I badged in and out." He paused, then said, "You know, you were a lot easier to handle when you were two years old."

She tilted her chin up. "I grew up some," she said. "Now tell me about this company. Who are the major players? I assume you're one? Do you guys get along? Is it all one big happy family, or more like our house growing up?"

Benny chewed some salad. "You know, I've mostly worked in academic medical centers, and then at Pfizer. That's a very different world from a biotech. Lots and lots of rules before, not so much now. That means smaller companies move a lot faster than big companies – not so many meetings, not so many people you have to listen to. But a lot less expertise in-house, and nowhere near the systems and processes you need to run research programs at the highest level. So biotechs cut corners where they can. And honestly, the big companies are so risk-averse that everything has a belts-and-suspenders approach that drove me nuts. But in a biotech, you get a lot more people shouting at one another." He forked a piece of grilled chicken. "Nobody ever yelled at me at Pfizer."

Maggie nodded. "So, not one big happy, then. Tell me who I need to know about. *Cui bono*?"

Benny raised an eyebrow. "A cop who speaks Latin?"

"Four years at Tufts as a Poli Sci major, and then the Police Academy. You pick up a few things. I might go to law school someday, but right now I'm having too much fun."

Benny smiled. "Well, who benefits? You know, drug discovery is this huge team sport. Each project is like a moonshot, and if you are lucky and have a good team, it's a blast. That's how you know things are going well. But Quercus isn't like that, at least not now. It's more like the '78 Red Sox: 25 guys, 25 cabs. Of course the guys who would benefit most aren't actually working in the company – they're the big outside investors. But of the people inside the company, it's the leadership that have the most shares, so when we go public they make a killing, at least on paper. But they can't sell for a year or more, or they're liable for insider trading investigations if they do something funny. Then it trickles down to the rest of us."

"The CEO is a guy named Art Kehoe. He's a VC guy – venture capital. He's not really strong on the biology, though he started out as a pharmacist. Figured out pretty quickly there's no money in that, I guess. He focuses on the financial part, and right now that's all about the IPO – the initial public offering. You know about that, right?"

Maggie said, "Sure, I live in Boston. Everybody and his cousin has an IPO coming. So right now you guys are private, and if you go public, Art and the investors make a bundle?"

"Yes. And the founders, a couple of scientists at Harvard and MIT, plus the early employees. There are a few, besides Kehoe. The CSO – that's Chief Scientific Officer – is a Dutch guy named Thomas van Haft. He was in the founders' lab when they developed the nanoparticle technology we're using, that they licensed to Quercus. It's special because they figured out a way to tag these nanoparticles so they can get into the brain. Normally, the brain is protected from the rest of the body by something called the blood-brain barrier. It lets nutrients and oxygen in, but it keeps harmful stuff – the riff-raff – out. Getting drugs into the brain is particularly hard. These nanoparticles have molecules on their surface that act like an address on an envelope, sending them into the brain. That's part of our special sauce at the company."

"Thomas really runs the place day to day, not just the science and the manufacturing parts but also things like Legal and Human Resources, that would normally report to the CEO in most places. Art's a big picture man – he prefers to focus on investor relations, and let's Thomas run the shop. And then there's my boss, Jorge Perez. He reports to Thomas, of course. He's a PhD biochemist from Argentina, been in the US just a few years. He's in charge of both Research and Development, but since he's not a clinician he's mostly been focused on the research side."

Maggie looked at him. "There's a difference? Between research and development, I mean?"

"In my world, research means everything before you go into humans – experiments in test tubes, and mice and so on. When I got here, he already had a basic research group, and toxicology, where Lilly was, plus pharmacology. He hired me to start up the development group, which means the people who put the drug into patients, or as they say in biotech, 'into the clinic', as if Dr. Schweizer was waiting in a white coat with a glass syringe and rubber tubing."

"Wow, this is a small company, but it already sounds complicated. How much is the IPO going to be worth?"

"We're hoping to get to unicorn status. Do you know what that is?"

She shook her head.

He said, "It's at least a billion valuation. We price it a bit below that and then hope the stock price pops – uh, goes up – on the first day. After the investors take their cut, it would leave enough to do the clinical trials and hopefully, if they're positive, we get an inflection up and a big buyout from one of the major pharmas."

Maggie chewed more pizza before saying, "We're looking into Lilly's personal life, to see if she had any enemies. And it could of course just be a random attack, a mugging gone bad, or sexual assault, but it doesn't feel like that. She certainly wasn't raped, based on what we've seen so far. She's not mixed up with anything illegal at first glance, but we'll check further. The husband, who's always the top suspect, is in China, which is a pretty solid alibi. So if she pissed off someone at work, someone might have had a billion reasons to get her out of the way."

"And that's why you want to become my secretary?"

Maggie allowed herself a small smile. "I think we call ourselves admins now, you know."

"OK, admin. But tell me, what pushed you from being a poly sci major at Tufts to the Police Academy? You must have been pretty unusual there."

"Careful, your East Coast elitism is showing." She paused. "In my senior year, a guy tried to rape me. I broke his arm for him, and he stopped. But I decided political science was too theoretical. The 12 years of martial arts I had turned out to be a lot more useful. So I took the civil service exam and went to the academy after graduation."

"Have you ever done anything like this before? Undercover work, I mean."

"Hah, yes. Eleven months working my way into a drug ring in Brockton, and then almost nine months there before we took them down. You might not have heard about the trial, since you were still in Connecticut back then. But I think I can handle admin at a biotech."

He raised his hands in surrender. "I didn't realize I had such a tough younger sister. But don't be too cocky – if someone really did kill Lilly, there's a murderer on the loose in Quercus Therapeutics. These people may be smoother and better dressed than the ones you dealt with in Brockton, but they can still be plenty dangerous."

"Is that brotherly concern? Then thank you." She paused. "By the way, I've been meaning to ask you for years. What is F60.4?"

Benny blinked. "Huh? It's an ICD-10 code – the billing code they use in hospitals and clinics – for histrionic personality disorder. Why?"

He doesn't remember that night, Maggie reflected, but at least he sounds sincere. "Never mind," she said. "You can introduce me to the vipers in the pit tomorrow, and let's see what happens, shall we?"

Chapter Four, Wednesday, May 24th

Maggie woke up early and did her three-mile run to the Charles River and back. The air was still brown, it still smelled like a charcoal grill that needed cleaning, and by the time she was done her eyes were tearing and the back of her throat was achy. Back home, she showered, dressed, and turned on the local TV news as she drank her coffee. 'Murder in the Fells' was the second lead after the ongoing Canadian forest fires and their impact on local air quality. The death of a woman in the dark woods sounded like something out of a television thriller. The Channel 4 reporter, Dan Beardsley, had been a year ahead of her at Tufts. Now he was standing in front of the Tudor Barn, his eyes tearing too, though probably not from empathy for the deceased. He didn't have much to say, as the police had not released the victim's name, but the story played up the dangerous-in-the-dark narrative.

As directed, she showed up at Quercus Therapeutics at 10 a.m. Benny met her downstairs, arranged for her to get a photo ID badge, and walked her around the second floor, introducing her to various staffers. Most of the floor consisted of 'open space' cubicles, with enclosed one- and two-person 'phone booths' for conference calls arranged haphazardly among them. Maggie thanked her lucky stars that she had veered off the poli sci track to police work. Otherwise she would be spending her life in a cubicle farm like this somewhere. Designed to "foster collaboration", she knew from experience that the desks were too close together to allow privacy, and too far apart to support easy communication. Mostly you just overheard other people's conversations whether you wanted to or not. Give me field work any day, she thought.

In the middle of the floor was a large common area with a kitchen, coffee machines, refrigerator, and storage cabinets. Two small conference rooms and one large one were ranged along two interior walls, while large glass windows on the outside walls gave light and relieved at least some of the claustrophobia caused by the crowded desks. There were splotchy modern paintings in bright acrylics on the walls, interspersed with scientific posters that boasted the Quercus logo in the upper right-hand corner. Obviously, the company had been publicizing some of their work at scientific meetings.

The third floor was all labs, Benny explained, and she would rarely need to go up there. The top two floors of the building were leased by Takeda, a pharmaceutical company that had several adjacent buildings; she would only see their employees in the elevators, as their badges worked solely for the fourth and fifth floors and hers wouldn't. So much for getting to know the neighbors, she thought. Welcome to Cambridge.

Benny left her with Dimitris Pappas, their self-declared "IT guy", who smilingly set her up with a work laptop, password, and access to Quercus's systems. Dimitris looked to be in his mid-forties, with black wavy hair and dark eyes that crinkled as he smiled, which was often. His accent was, he explained, from Thessaloniki, on the Adriatic, even though he'd been in the US for eleven years. She electronically signed a bunch of forms about confidentiality, non-compete, and agreeing to arbitration if she had a dispute with the employer. Fortunately for Maggie, the company used Microsoft stuff, so she was familiar with the software suite from her college days. He gave her access to Benny's calendar and plugged her laptop into a workstation at a desk next to Benny's.

"There's an all-hands meeting at noon today, with lunch, in the big conference room," Dimitris said. "They're talking about the IPO. I'll see you there."

She spent some time familiarizing herself with Benny's schedule. About half his day was taken up by various meetings, either one-on-ones or small groups, and there were several recurrent meetings that looked like they were for teams or committees. Before noon she joined the stream of people heading to the conference room, which was set up with sandwiches, bags of chips, water bottles, and a multicolored selection of soda cans on tables outside the door. The room had a large U-shaped conference table large enough to seat about half the audience, and additional chairs with folding half-desk writing surfaces had been set up along the wall on all three sides. The front wall was dominated by two large video screens, with a small lectern in one corner. Grabbing a tuna sandwich, salt-and-vinegar chips, and a diet Dr. Pepper, she sat in a chair along the wall next to Dimitris, who had smiled and waved her over.

Everyone was dressed casually, in jeans, T-shirts, and often a Quercus vest, black with the company logo over the left breast. At the lectern was a short, balding, middle-aged man with glasses and a booming voice, who could be heard over the general noise of conversation. Maggie guessed, and Dimitris confirmed, that this was the CEO, Art Kehoe. Kehoe was talking to a group of younger associates, some wearing white lab coats, who were nodding and smiling. Despite what Benny had told her at dinner the previous night, Quercus certainly seemed like "one big happy family" so far.

"Welcome, everyone," Kehoe boomed, silencing the room. "It's great to see everyone here today. We're close to a milestone for Quercus Therapeutics, as you all know. We've been working toward this for the past eight or nine months, and we're almost ready to give birth, ha ha. We've filed our S-1 with the Securities and Exchange Commission, and we are starting our road show in a couple of weeks. Our goal is thirty by thirty. Of course we hope it will go up from there. We're pretty confident we'll get a pop on the stock price, and that will put us in unicorn territory. And we go public in one month!"

There was a smattering of applause and a susurration of comments around the room. Kehoe was clearly dealing with a friendly audience. "I'll show you a few slides on the process, and then Thomas will give an update on where we are with QT-101. Jorge will talk about the preclinical programs, Anita will explain how this will work financially for you, and then we'll have a chance for Q&A."

Maggie concentrated on her lunch as Art Kehoe described the process of taking a private company public. Thirty by thirty, it turned out, meant 30 million shares at $30 a share. Nine hundred million dollars. A unicorn is an IPO that exceeds a billion dollars in market value, a pretty lofty goal. Her impression was of a smooth, even slick, fast-talking salesman.

Thomas van Haft, DVM, PhD, who followed Kehoe, was the opposite. He was about 6'3", had brush-cut dark blond hair, rimless glasses, and a mild northern European accent. He spoke calmly and deliberately. Maggie knew from his bio on the Quercus website that Thomas had grown up in Holland, trained as a veterinarian, and then gotten a doctorate in molecular biology, followed by a post-doc at MIT. He found he liked the unconstrained atmosphere of the United States, and stayed, moving first to Takeda Pharmaceuticals and then a few doors down to Quercus. Even from twenty feet away, his eyes were blue and piercing, and he alternately looked at his slides and the audience. Maggie couldn't follow the science in detail, but he seemed confident and persuasive. It sounded like Quercus was going to cure ALS, and it was just a matter of proving it. She saw Benny sitting at the main table, and he caught her eye, nodding approvingly. Well, Benny had come here from Pfizer, he had to be a believer at *some* level, Maggie thought, even if he's a natural-born sceptic.

Jorge followed Thomas. In the world of science, a melting pot of national backgrounds, accents, and physical features was normal, but Maggie found herself having to adjust to each speaker's cadence. Jorge, Maggie knew from her website surfing, was born and raised in Argentina, had trained there and in Spain and Sweden. This was his first American job, and his English was good but clearly not his first language. As he spoke, quickly and smoothly, with a Spanish accent that was a warm contrast to Thomas's northern European one, Maggie saw Benny's body language change. He was sitting up stiffly as Jorge described a new "small molecule program" that was going to be Quercus' next drug candidate, a pill instead of an injection. Admitting it was early days, and that the molecule was still several years from the clinic, Jorge still made it seem like a new and exciting opportunity for treating bad neurological diseases. Benny's expression was a neutral, but his face was flushed, and she could see a pulse throbbing at his temple. Now what's bothering *him*, she wondered. It certainly seemed like there was no love lost between Benny and his boss.

Benny relaxed as Anita stepped up to the microphone. She was a thin, wiry, fiftyish blond with a Tennessee accent and a smile that didn't touch her eyes. Checking on LinkedIn, Maggie had learned that Anita had been an HR executive at half a dozen companies, and she looked like a no-nonsense professional. She went through some details on the legal aspects of the IPO, sounding a lot like a kindergarten teacher laying down the law for her charges: no disclosures to outsiders; no discussion of stock price; no suggestion to relatives to buy – or sell – stock; no mention of any proprietary company information to anyone; no talking to reporters, and on and on. Maggie could feel the oxygen being sucked out of the room, even though Anita kept her tone light and mostly avoided sounding like a scold. But somebody had to be the heavy, she supposed, and Anita looked like she had no trouble with the role.

As the meeting ended, Benny took Maggie to meet the speakers. "In a company this size," he said as they waited for others who were talking to the company leaders, "everyone is on a first-name basis, and even the temps get to meet the CEO."

Closer up, Art Kehoe's salesman's smile was at odds with cold grey eyes that bored into Maggie's. He might have been considering which fish to buy at the supermarket as he welcomed her with a perfunctory greeting. Thomas van Haft was also a bit distant, she thought, but he gave her a smile and his full attention. His grip on her hand was firm, and though formal in a European way, he seemed friendly. Jorge looked her up and down in a way she was used to but didn't like; it faintly made her want to break his arm too.

These introductions done, Benny guided her to meet others on the R&D team. Rob Handler gave her a warm smile and genuine welcome that made her like him right away. She also met Antoine Dupree, the head of manufacturing and the only African-American in the room; Sandeep Mehta, Quercus's head of pharmacokinetics (whatever that was); Lisa Clark , the head of Research, which was evidently different from being head of "Research and Development"; Scott White, a large man who was the Quercus chief financial officer, in-house lawyer and patent expert; and Anita Mercer, the last of the day's speakers, who was head of HR.

Research means mice, rats, or test tubes, Benny explained. Development means patients before approval by FDA. Commercial means selling after approval. That's when patients and doctors become customers and the whole system goes to hell.

"There'll be a quiz later on all the names," Anita joked as they walked back to their cubicles.

"I know, it's a bit overwhelming," Maggie answered. "I'll go make a cheat sheet."

"Make me one too," Sandeep said. "This is only my second day, so I'm not far ahead of you."

She spent the next few hours poking through Quercus's electronic cloud-based file system, but not knowing what to look for didn't help. By about four-thirty in the afternoon, the second floor had mostly cleared out. Quercus allowed people to work from home as they wished, and some people had left right after the noon meeting. Others stayed a while, but left in time to beat the rush hour. Either way, they would work until dinner and most of them would log in again afterwards.

Looking around the empty cubicles, Maggie got up and ostentatiously went to the ladies' room. On the way back, instead of going to her desk she slipped into the chair behind Lilly Zhao's desk. Fortunately, it was against the back wall, so she was largely invisible unless someone walked around the partition in front of the desk. She tried the desk drawers, which were unlocked. The shallow drawer under the keyboard held various stationary items, while the two top side drawers were taken up with blank notepads, a box of Power Bars, a couple of instant ramen noodle soup containers, and a toothbrush and toothpaste in a small toiletry bag.

The file drawer at the bottom was locked. Maggie examined the drawer and the desk – it was made of particleboard, and the drawers, although they had a metal front, had loose, flimsy locks. She smiled to herself. If I were a TV detective, she thought, this is where I would pull out a couple of pieces of wire and pick the lock in ten seconds. As if. From an unobtrusive pocket along the side of her blue serge pants, she pulled out what looked like a hacksaw blade without teeth, about six inches long and 3/4" wide. Pushing the end of this tool between the drawer and the particleboard side panel of the desk at the height of the drawer lock, she applied lateral pressure steadily with one hand while pulling the drawer handle with the other. The wood gave way slowly, compressing around the metal blade without a sound. She popped the drawer open.

In the age of computers, paper files have largely disappeared. But Lilly Zhao seemed to be an old-fashioned sort, thought Maggie. She had lots of file folders, neatly labeled and alphabetized. Most of them looked old, with labels indicating manuscripts of technical papers published over the past fifteen years. Maggie walked her fingers through each hanging folder, stopping at an unlabeled manila folder that was stuck in the back of a file labeled "J Clin Investig 2007." Inside was a single piece of yellow notepaper, undated. It only had one word written on it, which made no sense to Maggie: "QTRD1014295." Looking around to confirm no one had come near, Maggie pulled out her iPhone and photographed the page, and then replaced the page and folder. Using her metal blade as a lever, she again forced the particleboard back and closed the drawer so it locked.

Standing up nonchalantly, she walked slowly toward her own desk and sat down. It was after 5 p.m. now, and the place was deserted, except for Benny, who was engrossed in his computer screen and didn't hear her come up.

"Hey, I'm leaving now," she said. "See you tomorrow? I think I'll work from home early in the morning and come in before noon. Sound ok?"

"Sure," he said without taking his eyes off the screen. "See you tomorrow."

* * *

Maggie dropped her unmarked police SUV off at her apartment building's garage and walked down Broadway to Bar Volpe, her favorite neighborhood hangout. Emily was already there at a four-top, with a Negroni in front of her and her eyes on her iPhone. She was a vivacious blond, about 5'2" with large brown eyes, a ready laugh, and a skeptical view of the world. They had been best friends since second grade, when Emily was the new girl whose parents had just moved to Brookline as part of the brain drain from Britain. Her father was an immunologist, her mother a statistician, and they both came for jobs at the nearby Longwood Medical Area. On the first day of school, with the kids in tables of four, Emily was seated across from

Maggie, and they started making faces at each other. Maggie was a METCO kid, meaning she lived in Boston but could go to the more highly rated Brookline schools because her father was a teacher there. That meant she was an outsider too. From that, a lifelong friendship was born.

Maggie was always impressed by Emily's ability to multi-task, juggling her real estate day job with an intense social life that was hard to keep up with from the outside. How Emily kept track of boyfriends was never clear to Maggie, but she never mixed them up – a large part of her process seemed to involve not taking things too seriously. Maggie was all about seriously. Maybe that's why the relationship train wrecks, she thought.

Maggie plopped into the seat next to Emily and gave her a hug. Emily looked at her, "Uh oh, you've got a new case, don't you?"

"Christ, you should be the detective, not me," she replied. "How can you tell?"

"Only on you, love. Something about the tilt of your chin, I think, and your energy. Like a dog on a scent. Anyway, I can read you like a book," Emily smiled. "Save the poker face for somebody else."

"And how are things with you?" Maggie asked, deflecting.

"Sold that haunted mansion in Chestnut Hill today," Emily said matter-of-factly, but Maggie could sense a bit of triumph in her tone. Emily had been flogging an 1890's Queen Anne house for seemingly months.

"Oh, wow, congratulations! That explains the Negroni," Maggie said with a grin. "A sale like that should help cover your rent for a few months, at least."

Emily shrugged. "Well, that or a vacation to Cabo," she said.

Maggie nodded noncommittally, knowing Emily rarely took vacations. "Okay, who is this fix-up you've dredged up now?"

"His name is Brad Something. He's a friend of Jeff's from work. They're coming over now from Vertex. Jeff says he's nice, he's straight, and he broke up with his last girlfriend like four months ago. Oh, and he says Brad's a hunk. How's your hoo-ha?"

"My what?" Maggie shook her head. Emily's mom – er, mum – was recalcitrantly British even after two-plus decades in the US, and after talking to her, Emily often came up with slang that caught Maggie off guard.

"I bet you haven't had sex since you broke up with Chris, right?"

"Er, yes, if that's any of your business."

"Well, then you can brush the cobwebs out of your hoo-ha with Brad," Emily gave her a locker room grin. Maggie rolled her eyes at her.

Vertex was a big biotech that had moved from Cambridge to the Boston Seaport District a few years earlier, bringing a slew of smaller biotechs in its wake into what had until then been a purely financial business scene. Now some of the big boys – Eli Lilly, Sanofi – were building in the Seaport, and it was threatening to become Cambridge East.

A few minutes later, Jeff, Emily's boyfriend *du jour*, walked in with another man, presumably the aforementioned Brad. He was about six feet tall, athletic, with wavy dark blond/light brown hair and hazel eyes. Hunky enough, Maggie thought. Introductions made, they all sat down and looked at menus.

Jeff expanded on the introductions. Brad Something was actually Brad Kitchener, and he had the accent of a Southie native. A waiter magically appeared and they ordered drinks: another Negroni for Emily, a Martini for Maggie, beers for the gentlemen.

"I already told Brad you're a cop, Maggie," Jeff said to her with a grin. "He didn't run away, at least."

"Thanks, Jeff," Maggie smiled. She looked at Brad. "It does put a lot of people off."

"Oh, I don't mind," Brad said seriously. "My dad was a Boston cop. I grew up here in Southie before it was gentrified into submission. He retired and now he heads up security at Novartis, in Cambridge."

"Well, it *is* a small town, isn't it?" Maggie said. "I was just over there today, visiting my brother. I saw the Novartis buildings when I was parking. Pretty fancy."

"He seems to like it…" Brad started, but Emily interrupted him. "You went to see Benny? No kidding? What happened?"

Maggie waved a hand vaguely. "Oh nothing, I was in the neighborhood."

Emily looked at her knowingly. The "uh huh" went unspoken, but Maggie could feel her skepticism. Instead, Emily asked Brad about his job, which turned out to be something complicated involving thousand-liter tanks for making antibodies to treat a disease Maggie had never heard of.

*　　　*　　　*

Maggie is three years old, Benny is 18 and leaving home for freshman year of college. He's excited, Maggie can see, but also upset. He's pacing up and down. Maggie starts crying. Benny turns to pick her up from the floor where she's sitting, but her mom is there first.

"I've got her," Jessica Thompson says. Benny's smile freezes, replaced by a deadpan scowl. Henry Mason comes down the hall of their house in West Roxbury, an unlit pipe in his mouth and a suitcase in each hand. He puts the suitcases down and takes Maggie from Jessica, whirling her around while holding her above his head, feet swinging above her head with the centrifugal force of it. Through her tears, she laughs, looking into her father's twinkling

eyes. Behind her, Benny takes the suitcases and turns toward the door.

* * *

Brad was looking at Maggie as if he expected her to say something.

"Sorry," she said. "I was spacing. What did you say?"

Brad made a don't-worry-about-it gesture with his lips and a headshake. "Just asking if you like police work."

"Um, yes, most of the time I love it. There's crap in every job, you know, but most of the time we help people, and sometimes we even catch the bad guys. And the State Police gives me a bit more scope for doing different things than the local forces, which is nice. I'm not bored."

Brad nodded, and Jeff asked, "So, what are you working on now?"

Maggie looked at Emily with a deadpan expression, willing her to stay mum. "Oh, you know, this and that."

"Oh, really? Anything we would have heard of?" Jeff asked.

Before Maggie could answer, Brad interjected, "Ha. Good luck getting anything out of her. My dad would never tell us anything about a case unless it was in the papers or TV first."

Emily looked at Maggie, who smiled. Brad Something was okay enough to see again, alone.

Chapter Five, Thursday Morning, May 25th

Maggie's "work from home" was an excuse to get up to Woburn and check in with the team at the Middlesex DA's office. It was fortunate that in the aftermath of the Covid-19 pandemic, nearly all biotechs allowed unlimited work from home for non-laboratory workers. The freedom to avoid Boston's soul-crushing rush hour was a major recruiting tool for startups trying to steal highly-trained employees away from their more staid, large-pharma brethren, who had gone back to requiring on-site presence routinely. If the big pharmas wanted to act like banks, the nimble startups were happy to take advantage and poach their talent, knowing that there was little price to pay in terms of productivity and a large gain to be made in terms of employee satisfaction.

The air was still brown, acrid, and brought tears to her eyes just walking across the parking lot. Being undercover spared her from rotating in the coffee detail, but it also meant no one would get her one, since they didn't know when she'd show up. BYO'ing it, she walked into the office in time for the 9 a.m. daily conference and sat down next to Eddie. Jimmy was on his other side, and Lieutenant Davis was at the front of the room with an Assistant DA named Adelle Watkins.

Maggie had been working with Eddie for over two years, and they had gotten to be as close as she had ever been with a partner. Maggie knew he was the divorced father of a sixteen year old daughter, who she'd met a few times. Of the ex-wife, Eddie didn't say and Maggie didn't ask. She also knew that Eddie had grown up in East Boston, a hardscrabble town best known as the location of Logan Airport, but to locals more treasured for the best pizza around.

Eddie was small and scruffy, just large enough to qualify for the Police Academy. He had more than compensated for his small size during his early days on the force by carefully cultivating a reputation as being, to put it bluntly, batshit crazy. Over time he had mellowed and matured into an effective investigator. Joining the police had gotten him away from the gangs in East Boston, but his roots in Eastie remained strong, and he coached Little League baseball and soccer there every year. East Boston was a landing place for immigrants, not just planes – from Italians and Jews in the nineteenth century to Salvadorans and Guatemalans more recently, it had always been a place to start building the American Dream. It still was, though Eddie groused that soccer was getting to be more popular than baseball.

Big and blond, Jimmy looked intimidating even without trying, but Maggie knew he was mild-mannered and even kind unless riled. He had grown up not far away in Melrose, a quiet middle class town that could have been on a different planet from East Boston, though they were only ten miles apart. Jimmy doted on his wife and twin nine-year-old boys, all similarly fair-skinned and blond but none over five feet tall, at least so far.

As the Zhao homicide was the newest and most serious case the office had, they started with that. "It bleeds, it leads" wasn't just for the TV news, Maggie reflected. There had been a few developments overnight. Jimmy had reached Vincent Chen early this morning, after getting confirmation from TSA that he had indeed flown to China several weeks before. It was a difficult conversation to have any time, but worse on the phone, Maggie knew. Vincent had seemed shocked on the phone, alternately speechless and tearful, but eventually he promised to let his daughter know and arrange to return to Boston as soon as possible. But as a suspect, short of hiring a hit-man, he was obviously in the clear.

Both Somerville PD and the State Police Narcotics Section came back with a clean sheet on the Shore Drive home and the neighboring houses. Credit checks on Vincent and Lilly were solid: they had a single mortgage on the house that they paid on time every month, a few credit cards with modest balances, and two cars that were several years old and paid for. There was no sign of Lilly's missing Camry yet. Mike Davis's instinct to focus on Lilly's work as the motive for her murder seemed to be gaining foundation.

Nothing more had come back from the crime lab, but it was early. The autopsy was scheduled for the next day, and results from that would come in dribs and drabs, taking from a day to several weeks. Somerville police had found one neighbor with a video-enabled doorbell, and were going to look at the video today. Maggie filled them in on what she had learned at Quercus so far, which honestly wasn't much.

"A fair bit of tension there, it seems. It's natural, with their IPO coming up in a couple of weeks. If any bad news comes out now, it can really mess it up for them. But what that has to do with Lilly Zhao is beyond me at the moment." She didn't mention her bit of breaking and entering into Lilly's desk, not with an assistant DA in the room.

"How much money are we talking about here?" asked ADA Watkins.

"It sounds like they want to go big – 30 million shares at $30 is what they're aiming for. That would give them the biggest biotech IPO in years, if not ever. They hope that it will go over a billion in value once the shares launch."

Eddie whistled. "Nine hundred million reasons to kill somebody, huh?"

Mike Davis, still standing at the front of the room, said, "We have to go public with more details about Lilly Zhao's death today, now that the next-of-kin has been notified. We've been lucky that there hasn't been too much media coverage of this so far, since it was on DCR property and there was no local police radio traffic for the scanners to pick up. You probably saw the stuff on TV about a woman jogger being attacked. I think that's fine for us – should keep the perp from thinking we're making a connection to Quercus. And the Canadian wildfire smoke has been the main story on all the networks and newspapers. But that's about to change. We won't release any details, just that we now have a name to the body that was discovered at the Fells, and that we are investigating. We'll let the reporters at the press conference ferret out that we think it was a random attack on a jogger in a lonely section of the park, nothing more complicated than that. I hope it will disappear into the background, but no doubt the murderer will be paying attention. If he was hoping to avoid discovery of the body for several more weeks, he's going to be disappointed, but hopefully not desperate."

Adelle Watkins raised an eyebrow. "You sure about the 'he', Mike?"

Davis shrugged. "I'm just playing the odds, Adelle. You know as well as I do, men outnumber women as murderers by about seven to one. And that blow to the head was pretty forceful, and it was a downward motion by a right-handed perp. Lilly wasn't very tall, so sure, it could be a woman. But still, playing the odds here."

Maggie took a breath. "Anyway, I'll get over to Quercus by eleven, so if you wait till then to release the news, maybe I can see some reactions when people there hear about it. And if you put out the office number for people to call if they have any information, L-T, let's see who reaches out to us," she said.

Davis nodded. "OK, Maggie. Be careful over there."

* * *

It was busy at Quercus when Maggie got to her desk around 10:30 a.m. She saw that Benny was working in his cubicle, and few other people she could now recognize, if not name, were at adjacent cubicles. She went to get coffee in the common area, only to find that most of the round tables were taken. As she waited for the Keurig machine to make its imitation of coffee, she picked up on nearby technical conversations that meant nothing to her.

"Look, a spray dried dispersion isn't going to have a high drug load. If we can get an API of 25% that would be success…"

"…and we still need a polymorph screen…"

"What's the anticipated human dose going to be?"

"…there are at least two active metabolites, S8 and S9. They're from oxidation of the piperidine ring in the south end of the molecule…"

"Look, the TPP calls for Q-day dosing, and I don't think this formulation can get us there…"

"We'll have to follow the new FDA guidance, and create estimands for the primary and key secondary endpoints…"

"We need to cover EC50 at trough – I think that's pretty unlikely, and we'll have a narrow window to cover the hERG liability…"

Rob Handler, Benny's clinical sidekick, sauntered over with an empty coffee cup. "How's it going, Maggie?" he asked.

"Wow, I guess they're speaking English but damned if I know what any of that means."

"I know, it's like Morse code – just flies by you if you don't know the language. So, have you got a handle on the TLA's yet?" he asked.

"Oh, Christ, another one. What's a TLA?"

He grinned. "Three-letter acronyms. Can't work in biotech without 'em. And I'm told, they're actually different in every company. But once you get the hang of it, you can't talk in complete sentences anymore."

"Exactly. But my work is about the same here as at my last job. Scheduling, travel, supplies, you know, stuff like that. What's a TPP?"

Rob laughed. "Target product profile. It describes what you want the drug to do when you finally get it approved. It's kind of like the destination you plug into Google Maps. Once you have that, you can figure out which route can get you there fastest."

"That sounds kinda vague."

"Ha, that's because it is. Benny once told me that a good drug developer is like Merlin. He lives backwards in time – think about the approved product and then work backwards to what you need to do in each step in order to get there, but in reverse order. The fun part of drug development, to me, is that there's never just one way to do anything. There are dozens of possible plans, each with its own plusses and minuses. The real pros are the ones who choose the fastest, cheapest plan that has the best chance of working."

"Is that your job?"

"It might be one day. Right now I'm just learning."

She nodded. "Well, Benny seems like a good guy to learn from."

Rob nodded. "Yes, he's really a brilliant clinician, and he knows all about early-phase clinical development."

"Funny," Maggie said, "he doesn't strike me as having, shall we say, the best bedside manner? He seems pretty low-affect, if you know what I mean."

"Yes, that's true. It's probably why he went into neuroscience, you know? Until very recently, there weren't any useful treatments in neurology – a lot of the people who went into it, to be honest, were more interested in the disease than the patient. Not everyone, mind you – I've known some wonderful, even saintly, neurologists. But it was all about making the diagnosis, though there was damn-all you could do about it in nearly all cases."

"And has that changed?" Maggie asked.

"Oh, yes. It started with multiple sclerosis. You know, MS. Twenty years ago, we just had steroids. They helped a little bit, but the disease kept on destroying brain cells. And the side effects were often just as bad – bone fractures, cataracts, stomach ulcers, weight gain, stretch marks, you name it. Today we have about fourteen drugs that really slow MS down or stop it, at least in the early phases. We still need better treatments for late-stage disease. And now there are a couple of drugs for Alzheimer's that sort of work, a few lousy ones for Parkinson's Disease, and so on. But the understanding of the biology has leapt forward amazingly in just the past twenty years. It feels like the tide is turning. There are actual cures – or at least long-term remissions – with gene therapy for some horrible childhood genetic disorders. I think we have a chance to have the first real DMD in ALS. Sorry, that's disease modifying drug. Not just buy a few months, but really stop the disease from progressing. That's why I'm here."

She saw the determination in his eyes, the set of his jaw. It was hard not to like Rob – in many ways he's the good side of biotech, she thought. The imagination to conceive of a treatment that totally changes patients' lives, and the determination to make it come true.

"And Benny?" she asked.

"Yes, he's the other reason I'm here. I agree, he's a bit on the spectrum, you know? But he's got amazing insight and judgment about what will and won't work, medically speaking. And he's totally fearless about saying what he thinks."

Maggie smiled. "That, I have seen," she said.

Benny called her over to his desk and showed her the travel itinerary for the IPO road show, which would start as soon as they could get the logistics sorted out. The idea was to visit as many potential deep pocketed investors as possible, give them "the spiel", and hope they'd buy in. In keeping with her cover, Maggie was to work with Lynn Seaver, Art Keough's admin, to make sure Benny had travel and hotel bookings along with the rest of the team. They would start in Boston, but then go to New York, Chicago, and Silicon Valley on a tour of the investors who they hoped would snap up Quercus's shares at above the asking price. The plan was that they would leave a week from Monday, ten days from today. Anyone they couldn't visit in person they would set up a video conference for the pitch, though that wasn't as optimal.

"I've done these road shows before," Benny said. "It's a tour of the world's most comfortable conference room chairs. The VC's sit on their butt all day, listening to pitches from startups and IPO hopefuls. They really need comfortable chairs, let me tell you."

As they were talking the volume of conversation around them suddenly rose. Maggie figured, correctly, that the news about Lilly had broken. Indeed, there were gasps, tears, questions throughout the room. Lilly had been a popular colleague, clearly, and she'd been with Quercus almost since the company began. Taking a coffee mug from her desk, Maggie walked to the café area in the middle of the floor, where others were already instinctively congregating. Washing out the mug and then waiting for her turn at the Keurig coffee machine, she could hear the shock and confusion around her.

There was a video screen suspended from the wall in a corner of the coffee area, which was tuned to the local news with the volume muted and the close captioning on. Once again, Maggie saw her friend Dan Beardsley, now standing in front of State Police headquarters in Framingham. The chyron below him read "Middlesex Fells Murder Victim Identified."

Art Keogh came out of one of the smaller conference rooms toward the coffee area, looking pale, lips compressed into a line. His voice much less booming than the day before, he was still easily audible as he told everyone that he didn't know any more than they did. The rest of the leadership team filtered into the café in his tracks – first the scientists – Thomas, Jorge, Lisa, Benny – followed by Scott White, the head of Legal, and Anita from HR. Anita was comforting a crying woman; Lisa was on her phone nodding and making soothing sounds; Thomas and Jorge were speaking to several associates in white lab coats. Benny was talking to Rob at a nearby table. Maggie didn't see any reactions that seemed forced or out of place. Several times she heard people saying things like "random attack" and "jogging" and "lonely area." Nobody shouted out "It was me! I killed her!"

Slowly the gathering broke up into smaller groups who headed out to find lunch in nearby Central Square. People were still visibly upset. Maggie managed to cut Benny out from the herd and pulled him into an empty conference room. Pulling out her phone, she showed him the photo she had taken the previous evening from the Lilly 's file folder.

"Does this mean anything to you?" she asked.

He studied the photo carefully. "Yes, I think so," he said slowly. "It's a research report number. QTRD1014295. QT is Quercus Therapeutics; RD is Research & Development, so it's a report on an unapproved molecule. Of course, that's the only kind we've got. 101 is our lead program, QT-101. And 4295 is the report number. Four means the toxicology department, and 295 is the sequence number."

"So is this a report Lilly would have been writing?" Maggie asked.

"I don't know, I'd have to pull it and see. It could have been her, but it could also have been someone in Research up on the third floor, or somebody in pharmacology. Either way, it's easy enough to find out. Let's go to my desk."

At his desk, Benny navigated through the Quercus file sharing system to the relevant folder. Maggie stood behind his chair, looking over his shoulder.

"Huh, that's strange. There is no report 4295. There's a 4296, it's dated about three months ago." He opened the file on his computer and scrolled through about 20 pages of text and tables. "Looks like it's a technical report for the PK assay for QT-101 in NHP's that's also the release assay validation. It was done by an outside vendor, and the sign-off internally was by someone who left the company a while ago. Routine."

"Wait, run that past me again. What's PK, what's a release assay, and what's NHP?"

"Oh, sorry. PK is pharmacokinetics. That's a specialty in the pharmacology unit. The point is to measure what happens to a drug in the body – how fast does it get in, how long does it stay, how does it get modified, or metabolized, how quickly does it go out, and by what exit – urine, feces, exhaled breath, whatever. NHP is non-human primate – that's pharmaspeak for monkeys…"

"Of course," Maggie said. "There's a TLA for that…"

Benny looked at her quizzically. "Yes, of course there is. When we have a molecule that is going to go into people, the FDA makes us test it in two non-human species, usually rat and one other, dog or monkey mostly, depending on which one metabolizes the drug most like how humans do. For QT-101, turns out that dog doesn't work, and we have to use monkeys. Very popular with the animal rights folks, we are."

"I bet. Not high on the hit list for English teachers, either, I bet. Do you guys ever go two breaths without some code word? Rob taught me – TLA's everywhere, right?"

Benny nodded without smiling. "Yes, TLA's. The key to communication."

Maggie rolled her eyes, but he continued, "When we make a biologic, rather than a chemical like a pill, it's a big complex molecule or set of molecules, and we have to prove that each batch is the same, or at least so close that it makes no difference. Otherwise the drug might work in one batch but not another. Or worse yet, be safe in one batch but toxic in another. So we need a really robust way of measuring that the drug is the same every time. That's the release assay – if the batch doesn't pass, it won't get released for use. With a pill, like aspirin say, we can just look at the chemical structure and if it's the same each time, then the drug will work the same way each time. Aspirin has 21 atoms, so making it is easy to control. But with a huge molecule like RNA in a lipid nanosuspension, it might have 20,000 atoms, and there's all sorts of things that can be slightly different each time. Most of them don't matter, but you don't want something harmful creeping in. So we need to show that it's clean, not contaminated with junk, and has the same three-dimensional structure as what we intended. So it's much more complicated. If we can use the same assay for the PK and the release, it's faster, cheaper, and we get the drug to patients sooner."

"And this report – um, 4296 – it says it's okay?"

"Yes."

"But where's 4295? Are they sequential?"

"I don't know. No, they aren't necessarily sequential, though every company does it a little differently. At Quercus, they're numbered by batches or experimental protocols that got to the stage of being done. Lots of ideas start and get a protocol number but then are canceled or changed, so they don't get reported out."

"Is there anything funny about these results? Something that could raise a red flag?"

"I don't know. I'll have to look at it more closely. Tell you what, I'll get a sandwich and then look at the numbers while I'm eating. I'll let you know."

"And was a 4295 report ever created? Is there any way to find out?"

"Well, if there was an experiment done here, it'll be in the electronic lab notebook. Those have to be Part 11 compliant, you know, so they can't be altered."

Maggie shook her head in frustration. "Argh, don't you people ever speak plain English? What's Part 11?"

"Oh, sorry again. 21 CFR Part 11 – it's a part of the FDA law, in the Code of Federal Regulations, Chapter 21, section 11 – that sets out the rules for electronic records so people can't fake data. You know, there are lots of scandals about falsifying research results, but nearly all of them are in hospitals and universities. Even the big, prestigious places. One of the biggest frauds ever was at Harvard. It's much less common in industry because we have to abide by Part 11 rules, so we have very expensive software that tracks every keystroke. We have things like electronic lab notebooks instead of paper ones, and archiving of all files continuously. The hospital and university labs are mostly overseen by NIH – the National Institutes of Health – not FDA, so they're exempt. And it's not pretty."

"So can you look at that too? If there was an experiment but no report, wouldn't that rouse suspicion?"

"Eventually it would, but it can be months after the end of an experiment before a report is completed. Sometimes you have to wait for final test results that take a long time, like pathology slides or some funky assay that only one lab in the world can do, or something like that. Other times there's a change of personnel and stuff gets put on the back burner. Or people are just overworked and put it off. Unless it's needed for a filing with FDA, people may not notice. But then there's a deadline or a question from management, and the shit hits the fan."

"OK, let's go get some sandwiches," Maggie said. "This could take a while."

*   *   *

They went around the corner through the brown air to a Flour Bakery on the ground floor of a Novartis building, and ordered sandwiches and decadent, mouthwatering, baked goods for dessert. The place was crowded and the line out the door, with people of all ages talking science, biology, chemistry, and relationships all at once.

"This is the real heart of the biotech world," Benny said with a smile as they waited for their order. "Come here at lunch and you can figure out what every company in the industry is doing."

Maggie nodded. "Sure, if you could understand their jargon. Oh, speaking of things I don't fully understand, that reminds me. I remembered something yesterday," she said. "Like a flashback. You were leaving for college. I must have been about three, so this could be my earliest memory, but I've never thought of it before last night. I was crying about you leaving. Mom picked me up and then Dad took me and whirled me around. That's all. Do you remember it?"

Benny looked at her with a rueful smile. "Oh yes. That was the day I left for Princeton. At least you were sad that I was leaving. I'm not sure anyone else was – including me, to be honest."

"You didn't come back much."

"No, I guess not. Your mom and I didn't really get along, and Henry kind of sided with her. It seemed simpler to just stay away."

"But I missed you, Benny. I was just a kid."

"I know. I see that now…and I'm sorry. I was too immature to think about you. And it seemed like the three of you were an iron triangle. I didn't fit."

"Dad missed you too, you know. He wouldn't say so directly, but he was always talking about how well you were doing, or what classes you were taking, or whatever. I think now that he loved your mother more than anyone, maybe more than us. Do you remember her much?"

"Only bits and pieces. I was five when she died. Sometimes it scares me that I can't remember her voice anymore. Then I watch some old home movies that dad had digitized, and I'm not sure if I remember those things, or I just think I do from watching them over and over on the screen."

"After Dad died, my mom went off the rails. She's been chasing one idiot boyfriend after another for the past two and a half years. Now she's in California. It's ironic that dad left the house to you, not her. Are you living there now?"

The house was a modest Cape Cod in West Roxbury, a middle-class residential neighborhood of Boston. Her father had lovingly maintained it, doing all the maintenance and renovations himself over the years. It had a small yard that was mostly perennials and tomato plants. Maggie blanched at the thought of it sitting empty.

"No, I would rattle around in that old pile. It's just me, you know. So I rented it out to the family of a visiting professor from Italy who's teaching at BU. I have an apartment a block away from here in Cambridge. It's an old factory where they used to make Fig Newtons. I like being able to walk to work whenever I want – no commute, no hassle."

Their order number was called, and they picked up the food and headed back to Quercus. "Where do you live?" Benny asked as they walked.

"In Southie, just by the Broadway T stop. When I moved there I was stationed in the Boston, so I could walk to work. A couple of years ago I was transferred out to Woburn, so now it's a grind, though at least it's a reverse commute. Sometimes that helps. But I love the neighborhood. I'm in a new building and the whole area is hopping. Between South Boston, Fort Point, and the Seaport, there must be a hundred restaurants and bars within a mile of me, and tons of new apartment buildings and condos. What's funny is I'm in the same block where thirty years ago Whitey Bulger used to run the Winter Hill gang, murdering all those people and blackmailing FBI agents to do his bidding. It's not the same Southie anymore."

Back in the office, they went to their separate desks. Maggie knew to leave Benny in peace if she wanted answers. It was also easier to think of him as not-a-suspect now, but was she just being swayed by long-ago memories? After all, how well did she really know the grown-up Benny? What had happened to him since he left home? He wasn't married, but had he ever been in a serious relationship? Or was he just too OCD, too compulsive, too geeky, to have a girlfriend? Funny how that memory had come back to her, after seeing him for the first time in years. And honestly, she thought, getting to know him as an adult and not as the little girl she had been when he left was going to be a longer-range project. She wondered if there were more buried memories out there, and what it would take to unearth them.

Chapter Six, Friday May 25th

Detective Trooper Jimmy O'Connor was waiting at baggage claim at Logan Terminal B at 5:10 a.m. on Friday morning for United 1871, the redeye from San Francisco, to discharge its passengers. Vincent Chen had taken a connecting flight from Shanghai to SFO, met his daughter at the airport, and together they flew home on the redeye. The terminal was still empty, just gearing up for the day's nonstop human traffic. The one exception was at the already open Dunkin Donuts, where Jimmy joined the line of airline employees, State Police troopers, and TSA guards desperate for their early morning caffeine fix. Chatting with a couple of uniformed troopers he knew, he kept an eye on the down escalator that would bring the passengers out to baggage claim.

It wasn't hard to spot the Chens. A very rumpled middle-aged Asian man with a sleepy young woman in black leggings, pink sweatshirt, and the footwear uniform of her generation, Nike slides. Jimmy identified himself and said the usual condolences. They waited in near silence for the suitcases, which eventually came, after the inevitable twenty minutes of MAFAT, as the cops called it. Mandatory airport fucking-around time.

After the introductions and a *pro forma* inquiry into their flight experience, Jimmy had suggested that they identify the body now, as the autopsy was scheduled for later that morning. Then he would take the Chens home to rest, accompanying them to confirm if anything was out of place or missing at the house. They agreed without enthusiasm, but to Jimmy they seemed overwhelmed, not indifferent.

"You don't both have to come," Jimmy said. "If you like, I can drop Stephanie off and just take you, Dr. Chen. Or you could wait in the car," he turned to Stephanie.

They looked at each other briefly but both nodded. "I think it's best if we both go, Detective," Vincent said. Jimmy nodded in return and led the way to the car. He would be much happier this way, able to keep them both in sight until they had not only identified the body, but also checked out the house together. Seeing their unrehearsed reactions, difficult though that might be, was just another part of the investigation.

*   *   *

It was a little after 6:30 a.m. when they pulled up to the faded red brick and beige limestone building on Albany Street near Boston Medical Center that housed the Office of the Chief Medical Examiner. Outside it was quiet and cool, the morning traffic still far from its daily crescendo and the usual roster of drug addicts, alcoholics, and schizophrenics holed up somewhere, off the streets for a few more hours.

Inside, Jimmy ushered Lilly Zhao's family into the waiting area. After a few minutes, Shirley Kung came out to meet them, already on site despite the hour and dressed in blue scrubs, with her hair covered by a disposable blue cap. Jimmy made introductions and Shirley led the group back to a small, bare room with a gurney in the middle. The walls were tiled in beige rectangles, the floor was a bilious green linoleum, and the lights were state of the art 1960's fluorescents, which hummed and buzzed in several registers. Covered with a sheet on the gurney were Lilly's mortal remains. Wordlessly, Shirley pulled back the sheet to the shoulders. Vincent, pale but calm, nodded once; Stephanie wept quietly.

"Yes," Vincent said in a raspy voice. "That is my wife." He reached out and cupped his hand on her cold cheek.

"Thank you," Shirley said gently. Jimmy, towering over them, put a large hand on each family member's shoulder and guided them back to the waiting room. In the hallway, Vincent asked, without looking at anyone, "Do you know how she died?"

"I'll know more after the autopsy," Shirley said. The automatic response of every medical examiner, thought Jimmy. But then she added, "It looks like a single blow to the head. I suspect loss of consciousness was immediate. She didn't suffer."

They hadn't seen the back of her head, thought Jimmy. It was a violent enough blow to break one of the thickest bones in the body. Even if Shirley was just trying to be kind, she was probably right. At least there's that much consolation, he thought.

*　　　*　　　*

Twenty minutes later he pulled up to the Chen's house on Shore Drive. It was still before 7:30 in the morning, and traffic had been light. The air seemed a little lighter today, too – a prevailing northeasterly breeze had pushed some of the smoke away from Boston. The house looked deserted, forlorn. A Somerville black-and-white was parked in front of it, a single officer inside drinking coffee. Jimmy went over to him, and confirmed that someone had been stationed there overnight, and that there had been no visitors. That won't last, Jimmy thought. If nothing else, the reporters will be circling soon. Thanking the officer, he told him he could go, now that the occupants were back.

Jimmy followed the Chens up the entry stairs, watching as Vincent unlocked the house and let them in. There was no alarm to reset, no video camera in the entry. Vincent put down his suitcase in the entry hall with a sigh. Jimmy could imagine his thoughts – their home will be without Lilly forever now. Stephanie pushed past them and went upstairs, presumably to her room.

"Please look around, Dr. Chen," Jimmy said. "I'm sure you're tired after such a long trip and a tough morning, but I really need to know if anything is missing, or out of place. Let's go through the house room by room."

Vincent walked through each room like a terrier sniffing for rats. It was only in the office he shared with Lilly that he stopped, almost pointing like a hunting dog, Jimmy thought. "My wife's computer is not here," he said. "She uses her work computer for everything, both work and personal accounts. It's gone."

Stopping himself from saying something fatuous like "Are you sure?" Jimmy reached for his phone and texted this to Maggie and Eddie. "Where does she…did she…keep her cell phone?" he asked Vincent.

Vincent pointed to her desk. "You can see, she has a charger here and also one on the nightstand of her bed. It wasn't in there, and it's not in here either. Did you find it, um, on her?"

Jimmy shook his head. "What kind was it? Was it an Apple phone, or Android?"

"She had an iPhone," Vincent said.

At that moment Stephanie came into the room. With a catch in her voice, she said hesitantly, "Mom always had this tracking app active on her phone. It keeps track of all three of us. When I was in high school she put it on my phone so she could see where I was without calling and nagging me."

She shuddered. "It was worth it to keep her from calling me on dates, and we kept it even after I left for college. It can show where her phone is now if it's on. And even if not, it can show her movements." She was crying again now, silently, letting the tears just rolling down her cheeks without any attempt to stop them. Vincent went to her and put his arms around her shoulders. Stephanie turned into him, burying her face in his jacket collar.

"Whoa," said Jimmy. "Are you kidding? That could be really helpful. But hang on a minute, we need to make this legal. Please don't look at the app on your phone yet. I'm going to call the ADA and get a warrant for her phone, and then we can get the State Police digital unit to do the checking. If we find this guy, we don't want him slipping away on a technicality."

*　　　　*　　　　*

It took a couple of hours to get the paperwork straight. By then the Chen's house had filled up. Maggie, Eddie, Jimmy, a Cyber Crime Services technician named Ted Sands, and the Chens were all sitting around the dining room table. Someone had made coffee in the kitchen pot, and Stephanie and Vincent were drinking tea.

Ted was a big man, six-five and 300 pounds, with mane of curly brown hair that blended seamlessly into a Z-Z-Top beard. He looked fearsome, but Maggie knew he was a big teddy bear. Now he and Stephanie Chen were side by side, almost touching foreheads, or more accurately her forehead to his chin, as they looked at the tracking app. Stephanie, obviously a digital native, was at least as facile as Ted, especially with this particular app. After a while they looked up, and Ted addressed the others in a surprisingly high-pitched tenor.

"Well, her phone is off now. It was last active on Monday evening, at 4:37 p.m.. At that point, it was located at Middlesex Fells, and it looks like it was near where you found the body. The app shows that the phone was here overnight Sunday, and that she took it when she went to work in Cambridge on Monday morning. The phone was on Sydney Street from about 8:30 a.m. to 3:00 p.m., and then she drove back here. Around 4:00 p.m. Monday, she left here and it looks like she drove up to the Fells – the trip took about ten minutes."

"Or was driven," Maggie said.

"Maybe, but it looks like she went for a jog after she got there. She went in a circle off the road, on what look like paths in the park. It was still light out, but it was raining."

"That wouldn't stop her," Stephanie said. "She ran every day, rain or shine, unless it was awful out. The Fells was one of her favorite places, especially now that the days are longer and it's warmer out."

"Okay, so she drives up there, with her phone, goes for a jog," Maggie thought out loud. "She meets somebody. Was it planned? Or did she just run into him? And what about her computer? She certainly didn't take it jogging."

"Maybe it was in the car, like in the trunk," said Eddie. "Maybe she was going to do some work on it after her jog. Would she go someplace afterwards, normally? Like a Starbucks or something? After all, she's home alone, maybe she wanted company."

Vincent answered, "She has a friend who owns a restaurant in Medford Square. A Chinese restaurant, Chili Garden. She goes there a lot, eats dinner and works on her computer or talks to her friend." Maggie noted that Vincent's accent was getting more noticeable, whether from fatigue or emotion or both.

"For that matter," Maggie said, turning to Vincent, "we're still looking for her car. I assume that's your Honda Accord in there?"

"Yes, I left it in the garage when I flew to China. Lilly's car is the Camry. It should be in the driveway. I didn't notice until now, but it's obviously gone."

"I don't suppose it has Lojack, does it, Vincent?"

"No," Vincent said. "We got it used, and it's not a car that people steal much."

"We've got a BOLO out on it," Jimmy said. Seeing Vincent's blank look, he explained, "It means 'be on the lookout', and it goes to State and local police all around New England. I'm sure we'll find it soon."

"Was Lilly upset lately? Did she say there was anything wrong at work?" Maggie asked.

"I don't really know," Vincent said. "I've been in China for three weeks, and we usually text every day, and call a couple of times a week. It's harder there, because everything you say or do is being watched by the government, especially for a scientist from America. We kept it pretty business-like. But no, she didn't say anything. She's always tense about her work, very careful not to make a mistake. She always says, if she screws up, it could kill somebody."

Based on what Benny had told her, Maggie believed Vincent. If a toxic molecule got into humans, it could make a sick person worse, or even kill them. "Yes, I get it," she said. "If I were a patient getting an experimental drug, I'd want some as conscientious as Lilly behind it." She turned to Stephanie, "Did your mom say anything to you about being worried or scared? Anyone stalking her? Any neighborhood troubles? Or at work?"

Stephanie shook her head, tears flowing silently down her cheeks. After a moment she was able to speak. "My mom was very private, she kept everything inside. She wasn't a typical Tiger Mom, you know? She was supportive but not crazy about making sure I studied and stuff. But there was always a push, unspoken expectations. She would never dream of telling me if something bothered her."

Maggie nodded. Opposite of my mom, she thought, who wanted to be my girlfriend when I needed a mother.

"Was she planning to go out to California to see you this week? Someone at her work mentioned that."

"Yes, my semester is over on Friday, and she was going to come help me pack up and come back here for the summer. I have a summer internship at Mass General."

The acorn not falling far from the tree, Maggie thought, Tiger Mom or not. Good for Stephanie, and a credit to Lilly. Another reason to find this killer…as if she needed one.

"Okay," she said. "We'll let you guys get some rest, and we'll be back in touch as soon as we have something. If you think of anything in the meantime, please call Jimmy." Jimmy gave them his card, and the police team filed out.

Outside on the sidewalk, Maggie turned to the others. "I think we have a time of death, then, don't we? On or about 4:37 pm on Monday."

At the end of the block, a man on a bike wearing a black helmet and reflective sunglasses casually turned his bike and pedaled away.

* * *

Benny had started looking at Research Report '4296 the previous afternoon. As usual in these documents, it was about twenty pages of text and a hundred pages of graphs and tables. Half the text was boilerplate – title page, table of contents, required regulatory language – and he had skimmed through it quickly. The body of the text explained how the release assay was created, what it measured, and then described triplicate repeat applications of the assay to three different batches of QT-101.

If there was something fishy about the report, Benny knew, it wouldn't be in the text, probably not in the graphs, but somewhere in the tables. Very few people had the patience to look through columns of numbers one by one without losing focus. Fortunately, Benny was one of those people. The advantage of a moderate case of obsessive-compulsive personality, OCD, he thought. If it was any worse, I'd have to call it CDO, just to put the letters in alphabetical order. Old joke, he told himself, but it amused him.

He had gotten through about half the tables the night before, until he realized that he was looking at the same column of figures for the third time. And because he'd been distracted by a memory he hadn't thought of in years.

Benny is five and a half. It's March, and his father wakes him up every morning for kindergarten with a kiss on his forehead. This morning he is awakened by a hug. He realizes his cheek is wet, but the tears are his father's. His mother is dead. She had died a few hours earlier, in the hospital, in the middle of the night. Instead of getting up, his father gets in bed with him, lies spooning him as they both cry. There would be no school that day.

He'd stopped for the night when his eyes were tearing up, but was now back at his workstation at 8 a.m. Friday morning. Having gotten a lemon-ginger scone and coffee from Flour Bakery on his way in, he chewed slowly as he scrolled through more numbers. An hour later he sat up, putting the last piece of the scone down and scrolling back and forth. He pulled a yellow pad to his lap and started jotting down numbers.

Two hours later he had three pages of numbers on his yellow pad, plus an Excel spreadsheet where he had copied and pasted data from the report. He looked around the room, surprised to find that there were now several other people in the office, though on a post-pandemic Friday most people would be working from home. Reaching for his cell phone, he opened an encoded messaging app and texted Maggie.

*　　　*　　　*

They decided to walk around, where they couldn't be heard. The air was still hazy, but no longer acrid, nor as brown as before. It was a milder day, sunny but not oppressive, and both of them felt good to be out of the canned air of the office. Benny led Maggie down Sydney Street toward the river, past one biotech after another. At Memorial Drive they walked upstream toward the Hyatt Regency and crossed to the riverbank at the light. As they walked he looked around, but didn't see anyone from Quercus. It was lunch time, and plenty of joggers passed by, hearing nicely blocked by earphones. A couple of eight-person crews were out rowing on the river. Finally, when they were out of earshot of anyone, he spoke.

"So it looks like this 4296 report has been manipulated. The data are a little too good – there are a bunch of numbers that repeat themselves, the standard deviations are all too tight, and most importantly the variability is the same across days and assays. That's not something that you would expect with real experimental results. Even good assays have error, and that error should be random. By chance alone, at least 5 percent of the data should be way off, and they aren't."

"Wow," Maggie said. "Can you tell who did it? And why did Lilly have a different report number in her files, but it's not in the system?"

"As far as who filed 4296, that's easy. It was Lilly. Or so the system believes. It could have been someone else using her login, of course. But there's another thing. The date on the cover page of 4296 is like I said, about a year ago. But the actual file was only created three months ago. My guess is, there really was an original 4295 report, and it's been deleted, and this new report was pre-dated to the time of the original. That's not supposed to be possible, but figuring out how that was done – or by whom – is beyond my I.T. skills."

"Why would anyone do that?" asked Maggie. "What would they gain?"

Benny followed an errant seagull with his eyes as it circled the riverbank.

"To know that, we'd have to find the original 4295 report. Maybe it's somewhere in the system, but your guess is as good as mine. Presumably, there's something on that report that would put QT-101 in a bad light, and possibly screw up the IPO. That's plenty of motive, isn't it?"

"OK, so two possibilities. One – Lilly wrote the fake report, and she's involved in a conspiracy. But if Lilly did write the fake report, why kill her? I guess she could have had second thoughts, or she could have been blackmailing someone else and got whacked for her trouble. The second possibility is that she didn't write it, but she discovered it, and discovered that someone had made it look like she wrote it. She's been at Quercus for three or four years now, right? So she could have seen the original 4295 report at some point. Even if she didn't remember the report numbers, she might have seen something on the new one that triggered her suspicions. Then the motive is obvious. And it fits with what her family said – and you said too, Benny – about what a goody-two-shoes she was."

"And it also fits with her writing down the original report number, 4295, and keeping it hidden in her desk drawer," said Benny. "If she'd actually written it, that would have taken her at least a few days and probably a couple of weeks, what with having to collect different assay results from different experiments, paste them in, collate everything so it reads properly, and all that. So she probably wouldn't need help to remember the report number."

"I sure wish we could find her laptop," said Maggie. "She could have had a copy of the original report on it, right? That would make a good reason for her, and her car and computer, to disappear."

"Yes," said Benny. "Because of Part 11 restrictions, she could have downloaded a PDF version of the file, but not one that could be edited. And she could have printed it, or emailed it, or put it on a memory stick and carried it home. Quercus isn't super-sophisticated in terms of electronic security. At Pfizer we couldn't copy files to portable drives, but in a small biotech like ours, it's not unusual."

"Did you see Lilly on Monday, Benny? Was she looking upset?"

"I remember she was there, because she walked by me to go to her desk around lunchtime. She and Tony were walking together – he's our head of manufacturing. It looked like they had come out of a meeting, but I didn't hear what they were talking about."

They turned without speaking and started walking back. Then Maggie said, "By the time we get back my colleagues from the Homicide Bureau should be there, asking questions. If they didn't show up soon, our perp would probably get suspicious. They won't identify me, so please don't either."

Benny nodded. After a pause, he said in a quiet voice, "I also remembered something from our childhood. It was the day my mom died, and dad came to tell me in my room. I hadn't thought about that in probably twenty-five years. Thanks a lot. This is part of why I avoided coming home after high school, you know. It's too painful. Even now, it's hard."

Maggie turned to look at him. He had rolled his lips inward, compressing them as if to prevent them from trembling. He looked straight ahead. "That must have been terrible," she said. "I know one thing, though. Dad loved your mother, Hue – and you, too – more than anything. I think it broke his heart when she died. Even years later, when I was old enough to understand, he could barely talk about her without a tremor in his voice. And he missed you something awful."

"Well, he had a whole new family by then. I was superfluous."

"Bull. You don't really believe that, do you? Sure, dad was a guy who rebuilt his life. He didn't go all Wuthering Heights, did he? More power to him – that literature stuff about pining for your one true love is bullshit. Life is for the living. He came back from Vietnam, he saved your mom from the wreckage, he built a career, and then after Hue died he built another family. Did he keep you out of it? Or did you exile yourself?"

"Some of each, maybe. I saw how he looked at you, and at Jessica. How was I supposed to feel?"

"Maybe like it's not a zero-sum game, you know? Look, I know you're a rules kind of guy. So am I – I'm a cop, right? But what rule of yours did he break by marrying Jessica? And anyway, I saw their relationship first-hand. It was okay, but I wouldn't say it was Romeo and Juliet. My impression is that he left that sort of love behind with Hue. Henry and Jessica were a good team, and I think they cared about each other a lot, but nobody would make a movie about them."

Benny sighed. "I'm sure you're right about a lot of that. I know I can be pretty rigid sometimes – I've gotten that feedback my whole life. In school, at the hospital, at work…that's why I like research – there are rules, there are experiments, there are results, and they either succeed or fail. Either way, you know what to do next. It's not like that in clinical medicine, which is mostly barely controlled chaos. I don't know much about Henry and Hue's life in Vietnam, or how they got out. I know how they met of course, when he was in a hospital after taking some shrapnel. But not much else."

Maggie said, "When my mom left for California, after she packed up the house, she left some boxes with me. I haven't opened those boxes, but from what she said, I think there are some of Dad's papers in there. I can call her and ask. Why don't you come over one evening and we can go through them together?"

"That would be good, thanks." They had arrived back in front of Quercus by now. As Maggie had promised, there were several State Police cruisers at the curb, placidly ignoring the "No Parking Any Time" signs.

* * *

Inside, Maggie ignored Jimmy while he was supervising several uniformed troopers and a Crime Scene Services technician who was sitting at Lilly's desk with what looked like a lot of fingerprint powder scattered around. Jimmy had his poker face on, he didn't even wink at Maggie as she walked by, though he did study her ass from behind a little more obviously than usual. One of the troopers approached Benny and took him aside for an interview.

Jimmy spoke to the Crime Scene tech loudly enough for Maggie to hear, "OK, Bill, if you're all set here, I'm going to interview Mr. Keogh, the CEO, and then the vic's supervisor. You can get going once you're done here." The technician nodded and went back to his work at Lilly's desk.

Maggie kept her head down and focused on her screen. She had enough windows open on her desktop – calendar, spreadsheet, email app, internet browser – so she looked genuinely busy. Another uniformed trooper – one she didn't know – came to her desk and collected her contact information, ascertaining that she had just joined the company and hadn't known the victim. The police stayed for a couple of hours, interviewed everyone in sight, collected names of people working from home to contact, and generally made a very good show of it, Maggie thought. She hoped it would be enough to lull someone into a false sense of security.

* * *

In Woburn, Eddie Bushell received a thumb drive containing video from a house two doors down from the Chens, a house equipped with an internet-linked doorbell camera. The conscientious citizen living there was more than happy to help the police try to find whoever had killed that nice Dr. Zhao.

Eddie connected the drive to his computer and brought up the video files. Realizing the files were only tagged with meaningless alphanumeric filenames, he resigned himself to going through them in date and time order. About thirty minutes into this review, he found footage of a silver Camry going by on Shore Drive at 4:04 p.m.. No other car followed the Camry for another minute and a half – that seemed too long to be a tail. He played the video again, back and forth, several times. There was a bicyclist, though, who had pedaled by a few seconds after the car. White bike, black helmet, black clothing, wearing reflective shades even in the rain. There are a lot of bikers in the greater Boston area, thought Eddie. Some of them might even wear sunglasses in the rain. Hard to keep up with a car on a bike, he thought. On the other hand, on a short ride like the one from Shore Drive to Middlesex Fells during afternoon rush hour, a bike probably *could* keep up, maybe even outpace a car if the traffic was bad. At that time, and with light rain falling, that was reasonably likely. He copied the file and went in search of Lieutenant Davis.

Chapter Seven, Memorial Day Weekend, May 27th -29th

Maggie didn't expect much from the holiday weekend. Friday night she collapsed on the couch with a pint of chocolate mint chip ice cream and a copy of Norman Rush's *Mating*, with the Red Sox game on TV as background. Around 1 a.m. she dragged herself to bed, and slept, happily alarm-free, until after 9.

Saturday morning she did her run, and then laundry. Brad called and asked her out for that evening, which seemed nice. They ate at Strega in the North End, and then walked around the old Italian neighborhood in the warm and almost-clear evening air. They found a sidewalk table to have an espresso, and stood in line at Modern Bakery for dessert. He was good company, cheerful and diplomatic, but the hazel eyes were warm and appraising. He asked enough to be clearly interested, but not so much as to seem nosy, and he didn't just talk about himself. As a professional interviewer of people who had secrets, Maggie was gently amused but also intrigued. She also found out that he kissed well, which was an important piece of information. Maybe she was past Chris enough by now. She didn't let it go further, but they agreed to see each other again at Emily's Memorial Day cookout on Monday.

Sunday afternoon she called her mother in Rancho Bernardo to ask about the papers that were in her storage room downstairs. Were there any of Henry's journals in there?

"Oh honey, yes, there were a slew of notebooks of his. I couldn't look at them after Henry passed, you know, so I just packed them up. If you want to look through them, feel free. It's too much for me."

Maggie wasn't surprised. Jessica was an expert at avoiding unpleasant topics, with death and dying at the top of the list. Her mother was not a devotee of Elisabeth Kubler-Ross, to say the least. That she had moved to a town famous for a decades-long study of human aging was an irony lost on Jessica.

"Well, it's not just for me, mom. Benny is going to come over and look at them too."

There was silence on the line. "Um, really? You and Benny? Well, wonders never cease. How did you two hook up?"

"We did not 'hook up', mother," said Maggie frostily. "I mean, eww."

"Oh, you know what I mean. He's avoided us for years."

Avoided *you* for years, Maggie thought.

"Well, we reconnected through work. Turns out I'm on a case that involves his new company."

"Oh? No kidding! Is he in any trouble?" Jessica's schadenfreude wafted through the Wi-Fi ether. Maggie rolled her eyes at the furniture. Maybe Jessica's attitude explained some of Benny's standoffishness. Feeling unwanted could have come from Jessica but deflected on to Henry. She wondered if Benny could tell the difference.

"No, he's fine, it's not related to him, just coincidence. So, how's Charles? What are you guys doing for Memorial Day?" Maggie redirected the conversation, knowing Jessica would happily talk about her new boyfriend for the next twenty minutes at least.

* * *

Benny came over around seven on Sunday evening. Maggie greeted him at the door to her apartment, wearing a faded pair of Tufts sweat pants and an oversized Bruins jersey. She had ordered pizza from Upper Crust, made salad, and offered cold beer. They ate companionably, talking about Lilly, her family, and the impact of her loss, but there was nothing new to say.

Maggie changed the subject: "So, Benny, how much are you going to make from this IPO?"

Benny looked at her owlishly. "Me personally? About two million, if we get the $30 price. I'm like employee number thirty – it's the founders and the early hires who get the most shares. And for perspective, if I'd stayed at Pfizer, I would make two million in maybe three or four years, with bonuses. I'm not bragging – I think I earn my keep. Ten years of either negative income or barely enough to get by, during medical school and internship and residency, and then mostly sixty-hour weeks ever since. Sure, it's a good living, but it's not like I'm sitting around eating bon-bons, is it? The IPO would be really nice, but it's not life-changing money. Money isn't really the motivator here. Why?"

"It's motive, obviously. How much will Art make?"

"About fifty million dollars, I guess. For Thomas, Jorge, Scott, Anita – the first employees really – it's twenty million plus apiece, I would say. We don't really talk about these things, but everyone knows the expectations, the ranges. That's enough to retire on, once they can sell. But they can't do that, usually, for one to two years, and even then they have to do it slowly, as part of a publicly disclosed plan, to avoid the SEC coming after them for insider trading. And of course, if they sell a lot of their stock and word gets out, it could tank the stock once it's public. After all, who knows more about the prospects of the company than insiders?"

"That's still a lot of money, even if it's just on paper," Maggie smiled. "I guess you're less of a suspect, at least."

Benny blinked. "Well, that's nice, thank you."

They went down to Maggie's storage room and brought up two cardboard storage boxes. Clearing her dining room table, they opened the boxes. The first one was full of photographs, the second one had manila folders, neatly labeled, and a dozen or so speckled black-and-white composition notebooks, the kind kids use in elementary school. These were labeled in Henry Mason's cramped handwriting and dated from 1968 to 1983. The older ones were frayed at the edges, water-stained here and there, and had clearly been toted around quite a bit before coming to rest in this box.

"Did you know Dad was a diarist?" Maggie asked. Benny shook his head, picking up the earliest notebook. They took a pile of the notebooks to Maggie's coffee table. She plopped down prone on the sofa, opening the first notebook. Benny sat on the floor, his back to the sofa by her head. Without thinking, they had adopted their childhood positions on the old black sofa in the family room of their father's house.

"This looks like it's from when he was in college. He had the hots for someone named Mary, but it doesn't sound like he got far. So much for Free Love, I guess."

"He was at a military school, Maggie. They weren't exactly hippies at Norwich."

"I know. For such a liberal guy as he was by the time we knew him, he sure started out with a very traditional background."

Benny nodded. "Yes, he had the opposite trajectory of Churchill, who said if a man is not a liberal at twenty he has no heart, and if he's not a conservative at forty he has no brain, or something to that effect. Henry got more liberal with age."

"I think his Vietnam experience changed him, and then teaching high school must have been more of the same," Maggie said, looking at the notebook labeled 1970. "Listen to this, it's from June 1970. He's been in Vietnam for three months now, a lieutenant with the 101st Airborne…"

June 26: I've been ordered to join my unit, the 2nd of the 506th, in the A Shau Valley, above Khe Sahn. A lot of scuttlebutt still about the mess at Kent State last month. Guys here don't understand either side – why the antiwar movement is so hostile to us grunts, or how National Guard troops could shoot civilians. Doesn't do much for morale either way…

July 2: At FSB Ripcord. We're surrounded by NVA and VC. They're constantly probing our perimeter. A lot of artillery fire last night. CO is Lt. Col. Lucas – good guy.

July 19: I've been evacuated to Saigon after being hit by artillery fire. Not sure what happened the last few days. They told me the enemy shot down a Chinook that crashed into our ammo dump, killing a bunch of guys and blowing up our howitzers. I guess I got off lucky – shrapnel in my legs, back, and left hip. I don't remember it.

July 24: I heard from the S-2 that we evacuated Ripcord yesterday. Col. Lucas died commanding the evac. They say they'll put him up for the CMH. He really was a hell of a leader.

"CMH?" Maggie asked.

"Congressional Medal of Honor," Benny said quietly. "Dad told me about this once, but I've never seen these journals. Henry said there were three CMH's from Ripcord, and Colonel Lucas's was posthumous. Ripcord was a cluster-fuck, the kind of stupid battle that showed how far the Army had deteriorated since World War II. The idea was to cut the enemy supply lines into South Vietnam, but we didn't have enough forces there to do it. By now heavy American losses in a victory were just as bad as a defeat, because of how it played back home. The North knew that, so they just shelled the hell out of Ripcord, and let the casualties mount. The answer would have been a major invasion of the whole valley in force, but we were drawing down our troops and not increasing them. Ripcord was the War in Vietnam in a nutshell – overcoming strategic folly through heroism doesn't really work."

"You want me to put on 'Born in the USA'?" Maggie asked.

"That came out like 15 years later," said Benny. "Try 'Ohio', by CSNY. That was about Kent State, which had happened two-three months earlier. It was such a tough time – antiwar movement led by college kids in the US, but same age kids without a college deferment from the draft dying in Vietnam."

"That's beyond sad," Maggie said. "But I guess this was where he met Hue. Listen."

> *July 25: I had a really cute nurse today. She's Vietnamese, but her English is good and she's very sweet. She said it's her first month on the job here. Her name tag says Hue Bac Nguyen, but I guess it's pronounced "Way Back When". How cool is that? I hope I see her again.*
>
> *July 27: I'm going to need another operation for a piece of shrapnel that's deeper in, near the nerve root. The docs say it explains the pain down my leg. If it works, I'll be out for about a month of rehab and PT. I hope Hue can be my nurse then.*
>
> *August 1: Looks like the operation was successful. I still have drains in my side and back, and I can't get out of bed for another couple of days. But the pain down the leg is gone – now it's just a dull ache – literally a pain in the butt.*
>
> *August 4: Hue wheeled me out to the sun porch today, and we ate lunch out there. It was really nice. Her parents are dead, killed by a VC bomb years ago. She was raised by nuns in a Catholic convent, which is how she speaks both English and French. She has a younger brother but doesn't know where he is. Her aunt and uncle are in Saigon, refugees from Quang Tri up north, but I guess she's not close to them. It's the tragedy of this country after 20 years of war. We thought we were here to save*

people from Communism, but we fell into a civil war that we can't win. I think she's amazing, she keeps her humanity and her open, loving nature even in the face of all these losses, all this horror. We have such different backgrounds, but I think she's as drawn to me as I am to her. I never believed in love at first sight, but maybe I need to rethink that. Being with her is like drinking from a cool mountain spring on a hot day.

"That's so sweet," Maggie said, eyes moist. "I never thought of Dad as such a romantic. Oh sure, he was always saying mushy things to me, and I would roll my eyes at him. When I went to college, he would send me clippings of poems, or cartoons from the New Yorker, but he was always a little distant, you know."

"I guess Henry never told you," Benny said, "but after he was diagnosed with leukemia he called me. After that, he and I would talk by phone every week. When I was in town, he and I would get together for lunch or dinner. I didn't want to walk out on him, you know. I wanted to get away from Jessica. I'm sorry you were collateral damage."

Maggie sat up on the sofa, staring at Benny. "Don't you remember?" she said slowly, "you kinda yelled that at Mom when you walked out after the funeral. I'm glad, you know, that you got back in touch with Dad, even if it was after all those years, and under such circumstances. You and me, maybe we can find a way to figure stuff out."

"Oh, yeah," Benny said. "I guess I did mention it, didn't I?"

Maggie nodded. "When Dad found out he had leukemia, three years before he died, he gave me a CD of Springsteen's *The Rising*. He told me it was something he was listening to, and that he would like it if I did too." She was crying now. "As he got sicker I listened to that album every time I went running. Sometimes I was crying so hard I couldn't see where I was going. Early on, I was focusing on

'Countin' on a Miracle'. Then it was 'Waitin' on a Sunny Day' and 'Mary's Place'. As he got sicker it was 'You're Missing' and 'Lonesome Day'. Finally, after he died, it was 'Further on Down the Road' and 'The Rising'. Those songs got me through a hopeless time, hokey as that sounds."

"It doesn't sound hokey at all. You know, he sent me the same CD. I don't think I listened to it so intently, but I liked it. Springsteen wrote it after the attacks on 9/11, so it resonates with loss and redemption." Benny wasn't a crier, but his voice was thick and his eyes red. Maggie came off the couch to give him a hug. He hesitated for a moment, then wrapped his arms awkwardly around her, standing rigidly as her shoulders shook with tears.

After a while Maggie got up, grabbed a Kleenex and brought back two more beers from the fridge. Benny was back in Henry's notebooks, and he read out loud:

> *September 14: I'm finally out of the hospital, but now reassigned to MACV. That means Hue and I can see each other, maybe even find a place to live together. I'm limping, but this is a desk job, and that's a relief. Oh, and I am getting promoted. Oh Captain, My Captain, etc. My DEROS is still six months away – I hope that's enough time to figure out how to take Hue with me. I think she'll come back with me.*

"What's MACV? And DEROS?" asked Maggie.

"Military Assistance Command Vietnam," Benny said. "Also known as 'Pentagon East'. And DEROS is 'Date of Expected Return from Overseas'. Henry told me all this years ago – it's the Army jargon for going home. I know it took him until after his discharge to get her out. Once he was out he came back to Saigon as a civilian and got her an exit visa. He never said, but I think he just bribed her way out."

Maggie started leafing through the contents of the second storage box, which included half a dozen photo albums and more manila folders. "Look, here's their marriage certificate – January 14, 1972, in Norwich, Vermont. And this photo album of their wedding – they were so young! According to the marriage certificate, Hue was only 22, and Dad was 24. They look so happy."

Benny looked over her shoulder as she turned the pages of the photo album. "Not a big wedding, huh? Uncle George is there, but not Grandma or Grandpa, and of course Hue didn't have any relatives in the U.S. It looks like some of Henry's college and Army buddies and their dates. And I think these two in the back are his old friends from high school. Wow, I wonder how that went."

"Well, we know some of that, right? It took years for Dad to talk to his parents again, though I met them when I was a kid, but they died before I was ten. Did you know them?"

"Not really. I think after my mom died they tried to make amends, but Henry had very little patience for them, and I can imagine why. By then he had moved to Boston and was teaching high school. He'd made his new life and he wasn't keen on looking back. Not too forgiving either, I guess."

She looked at him. "So they get out of Vietnam, he's discharged from the Army. He even gets a promotion to Captain before separation. Then they get married in Vermont, Dad gets his job in Boston, and then you're born in 1978. But during the pregnancy, Hue starts having kidney problems, and eventually she's diagnosed with lupus. It gets worse and worse, and she passes away in 1983. You're five years old. Do you remember much of it?"

Benny was looking out the window at the Broadway Red Line subway stop seven floors below them. There were people walking on the sidewalks, cars rolling by, a drunk leaning against the bus stop sign. Life in the big city. "Look, Maggie, it's late, and we've covered a lot of shit…I need to get going. Thanks for dinner, and for all this…it's a lot to process. Let's pick it up again another time."

*   *   *

Monday afternoon Maggie loaded up a twelve-pack of beer, four bottles of Petit Chablis 2020, and a two-quart container of homemade seafood salad into the Ford and drove to Emily's parents' house in Brookline. Spring was already well along, and the trees were glorious in their virescent foliage; tulips were seemingly in every garden, and rhododendrons were threatening to explode in purple and red blooms.

Her phone rang as she was stopped at a red light near the Boston-Brookline border. Glancing at the caller ID, she scoffed quietly, but answered with a shrug anyway.

"Dan Beardsley, has it been a year already?"

"Maggie Thompson, how the hell are you?"

"I'm fine, thank you. I only hear from you about once a year, Dan, so I figured it must be time. To what do I owe this dubious pleasure?"

"Now, Maggie, don't be sore. You know we're old friends by now. College is receding quickly."

Not quickly enough, Maggie thought. "And what can I do for Channel Four today?"

"Well, you know, I've been working on the murder in Middlesex Fells, and I wondered if you knew anything more than the official State Police line. Off the record, of course."

"Sounds like a Hallmark Channel movie, Dan. 'Murder in Middlesex Fells'. Are you auditioning for the role of leading man slash heartthrob?"

"Maggie, you know I love you. I'm just looking for an angle. Why would anyone want to kill Lilly Zhao? She seems to have been a regular girl scout."

"Dan, tell me the truth. Do you actually know any other cops besides me?"

"Umm…sure, just none that will actually talk to me. But you and me, we go back a long way…"

"I wouldn't call a couple of drunken dorm parties the basis for a lifelong friendship, Dan."

His voice grew more serious. "Well, we both know there was more to it than that, don't we?" he said.

One point to Dan, she thought. "True," she said out loud. "And what makes you think I'd know anything about this murder?"

"Well, I know you're working out of Woburn, right? That puts the Fells right in your patch, if you'll pardon the pun, doesn't it?"

"Well, yes, as a matter of fact. I can't tell you anything about an active investigation, as you know. But here's a clue. Her husband has been in China for the last three weeks. We think he might have run afoul of the Ministry of State Security…but at least he's not a suspect, right?"

"Oh wow, Maggie. Thanks."

"Off the record, right, Dan?"

"Yeah, yeah. Definitely. My lips are sealed. Thanks, Maggie."

"Bye, Dan." She hung up, suddenly cheerful. Well, that should cause a stir, if he's actually dumb enough to go with it, she thought. She'd better remember to let Vincent know, before he has a coronary. But deflecting the suspicion of whoever killed Lilly was worth a lot of incidental fluster just now. The investigation wasn't exactly speeding along, and she needed every bit of extra time she could get before the killer started worrying that they were on to him.

Emily lived in a "carriage house" behind her parents' home, which was large and grand even by Brookline standards. Every year she shamelessly commandeered the larger house's grounds for a freewheeling Memorial Day picnic that easily drew a hundred of her closest friends, though people came and went so it wasn't overwhelming. Maggie was jaded enough to think about the utility of this for

Emily's real estate business as well, but she put it out of her mind with a feeling of virtue enabled.

Despite the toney neighborhood, Emily's parties were strictly down-home affairs. She corralled a friend or two to mind the grill, prepared burgers, hot dogs, corn on the cob, beer, and fixings, and everyone knew to bring along something good. The ensuing feast was always amazing, running the gamut from Jamaican jerk chicken to many kinds of Indian and Middle Eastern specialties, salads, exotic wines, and dozens of desserts. Everyone went home happy, no one went hungry, and no one kept to their diet. It was the perfect way to start off the summer.

By the time Maggie arrived, there were cars parked up and down the road and onto several cross-streets. Taking her *droits de seigneur*, she parked in Emily's parents' driveway, pushing aside the inverted orange buckets that blocked it and then putting them back in place. Some traditions have to be maintained.

The party was in full swing, dance music blaring from speakers mounted above the large patio. The wisteria hanging from the pergola above the patio was vibrantly purple and fragrant. Maggie deposited her food and drink and found Emily chatting with several people Maggie didn't know. At an appropriate break they hugged and stepped to the side of the grill.

"Looks like another hit, hon," Maggie said. "This place is rockin'!"

Emily nodded, looking around critically but appreciatively. Her blond hair was swept back and held in a large clip, and she wore a flowered off-the-shoulder dress that showed her early-season tan to advantage.

"Your buddy Brad is over there, talking to Jeff and some other biotech bro's," she said with a smile. "How did you guys hit it off so far?"

Maggie shrugged, "No red flags yet, but no wedding bells either, okay?"

"Just remember the hoo-ha, honey, that's all I'm saying."

Maggie smiled. Not a bad motto, at that.

Chapter Eight, Tuesday Morning, May 30th

Antoine Dupree, called Tony by most everybody, had been the head of manufacturing at Quercus Therapeutics for about eighteen months. Tony had grown up in New Jersey, the son of a merchant marine sailor from Martinique and a Black woman from Newark who met her future husband when he was on leave in New York. One of three children, Tony had shown an aptitude for chemistry offset by a frustrated desire to play basketball. When he topped out at 5'8", he realized he'd better stick to science.

As one of the few Black men in biotech, an alumnus of Boston University undergraduate and doctorate programs, a veteran of several startup companies, and someone who had a big outgoing personality, Tony was well known not just at Quercus but all around the Cambridge research community. But on the last Friday in May, shortly after being interviewed by a State Police trooper, he left the building in Cambridge around 4:30 p.m. and vanished.

Tony was a bachelor, and he often took off for the weekend to his cabin in New Hampshire. Monday was Memorial Day, so he wasn't missed until Tuesday, when he failed to show up for his group's weekly staff meeting. Now that was unusual – Tony was always available by phone or in person – and he kept close tabs on all of Quercus's manufacturing processes and ongoing experiments.

Around two in the afternoon, Thomas van Haft stopped by Benny's desk, looking for Tony. Maggie, hunched down behind her computer monitor, listened in unashamedly. Benny hadn't seen Tony, and despite his European formality, Thomas sounded worried.

"Tony's always going off hiking in the White Mountains by himself," Thomas was saying. "I've told him that it's dangerous to hike alone, even in areas that have trails, but he says he needs to get away after a week with all of us! I hope he's ok, and not fallen down a ravine somewhere."

"Should we call somebody?" asked Benny, looking in Maggie's direction. Ugh, thought Maggie, my brother couldn't bluff his way out of a paper bag. Fortunately, Thomas, preoccupied, didn't seem to notice. "New Hampshire State Police? Or the park rangers? Do you have the address of his cabin up there? Or maybe he stayed home – we could check at his place here. He lives in Cambridge, doesn't he?"

Thomas seemed nonplussed by this barrage of questions. "That's a good idea. Let me get his address from Anita," he said. "I can go by his place in Cambridge, at least. She might know where his place in the mountains is, too. She and Tony are pretty close – they both worked at Millennium together, back in the day." Millennium Pharmaceuticals had been a legendary early biotech in Cambridge; it seemed that half the current crop of biotechs, along with several of the big venture capital firms, were staffed by Millennium alumni. It was a great place to be from.

After Thomas left, Maggie nonchalantly got up and walked to the ladies' room, her cell phone in the rear pocket of her jeans. Once in a stall, she texted the new information to Lieutenant Davis, asking for an address but no police drive-by yet. Instead, she asked for an unmarked car to stake out Dupree's apartment, and look for a visit from a Caucasian male, 6'3", blond brush cut, wire-rim glasses.

Coming out of the ladies' room, Maggie almost collided with a woman who was rushing in. She had a brief impression of black hair and teary cheeks, recognizing her after the fact as Lisa Clark. Now what's she upset about? Maggie wondered.

*　　　*　　　*

Trooper Rick Forster was based at the Boston Barracks of the State Police, next to a causeway between Cambridge and Boston, by the Museum of Science at the head of the Charles River. Offered a plain-clothes assignment, he jumped at the chance to get out of his marked sedan and uniform. Suffering the comments of his fellow troopers for driving his wife's five-year-old Honda Odyssey to work, he relished the idea of using it as the perfect undercover car it was. Nobody, but nobody, would expect a cop on stakeout to be in a minivan with a pink bunny hanging from the rear-view mirror.

He found a parking spot just past the Greek Orthodox Church across the street from Tony's apartment, turned off the motor and opened the windows a bit for air. It was a three-story brownstone that apparently had three apartments inside, judging from the buzzers by the front door. With the trained patience of cops everywhere, he settled down to wait.

About 20 minutes later a man matching the description Maggie had sent in – tall, athletic, short blond hair – cycled up to the door of 21 Magazine Street and locked his white bike against a lamppost. He walked up the entrance stairs from the sidewalk and pushed on one of the entryway buzzers. Rick could hear the buzzer, and that there was no answer. The man looked around, then pushed sharply on the outer hall door with his hip. It opened without difficulty and the man walked in. Rick looked down at his watch and started timing.

He came out a moment later speaking on his cell phone. Finishing one call, he peered at a small plaque at the top of the entry stairs, and dialed another number. This call was longer, and required several pauses, perhaps as he was put on hold. Rick waited some more, and presently a Cambridge Police black-and-white rolled up to the curb. Two uniformed officers stepped out of the car as the man waved to them. They spoke for a few moments – Rick watching the pantomime – and they went inside. A few moments later a panel truck emblazoned with the name of a large real estate management company pulled into the alley next to the house. An older, heavyset man in gray overalls stepped out of the truck and clomped up the stairs. Rick waited some more. The whole cast came out about ten minutes later, with the first man getting back on his bike and heading toward the river, the man in overalls returning to his truck, while the patrol car turned around and headed back toward Central Square.

Rick looked up the phone number he'd written down in his spiral notepad for Eddie Bushell, and called him from the Honda. After explaining what he'd seen and giving Eddie the Cambridge cruiser number, he signed off. Not exactly the most thrilling undercover work, he thought as he pulled away from the curb, but still a nice change of pace.

*   *   *

Jorge Perez was having his weekly direct-reports meeting in one of the second-floor conference rooms. He played absently with a bicycle clip that would hold his trouser leg away from the chain on his way home. The room had one glass wall along the corridor, but its upper half was covered with venetian blinds that blocked anyone walking in the corridor from seeing the contents of any slides being projected. Only disembodied legs could be seen through the lower half of the wall, so one could tell if the room were occupied without walking in, but a modicum of privacy was preserved. Around the table were Benny, Lisa Clark , and Sandeep Mehta. The empty chair for Lilly Zhao was a grim reminder of her death.

Like many meetings, this one was superfluous. The lead program, QT-101, was waiting for the safety studies in monkeys to finish, and for the next batch of drug to be ready. That would be the GMP batch, made under Good Manufacturing Process guidelines and suitable for injecting into humans in the upcoming Phase 1 study. It would cost about two million dollars. The actual production work was being done at Quercus's manufacturing site in central Massachusetts, about an hour away by car. It was for funding these studies and the subsequent ones that the IPO was needed. Neither of these activities technically counted as "Research" – they were further downstream in the development process and thus technically no longer under Jorge's direction. But scientists are people, and they have a hard time letting go of their babies, so Jorge still wanted updates on the progress of QT-101. The follow-up program, that they had just disagreed about last week, wasn't going anywhere until they had new data, and that would take several more weeks. But that was squarely in the Research wheelhouse, and by god they were going to talk about it.

Benny was bored, but he knew that Jorge wouldn't cancel the meeting, and that he would want to rehash Lisa's data in this small group setting. And so it proved. They went over the experimental results again, with each person taking their allotted role: Benny calm but determined; Lisa near tears; Jorge impatient; Sandeep wary. Finally, they ran out of steam and the meeting broke up.

Benny and Sandeep walked out together. In the hall, Sandeep put a hand on Benny's arm and said, "Benny, I am sorry about Lilly, even though I didn't know her. I hope I can help with the safety studies while we look for a new head of toxicology. Is there anything I can do?"

Benny shook his head. He knew he had to keep the questions about the missing study report at bay for as long as possible. "Thank you, Sandeep, I appreciate that. I think when the study reaches the end of the in-life phase in a couple of weeks, we'll need you to help write the report. At that point we'll be under a lot of time pressure for the IND. Of course it will still take a couple of months after the study ends to get all the data."

"Sure, Benny, I'll take a look at the study design in the meantime," Sandeep said as they walked around the corner to their desks.

*   *   *

Back in the conference room, Lisa was gathering her notes and computer when Jorge walked behind her, putting his hands on her shoulders and massaging them. She leaned back into his chest. They both looked around quickly to make sure the door was closed, then kissed passionately.

"Oh, I've missed you," Lisa said. "I've been so scared, thinking about Lilly. Who could have done this to her? Some psycho? Why did she choose to go out running in the rain, in a big empty park?"

"I know, Lisa. It's very sad, and scary. It must have been some psychopath – Lilly didn't have any enemies! I'm still not used to the violence in America, after so many years in Europe. In Argentina, we had crime of course, but not in the good neighborhoods. Don't worry, I'm sure the police will catch the person."

"And then there's everything we have to do here, without her. We have the final tox report coming for QT-101, and we have all this bullshit Benny put up about the new program. Arrgh. It makes me want to scream."

"Don't worry, *Cariño*, we'll get it all sorted. The tox report will be fine, we're just waiting for the CRO to finish the study, and I'm sure you, me and Thomas can write the report even without Lilly. We can find a consultant toxicologist to sign off."

"And us? What about getting us sorted, Jorge?"

"Us too, baby," he said, kissing her again, this time with his hands going down her back to her waist. "Us too."

"And when's that going to be, darling?" she pushed him away. "I can't wait forever."

"Look, you know I love you, right? My wife is coming back from Argentina tomorrow, and I'll tell her it's over, and that I want a divorce. It's going to be really unpleasant, and painful, but I don't care. You know that it's you that I want. You and me. We can still have one night before it all hits the fan. How about tonight? Dinner at your place?"

Her face softened. This was more like it. "Yes, ok. Come over by eight. We'd better get out of here before someone sees us."

*   *   *

Maggie had looked at Benny's calendar on her computer, and stationed herself outside the conference room at ten minutes before the end of the hour allotted for the meeting. She stood at the sink in the common area, about twenty feet from the conference room door, and had a nice view of everyone's legs as they sat around the conference table. By the time Benny and Sandeep left the room, she had the cleanest coffee cup in the Western Hemisphere, but the common area was empty, and no one objected to her obsessive washing. Jorge and Lisa's subsequent encounter was a like a silent-film ballet, as she saw their lower bodies come together, separate, and come together again in ways that could only mean some serious kissing was going on. It's good that they only had eyes for each other, she thought, and didn't notice that the venetian blind was only half-way down. Hmm, she thought, I wonder what Anita's response as head of Human Resources would be to this situation.

Chapter Nine, Tuesday Afternoon, May 30th

Telling Benny she was going to run some errands at lunch, Maggie drove up to the Middlesex DA's office in Woburn. She walked in to find the rest of the team gathered around a couple of half-eaten pizzas, snagged a slice, and sat down with them.

Lieutenant Davis was rolling a large Cuaba cigar in one hand, clearly wishing he could light it indoors. To Maggie it looked like a hot dog with two tapered ends. Without preamble, he said, "So we have one dead employee and now another missing. Maggie, we had the place staked out as you had asked. Eddie spoke to the Cambridge PD and they found nothing in his apartment. That is, no sign of Dupree, and nothing suspicious to suggest any violence or abduction. So, is Antoine run or done? I mean, does he know something and he decided to run? Or did our guy strike again?"

"If he wanted to run," Eddie said, "he picked a good time to do it. With the long weekend, he got a 72-hour head start before anyone would miss him."

"The same applies to someone wanting to off him," said Jimmy. "I just heard back from New Hampshire State Police. They sent a car to his cabin. It's on Newfound Lake. They said it's a nice place, and not one of these super-fancy mansions. It's empty. The neighbors know him, but say they haven't seen him in a couple of weeks."

"Do we know if he was close to our victim?" Davis asked. They looked at Maggie, who shook her head. "I don't know, but I'll ask when I get back. I don't know how much their jobs overlapped – I mean, he does manufacturing and she ran toxicology. They don't sound very related, but it's a small company and everybody does a little bit of everything. I'll find out."

Davis nodded. "Jimmy, let's get a search warrant for his apartment in Cambridge. The wellness check by Cambridge PD was fine and good, but they weren't there to look for clues, just bodies. I also want to know what bank he uses, what credit cards, and let's see if we can track him that way. I don't think he's on the run from us, so he might have used a card to buy gas or check into a hotel. What kind of car does he drive? And where is it?"

Eddie turned to his computer and pecked away for a bit. "There's a 2022 Audi S5 registered to Antoine Dupree. No traffic violations." He jotted down the license plate and started typing a BOLO request.

Maggie said, "There aren't garages in those apartment houses on Magazine Street, as far as I know. He could street-park, but I'll bet you dollars to donuts that he has a long-term contract with one of the garages. The one on Greene Street is nearest. Let's ask Cambridge PD to check there first." Jimmy nodded and picked up the phone.

Maggie turned to the Lieutenant. "What about the autopsy? Anything new?"

"No," he said. "Death was due to a blow to the occipital fossa, according to the M.E. No drugs in her system. No recent intercourse, no pubic trauma. Hadn't eaten within the previous six hours. If she was going jogging and then planning to eat at her friend's restaurant in Medford Square, that would fit. It all suggests the suspect either followed her or met her at the park."

Eddie cleared his throat. "We got the doorbell camera footage uploaded and analyzed, by yours truly. There was someone on a bike who followed Lilly on Shore Drive on her way to the Fells. Can't tell if that's a coincidence or not, but she wasn't followed by any cars within five minutes of leaving. So either this is our suspect following her car on his bike, or he met her at the Fells and this is a red herring."

"Or he was already in the car. Could you tell if there was more than one person in the car when Lilly drove by?" said Maggie.

"No, from the few frames we have of her car, we can just see the outlines of the car itself. There were raindrops on the camera lens, which limited the quality even more. I'll take it to Ted and see if he can get any more out of it, though."

Maggie brought them up to date on the potential love affair at Quercus, and on the doctored research report that Benny had uncovered. No one was sure what to make of the relationship between Lisa and Jorge. It might be an HR violation, but it wasn't State Police business unless it connected to the murder.

Eddie chuckled. "So Lilly finds out that Lisa and Jorge are doing the dirty, and she blackmails one or both of them, so they off her? Seems a little far-fetched."

"Maybe so," Davis said, "but it gives them something to hide, and that can be a motive. Maggie, maybe it's worth having a little heart-to-heart with this Lisa Clark."

Maggie shrugged. "From what I've seen of her so far, she's not exactly warm and fuzzy. I'm not sure if she'll give me the time of day without my showing a badge, but I'll see what I can do."

They all agreed the research report sounded like a more likely motive, though the ins and outs of pharmaceutical development were a bit hazy to everyone.

"Let's assume that missing report had something bad in it," Maggie said. "Something that would mess up their lead program, or the IPO. Anything important would affect both, really – they're intertwined. So the people most interested in having that bit of information buried are the ones at the top of the leadership team, and the investors. They would lose the most if the IPO goes sour. That's Art Kehoe, the CEO; Thomas van Haft, the CSO; Jorge Perez, the head of research and development; Anita Mercer, the head of HR; Scott White, the head of Legal; and our missing friend, Antoine Dupree."

Davis stirred. "Jimmy, when you interviewed Kehoe, did you ask him for the documents that show who gets how much of the IPO?"

Jimmy smiled. "Oh, yeah. He hemmed and hawed and told me how confidential all this was, and how he wasn't sure if he could share it, and on and on. I gave him the 'this is a murder investigation' line, and that I would be happy to get search warrants for every computer they have, so he agreed to play nice."

He looked down at his notepad. "The investors get about 75% of the proceeds, and the founders – two scientists at Harvard – share 5 percent. That leaves Art with 4%; White, the lawyer and financial guy, gets 3%; van Haft with 3%; Perez, Mercer, and Dupree with 1% each; and the rest of the employees split the final 7%."

"Wow, it's good to be king," said Eddie.

"In this case, it's not bad to be a serf, either," said Maggie. "Seven percent of a billion is 70 million dollars, split among 34 employees, and with the hope of more if their drug works. And it's not like their salaries are at minimum wage, either."

Assistant DA Adele Watkins looked up from her notes. "You guys are forgetting something. When they say they're selling $900 million worth of shares, or whatever, that's not the total value of the company. Usually these IPO's, in biotech or whatever tech, they only sell about 20% of the company's voting shares. That means the companies valuation will be more like four or five billion dollars. These guys all stand to make much more if the drug succeeds and the VC's do what's called an 'exit' – they sell the rest of their shares either on the stock market or to some big pharma. So this is just the tip of the iceberg."

There was silence for a moment. Jimmy let out a low whistle. "Now, that's what I call a motive," he said.

"No wonder there are so many biotechs around here," Eddie said. "Adele, how do you know so much about this stuff?"

Adele smiled. "My mom works at Biogen. Like we always say, biotech is a small town."

"Well, don't forget," Maggie said, "nine out of ten drug programs fail, and so do a lot of these small companies. My brother told me the winners pay for the losers. That's why the successes are called unicorns, I guess."

Eddie shrugged, dismissing the woes of would-be millionaires and biotech bros. "Would the founders be suspects, too?"

Maggie shook her head. "I don't think they'd be very high on my list. Both are over seventy, one has a Nobel prize, and they don't have access to the internal file servers. No, I think we look at the management very closely."

"How about the investors? They're whaddayacallit, VC's, aren't they? Venture capital guys, right?"

"Yes, venture or vulture, depending on your point of view. They also don't have access to the systems, though. They sit on the board of directors, and they get monthly or quarterly reports on the progress, but they're not involved in the day-to-day operations. Again, I don't think they're high on our list."

Davis nodded. "I'll call Cybercrimes and ask them to loan us someone to do a deep digital dive on these guys," he said, referring to the Cyber Crimes Unit of the State Police. "Meanwhile, let's put out a BOLO for Antoine Dupree, and get that search warrant going on his apartment. Jimmy, get on to Verizon or whoever was her phone provider, and get a list of all the calls Lilly made from her cell phone and home phone since the week before she was killed. Maggie, you get back to Cambridge and see if you can connect Lilly to Antoine, and to this missing or doctored research report. And try to find out if there's a connection to our lovebirds, Jorge and Lisa. There has to be a link somewhere."

*   *   *

The Cybercrimes tech assigned to the case turned out to be Ted Sands, who had already been at the Chen's home and felt a kinship to the case, so he volunteered. It didn't take him long to hit pay dirt.

Kehoe, it turned out, wasn't Art's real name. Or at least not the one his parents had given him, which was Kauffman. Fifteen years earlier, he had started his business career in another aspect of health care, selling medical equipment to hospitals and clinics in Florida and the Gulf Coast. The confluence of easy money before the 2008 financial Crash, and intentionally myopic state oversight in the name of business-friendliness, created something of a gold rush in hospital and clinic building through the Southeast. That meant lots of deals were greased with kickbacks and even outright bribes.

When the first inklings of the coming financial meltdown began appearing, an astute Art Kauffman promptly switched sides, filing a whistleblower suit with the Department of Justice under the False Claims Act. Since much of the equipment was charged to the government under Medicare, DOJ took an interest and eventually won a $300 million settlement against Art's erstwhile friends and colleagues. Under the FCA, Art got twenty percent of that. He thought it prudent to disappear for a while, and change his name, business, and location. He surfaced again in 2018 with his new name, 30 pounds heavier, and a new job – CEO of the newly formed Quercus Therapeutics.

When Ted brought this information to light, Eddie, Jimmy, and Mike Davis exchanged glances, and the lieutenant blew out his cheeks in a silent exhalation.

"Wow," Eddie said, "this Quercus place is really a viper's nest. Who else is a crook around there?"

Jimmy was doodling on his notepad, shaking his head. "And I thought the real crime was on the streets."

"So the CEO has a past, and he's already gotten sixty million bucks from Uncle Sam for outsmarting his fellow crooks. Yet here he is, back at the trough. Hmmm…Ted, call Maggie and let her know. Jimmy, see if you can trace Mr. Keogh's whereabouts on Monday night and Tuesday morning."

Eddie's phone rang and he walked away to answer it. He came back with a grim smile. "That was Stoneham Police. They found Lilly's Camry. It wasn't far from her body, about a mile away, behind the old Boston Regional Medical Center building on the other side of Woodland Road from where she was found. I'm headed over there now. Crime Scene's already on the way."

Davis nodded in agreement. "See if there's a computer in the car!" he called to Eddie's back.

*　　　*　　　*

Boston Regional Medical Center, despite the fancy name, had been a small community hospital in the town of Stoneham, north of Boston, but it had closed over twenty years earlier. Situated on the eastern border of Middlesex Fells, the property had been mired in lawsuits, zoning hearings, and various unfulfilled plans for redevelopment ever since. Part of the land had been used for a long-term care facility, a nice term for nursing home, but the old hospital was quietly and sadly deteriorating behind a "temporary" chain-link fence that only added to the forlorn look of the place. At night, it wasn't even lit, except from distant streetlights and scattered floodlights on the next-door nursing home building.

The entrance was a driveway off Woodland Road, less than a mile north of the Tudor Barn. From the entrance, to the left were empty parking lots around the old hospital building, and to the right was an access road to the nursing home. Other than signs forbidding trespassing there was nothing to stop anyone from coming and going. Eddie noted that the nearest video camera was on the corner of the nursing home complex, but it was pointed away from the old hospital lots and toward the nursing home entrance.

The Camry was parked around the back of the former hospital, partially hidden by the chain-link fence and some bushes and low trees. A Stoneham patrol car and State Police Crime Scene Services van were already there. Eddie parked, got out, and introduced himself. They all gathered around the Toyota as the Crime Scene technicians dusted the outside for fingerprints before jimmying open the driver's side door.

Eddie had low expectations, and they were certainly met. There was no computer in the passenger cabin or the trunk of the car, no blood spatter or evidence of any struggle in the car. The ground around the car was grayed-out, cracked, granular asphalt, a surface that would not hold any footprints or any clue more subtle than a bucket of blood. Thanking the local police for their help in finding it, he left the technicians to finish their work and arrange for the car to be transported to the Crime Lab before it could be returned to Vincent Chen, if he even wanted it back.

*　　　*　　　*

Maggie got back to Quercus at about 3:30 in the afternoon. On the way she heard from Eddie that Cambridge Police had reached the manager of the Green Street garage, who confirmed that Antoine Dupree's Audi had a monthly spot there, and that it was not currently in the garage. So that could mean that Tony had run, of his own volition, rather than being done in by person or persons unknown. Jimmy was on the phone with Anita tracking down Tony's direct deposit account and would then contact the bank's fraud unit to track expenditures. That would work if Tony used a debit card, and another trooper would check with American Express, Visa, and Mastercard in the meantime.

Maggie grabbed a yellow pad from her desk and went directly to the third-floor office of Lisa Clark. Sticking her head in at Lisa's door, she said, "Excuse me, I'm Maggie, Benny's temp admin? He asked me to ask you if you have a research report that he can't find. Could you help me, or direct me to who could?"

Lisa was behind a wall of three computer screens, but Maggie could hear her exhale with annoyance. Still, she kept her voice calm.

"Sure," Lisa said, "what's the report number?"

"Um, it's QTRD1014295. He said he couldn't find it in the system."

"OK, let me take a look…No, I don't have anything with that number. I see QTRD1014296, maybe that's the one he meant?"

"Oh, maybe he mixed up the numbers. Thanks, I'll check with him again," Maggie said lightly. We'll see if Lisa goes running to Jorge with this, she thought. She walked noisily down the hall to the curving stairway to the second floor, wishing she had some bubble gum she could snap. Halfway down the stairs she stopped to jot something down on her yellow pad, then silently went back up the stairs. Approaching Lisa's office from the other side, along the wall that held her office door, she could see that Lisa was back behind her screens, head down and keyboard clacking away. No sign of panic so far, at least. Maintaining her position for a few minutes, until she felt too exposed, Maggie slipped down the hall to a fire exit that debouched onto a gray concrete stairwell, and went down to the second floor from the back of the building.

Back at her desk, she dropped the yellow pad and walked over to Benny's cubicle. Suddenly she felt a little abashed, seeing him here after their rather raw emotional review of their father's journals, a cognitive dissonance with her police investigator persona. Was she pushing him too hard? He obviously didn't like to expose himself to feelings, and here she was demanding exactly that from him, both on a personal front and about his work. He obviously cared deeply about Henry, and maybe even more about his work, which seemed to define him. She needed him on her side, and not cracking up, but she had a job to do and not much time to do it. Take a deep breath, she told herself. Benny's a big boy, after all.

Benny was reading a journal article, one that was actually printed out on paper and that he was highlighting with a yellow marker. He was completely immersed in it, unaware that she was standing before him. She had seen him do this when she was a little girl – it came back to her now – this preternatural ability to focus his entire being on the task in front of him. She had never had this ability, she knew. Dad said she was easily distracted, but she preferred to think of it as 'situational awareness', an important survival skill in her line of work.

"Ahem," she said, and repeated it until Benny, startled, looked up. "Your pants are on fire."

"Ha ha," he said. "Nice regression. You last said that to me when you were what? Six?"

She ignored him. "A lot's been happening. We should catch up. Maybe time for another Flour Bakery run?"

He nodded, looking around. There were a few occupied desks around them, but none immediately nearby, and no one paid them any attention. They walked down the curving staircase to the ground floor and out to Sidney Street. It definitely felt like summer now – close to 90 degrees, and clear.

"At least the air is better now," he said. "The smoke seems to have shifted away from here, at least for now."

Maggie didn't waste time on small talk. "Lilly Zhao was killed by a blow to the head, wrapped in laboratory film, and stored in a barn. Tony Dupree is missing, his car is gone, and we've got a BOLO out for him. We found Lilly's car up by the Fells, but not her phone or computer. She may have been followed by someone on a bicycle on the evening she was killed. Or not. There's a missing research report that could have an impact on the billion-dollar IPO you guys are planning, and no one can find a copy of it. The CEO is using an alias and has a criminal background, and Jorge Perez is screwing Lisa Clark. What kind of company is this, Benny?"

Benny stopped walking, looking pale despite the warm day. He stumbled over to a curved granite bench that fronted a small lawn next to the Cambridge Fire Station at the corner of Sydney Street and Massachusetts Avenue. Maggie sat down next to him. It was clear he was shaken, and that he didn't know most of what she had just dumped on him. It helped her with trusting him. So did knowing he didn't need the money, though there could be other motives, too. Hating to lose, for example. Shame of failure, whatever. She outlined more of the details of what she knew so far.

As Benny recovered, adjusting to the new information as he would to new and unwelcome experimental results, he looked grim.

"Jorge and Lisa?" he asked. "You're kidding, right?"

"Everything I just told you, and *that's* what you focus on? Seriously?"

"Well, it seems the easiest to come to terms with. Explains a lot about their pushing that second program…"

Maggie rolled her eyes. "Can we keep our eyes on the prize here? Lilly is dead, and Tony is either dead or abducted or on the run. What about that report could connect the two of them?"

"Oh, that's pretty clear. The assay that Lilly needed for her toxicology studies is basically the same one that Tony would use to approve release of new batches of drug. It's used in a slightly different format, but the basics are the same. There's an antibody made against the drug, and there's a bioluminescent tag. That's a small molecule that glows in the dark if exposed to ultraviolet light. If the antibody binds to the drug it changes shape, releases the tag into the fluid around it, and it glows when it goes under ultraviolet light in a UV plate reader. The more drug, the more antibody binds to it. The more antibody, the more tag is released. The more tag is released, the stronger the color. We can read 384 wells at a time with duplicate sampling, so that means we have a fast way to measure how much drug is there."

Maggie shook her head. "You know, you take it for granted, but it sounds like magic."

Benny smiled. "Well, there's a line from Arthur C. Clarke, you know – 'any sufficiently advanced technology is indistinguishable from magic.' People in Cambridge say that a lot."

He continued, "But the point is that if Lilly found out that there was something wrong with the assay, she would naturally take it to Tony. Her problem is his problem, you see. If it was just a technical issue with the assay, that's not so bad, it could be fixed given enough time and money, probably a few months and modest expense. But if the assay worked and the results showed something bad – like not enough drug getting into the rats Lilly was testing, or an unexpected metabolic pattern – well that would be a much bigger deal. In that case, it would work for Tony, because he just measures drug in water from the vial, but not for Lilly, who's measuring it in blood after it was injected into a rat. That could mean reworking the drug itself, and that could take years. Bye-bye, IPO."

Maggie nodded. "So if we can figure out how Lilly shared the report with Tony, we could get a lead on finding a copy. If she just printed it and gave it to him, we'd have to find him first. If she sent it electronically, there might be a trail. Meanwhile, we're looking for Tony of course, and I think we're going to show up in force at Quercus tomorrow."

Benny suddenly sat up, slapped his forehead, and said, "Of course. I should have thought of this earlier. Let me do some digging, I'll let you know in the morning if there's another way to get this report. I think I've got one."

Chapter Ten, Wednesday, May 31st

The team met in the Woburn office at 7:30 on Wednesday morning, Lt. Davis providing coffee and donuts. Somewhere two miles up and two thousand miles away, the winds had shifted again, and the sky had an amber haze once more. Not as bad as the previous week, but it still smelled like cold cigarette butts. The cast had grown to include the three detectives, Davis, Ted Sands from Cybercrimes, Adele Watkins, and three uniformed troopers who were working the search for Tony.

Normally, Maggie would be leading the team on a minute-to-minute basis, with guidance from the Lieutenant, who acted like a coach to Maggie's quarterback. But with her undercover role limiting Maggie's presence with the team in Woburn or in the field, Mike Davis had stepped back into a more active 'player' role. He clearly enjoyed getting back into the action, though whether the others agreed was unclear.

If Maggie had any concerns about being supplanted, she didn't voice them. Eddie, however, had no hesitation in commenting. Putting on his best Down East accent, he said, "Ayep, it's like old Doc Johnson said of the three-legged dancing dog – the impressive thing is not that he does it well, but that he does it at all. Right, Lieutenant?"

Ignoring Eddie, Mike Davis handed out coffees and everyone grabbed a donut. He opened the meeting by saying, "I think it's time to start putting more pressure on this situation, see if we can pop something loose. Jimmy and I will go into Quercus today and interview Keogh, van Haft, and the whole leadership team. We're going informally, trying not to have anybody lawyer up. We'll search Tony's desk, and also his computer if it's there. Maggie, I think you need to stay under cover for a bit longer, see what happens after we leave. Eddie, you and the others concentrate on finding Tony. Any updates overnight?"

Eddie pointed at Heather Martin, a uniformed corporal with brown eyes, curly brown hair, and a serious expression. Consulting her spiral notebook, she said, "Tony's last gas station receipt is from Friday afternoon at the Sunoco station right by his work. He took out $1000 in cash at the Bank of America in Central Square after that. No credit card activity since then. No highway toll pass activity, so he's not on an interstate toll road, though he could be anywhere along I-95, of course."

"So it looks like he's on the lam, rather than being another body somewhere," said Maggie. "That's good for him, and for us. How about his cell phone?"

"It's been off since last Friday. Do you want us to leave a voicemail or text in case he checks it?" asked Heather.

"I think it's worth it," Maggie answered. "It's a risk in case the phone is in the hands of someone else, though it seems more likely to be with him, but switched off. I bet he'll try to check when he gets on Wi-Fi somewhere but can stay off the cellular network. If he's really an innocent in this, he might call in. I can leave him a message with my name and number; he could check up on me with Benny if he wanted to. Of course, if he's the one who faked the research report, and he's running because he's guilty, and he's actually the one who killed Lilly, then this will just tip him off."

Jimmy grunted. "If he's the bad guy, he's gonna assume *someone* is after him, it doesn't matter if you give him a name. But why would he run now? We're not exactly hot on the heels of anyone. There hasn't been any publicity to suggest he's been identified as the killer."

"Yes," Maggie said slowly. "It seems more likely that he's running because Lilly is dead, not because he killed her. I think."

She turned to Mike Davis. "How do you want to handle the Perez-Clark affair? We could use it to our advantage. If they're found out, they could both lose their jobs. These biotechs all have very strict policies about relationships between supervisors and employees."

"Yes, and it could also be a motive for murder, couldn't it?" Davis replied. "I think we bring it up when we interview Perez, let's see how shaken he gets. Then we talk to Clark right after, before Perez can warn her."

* * *

Maggie drove through rush hour traffic to Cambridge, tuning in the radio news on her way. To her surprise, Dan Beardsley had run with the wacky story she had given him, telling his audience about 'unnamed sources near the investigation' voicing concern about Chinese Communist Party agents suspected of a role in the 'Middlesex Fells Murder.'

Oh, shit, she thought, I forgot to call Vincent. Taking advantage of the stop and go traffic, she dialed Vincent Chen's number and explained-apologized for the story on the news. Fortunately, he hadn't heard it, and also, it seems, he had finally gotten some sleep and was bemused but not upset. She only hoped Mike Davis would be as forbearing.

She got to her desk at Quercus by 8:45, but was surprised to find Benny was already there, and on the phone. He waved to her almost gaily, gesturing that he would be off shortly and had something to tell her. She nodded, got coffee, and fired up her computer. There were definitely more people around today, as Wednesday was normally the day for the weekly noon science lecture with pizza, the same one that had been supplanted by the business meeting the previous week.

A few minutes later, Benny came over, smiling. "I got it!" he said loudly.

"Shh! Got what, Benny?" Maggie said at a much lower volume. Benny grimaced, looking around in a way guaranteed to raise the suspicion of anyone with evil intent.

Maggie groaned to herself, again reassured that he was a pretty unlikely suspect himself.

In a more confidential tone that couldn't be heard three feet away but still betrayed his obvious excitement, Benny said, "I've got the 4295 report. Or at least the raw data for it. A small company like Quercus doesn't have GLP facilities – we can't do our own toxicology studies at the level of control the FDA requires. So we outsource them to a CRO."

Maggie held up a hand in a 'stop' motion.

"TLA's, Benny, TLA's. I barely know what FDA is. What's GLP? What's a CRO?"

He put a hand to his forehead. "Sorry, sorry. GLP is Good Laboratory Practice, it's a set of regulations about how to do research and especially how to document what you did, so it's clear and reproducible. And auditable, which is what FDA cares about. They pretty much assume we fake stuff if we can't prove we didn't. And CRO is a contract research organization. They work for dozens of companies – both biotechs and big pharmas – and they have all the GLP bells and whistles in place so that their reports can be submitted without a problem. That's why I couldn't find anything in our ELN here…"

He saw her frown at him and added, "…our electronic lab notebook. That would have been impossible to fake or erase. But there were no data, no protocols, no statistical code at Quercus. Those are things that are probably impossible to erase or change because of the Part 11 software I was telling you about the other day. Every file is permanently stored, so even when there are evolving versions of them, each one is saved in the system, even if there was only one keystroke different from the previous version. But a report isn't primary data – it doesn't sit in multiple places, just one. You can overwrite it like any Word document. If someone had the IT clearance, I think they could have figured out how to delete it. Yesterday when we were outside and I thought about it more, and realized there had to be a CRO involved. The original report – 4295 – was probably done by one of our regular partners. We mostly use a company called PTS, Preclinical Toxicology Solutions. I have a contact there who I know pretty well from my Pfizer days, so I called him. He doesn't have the final report, but he has the experimental protocol and the raw data. They also have the full 4295 study contract, so it's definitely the right one. He's sending that to me now. So I should be able to basically write the report for us, and compare it to the 4296 version."

"That's great, Benny, well done!" Maggie said. "How long do you think it will take to figure it all out?"

"I'm not sure, it depends on what's going on. You know how it is, work expands to time allotted. But I should have it done by the end of the day, I would guess."

At that moment Mike Davis and Jimmy O'Connor came up the curving staircase from the first floor, and proceeded – police always proceed, they never just walk – to Art Keogh's corner office at the front of the building, overlooking Sydney Street and the garden below. Davis ignored Maggie, but Jimmy gave her a quick side-eye glance, and tapped his cell phone with his forefinger. She gave a single short nod. Benny looked at her curiously but didn't say anything. Maggie gave him a little smile as she turned away and put her headphones on her head, answering the incoming call from Jimmy at the same time. Jimmy had put his phone in his blazer breast pocket, so the microphone and camera were looking forward over the edge of the seam, making Maggie a surreptitious eyewitness to their interview with Keogh without blowing her secretarial cover. As long as Maggie kept her own microphone on mute, she could see and hear without being seen or heard herself.

Art Keogh was at his desk, eating a Danish pastry and reviewing documents, when Davis and Jimmy walked in. He was wearing the CEO man-of-the-people uniform, white oxford shirt and dark blue jeans with a pressed crease down the front, and white Nikes. The room smelled rather strongly of Dior Sauvage. He looked up, surprise and annoyance chasing each other across his round face. Mike Davis introduced himself and Jimmy, and explained that they needed Keogh's help with their investigation. His tone was placatory but his stance, with Jimmy towering behind him, gave a different non-verbal message. There was a deft but unspoken threat, the mailed fist inside the velvet glove.

"Of course, Lieutenant," Keogh said in his booming voice, even though he was keeping it down to minimize interest from curious colleagues. "What can I do for you?"

"We're trying to understand if there was a motive for Lilly's murder in her activities here at work, Mr. Keogh," Davis began. "Do you know if she had any issues here? Any trouble? We'll ask your HR director, of course, but I'd like to hear your thoughts."

Keogh drummed the desk with three fingers. "No, I don't think so. Certainly nothing that reached me. Anita and Thomas – that is, Anita Mercer the head of HR, and Thomas van Haft, our CSO – would be the best ones to ask. As I'm sure you will, I'm sure you will…" he trailed off.

"If she found something wrong in her toxicology study, would that potentially derail your IPO, Mr. Keogh?" asked Davis disingenuously.

"Well…I suppose it could, but we've not seen anything of concern, you know. Everything has been moving ahead according to plan. We should have the final toxicology in a few weeks, and then we'll be filing our IND. Uh, that's Investigational New Drug application to the FDA – that will give us permission to start treating humans. Our IPO is coincident with that so we can ensure the funding for the clinical trials. For these sort of gene therapies like QT-101, a lot of the costs are front-loaded, you know. The manufacturing alone will be over $20 million."

"We understand that a research report relating to this QT-101 is missing, Mr. Keogh," Davis was sitting down now, leaning forward. Maggie had a view of his back and Art's face from where Jimmy was still standing, behind

Davis. She imagined him with his arms akimbo, face impassive, looking like a stone-cold vision of the long arm of the law. Should scare the hell out of Art, she thought.

Keogh was clearly surprised by this announcement, his mouth gaped and he pulled his head back like a shying horse. "Wh…what? What do you mean? How could that be? We have systems in place to preserve all our documents, you know. Where did you get this information? You must be mistaken!"

"No, I don't think so," Davis said grimly. "We'll keep our sources confidential for now, if you don't mind. But I think we'll be asking for your permission to have our Cybercrimes Unit send someone over to look at your systems with a fine-tooth comb. I'd like that permission voluntarily, of course, and in writing, but if you prefer, we can get a search warrant. Of course, that would shut you down for a few days…or weeks." Maggie grinned on her end of the phone as she saw Keogh go even whiter.

"Of course, we're happy to cooperate, Lieutenant. Lilly was one of our own. Anything we can do to help," Keogh said.

"Thank you. Detective O'Connor will fill out a permission release for your signature. Now on another topic, we've also learned that you have a somewhat checkered career in healthcare, don't you, Mr. Keogh? Or should I say, Mr. Kauffman?" Davis sat back to see the effect of this line of questioning.

Keogh's complexion turned from white to red. "Now see here, Lieutenant, what does that have to do with anything? I was young and I got caught up in something that turned out to be rotten. Once I realized it, I turned to the authorities and helped them close the whole thing down. Sure, I made some money out of it, but I didn't make the rules – I just followed them."

"I don't know, Mr. Keogh. I looked into that case. You were neck deep in these illegal kickback schemes for several years, weren't you? You were smart enough to see the end was coming, and then you ratted out your fellow crooks. Isn't that an equally fair characterization of what happened?"

Keogh sat back and exhaled loudly, looking at Davis from under lowered brows. His voice was quieter when he answered, totally in control again. "How much do you know about the American healthcare system, Lieutenant?"

Davis shrugged. "I know enough to try and avoid it as much as possible," he said.

"Exactly, and that's the right response. But do you know why? It's because taking care of the sick in America went from being a profession – medicine – to being a business – healthcare – slowly at first but faster and faster since the 1980's. Do you know why there are no more country doctors with a shingle on Main Street? No more Norman Rockwell doctors? Because there's no profit in it, and the whole system is designed to maximize profit, not maximize health. Healthcare in the US costs much more than anywhere else, for results that are no better, and certainly are a lot less equitably distributed. The whole system is immoral, sure, but I didn't create it. I just rode that wave for a while, Lieutenant, that's all."

Davis shrugged. "We all know the healthcare system is dysfunctional, Mr. Keogh. That's hardly news."

Keogh shook his head. "Don't you believe it. There are no dysfunctional systems, Lieutenant. Every system is designed to give exactly the results that it produces. Like I said, the goal of the American system is not to maximize health, it's to maximize profits."

He continued, "And you know what's really ironic? While we've created this horrible system that grinds individual patients up for bait, it's also created the greatest explosion of new medicine, new treatments, and new knowledge in the history of mankind. Do you have any idea how much things have changed? Today there are almost 20,000 FDA-approved medicines. We have not just pills, but antibodies, and proteins, and RNA drugs, and gene therapies, and even therapeutic apps on your phone. Things we couldn't even dream of 30 years ago. It's all a byproduct of the greed of the system. Sometimes, greed really is good. Do you think we could have made a vaccine against Covid in less than a year at any other time in human history? Not a chance. And it worked really well, didn't it? Saved millions of lives."

He looked up at the ceiling. "You know, we're building something really important here. ALS is a horrible disease. It kills people in the prime of their lives, and it does it slowly and cruelly, scarring the survivors as it does so. QT-101 could change that, you know. And I'm going to make damn sure it gets a chance."

Davis looked at him. "Very noble, Mr. Keogh. I'm sure you're right about all of that. But if Lilly found out something that would stop QT-101 from going forward, maybe for a very good reason, like it doesn't work as advertised or it's not safe, then you have a very good motive for murder, don't you? And so does your whole management team. By the way, where were you on Monday evening?"

"I was here until about 6:30, I think. Yes, that's right. And then Scott White and I went to dinner with our investment bankers from Morgan Stanley. Thomas was there with us, though he came a little later. We were at Harvest in Harvard Square. I can get the receipt if you like. I had the scampi."

"We will certainly check, don't worry. Why was Dr. van Haft late?"

"Oh, he bikes everywhere," Keogh waved a hand to show how crazy that was. "So do a lot of our folks. Jorge bikes in from Wellesley every day, for God's sake. Several of our associates do Ironman competitions. Anyway, Thomas said he had a flat tire. He looked like he'd been changing a tire, too – had to wash the black marks off his hands before he could eat."

Jimmy noted it all down. "Meantime, here's what we're going to do, Mr. Keogh," Davis said. "Detective O'Connor and I are going to talk to your team, one at a time. Then we're going to get our cybercrimes people in here to look at the Quercus document system. And you're not going to say one word to anybody until I come back here after I've talked to the others. I'm going to have a very nice policewoman come up and sit with you. She's cute, you'll like her. But if you pick up that phone and call anyone and mention this investigation, you'll be up on obstruction of justice charges so fast it'll make your head spin. *Capisce?*"

Keogh nodded, looking deflated. "Yes, Lieutenant. I have more sense than to get in the way of a murder investigation, thank you very much. I want this sorted as much as you do, both for Lilly and for QT-101, and all the people here who've put their heart and souls into this drug. I'm willing to stand behind our science, no matter what."

Despite herself, Maggie was a little impressed with old Art. Either he wasn't all sleazebag, or he was a hell of an actor. Upon reflection, she realized the two were not mutually exclusive.

*　　　*　　　*

Davis and O'Connor next met with Anita Mercer in her office. Jimmy kept Maggie dialed in via their cell phones. They introduced themselves and started by asking Anita to tell them about herself. She looked to be in her early fifties, a little on the heavy side, with streaked blond hair pulled back in a loose chignon, green eyes that looked like they'd seen it all, and wearing red lipstick that stood out against pale foundation and muted eye shadow. She was dressed a cut above the studied casual-slob of the scientists, in a light green silk blouse that favored her eyes, and a beige skirt with matching heels. After Keogh's overpowering cologne, Anita's subdued Chanel No. 5 was a welcome relief.

"Not much to tell, really, officers," she said, taking sips of coffee from a remarkably large travel cup. "I've been doing HR work – now we call it 'People and Organizations' but it's still the same human relationship stuff – for over twenty years. I started in retail, at TJ Maxx in Framingham, and then went to biotech about 10 years ago. I've been at a few of them. It's a funny business – a combination of idealistic scientists out to save the world and arrogant venture capital types who think they're 'disruptors' but really just want to become billionaires. There's always tension between the two groups. The closer a drug gets to approval, the greater the friction, and the more the real world intervenes, and the more power shifts from the scientists to the commercial people."

"How is it here at Quercus?" asked Davis. "Is it more fraught than usual?"

Anita thought about this. "Nooo, I wouldn't say that exactly. But the frictions have emerged sooner than usual because of this IPO. We're just entering the clinic with our lead drug, and everyone's very excited about it, but there's all this tension around getting the IPO done, priced right, and the stock launched. Not so many companies even get this far, you know."

"How about you, Ms. Mercer?" asked Davis. "You're on the leadership team. How much do you stand to gain or lose with this IPO?"

"Ha, I wish," Anita said. "Sure, I'm on the management team, but HR people are interchangeable, you know? They don't matter to the reputation of the company or the ability to attract investors or marquis employees. I'll get about one percent, and I'll be very happy with it. We don't have any kids to hold us back, so my husband and I are talking about moving to North Carolina, where his family is from. I'll be fine even if the IPO disappears."

"Still, that's ten million dollars if all goes well," Davis said.

She didn't reply, so he pressed on. "And does this management team get along? Do they work well together?"

"That's not the same thing, you know. They do work well together, but mostly because they have good fences. I don't think they're buddy-buddy in any way. Art is purely focused on the business aspects, he and Scott really handle all that, and Art lets Thomas run the scientific enterprise as he sees fit. Scott handles the contracts, and especially the patent stuff, which is really complicated. Fortunately, Thomas is a cool and efficient manager of everything else, he's very smart and knows the details of the research programs. He has an eidetic memory, you know."

Davis looked askance. "A photographic memory, in other words," Anita explained.

Davis shrugged. "So did Stalin," he said.

Anita smiled, but it didn't reach her eyes. "Thomas also hires well – Jorge, Tony, and Benny really know their stuff. Anyway, there's not much socializing outside of work, though, except at Christmas parties and the like. The company's grown rapidly, you know. We were ten people two years ago and now we're forty and still hiring. It'll really take off after the IPO, because we'll need to bring in more clinical expertise, and people to do the manufacturing, and hire commercial people for the first time to start planning for late-phase development and – we hope – approval and launch. Right now we only have Benny Mason and Rob Handler on the clinical side, and nobody on commercial. Art mostly handles that along with Scott, but it's all very high-level, theoretical stuff at the moment."

"Are there any hostilities?" asked Jimmy, speaking up for the first time. "Anyone who can't stand each other?"

"Well, not obviously. I don't think Benny likes Jorge much, but it's not anything dysfunctional. Thomas and Scott often see things differently, but that's kind of expected with their different roles and backgrounds. It's always been amicable, though."

She paused for a minute, then said, "Look, these biotechs, there's a lot of arrogance here, you know? Some of it is justified, they're making medicines for incurable diseases, but some of it is defensive, because they're scared they'll fuck up. And some of them are just assholes. For the most part, though, I'd say 90 percent of the people, they're young and idealistic and looking to change the world. A biotech is like a diamond mine in a pigsty – there's the hope of a great treasure, but it doesn't necessarily smell so good. Also, there are a lot of introverts in science, and you see that here. It means people aren't necessarily very good at communicating, except in a very technical sense. The extroverts are in sales and marketing. Like I said, we don't have any of those folks here yet, but that's what the IPO will bring."

"Really?" asked Davis, "there are no extroverted scientists?"

"Well, sure there are, but they tend to gravitate toward medicine, or the business side of biotech. You know the joke don't you? What's the difference between an introverted scientist and an extroverted one? The introvert looks at his shoes when he's talking to you, and the extrovert looks at your shoes."

She smiled to dilute the force of what she was saying. "You know, the biotech workforce's average age is like 35 or something – this is still an age when people are trying to find themselves. The executives are older, of course, late 40's to mid-50's, so they don't have as much excuse."

"How about Lilly Zhao, Ms. Mercer?" asked Davis as Jimmy was taking notes. "Did she ever come to you with any issues? Was she having trouble with anyone?"

"No, she never did. She was such a classic introvert, dedicated, as far as I could tell, to her family and her work. She had come from China, where she had a very traditional upbringing, and she excelled because she was smart and worked really hard. You don't succeed there if you don't keep out of trouble, stay off the Communist Party radar.

Though I heard on the radio coming in, that she might in fact have gotten in some hot water with them. I'm sure you'd know more about that than I would."

At her desk, Maggie grimaced. She hadn't mentioned that Dan Beardsley item to Davis yet, and was willing to bet he hadn't been listening to the news in the car coming down here.

Maggie guessed that both Davis and Jimmy had kept a poker face, because Anita continued. "If she was having any issues here, she would probably keep them to herself, you know? She would worry more about getting in trouble by complaining than about an interpersonal issue. But from what I saw of her, she also had a very strong, almost rigid, sense of right and wrong, good and bad. Again, maybe that's the Communist childhood, but if she thought something was wrong it would really bother her. I'm going to miss her."

* * *

Scott White, the lawyer, was a large, friendly-seeming man who reminded Mike Davis of John Candy. Despite his size, he moved gracefully around his desk to meet the detectives, close his office door, and take them to a small round table with four chairs. The shrewd brown eyes behind silver wire-rim glasses appeared unfazed by having the State Police in his office. Definitely a cool customer, but then, he's a lawyer, thought Davis, as he ran through his now well-rehearsed introduction.

"I don't know that there's much I can tell you, gentlemen," White said. His voice was as calm and unflustered as his gaze. "I'm not the scientist around here, but I did train as a chemist before going to law school, so I could understand how to get the patents right. I certainly know Lilly Zhao, but no more or less than any of the other people in such a small company. You know, it's pretty intense here, with everything moving toward the clinic, exciting data coming out, and of course the IPO."

"You're one of the original employees around here, aren't you?" Davis asked neutrally.

"Yes, I think I was number five. Once the founders decided they needed to get out of the academic sphere to move their ideas forward, and agreed to found the company, they went to our original investors and hired Art, Thomas, me, and a couple of techs to get things going. My part was tech transfer – getting the IP from the university to Quercus cleanly, and patenting our new inventions as they started coming out."

"IP?" Jimmy asked. "What's that?"

"Oh, sorry, that's biotech alphabet soup. Intellectual Property, a fancy name for patents and knowhow that protects research from being stolen."

Davis looked up. "But it creates a monopoly, right?"

White beamed. "Yes, exactly. Twenty years, though with additional patents and patent extensions, you can sometime go substantially longer."

"And charge substantial prices," Davis said.

"Yes, that's what makes the system work, you know. Without the profit motive, nothing gets done. No such thing as altruism, really."

"But with it, you charge so much that lots of people can't afford the drugs you create, right?"

"We offer discounts and even free medicine under certain circumstances," White said patiently. "But if the drug was never invented, it wouldn't do anyone any good, would it?"

Back at her desk, Maggie shook her head. She'd heard variations on this theme three times now, and it was getting old. Biotech was both an amazing producer of cures and a deal with the devil in terms of expense and inequity.

Davis was ready to move on. "So as one of the earliest employees, and a member of the management team, you stand to do very well from this IPO, don't you, Mr. White?"

"Um, yes, I would say so. But I've been working here over five years, I've put in my sweat equity too."

Jimmy tilted his head at White. "We're told you get about three percent of the company. That's $30 million if the IPO goes well, isn't it?"

"Yes," White answered. He didn't add any more.

Lawyer, thought Maggie. Trained in the art of staying quiet.

"And that's a pretty good motive for murder, if someone was going to spoil the IPO," Davis said, inflecting it a bit into a question.

White nodded. "Yes, I suppose it would be. But why do you think that's the case? It's not in anyone's interest here to mess up the IPO. It would ruin the company."

"Well, Lilly Zhao found that a key technical report on the quality of your lead drug wasn't right. She was trying to track down the real results, and she wound up dead. From what we've heard about her, Lilly was a very straight arrow. Someone who would do what was right even if it cost a lot. It looks like it cost her everything."

"Well, Lieutenant, it's the first I'm hearing of it," Scott White said firmly. "It sounds awful, but I can't imagine anyone here harming her. We're a tight-knit group – that's what comes of working for so long to try and make a new drug. It's a bonding experience. If you don't believe in the program, it's too much hard work and takes too long to see results to stay with it. People who haven't drunk the Kool-Aid, they don't stay."

"Where were you on Monday night, May 23rd?" asked Davis.

"Art and I had dinner with our investment bankers at Harvest, as I'm sure you know by now," White replied. "We finished up around 9:30 or a little after, and Art and I each drove home. Thomas had his bike, as usual."

"Did you drive to the restaurant separately, or did you leave your cars here and come back for them?" Jimmy asked.

"We drove separately, because we both live in the other direction from here, and not near each other."

"So you didn't come back to the office after dinner?"

"That's right. I went straight home."

"Thank you, Mr. White," Mike Davis got up. "I'm sure we'll have more questions as our investigation proceeds. Please don't leave town without talking to us first." He put his business card on White's desk as they left.

*　　　*　　　*

They moved on to Thomas, who sat with them in his office. Behind his desk was a large picture window overlooking Sydney Street and the gardens in front of the Quercus building. In front of the window was a credenza with a fancy espresso machine, all shiny chrome and black knobs, that was working industriously to produce a thimbleful of coffee as they walked in. Thomas was wearing narrow, tailored, expensive-looking beige gabardine slacks and a midnight-blue polo shirt without any logo. He looked fit and relaxed as he took up his coffee. He didn't offer them any. Jimmy still had his open phone connection with Maggie, and they did their now routine introductions and explanation of the purpose of the meeting.

"I am happy to try and help you, Lieutenant," Thomas said, sounding somewhat formal with his Dutch accent a little more prominent than usual. "I am shocked by what happened to Lilly, and of course now I'm worried about Tony as well."

"Did Lilly say anything about finding a problem with a research report, Dr. van Haft?" Davis asked, matching Thomas's formality.

"Um, no, not that she told me. She reports…reported to Jorge, so I would generally only speak with her in group meetings or if she had a specific question where I could help. My research background is in lipid nanoparticles, that's a little different from Lilly or Jorge, you see."

He paused, then continued, "Maybe I should clarify, officers, that what we do here is like trying to put a man on the moon. I'm a bit of an amateur historian, so perhaps you'll forgive me a little lecture? You see, two hundred years ago, medicine was one step removed from voodoo. Doctors were atrociously trained, often with just a few months of medical 'education' even at the better medical schools, and they learned by apprenticeship to older doctors who knew very little biology. They used texts written hundreds of years earlier, and they had only a few drugs that did anything at all, mostly from plants. The poppy gave opium, wintergreen gave a precursor of aspirin, quinine from a bush from Peru could treat malaria. Otherwise they used poison – mercury and arsenic, among others – hoping the dose that helped the disease was just a little less than the dose that killed the patient…it was a shambles."

Davis sat back and watched Thomas as he spoke. Jimmy was making indecipherable doodles in his pad.

"Then, a few breakthroughs: Jenner's vaccine for smallpox was about 200 years ago. Across the river in Boston in the 1840's, Warren and Morton demonstrated that you could use ether to anesthetize a surgical patient. A few years later Semmelweis in Vienna figured out that washing hands was a good idea before delivering a baby, and from there we got to germ theory with Pasteur and Lister. But it was the chemists who really brought us into the modern age. Paul Ehrlich invented the first antibiotic in 1907. He called it the 'magic bullet', because it killed the bacteria but not the host. And you know what it was for? Hah – syphilis!"

Thomas's face was flushed, his eyes glittered, but he wasn't really looking at either policeman. He seemed to be looking into the past. Jimmy noted that he seemed relaxed, unflustered. His hands were perfectly still on the arms of his chair.

"The entire pharmaceutical industry grew out of the companies those chemists founded, mostly between 1860 and 1900. They didn't start out trying to make drugs – most of them were working on a much more important topic – fashion! They were making dyes, aniline dyes, to make dresses in bright colors for women who were sick and tired of wearing drab clothes in black or beige. Some of those dyes – gentian violet, crystal green – turned out to cure skin infections. But most importantly, the chemistry that made dyes possible was also applicable to making medicines. Salvarsan, aspirin, cocaine, morphine, heroin – that was just a better painkiller, once – all came out of chemical companies that transformed themselves into drug companies by the early twentieth century. And then insulin, and sulfa and penicillin, and eventually drugs for high blood pressure and depression and birth control, but most of those are only since the 1960's."

Thomas sipped some of his espresso. Davis was about to interrupt him when he resumed his lecture.

"For the first hundred years of the pharmaceutical industry, gentlemen, all those chemists worked on about fifty drug targets. But then in the 1980's it became possible to make drugs out of antibodies. Man-made antibodies, designed to hit a chosen target, not just random ones like buckshot from a shotgun. And then about twenty years ago, with the Human Genome Project, all of a sudden we had thousands of targets. Thousands! We didn't even know what most of them did, but we could see that mistakes in the genetic code could predict diseases, and the race to find ways to fix those mistakes – either with a pill, or with a protein, or now by fixing the DNA itself – that's the gold rush we're in now, and it will change everything. All the eons of human misery caused by disease – we have a chance to end that. Cancer? I'll bet you in twenty years nearly all of it will be curable. Babies born with genetic disorders that leave them vegetables? I'm sure they'll become treatable, probably even before birth. Dementia? It may take longer, but we're beginning to crack it. And here in our little company, we think we can cure Lou Gehrig's disease, ALS – maybe the cruelest way to die of them all."

"That's a lovely history lesson, Doctor…" Davis began, but Thomas raised a hand.

"Indulge me for another moment, Lieutenant. I promise to answer all your questions after that. Do you know why all these biotechs are here, in Cambridge? It's because of the nearby universities and hospitals – that's where the original ideas came from over the past forty years, the original technology that became *bio*-technology. And it's the ability of researchers to go back and forth between the two – between academic centers and companies – that made all this possible. It happened here and in San Francisco mostly, a little bit in San Diego and Cambridge, England and here and there in Europe. A few brilliant researchers at MIT or Harvard or Stanford or Berkeley decided they needed to start a company to make their ideas into reality, and that became Biogen, or Genzyme, or Genentech. Once those first-wave companies got established in the 1980's, more followed. There are professors at MIT, for example, Phil Sharp and Bob Langer and others, who have started dozens of biotechs between them, not to mention winning a Nobel prize here and there. The big pharma companies noticed, and the first one that moved here, Novartis, got a big advantage over their peers. Today, they're all here too, or in San Francisco. It's another industrial revolution, you know, but not with steam engines and the telegraph – now it's pills and shots."

"Each drug program is an enormously complicated, years-long project that has only a small chance of success. Less than ten percent. And it takes a huge range of expertise in everything from biochemistry to medicine to patent law. So each person on the team brings special knowledge that the others don't have. And people like me – people who run the show – are really just trying to keep track of what's going on and ask the right questions so things don't go off the rails.

Since it costs a couple of hundred million dollars to make a drug – and it does – we can't afford to make too many wrong choices. Even the big companies don't have that kind of money, and at a biotech like Quercus, we basically have one shot at it. If Lilly found something wrong in her particular area, it's unlikely that anyone else on the team would know until she brought it up. No one else would have her exact expertise. But with what I've just told you, you can imagine that if what she found was dangerous enough, someone could think it enough reason for murder."

"Thank you for the history lesson, Doctor. That's what we're interested in – what did Lilly find? She seemed to be focusing on a report number…" he looked down at his notes, "…QTRD1014295. Have you heard of that one?"

Thomas looked into the middle distance. "No, I don't think so. I don't know reports by their numbers, generally. What was it about?"

"I'm told it's a release assay for your lead program, QT-101. It's missing."

"Missing? How can that be?"

"You tell me, Doctor. This is your shop. There seems to be another report in its place, ending in 4296, but we have reason to believe it's been, ah, altered."

"Altered?" Thomas sat forward, opening the laptop sitting on the desk in front of him as his face flushed a bit. "That's impossible, Lieutenant. We have systems in place…"

"Yes, yes, that's what everyone keeps telling me," Davis said. "Yet here we are, the impossible seems to have happened. Not to mention the murder of the woman who was looking into it."

"Murder?" Thomas was on a roll with the one-word repetitions, Maggie thought on the other side of the phone link. "I thought she was mugged while she was jogging. Surely you don't think her death had anything to do with her work here?"

"That's what we're trying to figure out, Dr. van Haft," Mike Davis said. "They say you're in charge of all the research around here, and you know everything that's going on. So what about it? What did Lilly discover that got her killed?"

Thomas was staring at his computer screen. He turned it around to show Davis and Jimmy the file storage system. As Maggie and Benny had already discovered, report '4296 was there, and '4295 was not. He exhaled audibly.

"I'm afraid I have no idea, Lieutenant," he said quietly. "I'll have to look into it, and work with our IT expert to see if I can find any evidence of this missing report. How did you find out about it anyway? If it's missing, I mean…"

"We'll keep that to ourselves for now, if you don't mind," Davis said evenly. "For the record, where were you on Monday evening?"

"I was here until about three, I think, and then I went home to drop off my work bag and computer, and to work out a little bit before I left to join Art for dinner with the bankers at Harvest. When I have these dinners, I like to exercise a bit first so I don't over-eat. Then I took my bike to Harvard Square. I got a flat tire on Mass Ave, near the Post Office. There's always glass and stuff on the road, and it was rainy, and the road was shiny so I didn't see whatever it was that cut the tire. I have a patch kit and a pump, so I fixed it myself. But I missed the first course."

"That's fine. This afternoon I'll need to bring in forensic experts from our Cybercrimes unit to look at your systems very closely indeed. Mr. Keogh already granted that access. They'll be here this afternoon."

Maggie smiled to herself. Davis was having a good old time pushing people's buttons. If they were going to shake anyone into making a mistake, this was a good start. None of them had expected to learn anything from these interviews, just to tighten the screws. But there was still Jorge – and Lisa – to go.

*　　　*　　　*

Jorge Perez was nervous. He met them in one of the small conference rooms, large enough to hold a round table and four chairs but not much more. He had a coffee and his laptop on the table, but kept his hands out of sight on his lap. His knee was jiggling, and his eyes kept darting around the room. Davis and Jimmy exchanged glances, looking a bit like wolves smelling a deer. Nervous witnesses – and suspects – made mistakes.

Jorge was, in contrast to Thomas, dressed in the biotech bro uniform of slightly ratty black jeans and a black T-shirt. The shirt was tight and showed his athletic build. Davis did his introductions, and Jimmy already had Maggie dialed in.

"I hear you're a big bicyclist," Mike Davis said. "Is that right?"

"Well yes," Jorge seemed surprised by this opening topic. "I ride in from my house in Wellesley. It's a good way to keep fit – the American lifestyle is designed to create obesity, you know. Plus, that way my wife can have the car, and we only need one instead of two."

Davis shrugged. "Were you biking in Somerville last week, by any chance?"

Now Jorge seemed more confused than anything. "Um, no, just to work and home, why?"

"No matter. Tell me, Dr. Perez," Davis dove right in the deep end, "how long have you been having an affair with Dr. Clark?"

Jorge turned pale, but kept his composure. "I don't know what you mean," he said weakly.

"We have our sources, Dr. Perez," Davis continued, inexorable. "And if we know about it, how long till HR gets wind of it? I'm sure you have policies against that sort of thing, don't you? After all, you *are* her supervisor."

"Look, it's not how it seems. We're in love, and we want to be together. My marriage…my marriage has been in difficulties for a long time. My wife is spending the week back home in Argentina, but she will be back tonight, and I expect that she will be asking me for a divorce anyway. If not, I will ask her for one. Lisa and I – it just happened." He tried to smile. "I don't think we have a policy against falling in love, Lieutenant."

Maggie rolled her eyes. So Jorge was supposed to be such a romantic, was he? A man in love? Not just a Latin Lothario, cheating on his wife? Or maybe he was just quick on his feet and not one to worry about a few rules…

Meanwhile, Davis nodded, and switched gears to ask about the missing report. Jorge also denied knowing anything about it, or that Lilly had come to him about it. Then he added, "But you know, now that I think about it, Lilly and Tony had been meeting together quite a bit over the last few weeks. They wouldn't normally have a lot of areas in common – their experiments are quite separate. Nothing wrong with it, I suppose, but now she's dead and he's not turned up for work."

*　　　*　　　*

Lisa Clark, in turn, was coldly composed and didn't bat an eye at Davis's Dutch Uncle impression. Since Lisa had a desk in the common area on the third floor, by the labs, the two detectives approached her more circumspectly. Davis introduced himself and Jimmy, and suggested they speak privately.

Lisa, wearing jeans and a silky peach-colored top under a white lab coat, led them past the lab area to an empty conference room. She wore no makeup except pale lipstick. She sat at one of the chairs, crossed her arms and waited while Davis gave his spiel.

"Are you being harassed by your supervisor, Dr. Clark?"

"I beg your pardon?"

"We understand that you and Jorge Perez are, um, in a relationship. That would of course be against your company policy, and could be against the law if you feel that you are being pressured into something you don't want to do."

"I'm not aware that there's anything here that's State Police business, Lieutenant, is there?" she said. "If Anita has an issue, I'm sure she'll come talk to me."

Well, that was a bust, thought Maggie. Lisa Clark is one cool customer.

"Are you aware that Lilly Zhao had uncovered a missing research report, that had been replaced by a fabricated one?"

Unlike the personal allegations, Lisa's reaction to this was much more pronounced. She turned pale, then flushed. Davis watched closely as she opened her mouth as if to speak and closed it again several times. Finally she said, "No, no, not at all. What are you talking about? What report? Whose experiment? That can't be…"

Davis explained about the reports, the missing 4295 and the substituted 4296.

"That's not really my part of the work around here, Lieutenant. I'm working on basic research, and leading a follow-up program to QT-101. I'm not on the team for the lead program, and I wouldn't have access to the reports, you know."

"We believe Dr. Zhao was murdered because of that discovery, Dr. Clark. So you see, we are taking this extremely seriously. And your, um, relationship with Dr. Perez is a secret that can be exploited. You can be blackmailed easily. Were you and Lilly close? Did she know about your affair? Was she suspicious of what you and Jorge were up to?"

Back at her desk, Maggie rolled her eyes. Davis was fishing, anyone could tell that. But now Lisa Clark was rattled enough that pushing her might be effective.

"No, Lilly and I had a good working relationship, but it wasn't close. Like I said, we didn't work on the same project team. And we weren't friends outside of work, if that's what you're getting at. She was a very private person, very quiet. She told me about her daughter, of course – she told *everybody* about her daughter, she was so proud of her. And I think her husband is a cancer researcher at Dana Farber. But otherwise I know nothing about her, and as far as I know, she knew nothing about me."

It struck Maggie that Lisa was the only person interviewed who hadn't spoken about Lilly in the present tense. Not even once.

*　　　　*　　　　*

By now it was almost 1 p.m., and Maggie realized she was hungry. Ted Sands had joined Mike Davis and Jimmy O'Connor in one of the small second floor conference rooms, and they brought in Dimitris, the Quercus one-man "IT Department", to get Ted full access to the Quercus systems. Dimitris was hesitant until they pulled Art Keogh out of his office to confirm that he was to cooperate fully, and that settled the issue. Once Ted had access, Davis and Jimmy left for lunch.

A moment later, Maggie's cell phone buzzed, and she saw "Mike Davis" on the caller ID. Looking over the wall of her cubicle she saw she was out of earshot of everyone but Benny. She answered the call with a *sotto voce*, "Hello?"

"What the fuck is this about the Chinese Communist Party, Thompson?"

Maggie winced. When he was happy, Davis called her Maggie. When he was irate, it was Sergeant. When he was *really* pissed off, they were on a last name basis.

"Sorry, I had to keep Dan off the trail," she said as blandly as she could.

"Well, if you cause an international incident, I will pull you off this case. Even one peep from the State Department, Thompson, and you're going back on patrol."

Someone came up to speak to Benny at his nearby desk, so Maggie raised her voice and lifted her pitch half an octave.

"OK, mom, thanks for letting me know! Talk to you later!" She hung up, shaking her head.

Once the conference at Benny's desk had ended, Maggie sought him out, finding that he was still working on reconstructing the '4295 report. He agreed that lunch was in order, so he locked down his computer and they went out to Mass Ave. It was warmer than before, and the air was still the color of nicotine-stained fingers. They decided on Roxy's, where the grilled cheese sandwiches were sinfully good. It was past the lunchtime rush, and they found two seats away from the window.

"So it looks…" Benny started, but Maggie interrupted him.

"Is this a biotech thing? To start every conversation with 'So'?" she asked.

He smiled. "Yeah, I guess it is. Specifically a Cambridge thing. It's as if we're picking up a continuous conversation from before, not starting a new one. Once you've been here a few months, you do it without noticing, because everybody talks like that."

She rolled her eyes. "So…?" she said.

"The original data show that the drug doesn't seem to behave in the monkeys the way it did in *ex vivo* experiments…"

"What does that mean?"

"*Ex vivo*? Like test tube, but no one uses test tubes anymore. An experiment in a dish, *ex vivo* – outside of life – as opposed to *in vivo* – in life – like in a mouse or human. We did a lot of work in mice, of course, to get the drug candidate. And in rats too. But now that Lilly was doing the formal toxicology studies for the FDA in monkeys, for some reason she went back to review the report of the release assay validation study, which was also the study that was supposed to show we could measure drug in monkeys. And, it would be the same assay, more or less, that we would be using in humans when we start the first clinical study. So, I've got to assume that all of a sudden she's not detecting drug, or the results are funny in some way, you know, erratic. And when I looked at the raw data from '4295, that's exactly what's happening. The assay isn't working in monkey serum, in fact – it's not detecting the QT-101 levels that should be there. There could be interference with the assay from something in monkey blood that isn't in rodents, or it could be that the drug is being inactivated somehow in monkeys. That would be much worse, of course. And most importantly, since monkeys are closer to humans than mice and rats are, this could also be a problem for the human clinical trials."

"Can you tell what is causing it? And what happens in the second report?" Maggie asked as she bit into her sandwich, pulling a gooey string of cheese from her mouth to the plate as she put the sandwich down.

"In the new report, '4296, the assay works beautifully, but of course that's not real. I also went back to the old research assay, and that one really did work, but it was only used in rats and mice. Different species have different interfering substances in their blood, so it's not a slam dunk that an assay that works in one species will work in another."

"So why not just make a new assay?" Maggie asked.

"Sure, that's what anyone would do," Benny said, chewing intermittently as he spoke. "If the issue is just an assay problem, we could solve it with a better detection system. But it would take months, and delay the IPO. The company is basically out of money now, we're running on credit until the stock sale. And developing, testing, and validating a new assay also delays the manufacturing, and the clinical trials, and would spook the investors. With rising interest rates and tight funding – biotechs are laying off people all over the place, if you've seen the headlines – it could sink Quercus even if it turns out to be a fixable problem. Or the company would get bought by somebody at a fire sale, for pennies on the dollar."

"And if the problem isn't just the assay, but that the drug actually gets inactivated in monkeys somehow?"

"Well, that's much worse, of course. That usually means neutralizing antibodies, and if that were to also happen in humans, it could stop the program. It's also pretty unusual, especially on first exposure to the drug, so I think it's much less likely. But if you think an assay delay would spook the investors, can you imagine what a failed drug would do? It would be a stampede for the exits."

"So somebody saw these results, and decided to change the report to '4296, make '4295 disappear, get the IPO done, and then worry about it later?"

Benny nodded slowly. "Yes, I think that must be it. With millions in the bank, they could announce a delay, and even if the stock dropped, they would still have the money to keep going. It would only be a paper loss. The delay would just be a business-as-usual blip, and not a company-threatening event. They could even postpone announcing it until they had a solution, if it was just the assay."

"And Lilly stumbles across this, and she says something to the wrong person, or overheard by the wrong person, and it's lights out."

"Yes," Benny agreed, pulling gooey grilled cheese away from his remaining sandwich. "And she must have said something to Tony. He's depending on that assay as much as she is. He's the QP. If it's not working, he can't certify how much drug there is in a vial, and there's no clinical trial."

"What the fuck is a QP, Benny?" Maggie was getting pretty tired of biotech alphabet soup.

"Oh sorry. It just means Qualified Person, believe it or not. Someone approved by the regulators – FDA in this case – to authorize release of drug for human investigation. He has to certify that the stuff we put into patients is what we think it is, that it's pure, not contaminated, and meets specifications that FDA agreed to. If he screws up, FDA puts us on hold, and he can be in serious trouble. If they decide he's falsifying records, that means fines, jail time, the works. The whole point of having a QP is to make someone who is qualified and trained also personally responsible for ensuring the drug is good. Tony quite literally has skin in this game."

"I think we have a couple of ways to get at this, Benny," Maggie said, holding up a French fry as a pointer. "First, the IT side. Somebody made a report disappear, and I don't see how they could do that without software expertise. That means Dimitris, right? Is there anyone else doing IT at Quercus?"

"No, he's a one-man show. He's not someone I would suspect, though, he seems like a straightforward, friendly guy."

Maggie nodded. "We'll see. Our Cybercrimes guy, Ted, is there now, and he's very, very, good. Second, tracking Tony. We've got three troopers working on that, and an alert out to all the surrounding police departments. I hope we'll get a lead on him soon. That Audi has to be somewhere."

"Third, the stirring of the executive team pot that Mike and Jimmy did today. You didn't witness it, but I did." She explained briefly about listening in to the interviews with the management team members. "I think if one of them is involved, they might just panic enough to make a mistake."

"Did you get anything out of them?" Benny asked.

"It was sort of like reading the Gospels," Maggie answered. "Four versions of the same story, but each a little different. And a whole lot of pontificating about the virtue of biotech as the savior of mankind. You guys really have some swelled heads."

Benny smiled. "Well, some of it is justified. But yes, it's also a game, and the people who play it will cheat if they have to."

*　　　*　　　*

In Woburn, Corporal Heather Martin was dining *al desko*, eating a tuna sandwich and scanning her monitors for any traces of Tony Dupree, when her screen suddenly lit up. Tony's cell phone had switched on, pinging a cell tower near Rangeley, Maine. The phone had switched off again less than a minute later. Quickly Heather looked up the number for the local police there, and then the Maine State Police. She called Verizon as well, and asked for more precise coordinates of the phone and whether any text messages or calls had gone out in the past few minutes.

Next she called the Rangeley Police Department and asked for a unit to go to the location indicated by Verizon.

"We don't think he's a fugitive," she told the desk sergeant in Maine after giving him the Audi description and license plate. "We do think he's on the run because a colleague of his was murdered, and he's afraid he might be next. Still, approach with caution. There's no warrant for him, but we could get one if he won't cooperate. For now, he's a person of interest, not a suspect."

While that was in progress, she texted Mike Davis and Maggie to bring them up to speed. She got a call back from Rangeley PD about half an hour later.

"We didn't have to go far," laughed the dispatcher from Maine. "He was at Sarge's. It's a local bar, about half a mile away. He was eating a pastrami sandwich. He came with Officer Pennyman without any problems, seems relieved that you're looking for him. Do you want to talk to him?"

"Uh, sure, I guess," said Heather.

"Hello?" a soft, hesitant voice. "This is Tony Dupree."

"Hi, Dr. Dupree, this is Corporal Martin, Massachusetts State Police. We're working on the death of Lilly Zhao, and we're worried that you may be in some danger. Are you okay?"

"Yes, I'm fine. But how…how did you know?"

"You were missed at work, Doctor. It's not like you to be out of touch, as I understand it."

"Well, I'm glad you contacted me, I guess. I just had to get out of town and think. To try and understand what happened to Lilly. Do you know any more about it?"

"Not yet, but we've got a big team working on it. Did she talk to you about anything that was bothering her recently?"

"Yes, she showed me a report that had been removed from the system. She said it was the release assay, and it wasn't working right. That the report had been replaced by one that made the assay look good, but that it wasn't true. She was very upset because the second report was in the system under her name, as if she had uploaded it, but she knew she hadn't done that. She said she suspected who to ask about it, but she didn't tell me who."

"Look," Heather said, "I can have someone there in about 4 hours, and we can bring you back safely to Boston. We'll have another trooper drive your car back. Does that sound okay to you?"

"Um…yeah, I guess so," Tony said.

"We're down to a pretty short list of suspects," Heather said, ad libbing, looking up at the ceiling and hoping she wasn't going too far out on a limb. "We'll make sure you're safe. And once you've talked to us you won't be in danger anymore – there's nothing to be gained by harming you."

"Okay, thanks, that sounds good," said Tony.

"We're on our way," Heather said. She grabbed her Smokey the Bear hat and went to get Eddie. "C'mon, detective," she said. "We're going to Maine. At State Police speed." Eddie stared, then scrambled after her, gathering his phone, ever-present coffee cup, and a windbreaker jacket with 'State Police' in yellow block letters on the back.

"Where are we going?" he asked, while trying to figure out how a uniformed cop was giving the orders all of a sudden.

*　　　*　　　*

Maggie was still at Quercus at 5 p.m., wishing people still stored papers in file cabinets so she could look busy. Instead, she sat behind her keyboard and typed random words into an email that she periodically deleted. She was waiting for Ted to emerge from his cloister in the small conference room. The rest of the floor was practically empty, except for Benny at the desk next to hers, and Jorge, Thomas, and Art in their offices. One effect of Davis's ministrations was obviously a renewed dedication to working late in the office among the members of the management team. She mentally crossed Benny off her suspects list, which only left about half a dozen others.

Finally Ted emerged and walked past her without a glance in her direction. As he passed her, she could see his index finger pointing to the back of the building, in the direction of the toilets. He himself was ostentatiously steaming toward the men's room. Given his 6'5", 300 pound frame, it was kind of like cruise ship going upriver. Only thing missing is the tugboats, Maggie thought. She waited a ten-count and then got up unhurriedly and sauntered after Ted.

There were three doors along the back corridor, one for each toilet and one for the emergency stairs. Not seeing Ted, she hesitated but then saw the Ladies' Room door open slightly and Ted's size 14 hand come out, finger curling in an inviting motion. Shaking her head, she walked into the bathroom.

"Aren't you worried about being thought a pervert?" she asked.

"You're the only woman on the floor now, aren't you?" Ted said. "And you already know me…wait, that didn't come out right."

"Yeah, whatever. So, what did you find? Jesus, I'm talking like *them* now."

He shot her a quizzical glance. Whatever, indeed. "First, I can confirm that Lilly badged in at 8:32 Monday morning, and badged out again at 3:07. Second, we need to get hold of Dimitris. I looked around but he seems to be gone for the day. This file you're looking for – it was in fact removed, and the only person who could do that would be the system administrator. He covered his tracks pretty well, and used an alias that links to a non-existent employee, but it still needs top-level access to do it. Dimitris is the system admin, and I gather he disappeared after lunch. His phone is off the grid, according to a quick look I had online, using methods that you don't want to know about. I'd bet you a dozen donuts that he's on the run."

"And he's such a friendly guy, too," said Maggie, deadpan. "Benny even noticed it. Have you got any idea of timing? When did the file get deleted? Was the other file, 4296, inserted at the same time or later? Who else accessed either file? Can you see when Lilly found it?"

Ted looked at her sadly. "I would not want to be your dog, Sarge. Here I bring you this beautiful bird I just caught, and instead you want a flamingo… I will keep looking. I should be able to get those answers in a couple of hours."

Maggie put a hand on Ted's big arm. "I'm sorry, Ted, you're right. This is fantastic – you've really given us a huge lead. I was just thinking out loud about how to follow that lead. Get hold of L-T and let's get a BOLO out on Dimitris, and send a car to his home. Ask them to get a search warrant going for it. You *know* I totally appreciate what you've done here."

Ted smiled and walked out of the Ladies' Room purposefully. Maggie waited a few beats and then followed. She stopped at her desk and jotted something on a yellow sticky note pad. Pulling off the top page, she walked over to Benny's desk and said, loud enough to be heard in the middle of the room.

"OK, boss, I'm heading out, unless you need anything else tonight." She reached over and stuck the note on Benny's monitor as she spoke.

Benny had been focused on his screen and seemed startled to see her. He looked down at the note absently, saying "Oh, thanks, Maggie. I'm all set, see you tomorrow." Then, as he read the note silently he swallowed and nodded.

"Bye," said Maggie, "have a good evening."

"Uh, you too," Benny said, starting to put his computer away in his backpack. The note, which was still on his screen, said 'Meet at your place. Bring this note.' He crumpled it up and tossed it in his bag.

Chapter Eleven, Wednesday Evening, May 31st

As Benny's 'admin', Maggie had found his home address in the files, and she went there by a circuitous route to make sure she wasn't followed. After about twenty minutes of wandering through Central Square, she found herself back near Quercus Therapeutics, and outside Benny's building on Franklin Street. He lived in a former biscuit factory that had been converted into expensive lofts and duplexes. He was waiting for her outside the entrance.

"Come on in," he said with a gesture toward the front entrance.

"What is this place?" she asked. "Looks a little steampunk."

"It's an old bakery. They used to make Fig Newtons here, and Lorna Doons." He pointed to ceramic oversized Lorna Doon biscuits in the newel post of the entryway.

"Ooh, I love Lorna Doons," she said. "I had no idea they were from here."

"Well, it was a long time ago, and they totally renovated it. You'll see."

Benny led the way to a two-story apartment, very modern inside with exposed brick interior walls, 18-foot-high ceilings, and lots of daylight. They walked into a living room that was also a library, housing shelves on three walls of what Maggie later learned were mostly antique medical textbooks, some of them from as far back as the 1600's, and many at least a century old. Interspersed with the books were antique pharmacists' mortar and pestles, glass apothecary jars, patent medicine bottles, and an old-fashioned brass balance beam scale. These made a warm contrast to the kitchen, separated from the living room by an island with a black glass induction cooktop set in a white granite counter and fronted by two black bar stools. Behind it, the kitchen was all stainless steel, with white cabinets boasting frosted glass fronts, and still more polished white granite counters. At the right far corner of the living room a circular stairway led up to the main bedroom, while there was a guest bedroom behind a door on the left-hand wall of the living room.

"Wow, very nice, Benny," Maggie said. She dropped her backpack on the white nubbly sofa in the living room and walked around, admiring the contents of the shelves. "This is quite a collection you've got here."

Benny smiled. "Yes, a little geeky, maybe, but it's a hobby. That's a first edition of Vesalius's textbook of anatomy up there, and there's one of Darwin's *Origin of Species* on your left."

Maggie nodded, running her finger down the spine of the book. "Our Cybercrimes expert, Ted, has found evidence that the Quercus IT guy, Dimitris, was responsible for changing the research report files, Benny. We're looking for him now. And also, we've found Tony. He was up in northern Maine, but he's agreed to come back and speak with us. I've got people going to fetch him now, and they should be back by 11 o'clock tonight. I'm going to interview him then, and I'd like you to come with me."

Benny nodded, "Sure, if you think I can help."

"Yes, having someone there he knows can reassure him that he's not a suspect – at least, I don't think he is at this point – and that should help him speak more freely. But you'll have to take my lead on this, even if I sound hostile or put pressure on him. I hope that won't be necessary, if he's cooperating. But either way, you sit tight, don't answer for him whatever you do, or I'll have to boot you out."

Benny nodded again, more somberly. "Okay, well, we should eat something, then." He walked into the kitchen and started opening cabinets and the fridge. "Do you cook?" he asked.

"I can barely boil water," Maggie said. "Coffee, eggs, and delivery are my limits."

"No problem, I can manage," he said. "You have any allergies?"

She shook her head no. "Can I help?"

He grinned. "Sure, there's some bread in that cupboard. Take out four slices and toast them in that toaster over there. Then cut off the crusts and then put them out two to a plate. Plates are up there, and then if you can grab silverware and placemats, they're in the drawers to the left."

He pulled out eggs, butter, oil, a container of potato starch, some corned beef, a can of evaporated milk, and a bag of green beans. The wall behind him held an oven and a smaller steam oven above it. He washed the beans, spread them out on a perforated baking pan, and put it into the steam oven, setting it to start. There was a gurgling sound and a faint chugging from the upper oven. Pulling some scallions out of the fridge, he quickly washed one or two and chopped them on a cutting board. Turning to the cooktop, he pulled out a large skillet from under the island, turned on the heat and let it warm up. In a small bowl he mixed starch and water while in the larger one he whisked four eggs, the evaporated milk, oil, white pepper, salt, the corn beef in small pieces, and finally the potato starch slurry from the first bowl. Adding oil to the now hot skillet, he waited for it to heat up, turning on the downdraft fan in the island in the meantime. Then he added the mixture from the bowl to the pan slowly, pushing it around with a rubber spatula so it cooked in thin layers. When all the mixture was cooked, he shook it out onto the toast, folding the layers back and forth so they looked like sheets. He was sprinkling the scallions on top as the steam oven pinged to announce that the beans were done. He pulled out the beans, shook kosher salt and black pepper and the rest of the scallions onto them, and plated the mixture next to the sandwiches. He put the plates on the living room side of the island in front of the bar stools, where Maggie had set placemats and silverware.

"Voila," he said. "Hong Kong Egg Sandwiches with steamed green beans à la Benny."

"Wow," Maggie said. "Doctor, scientist, and short order cook. I'm impressed."

He shot her a glance, blushing slightly. "Well, when you live alone, you either decide to make cooking fun, or you get fat. At least, that's my experience. Too much pizza and I start looking like a beach ball, and I'm not tall enough to carry that off."

He went to the corner of the kitchen, where there was a tall wine fridge, selected a 2015 Chablis and uncorked it. Grabbing two wine glasses he poured the wine and set the bottle down.

"Cheers," he said, settling into one stool.

Maggie raised her glass. "Cheers, Benny. Here's to family reunions."

It was delicious. Maggie moaned with the first bite, not speaking again till she was done. Benny looked pleased at her reaction, and ate at a more moderate pace. They drank their wine and nodded. Benny made espresso from a Rocket Mozzafiato machine that Maggie figured cost more than she made in a month, but the coffee was amazing.

"Benny, that was terrific, thank you, just what I needed," she said. "Now, we have some time until Tony's back. Heather – one of the troopers on the investigative team – is going to bring him to the Boston State Police barracks, near the Museum of Science. We can talk to him there."

"Meantime," she continued, reaching for her backpack, "I brought along some more of Dad's diaries. I've been looking at them, and I found some things I don't understand. I thought we could look at them together." She looked at Benny while rummaging through her backpack. He was doing his deer-in-the-headlights impression, but at least he didn't walk away or refuse. After a moment, he nodded, and said "Okay, sure."

Maggie pulled out three of the notebooks containing Henry's journals, along with a large envelope that was filled with photographs, partially visible through a clear plastic address window. She spread out a handful of snapshots – a smiling Henry with Hue, both looking ridiculously young, dated August 1970; a baby photo of Benny in a crib, standing up and gripping the bars with a handwritten caption on the back of "Planning his escape"; Benny on what looked like his first day of kindergarten; an older Henry, smiling but more guardedly, with Jessica holding baby Maggie; Henry with Benny, who was wearing bright blue graduation robes from high school.

"There are more photos back at my place, but I thought a few of these were worth a look. This family has had its share of ups and down, just like every other family," she said. Benny sifted through the photos but didn't answer.

"Look, we stopped reading when Dad was out of the hospital in September 1970, right? I looked through the next few pages last night." She paged to a purple sticky page flag in a notebook marked '1971', and read out loud.

> *March 26, 1971:* *DEROS Day!*
>
> *I can't believe it, I'm on the tarmac at Tan Son Nhut, sitting and waiting to board the Freedom Bird – in this case a Pan Am charter to Manila, Guam, Honolulu, and San Francisco. 0900 and already 85 degrees – I won't miss that! I'm only sorry Hue can't come with me – yet! I promised her I would come back for her, and I swear I will. She was very upset when I left, of course. So was I. She hates to cry in front of me, she's so stoic. But at the end, we could only hug and hold each other as hard as we could. I asked Dave and Dan to look in on her, make sure she's o.k. – I'm sure they will. Plus she'll be working at the base hospital again, so she'll be fine.*
>
> *I've written to Larry Berman at the Concord Daily Monitor, asking if he would credential me as a reporter for the paper, so I can come back here without getting hassled. I gave him the old*

folks' address, so I hope there'll be an answer there waiting for me when I get back.

"Then we skip ahead a few weeks. He's shipped back to Fort Campbell, and then he's given an honorable discharge along with his Purple Heart. Now listen to this."

> *May 13, 1971: I'm officially a civilian again! Hooray! And back in Vermont, to boot. Mom and Dad have gotten older while I was away – probably worrying about me and George. At least he got a 4F on account of his heart murmur, but he's turned into a hippy while I was gone! Long hair, mustache, all this anti-war stuff he's spouting. He seems to be playing in a rock 'n roll band, of all things. He does go on and on about that business at Kent State last year that was so awful – it's turned even more people against the war. I'm already against it, I'm just glad I'm out but I'm worried about my buddies who are still there. I'm sure George is right that we should get out of Vietnam, but he doesn't have a clue what it's really like, does he?*
>
> *Anyway, Larry Berman came through! I can have press credentials and go back to Saigon as a correspondent of the Concord Monitor! (They dropped the 'Daily' while I was gone, too – everything's changing around here). Dad thinks I'm nuts to go back there, he thinks I should get a job, or go back to school.*
>
> *I've only seen a few of the old gang from high school or college since I've been back. Some folks have left town, a couple are in the Army – Vietnam or Germany – and some I haven't tracked down yet. People are nice, but coming home as a veteran is weird – there's a reserve, a reluctance of people to engage, like they're embarrassed to see me. I had somebody*

cross the street when they saw me coming. Somehow, I don't think it was like this after WWII or Korea.

May 15, 1971: Hue is pregnant!! Holy cow, how did that happen? Well, duh, I know how it happened, but but but…Now I really have to get back there. She doesn't say much except she feels fine, it's only the first trimester, things could still go wrong, blah blah blah. I'm guessing Uncle Quan and Aunt Trang are not super enthusiastic about this – a mixed-blood American-Vietnamese baby. But, hell, I'm excited! Wow!

May 20, 1971: Well, no surprise, the Old Man was apoplectic. Something about keeping my pecker in my pants. Something else about yellow grandchildren. Mom was quieter, but I think she's both horrified at out-of-wedlock children and kinda pleased about being a grandma. Of course I had to ask them for the money to fly back there – it's crazy - $400 for a one-way ticket! And I need more money to bribe Hue's way out – and the baby's, of course. From what I hear, it's like $2000. That's a lot of money! I got it in the end, but the Old Man definitely ain't happy. Mom finally put her foot down and insisted, so that did it. At least I'll get something from the Monitor as a reporter, $50 a week and five cents a word for what they publish. The salary is about half what I got from the Army, so I better get verbose. "I shall have to enhance my verbosity in order to maximize the pecuniary impact of my thoughtful and insightful missives from the proximity of the front lines where our brave boys are beating back the Communist menace every hour of every day." There, that's $2.10.

Maggie looked up. "Did you know about another sibling, Benny? It's the first I'm hearing of it. Certainly mom never said anything about it, if she even knows."

Benny shook his head. "No! This is wild – I had no idea. Henry never said anything, nor Grandma. I wonder if George knows – he must. We should talk to him."

"Do you think we have a brother or sister somewhere? In Vietnam, maybe? Or maybe even here in the US? Not that there's much inheritance, but I can't imagine Dad leaving her out of his will, if she's here…or even alive."

Benny shook his head again. "What else does it say? What happened next?"

"I don't know, that's as far as I got last night. I had to digest all this, and thought we should go through it together anyway. I brought more notebooks with me, but I haven't had a chance to go through them yet." She glanced at her watch – it was 8:45. She checked her texts and saw one from Heather indicating an ETA of 10:10 at Station H-4, the State Police Boston Barracks at the confluence of Storrow Drive and Monsignor O'Brien Highway. They had time.

June 7, 1971: Back in San Francisco airport. Waiting to board Pan Am 841 to Saigon. Same milk run I took to get out, only in reverse. Honolulu to Guam to Manila to Saigon. My back hurts just thinking about it. That could also be the money belt I'm wearing. But I can't wait to see Hue! I hope we're still o.k. What if she doesn't love me anymore? I couldn't stand it.

June 10, 1971: Wow, I didn't know pregnant ladies could screw like that! It's like I never left, we're back together and can't get enough of each other. I was silly to worry. She'll soon be showing, and she might lose her job if the brass get wind of it.

On the other hand, they're short-handed anyway for nurses, and she's really good, so I don't think she'll be in any real trouble. Of course, Hue is now three months pregnant, she thinks, so she'll have to quit working at some point. It looks like we might have a Christmas baby! I need to get her out before then.

"Yeesh, I'm not sure I'm ready to read about Dad's sex life, you know?" said Maggie. "Still, I'm glad they were happy."

Benny was blushing, looking at the bookcase behind and above her. "Yes, exactly," he said. Glancing at him, Maggie put her nose back in the notebook, mumbling to herself as she skimmed the pages.

"Yada, yada, yada, everyone's happy, trying to get the exit permits, government office here, government office there…ooh, looks like they got married in Vietnam first, there's a photo of them here in front of the church. On the back it says, Notre Dame Cathedral – it looks like it could be in Boston, actually. I guess they had what was actually their second wedding later – the one in Vermont. I haven't found a marriage certificate from either one, at least so far."

"That could be in the safe deposit box," Benny said, walking over to a light switch and turning off the overhead lamp, a white sleek twisty modern confection. Then he walked to another switch on the opposite side of the room and turned the lamp on again. "He had one when I was growing up, it could still be at the bank branch in Brookline. You can ask Jessica."

Maggie glanced up, but his voice and his expression were both neutral. She said, "Why did you turn the lamp on and off again?"

"Oh," he blushed again. "Sorry, my OCD kicking in, I guess. I like both switches on a panel to be aligned the same way. Do you ever do that?"

Maggie shook her head, keeping a poker face. "No, I don't. I'm mostly a slob. I cleaned up my apartment before you came over the other day, but normally it's a mess. Is your OCD bad?"

"No, it's just a habit. When something I'm using – toothpaste or shampoo – gets below half-full, I need to make sure there's a backup in the house, stuff like that. I guess you didn't get that gene either?"

"No, I didn't. I run out of stuff all the time. I guess it's the difference between having Hue and Jessica as a mother, genetically speaking."

Benny shrugged. "Anyway, what's next in the adventures of Henry and Hue?"

Maggie turned back to the notebook, leafing ahead.

> *August 17, 1971: We're totally getting stonewalled by the South Vietnamese government. The US part is actually pretty straightforward – we submitted the forms, and since we are officially married here, the clerk said it would take a couple of months to get Hue a visa, but we also need an exit permit from the locals. That's the part that's still a problem. We spent hours at the Ministry of Foreign Affairs today, only to be told we need a form from the Interior Ministry first. Went over there and they won't see us without an appointment, and it will take three more weeks to get one. Hue is going to see if her uncle can help us grease the wheels a bit. She hasn't seen him in over a year, because I guess he's somehow connected to the VC, but since her parents are dead he's the head of the family.*

> *September 5, 1971: Well, I met Uncle Quan today. Quan Van Nguyen, to be exact. He's a small man, about 5'5", but he has a commanding presence, maybe in part because he's so still and silent most of the time. He was a colonel in the ARVN until he was wounded in an ambush during the Tet Offensive, and he's been retired since. Hue thinks*

he's actually a spy for the North, but she doesn't ask and I certainly didn't either. He was wearing civilian clothing, a white shirt and grey slacks, but he seems to be at attention even when he's sitting, back ramrod straight, hair regulation length, eyes front. Because of his military background, he seems to have some pull with the Ministry, and promises to try and help. He's a tough character to read, very stoic and unemotional, doesn't speak if a grunt will do.

His wife, Aunt Trang, is just as distant. She's even smaller than Uncle Quan, about 5'1", with short dark hair. She can't be much over forty-five, and she has an air of sadness, somehow. She dresses traditionally, today she came in the Áo dài, a sort of long over-jacket in jade green with wide white pants. She is Hue's mother's older sister, and she doesn't seem to approve of me, or of Hue being pregnant, I guess. I can see why Hue avoided them until now.

They don't like mixed-race children here, call them 'bui doi' – 'dust of life' – and say they are worthless like dust. A lot of them wind up in orphanages, or on the street. That's another reason to get Hue back to the USA – at least there the kid will have a chance.

There's a third reason, too: with the US troop reduction finally happening, there are less than half as many Americans here now as a year ago. It's hard to know how long this country will stay independent once we're gone. We've got to get out of here before the North attacks again.

October 8, 1971: I'm writing a lot of stuff for the Concord Monitor, and they're printing most of it. The election here last week was a good topic – got a thousand words out of that one. Of course Thieu won – running unopposed can help – but there's not a lot of enthusiasm for him in the streets. I'm learning some Vietnamese slowly, and it helps break the ice a bit when I interview people, though of course I still need a translator.

The foreign correspondent gig is a big part of our income now, because Hue has lost her job. And on top of it, her blood pressure is up, her ankles are swelling some, and the doctor thinks she has preeclampsia. Evidently the treatment for that is bedrest, and so she's in our tiny apartment supposedly lying down, but actually getting up and doing stuff every time I go out and I'm not here to stop her. I'm supposed to believe she's in bed all day and somehow dinner has cooked itself by the time I come back. Sigh...

Still no luck with exit visa from RVN. Uncle Quan says another few hundred dollars ought to do it, but I'm not so sure. We've got another appointment on Tuesday next week, so maybe we'll get something then.

November 1, 1971: Well, we finally got the exit visa today! It cost almost $1000 in bribes, plus innumerable hours in line and a lot of running around, but it's done. It's only good for the next two weeks! I'm going to the Pan Am office tomorrow to book a flight!

November 4, 1971: The last few days have been a whirlwind. I was going to go to the airline office on Tuesday, but Hue went into labor prematurely that morning! I got her to the 3rd Army Field Hospital in time – it's where I had been a patient and she had been a nurse. It's where we met, and it was only fitting that it would be where our child was born. Dr. Auerbach was still stationed there, and he pulled some strings to get her in. Labor took about 12 hours – I was sweating bullets but Hue was calm, and the nurses were great (most of them knew her anyway). Finally, the baby was born about 11 at night. A girl! We decided to name her Mai. It means 'flower' in Vietnamese, and of course it would work in English too. Mai Nguyen Mason. She's gorgeous, just like her mother.

"Hear that Benny? We have an older sister. Somewhere, that is," Maggie said, grinning. "Isn't that cool?"

"Maybe," said Benny. "But what happened to her? I've never heard one word about this. Talk about a family keeping secrets. I have a bad feeling about this, Maggie. Keep reading."

"Look, Benny, it's already 9:30. We'd better get going, the troopers will be back with Tony in about half an hour. All of this stuff is fifty years old or more, it will keep another day or two."

Chapter Twelve, Wednesday Night – Thursday Morning, May 31st to June 1st

Maggie drove them to Station H-4, at the mouth of the Charles River and the start of Storrow Drive. Parking the Explorer in the small lot behind the Station was easy – the lot wasn't close to full this time of night. She badged in and they entered by the side door, and she introduced Benny to the duty sergeant at the front of the building as Dr. Mason. The station had been built decades earlier, and had cream-colored tiles accented by blue metal door and window frames. Although it wasn't new, and it reminded Maggie of an inner city junior high school, it was clean and orderly. The sergeant pointed them to an interview room, and Maggie got them some evil-smelling coffee from a half-full pot in the mostly deserted duty room.

"Any results for the BOLO on Dimitris Pappas?" she asked the sergeant. He pecked at his keyboard and said, "Nothing so far. Home visit negative, cell phone not on the grid, no car found."

As they waited, Maggie said, "When I was looking through the box of photos from my storage room, d'you know what I found? Do you remember Dad's notebook of all our art projects, and his stories, and such?"

Benny smiled. "You mean, 'The Electric Book of Happy'? It still exists?"

Maggie nodded, smiling too. "Yes, both of them. Yours and mine. Big three-ring binders with Christmas lights around the cover and a battery inside the spine of the notebook. I had never seen yours. I hope you don't mind that I peeked."

Benny sniffed the coffee in the paper cup Maggie had given him, grimaced, and put it down. "Oh my gawd, there's nothing to write home about in there. I was never very creative. But I'd like to see yours."

"You were fine. Anyway, the best thing was all the stories Dad wrote for us – bedtime stories, school vacation stories, letters when we were at camp. All that's in there. It was an electric book of love, really. Despite all the drama in the family, he really did try to give us some stability, to make sure we knew we were loved. A lot of kids have far less."

Benny didn't answer, he just nodded slowly.

About ten minutes later they heard a police siren winding down and saw flashing red and blue lights reflecting off the ceramic wall tiles. A moment later Heather and Eddie walked in with a short Afro-Caribbean man between them, the previously missing Antoine Dupree.

She looked at Eddie. "Any trouble on the way down?" she asked.

He shook his head. "No, all good. Heather had Tony in the cruiser, and I followed behind them in his Audi. Sweet ride."

Tony had short dark hair just beginning to gray at the temples, and wore gold-rimmed glasses, blue jeans and a lilac polo shirt. He looked tired. If he was surprised to see Benny and Maggie there, he didn't show it.

"Coffee?" Maggie offered. "I can't really recommend it. Maybe a Coke?"

"Thanks," Tony said. "A Coke sounds safer." Heather went over to a vending machine and got sodas for everyone, and they filed into the interview room with the same cream-colored tile and institutional feel of the rest of the station. They found seats around a small rectangular gray metal table that was bolted to the floor. Eddie pulled out a tape recorder and put it on the table.

"Dr. Dupree, okay with you if we record this?" he asked. "You're not a suspect, and you're not under arrest."

Tony rubbed his face with a hand and nodded. "Um, you can call me Tony. Sure," he said. "What do you want to know?"

Maggie leaned forward. "Tony, I'm Sergeant Maggie Thompson of the State Police, and we're investigating the murder of your colleague, Lilly Zhao. I'm sure you're aware of her death. What can you tell us about that?"

Tony looked from Benny to Maggie and back again. "Wait a minute, didn't I see you at Quercus? I thought you were a new admin or something? And Benny, how are you involved in this?"

"Yes, that's right. I was – still am – working undercover," Maggie smiled. "Benny and I know each other from way back, and I asked him to help us out. He's been my sherpa through the biotech mountains."

Benny nodded encouragingly to Tony, but didn't say anything. Maggie eyed him approvingly. At least this time he's following directions, she thought.

Tony was silent, marshalling his thoughts. Then he said, "Lilly came to me last week – no, the week before last – it was a week ago Thursday. She said she thought there was a problem with the PK assay that she was using in the QT-101 monkey tox study. It's also the release assay for QT-101, so I was familiar with it. She asked if I would look it over with her. I said sure, and we sat down together and went over the data."

"Where did you do that? I mean in what room?" Maggie asked.

"We were in the large conference room, because it was empty, and the small ones were being used."

"I've seen that room," Maggie said. "Please think – were the blinds up or down on the glass wall to the hallway?"

Tony closed his eyes, as they waited. "Um, I'm pretty sure that they were up – that's how we knew the room was empty. We sat at the table with her computer between us."

"Were you facing the glass wall, or with your back to it?"

Tony paused, his eyes shut again for a moment. "I think…with our back to it. We just took the first two seats once you come in through the door, you know?"

Maggie nodded. "So anyone walking by could have seen the screen over your shoulders, and you might not have noticed, right?"

Tony nodded tiredly. Maggie pressed on. "Do you remember who was in the office that day?"

Tony shook his head, looking at Benny, as if asking for confirmation. "No, I think it wasn't very full, but I'm really not sure." Benny nodded in agreement.

"What time was this meeting between you and Lilly?" Maggie asked.

"About ten in the morning. It wasn't anything scheduled in advance. I was getting a coffee in the common area, and she came up and asked if I had a few minutes. I said sure, and we took our stuff and went into the room."

Maggie turned to Eddie. "Tomorrow, let's cross-check who had already badged into Quercus by 10 a.m. on May 18th." Eddie nodded and jotted something in his notebook.

"So what did she tell you, Tony?" Maggie asked quietly. There was a general hush in the room, people seeming to lean forward without moving.

"Lilly had some preliminary data from the cyno tox study with QT-101, just an interim PK bleed that had been done at PTS. It should have been at steady state, but all the results she was seeing were BLQ – only concentrations below detection."

Maggie cast a look at Benny, who leaned forward. "Tony, let me translate for a minute. Maggie, this is from the monkey study – the breed of monkey is called cynomolgus, or cyno for short. As part of the study, the company running it at their research facility, Preclinical Toxicology Solutions, or PTS, did a monitoring blood draw where they took samples at a time when there should have been drug in the blood, and ran the assay that was supposed to detect it, as shown in the research report, number 4295. The analysis of drug concentration is called pharmacokinetics, or PK. And all the values were below the lower limit of quantification, BLQ."

Tony nodded. "Thanks, Benny. Yeah, it should have been there. The drug I mean. It should have been in their blood in easily detectable concentrations, given the timing since they were dosed. So she was wondering if there was a stability problem with the DS."

He looked around. "That's Drug Substance, the chemical makeup of the drug. But I showed her that our stability data from a bunch of different batches, including the one she was using in the monkeys, and those were fine. So then I said maybe it's the assay, and she pulled up the assay validation report. I knew that report, because it's also the validation for the release assay. Lilly pulled it up from the system, and it looked fine. But then she said there was something wrong with the report, that it couldn't be right. That's because, according to the system, Lilly was the one who uploaded this report. But she was sure she hadn't done that. That she had never seen that report before. She was very upset."

Benny sat up. "Yes, I can see that. She would be – anyone would be, if a report suddenly appeared linked to them that they had no idea about. These are all open to audit by FDA, and there are criminal penalties for faking data."

Maggie turned to look at Benny. "But didn't you say before that someone else had signed the report? Not Lilly, right?"

Benny nodded. "Yes, it was Richard Sinsky. He left at the end of last year – he's over at Moderna now." He frowned. "Wait a minute, that report was from February of this year. Sinsky wasn't even here anymore. That must be what Lilly saw. She must have realized someone had doctored the report, and put her name on the file metadata, because they couldn't use Sinsky's credentials to upload a file once he left the company, even though they could type in his name on the report and even fake his signature if they had to. But the system credentials would have been disabled and deleted when he left. I doubt she figured out the whole thing, but even if it was just trying to cover up an overdue report, Lilly was such a stickler for proper procedure that this would have been a big deal to her."

Maggie asked, "Who would be the natural person to be in charge of this report? What did this guy Sinsky do at Quercus?"

Tony answered. "He was our last head of PK, before Sandeep. We were without anyone in PK for the first part of the year, but since nearly all of it is outsourced to CRO's – um, contract research organizations – the work could keep going. I bet Sandeep hasn't had enough time to get around to looking at everything yet, especially an old, routine technical report like this. So someone sneaking a report into the system could be pretty confident it wouldn't be noticed."

"So with Sinsky gone and Sandeep not here yet, who would be getting the report updates from the contractor?"

"Well that would be Jorge – he was Sinsky's boss and the system would forward stuff to him."

Maggie nodded as Eddie was scribbling in his notepad. She saw Benny bite his lower lip. Probably adding another reason to dislike Jorge to his list, she thought.

"What did Lilly do next? Did she say anything about trying to track this down further?"

Tony looked sadder and even more tired. "She said she would talk to Dimitris about how this report got under her name in the system. And that she had an idea where she could find an earlier draft version of it to compare to what's on file. But she didn't tell me any more about how she could do that."

"Can you remember her exact words, Tony?" Maggie persisted. "It could be important."

"Um, she was pretty upset, like I said. It made her accent more pronounced, you know? A lot harder to understand. This was all as she was gathering her stuff and leaving the room, but I'm pretty sure she said, 'I must see the draft'."

"OK, so this is Thursday at about what, 11 a.m.?" Maggie asked. "Did you see her again after that?"

"No, I had some meetings and then I went to a research lecture at Harvard Medical School. So I didn't see her again on Thursday, and then I took that Friday as a work-from-home day."

Crap, Maggie thought. Every lead on this case peters out before it gets us anywhere. It's like that damn smoke in the air – it clears a bit, and we think it's done, and then it comes back. We're playing hopscotch from one clue to another, hoping that we're guessing right. At least we can question Jorge again, but we don't have a way to get around any denials at this point. Externally, though, she didn't vary her tone.

"Thank you, Tony. That's really helpful. If there's nothing else that comes to mind, we can let you go home. We'll transcribe the tape in the next day or so, and ask you to review and sign it. And we'll post a uniformed patrol outside the house, and they'll check out the inside before you go in. I don't think you're in any danger now that you've spoken to us, though. There's nothing to be gained by harming you now."

Tony didn't look very reassured. Benny said, "Tony, if you want to bunk at my place for a couple of days, I have an empty guest room. You're more than welcome."

Tony brightened at that, nodding gratefully. "Thanks, Benny. That sounds nicer than going back to an empty apartment and starting at every noise. Is that okay with you, Sergeant?"

"Sure," Maggie said. "Sounds like a good idea. It's close to midnight now, so you can both go. Tony can drive the Audi with you Benny, since you came with me, and we'll send a trooper to escort you and make sure everything is ok at your apartment. I still have some paperwork to do here."

*　　　*　　　*

A little after 1 a.m., Maggie had finished her report and was sitting back in a borrowed desk chair rubbing her eyes. Eddie came in with another – or the same – cup of abominable coffee in his hand. As usual, he looked the same in the middle of the night as he did first thing in the morning – slightly disheveled, apparently bemused, but missing nothing. His thinning brown hair was a bit more tousled, his shirt a bit more baggy around his waist, his chin a bit more bristly, but you had to look to see the difference. Eddie didn't look happy.

"They found Dimitris," he said. "And not in a good way."

Maggie raised an eyebrow. "Oh?"

"Down by the Muddy River in the Fenway, near the old Sears Kenmore building. Somebody out late walking their dog saw something floating in the marsh and called it in."

Maggie was already gathering her jacket and belongings. "OK, you drive," she said, tossing him the keys to her Explorer.

The Muddy River, a river by courtesy but actually a series of estuaries now funneled into culverts, creates the border between Boston and Brookline. In the 19th century, to control its periodic flooding, Frederick Law Olmsted had enfolded it into the Emerald Necklace, his network of parks throughout Boston, stretching from the Public Garden downtown to Franklin Park at the southern edge of the city. Near Kenmore Square it widened into a marshy area called the Riverway, with pedestrian and bike paths on either side below a busy roadway.

Eddie drove through Kenmore Square with its Citgo sign now dark, past Fenway Park, and parked near the Longwood T stop on the Brookline side. Maggie and Eddie crossed the Green Line trolley tracks and walked along the placid water of the Muddy River to an elegant arched stone pedestrian bridge that spanned the marshy water. Downstream, toward Kenmore Square, the river bifurcated and broadened into a wide pool covered with lily pads, tall grasses, and cattails. From the Boston side of the water, below the embankment that separated the nature preserve from the busy roadway of the Riverway, they hiked down to where klieg lights had been set up illuminating the tall reeds and brownish green water that gave the river its name. Although the body was found only 20 yards from the busy roadway, with a high school, synagogue, and the Longwood Medical Area hospitals just beyond it, the river was invisible from the road, secluded by trees and the downhill terrain.

Boston Police had been called first, and had fished the body out of the water and onto the muddy edge of the river. They had found a wallet and ID on the body, and recognized Dimitris's name from the BOLO sent out earlier by the State Police. That had led them eventually to Eddie and Maggie, and they were happy to relinquish jurisdiction to the ongoing State Police investigation. A Medical Examiner's truck was also at the scene, parked on the Boston side near the pedestrian bridge that led across the stream to the Riverway at Short Street. The always-on lights of the world-famous hospitals in the Longwood Medical Area twinkled in the background. A bleary-eyed Dr. Shirley Kung was standing at the edge of the water, sipping from a Dunkin' Donuts cup, watching as the Crime Scene technicians moved the body to a gurney for examination.

"Just my luck to be on call," she said to Maggie. "Your case is getting a little too busy, isn't it?"

Maggie lifted her shoulders. "Oh, yeah, you could definitely say that. Have you examined him yet?"

"No," Shirley said. "I was waiting for you, and for the coffee to kick in. If I wanted to work in the middle of the night, I would have gone into OB-Gyn."

They moved over to the body together with Eddie, making room for the tech who was photographing the scene. Shirley turned on a recorder, and started speaking into it. "Deceased is a white male, approximately 30-40 years of age, appears to be in good premorbid health. Roughly five foot eleven, 180 pounds. Wearing jogging clothes – short-sleeve shirt and running pants. No obvious signs of trauma but facial grimacing and rictus are evident. Rigor mortis present in full. Eyes are open. Corneal clouding present, pupils dilated. Body temperature is…" she pushed an instant-read thermometer into the liver "…94.2 degree Fahrenheit. Ambient temperature is…" she looked at one of the technicians who said, "Fifty-eight degrees now."

"…Fifty-eight degrees. There is a small tear in the shirt anteriorly at the left shoulder, at the deltoid below the acromion. There appears to be an injection mark on the skin there, with petechial hemorrhage but no bruising." She turned off the recorder.

Maggie was still looking at Dimitris's face. For it was certainly Dimitris, but there was a look of horror and fear on his face that was straight out of a nightmare. His lips were pulled back – Shirley's clinical description of 'rictus' seemed ludicrously inadequate to capture the horror of it. His eyes were not just open, but open wide in a caricature of horror; the pupils were wide, the irises reduced to a millimeter or so of circumferential brown. Dimitris had died knowing he was dying, and slowly enough to make it torture. She shuddered.

Shirley saw that, and put a hand on Maggie's arm. "I'm sorry, this is a gruesome one. It's almost certainly murder, but I'll know more when I get him into autopsy. I would guess time of death was three to four hours ago, and I'm betting on poison. We'll get blood and urine samples now, before there's any further deterioration," she motioned to another technician, who moved forward with needles and syringes, "but there's only a short list of things that can do this. We'll get the mass spec readings by morning. This guy is pissing me off." There was an intensity to her tone that made Maggie smile grimly. She felt the same way.

"What was he carrying?" asked Maggie.

Eddie answered, "We found wallet, keys, and phone. Not like the last one. I guess our perp wasn't trying to hide this body, just get away without being seen."

"Yes," Maggie said, "but some things are similar. Look, this is a hidden spot in the middle of the city. Even more so than at Middlesex Fells. Again, he found a place that was secluded but accessible. I would bet that they met on the bridge, the attacker struck Dimitris and then pushed him over the railing into the water. The whole thing would only take a few seconds. Then he walks away and disappears. No cameras, no lights, no witnesses. Cars whizzing by 30 yards away but they can't be seen, and drivers or pedestrians can't see down here."

"Where did Dimitris live?" asked Maggie.

Again, Eddie answered, looking at the wallet in his gloved hands. "According to the driver's license, he has a place in Longwood Towers apartments. That's just across the river, on the Brookline side. If you stand a few feet higher on the bank you can see the building from here. We sent someone there this afternoon once the BOLO went out, but he wasn't home. He probably showed up later – we can ask the doorman, they have someone there 24-7. It's only a short jog from here, across from where we parked. Not safe to go jogging on dark paths at night."

"But he disappeared from Quercus and shut off his phone. If he was on the run, why would he go home? And then go jogging? No, I don't think so. I think he was hiding somewhere, and he came out to meet the killer. So he couldn't have been scared of him – not like Tony. Remember, Ted said Dimitris had to be involved in faking the research report. He was scared of *us*, more likely. I think he was in cahoots with the killer, and was meeting him to plan the next steps. But the other guy had already made up his mind that Dimitris was a liability, and that's the end of him. Our perp is a very cool, very vicious customer."

By the time the crime scene was processed – a relatively quick procedure since the body was found in the water – and the corpse transported to the morgue, it was close to 5 a.m. A couple of TV trucks had shown up even though it was the middle of the night, but were being kept behind yellow police tape by a couple of uniformed Boston officers.

"Maggie! Maggie! Can you tell us anything about what's going on here?" she heard a familiar voice call from behind the tape.

Oh, shit, she thought. Just what I need. She turned around to see Dan Beardsley, a pudgy pale man with receding sandy hair, wearing a black Channel 4 jacket, waving her over. Eddie put a hand on her arm, saying, "You know, you can just ignore these creeps, right?"

Maggie grimaced. "Yes, in theory, but I owe this guy something. You go ahead home – see if one of the uniforms will give you a ride. I'll take the car back after I'm done with this."

Eddie nodded, ducking under the crime scene tape, and walked away to the Brookline side. Maggie turned around and walked toward the TV vans.

"No cameras, Dan. No naming me or anyone else involved in the investigation. Off the record only, got it?" she said.

Dan nodded, and three other reporters did too. She recognized someone from the *Boston Globe*, another from the *Herald*, and someone else from Channel 7. The cameramen killed their lights and walked away, the sudden darkness giving Maggie some anonymity to match her off-the-record demand.

"Guys, this is Sergeant Maggie Thompson, Mass State Police," Dan said. "We're old friends, right, Maggie?"

"Sure, Dan. Sort of." In fact, Dan Beardsley had been the roommate of Maggie's boyfriend in college. A short-lived relationship that ended when she had broken the man's arm after he assaulted her in a drunken fury caused by her reluctance to have sex with him on demand. When the man had threatened to accuse Maggie of assault, it was Dan who had come forward to confirm Maggie's version of part of the events of the night. Enough to make it clear that criminal charges would go very much the other way if the roommate persisted. So yes, Maggie thought, I owe Dan, even if seeing him raises some PTSD issues.

"What's going on here, Maggie? We heard about a body on the scanner, and we saw the Medical Examiner's truck pull out. Can you tell us who the victim is?"

Maggie sighed. "Not yet, I'm sorry. We have to notify the family first." She actually had no idea if Dimitris had any family, or if so, which continent they might be on. "But we can say that there was a body found in the river, and we are investigating the cause of death. You can say it was a white male in his thirties."

"Is it suspicious? Was there any evidence of violence? Suicide?" all the reporters were in the scrum now.

"It's the second death in a State Park in less than two weeks, Sergeant. Is this related to the Middlesex Fells Murder?"

Maggie ignored them, looking at Dan. "That's all I can tell you right now, guys, sorry. It's been a long night. Check with MSP Public Affairs in the morning, okay?"

"Thank you, Maggie," Dan said, subdued for once. "Hey, I'll call you later!" he shouted after her as she walked away. This time, she didn't answer.

Chapter Thirteen, Thursday, June 1

Maggie's phone woke her at 9:30 a.m. Groggily she reached for it, but it wasn't the alarm function but an incoming call, handily identified on the screen as coming from the Medical Examiner's office. At least it's not a spam call, she thought wearily as she answered.

"Yes?" she spoke to the ceiling and closed her eyes.

"Hi, Maggie, it's Shirley. I've got the mass spec results from your second victim. Are you awake enough to hear it?"

"Um, yes, sure, Shirley. Four hours of sleep and I'm raring to go," Maggie sat up in bed, reaching for pencil and notebook from the bedside table. "Shoot."

"It was succinylcholine, a big dose." She spelled it out. "There was detectable metabolite in the urine and parent drug in the blood. It's a neuromuscular blocking agent, we call it sux for short. Basically it short-circuits your nerve endings so they can't activate the muscles, and the muscles become paralyzed. It's used after people are anesthetized to relax the muscles for surgery, but we always, always, always knock people out beforehand. To use it without anesthesia is horrific. The victim can't breathe or move but is fully awake and aware until he asphyxiates. It's inhuman."

"All too human, obviously," Maggie answered. "Is it hard to get?"

"No, not really. It's an old drug and not expensive. You have to have a medical or veterinary license, but it's used in human and animal surgery all the time. You don't want muscle to twitch when you cut into it during surgery, it becomes a moving target – all sorts of bad things can happen. But it's short acting, so when the operation is over, it wears off before the patient wakes up. You can reverse it, too, with another drug."

"So would a research lab have this?" Maggie asked.

"Yes, they could if they're doing experiments where they need to put catheters in animals or to operate on them to create a model of a human disease," Shirley answered. "But for animals, too, no one would use sux without first putting the animal to sleep. They would have animal rights protesters at their door, and the ethics committee would pull their permit in a heartbeat."

"Thanks, Shirley. That's really helpful. I'll track down whether there's any sux at Quercus. Talk to you later."

Groaning, she lifted the covers and struggled out of bed.

* * *

A little after 11 a.m., freshly showered and repeating to herself the dictum that a shower is worth two hours' sleep, Maggie walked into Quercus's 2nd floor office area, Dunkin Donuts cup in hand. She walked directly to Benny's desk, where he was in his usual slouch behind the computer monitors. There was no one else within earshot.

Speaking *sotto voce*, she explained to Benny about Dimitris, and what Shirley had found. He looked dumbfounded, but at least had the presence of mind not to say anything out loud. Medical training, Maggie figured, gave one practice at absorbing bad news without flinching or running around in circles.

She asked, "So how do we find out if there is sux on hand here, and who would have access to it?"

"Hmm…realistically, we have to ask Jorge. Do you want to go there? It would certainly tip him off, if he's involved in this."

"No, definitely not. We'll have to be sneaky about it, or else bring in the troops and have them go through the books officially. That would also tip anybody off, wouldn't it? Who in Research would you trust?"

Benny shrugged. "I wouldn't trust anyone, if I were you. We could go up to the third floor and look in the drug cabinet. It's kept locked, or it should be, and we'd have to get a key."

"Wait a minute. Would Lilly have had a key? I seem to remember some keys on the lanyard with her Quercus ID. It was in her desk at her house. What if I get it and we take a wander upstairs later on, after people are gone?"

"That's a great idea, Maggie. She should have one. I think by 5:30-6 o'clock it'll be empty up there."

She looked at her watch.

"OK, I'll head up to her house and then check in with the Woburn office, and I'll meet you back here after five."

* * *

Maggie called Vincent Chen from her car and explained what she needed. As she pulled up to the house on Shore Drive, he came out with Lilly's lanyard, ID, and keys.

"How are you doing, Vincent?" Maggie asked, eyeing him closely. He still looked gray and tired, but not as wan has he had the previous Friday. Well, she thought, at least he's over his jet lag, and the first shock of losing his wife.

"I'm okay, thank you," he said carefully. "My doctor gave me some sleeping pills, and they help. Stephanie is having a really hard time, but two of her close friends are just back from college this week, and I hope that will help. In many ways, she is more American than Chinese, you know, and she needs the connection with her friends more than with me."

"Don't sell yourself short, Vincent," Maggie said. "Even if she doesn't show it, knowing you're here and you support her is something she knows she can count on. It's like she's treading water, facing her friends, but you are the rock her feet can reach and touch when she needs a rest. You save her strength for when she needs to swim."

Vincent smiled gently, but even the smile seemed tired. "Thank you, Sergeant Thompson. That is very wise."

"Maggie, please. Not wise – my dad died three years ago, and I also turned to my friends for comfort. But I knew my mom was there for me, even though I wasn't particularly appreciative at the time."

He nodded. "Well, perhaps when you have a chance, you can tell your mother that, if you haven't already. I'm sure she would be happy to know it."

With a pang Maggie realized she had never said anything like that to her mom. Given Jessica's current efforts to run away from the past, Maggie wondered if her mother would want to hear even a "thank you" that reminded her of that past. Probably worth a try, though, she thought. I owe her that. Shifting gears, she said, "I'm sorry about blindsiding you with that news item about the Chinese Communist Party. I was just trying to throw a reporter off the scent about something at Lilly's work. I hope that didn't cause you any worry or difficulty."

Vincent shook his head. "I hope not too. There has been nothing so far, at least. You never know with the government, but I hope this will just disappear into the noise on social media."

He changed the subject. "Tell me, Maggie, why do you want Lilly's ID?"

"It's actually the keys I need," Maggie said, the habit of compartmentalizing information bred into her from the first day at the Police Academy. "I want to take a look at some locked cabinets in her office, and it's much easier to get the keys from you than to either break in or possibly tip someone off by asking for a new key." Never mind that she had already broken into Lilly's desk, she thought.

Vincent nodded without much interest. "I hope this helps. I hope you catch whoever did this to Lilly."

* * *

The 'Murder on the Muddy River' led the radio news as Maggie drove to Woburn. The link to the 'Murder at Middlesex Fells' got a lot of play as well. The police had not released Dimitris's name yet, 'pending notification of family', so the newscast was relatively vague. But enough, she thought, to tell the murderer that his handiwork had been detected. They could only withhold the details for another day or so, then the publication of Dimitris's name would link this murder to Lilly's and to Quercus, and the whole three ring media circus would be under way.

The combination of the news reports on the radio, driving by the Tufts campus, and her short night lowered Maggie's defenses and led her to memories she generally locked down and avoided.

As a freshman in college, Maggie had met Dan Beardsley on the first day of school, when only the freshmen were already on campus. It was on the stairs of the Campus Center, as the student union building was known. She had a few high school classmates who were also in her freshman class, and they met for lunch. Dan was a friend of a friend, but they hit it off well enough to become friends themselves through all four years of college.

Fast forward to senior year. Maggie was living off-campus in an apartment with two other girls, and Dan was in the same building with one male roommate. When Dan's roommate asked her out, she was flattered. He was tall, handsome, a jock, and had a nice-guy demeanor that she was too naïve to question. They went out for a few weeks, but the more she got to know him, the more uneasy she became. He had a way of trying to control her – she later learned that was true with other women as well – and her natural contrariness made her resist. Eventually, that led to what Emily later called "The Night You Said No." Neither of them ever used his name, and NYSN became their shorthand for the events of that evening.

The evening in question was a bit of a blur now, almost a decade later. They went out to dinner, had a couple of drinks, went to a club, and another bar, and eventually came back to the guy's apartment. Dan was out. Maggie had as usual limited herself to a couple of glasses of wine, but the guy was pretty drunk, belligerent, and demanding. Demanding a blow job, actually. When Maggie told him he was too drunk, and gross, he tried to force her. Neither of them saw Dan unlock the apartment door at that moment. The guy was too enraged to care, and Maggie's martial arts training had kicked in. Literally. She already had a black belt in Kyokushin karate, which emphasizes kicking rather than arm strikes.

When he first came at her, she tried to evade him, but in a small room, fenced in by a sofa, a table, and the walls, that wasn't much of an option. She did a simple crescent kick as he charged at her, using his momentum to propel him harmlessly past her and into the wall. It knocked the breath out of him for a moment, but seemed to only make him angrier. She heard Dan shout something, but the guy was coming at her again. This time she executed a double roundhouse kick, landing one in his ribs and the other on his upraised arm, which snapped audibly. That was the end of the NYSN.

A day or two after the guy got his arm casted, he showed up at Maggie's apartment door. First he tried to convince her that nothing had happened, that it had been an accident, that she had overreacted. When she told him she didn't want to see him again, he grew angry, and threatened to go to campus police and accuse her of assault. Things were getting heated when Dan showed up, took his roommate by the uncasted arm and reminded him that although he had been too drunk to remember what happened, that was true of neither Maggie nor Dan, and he was willing to testify to Maggie's version. That's why, Maggie knew, she still owed him years later.

She stopped to pick up a late lunch at Bill & Bob's Roast Beef, a squat building on Main Street of such a bright red hue that it was probably visible from the International Space Station. The Super Pastrami sandwich with onion rings filled the car with the scent of impending coronary occlusion, but Maggie was salivating on the short drive to the Fort. She parked in the lot next to the Woburn office building and walked into the Homicide & Unsolved offices, trailing the scent that turned heads as she went.

The team were at their desks, pecking away at their keyboards. Dropping into her chair, she focused first on lunch, then came up for air and motioned to Eddie and Jimmy to huddle up. Mike Davis and Heather Martin joined them.

Davis shook his head sadly. "I don't know how you eat like that and don't look like me," he said, pointing at the remaining half of the pastrami glistening unctuously on its bulkie roll.

Maggie shrugged. "It's because my heart is pure. Or good genes. Or just a matter of time."

Davis sighed. "Youth," he said, "is wasted on the young. Tell us about the discussion with Tony Dupree."

Maggie reviewed Tony's report of his meeting with Lilly and her reaction to finding the study report attributed to her, ending with, "So I think you or Jimmy or Eddie should interview Jorge again as soon as possible, either this afternoon or tomorrow morning. We need to establish if he got this report notification – or at least get it on the record that he lied to us if that's what it turns out to be."

Next, Maggie reviewed the call with Shirley and the plan to investigate the third-floor labs. Eddie had come up with a list of everyone who had been badged into the office at the time of Lilly and Tony's meeting. It seemed about half the company was on site that day, including all of the leadership team. Maggie sighed. Another dead end.

"So we have a second murder," Lieutenant Davis summarized. "Same pattern of a jogger at night, but different cause of death. First one was blunt trauma to the head, second one is Soviet-style poisoning, more or less. And the first time the body is dressed up like a modern-day mummy. This time it's dumped in the Muddy River without any fancy stuff. Do we assume it's the same perp, or do we have a second killer?"

"I'm betting it's one killer, but he's more aggressive now," Maggie answered. "The first time he's had the weekend to prepare. If Lilly says something to somebody on Thursday or Friday, and she's killed on Monday evening, that's plenty of time to at least plan the murder. He must have known something about Lilly's routines, like jogging after work, up at the Fells. Maybe he staked her out over the weekend, to learn about that, and maybe he knew or found out that both her husband and daughter were away. The perp doesn't have time to dispose of the first body, so he wraps it up until he can come back to it. Remember, if it weren't for the smoke closing the park, we probably wouldn't have found Lilly. He would have had time to get back there and remove the body, take it somewhere and make it disappear."

"On the other hand, Dimitris walks out of Quercus at noon on the following Wednesday, and he's dead hours later. This time, our perp is ad-libbing, making it up as he goes along. So he prepares this lethal injection, pretty much on the fly. He must have enough biology or medicine background to know what to do, and he doesn't care how horrible and excruciating a death it causes, either. Now that we've found the first body, there's not much upside to taking the risk and time to dispose of Dimitris. We would assume if he's missing, he's either on the run or dead, and we'd be looking for him anyway. A real cold-blooded psycho, this guy."

Jimmy stirred in his seat. "Eddie found this video of a bicyclist following Lilly's car when she left home for the park. If that's our guy, he might have been staking the place out, trying to figure out how to accost the vic. Then she drives off to the Fells and he follows her, and finds an isolated spot where he can kill her."

"He was prepared enough to have the blue wrapping with him, and gloves too, since we didn't find any prints," Eddie pointed out.

"True," Maggie answered, "but if he's a lab rat, he would have had access to those things at Quercus, and could just plop them in his bike saddlebag, ready for whatever exactly turned out to be the scenario when he caught up with Lilly. Those guys are geeky enough to carry anything."

"If you're going to go snooping around their labs, you'll have to wear gloves too," Eddie smiled. "If you find something that's evidence, we'll have to go back there and get it with a warrant, and you can't contaminate it."

"Yes, I will," Maggie said. "As long as it's still an undercover assignment, we should be okay. All I want to establish is if they have sux on the premises. I don't think it's likely we can find fingerprint evidence if they do – this guy is too smart for that. But we'll still have to test everything."

"Why not just get a warrant now and go in with lights and sirens?" asked Heather. "Seems simpler."

"Yes, it definitely is simpler," Maggie said, "but then it tips off our perp that we're aware of the sux and that we suspect it came from Quercus. The longer we can keep him in the dark about how much we know, the more confident he'll be that he's getting away with it. Maybe he'll make a mistake. Or at least he won't get even more desperate and hurt someone else. You guys will be going in there anyway to interview Jorge."

"Okay," Davis said. "Let's do it Maggie's way. But Maggie, I want to hear from you as soon as you're out of there, both that you're alright and what you found, if anything. Otherwise, we *will* go in with lights and sirens."

* * *

Maggie was back at Quercus a little before 5 p.m. With most people leaving earlier than that to beat the rush hour, she was able to park right in front of the building, then walked in and slid behind her desk, nodding to Benny. She sat at her computer, typing, while keeping her jacket on. There were only a few other staffers on the second floor, and they gradually filtered out over the next half an hour. Once they were the last ones left, Maggie texted Benny:

"Shall we?"

"No, not yet, I would give it another ½ hour. The lab guys often stay later."

They waited until 6:15, then walked upstairs. The third floor was very different from the second. There were desks and carrels and a coffee area by the elevators. From either side of the elevator bank a corridor ran around the entire perimeter of the building. The inside wall of this corridor was glass-enclosed from chest-height up, and showed three aisles of lab benches, with scattered tanks labelled liquid nitrogen or oxygen or carbon dioxide, as well as centrifuges, ceiling-high freezers, and other equipment that Maggie didn't recognize. There was a small conference room in each corner for people to have meetings without changing out of their lab clothes and shoes. Everything was blindingly white under bright LED lights, with scattered yellow and red warning signs providing contrast. There were closed beige cabinets below the lab benches, and open beige metal shelves full of bottles, pipette tips, tubes, scintillation vials, and other supplies. No one was about – the place looked deserted.

Entry to the lab area was through locked doors in each side of the building, accessible by badging in. Benny pulled blue nitrile gloves from a box clipped to the wall next to the nearest door, and handed two to Maggie. Putting on his own gloves, he touched his badge to the card reader next to the door, and it opened with a ping.

"Well, now we've rung the front doorbell," he said, keeping his voice low. "The system will record that I was here, if anyone wanted to look."

"Come up with a good excuse, Benny," Maggie said, almost whispering, though she wasn't sure why it was necessary. "You needed some document for your next FDA filing, or something."

"Pretty good, Mags," Benny said. "I can work with that."

They went inside. "Since I'm the senior MD on the staff, I have to sign for prescription drugs for animal research, like anesthetics and such, when they're delivered. But I don't deal with them again until someone runs out and they need another shipment. They're kept in a cabinet and a refrigerator back there, on the left," Benny pointed down the left-hand aisle of lab benches to a beige cabinet with a padlock, and next to it an ordinary white household refrigerator with a freezer above and fridge below. Both doors of the fridge had been fitted with padlocks and hasps, the kind you could get at any Home Depot.

Maggie took Lilly's keys out of her jacket pocket. "Who else would have a key like this?" she asked.

"Just about anybody who works up here. We keep isoflurane, lidocaine, sux, heparin, lots of reagents needed for animal experiments."

"Boy, you guys have like zero security, you know that? Well, let's see what's inside."

Benny tried a couple of keys until the lock opened with a click. He pulled the cabinet door back, revealing shelves of medicines, needles of various sizes, and on the bottom shelf, gallon-sized brown glass bottles of hydrochloric and sulfuric acid.

"We keep the acids locked up too," Benny said. "Avoids accidental spills, or at least it should."

"So where is the sux?" Maggie asked.

"That has to be kept refrigerated, so it would be in here," Benny said. He played around with another padlock until it clicked, and opened the fridge door.

Benny stooped to look more closely, and pointed to a white rectangular box labeled 'Succinylcholine chloride injection, USP' and 'Rx Only'. He opened it to show seven glass vials, each about two inches high, with bright red metal seals. Three vials were missing.

"Is there a log when someone takes out something from here?" Maggie asked.

Benny pointed to a clipboard hanging from a nail on the wall. There was a sheaf of papers marked 'Drug Log' with columns for the substance, date, amount, and signature. There were listings for various substances, but no one had signed out any sux in the past six weeks. Maggie took photos of the log, the fridge and the box, and Benny locked things up again.

"You know," he said quietly, "one vial is more than enough to kill a human. If someone took out three vials, he's got two lethal injections left."

Maggie sighed. "Oh great, just what we need. We'll have to get a warrant for this before we can officially look at it. Let's just keep that to ourselves, shall we? I'll have the detectives come back and take custody of this in the morning. Until then, we can keep an eye on it." She reached into her jacket pocket and pulled out a small round black object, about one inch in diameter. "This is an upgraded version of a nanny cam," she said. "I borrowed it from the Narcotics Unit once, and keep forgetting to return it. It's got a battery that's good for about 72 hours, which should be fine for our purposes."

"Do these things really work?" Benny asked.

"The ones you get on line for fourteen bucks probably don't, but the ones we get for fourteen hundred bucks, yeah, they work just fine."

Maggie peeled the nonstick backing off an adhesive pad mounted on the rear of the camera, and attached it to a whiteboard affixed to the wall across the aisle from the refrigerator. There were various formulas and chemical names scrawled on the whiteboard, along with half a dozen round magnets in various colors, some holding printed pages of announcements in place. The camera looked like just another magnet. She checked her phone that the appropriate app was active and showed Benny the video of the fridge on the screen.

"That will record continuously until the battery runs out. If someone comes to get more sux, we'll see them. I'll call about the warrant once we're out of here, and we'll take possession of the sux tomorrow. I think that's more reasonable than rousting a judge and bursting in here like a herd of buffalo at midnight. If we can delay tipping off our perp that we're on to the sux as a cause of death, that could be helpful."

Benny led the way back downstairs. They had the place to themselves, but there was no point to staying.

"How about some dinner?" Maggie asked. "I'm starving. Come to my place, and we can get takeout from downstairs. We've still got a bunch of Dad's diaries to look at."

Benny nodded. "Lloyd's Law," he said.

"Huh? What's that?"

"It's an old intern's maxim – food plus sleep equals a constant. So if you sleep less, you eat more. We all gained about 15 pounds as interns. My friend Lloyd made an equation out of it."

"I guess so. Either way, I'm still starving."

"What about Tony?" Benny asked. "I hope he's not going stir-crazy in my apartment all day."

"I'm sure he's fine. You'll be back to check on him in a couple of hours."

"Yeah, I guess you're right. Let's go, I'm hungry too."

Maggie ordered from Fox & the Knife before starting the car, and texted Mike Davis that they were safely out of the building so he wouldn't send in the cavalry. She also asked him to organize the warrant for the sux in the morning. Then she pulled away from the curb. Neither she nor Benny noticed a figure in black jacket and bike helmet on a sleek white bicycle waiting at the corner of Sydney and Franklin Streets. As Maggie drove by toward Massachusetts Avenue, the biker casually followed. Given the traffic and number of red lights, he overtook them before they got to the Mass Ave Bridge, then accelerated to keep up as they passed him going over the Charles River.

* * *

Maggie sent Benny into Fox & the Knife to get the food while she double-parked outside the restaurant. Then they drove around the block to her building and left the car in the garage. Upstairs, she unpacked harissa-marinated olives and homemade ricotta as appetizers, a pomodoro salad to share, whole branzino fritto for Benny and *cacio e pepe* for herself. There was chocolate olive oil torta for dessert. She pulled a bottle of pinot grigio from her fridge and Benny opened it. Less than half an hour after leaving Cambridge, they were eating.

Happily full, they took their wine glasses to the sofa. On the coffee table, Maggie had more of Henry's diaries open and flagged with sticky notes. Taking a Kleenex from the table, Benny took off his glasses to blow his nose. She had a sudden sharp memory of him doing the same thing when she was a child.

"Okay, here's where we left off, Benny," she said, rereading the section:

November 4, 1971: The last few days have been a whirlwind. I was going to go to the airline office on Tuesday, but Hue went into labor prematurely at about 5 that morning! I got her to the 3rd Army Field Hospital in time – it's where I was a patient and she had been a nurse. It's where we met, and it was only fitting that it would be where our child was born. Dr. Auerbach was still stationed there, and he pulled some strings to get her in. Labor took about forever – I was sweating bullets but Hue was calm, and the nurses were great (most of them knew her anyway). Finally, the baby was born about 11 at night. A girl! We decided to name her Mai. It means 'flower' in Vietnamese, and of course it would work in English too. Mai Nguyen Mason. She's gorgeous, just like her mother.

"It's bad enough we have a mystery at work," Benny said. "Now we also have a fifty-year-old mystery in the family? And both women named after flowers. You might be in your element, but I'm exhausted already."

"You don't like mysteries?" Maggie asked.

"No. I like hypotheses. Testable ones. Answered by experiments that are rationally designed and lead to clear answers. Haven't seen much of that in your line of work."

"No, I suppose not. We *do* have hypotheses, I suppose – sometimes just based on hunches, or process of elimination of who could be at the place of a murder at the time we think it happened. At least, we have a list of suspects in some sort of order of expected likelihood that they did it. I don't know about experiments, though. Mostly I bumble around until the answer becomes obvious or we flush out the bad guy."

"And which one do you think will apply here – at Quercus, I mean?" Benny asked.

"I'm not sure. Whoever is behind the murders is a very cool customer. Probably not much given to panicking or making mistakes, which is what leads to being flushed out. I predict more bumbling."

"Oh, great. Maybe we'll have more luck with the past," he said. "Looks like you cheated and read ahead."

"A little. So Mai is born in November 1971, and Hue and Dad are married in January 1972. What we have to do is trace their progress from one to the other. If we can account for their whereabouts and activities in that period, maybe we'll have our answer." She turned the page in the diary to the next flagged page and read:

> *November 8, 1971: Hue and Mai came home today. Hue is sore and moving slowly but says she feels fine. Her ankles are already less swollen, but boy her boobs sure make up for it! Mai isn't very fussy, but she is still trying to figure out the whole breast-feeding thing. Me too. I told Hue we could just get formula from the base PX, but she says we can't afford it, and anyway breastfeeding is natural and better for the baby. I'm sure she's right on both counts, but back home every woman bottle feeds.*
>
> *This also messes up our exit visa plans. I don't know if the baby needs her own papers – I'm going to ask Uncle Quan tonight when he and Aunt Trang come to meet Mai. The clock is ticking – we have to leave by November 15, or our visas expire and we have to start all over again. We can't afford to do that – Dad will never give me that kind of money twice.*

"Yikes," Benny said. "I can see how they could get stuck there. What happened?"

Maggie turned the page and read:

> *November 9, 1971: Uncle Quan says we need new papers and an American passport for Mai. That would take months, of course, and another round of bribes for the exit visa.*

I'm going to MACV this morning to try and find Dan. I think he's still here, though Dave rotated out to Tokyo and will be going home soon. I'll see if there's a way around this. Otherwise, we've got real trouble!

"Here's the next entry," Maggie said:

November 11, 1971: The last two days have been a blur. Found Dan at MACV, and he confirmed that we'd need new papers, but Mai doesn't need a passport as long as we have her birth certificate with both our names. A new exit visa would take weeks, and probably cost more money than we have. When I got back, I found Uncle Quan talking very fiercely with Hue. After some back and forth it seems he's worried that there will be another PAVN attack at Christmas, and we could be trapped in Vietnam. He says he has a friend who can forge a document for Mai, that it would only be $200, and that it would be safer to get out now. I don't know how he knows about North Vietnamese plans, but it sure sounds like he's VC, even if he's an ARVN veteran. Not surprising – probably half the damn South Vietnamese Army would flip if they could.

Hue and I went back and forth on it all afternoon. In the end, we decided it was worth a try. We still have about $800 left from Dad, so if this works we can get home, and if not, I'll have to figure out how to raise another thousand or more for legit papers. After all, it's for a baby – how much could they care about letting a baby – especially a 'bui doi' girl – out of Saigon?

Anyway, after we finally agreed, there was still time so I went down to the Pan Am office and got tickets on the flight out for Sunday, the 14th. That's the last of Dad's money, though. We're committed now – either we get on this flight or we're stuck here, maybe for months, maybe longer. On the other hand – wow – we could be home for our first Thanksgiving together!

"Jeesh – 'especially a girl'? Is he kidding?" Maggie grumbled. "And more damn acronyms. ARVN is the South, right? I'm guessing PAVN is the North?"

Benny shrugged. "I think in the Vietnamese culture – especially then – boys were more valued than girls. But a mixed-marriage baby was of no value – 'bui doi', remember? 'Dust of life'. And yes, ARVN was the Army of the Republic of Vietnam, that's the South; and PAVN was the People's Army of Viet Nam, meaning the North. And VC meant the Viet Cong, the North's underground guerillas. Dictatorships have to operate in the name of 'the People', and the North was officially the Democratic Republic of Vietnam, even though it was neither."

Maggie nodded, and went back to the notebook:

> *November 12, 1971: I gave Uncle Quan the money yesterday and he came back tonight with Mai's exit visa. I think it looks okay, though the paper isn't as good as ours, it's flimsier, and a little more beige than white. Hue is packing her suitcase, though we still have a couple of days. The hardest part was actually getting Mai to lie still for a photo. We went first thing in the morning to the camera shop Uncle Quan recommended. She kept cooing and smacking her lips, and the photographer had to take a dozen shots to get one that looked sufficiently serious for a visa. Of course, I had to pay for all of them. At least he did a rush job on developing the film and printing the photos, and I had them by noon. So now we have Mai's first baby photos!*

"I wonder if those photos are in the other box," Maggie said. "I haven't searched through all of it yet."

> *November 15, 1971: It's been a terrible couple of days. Where do I start? We got to the airport on Sunday morning. Me, Hue, Mai, Uncle Quan and Aunt Trang. We checked our bags and got our seats at the Pan Am counter, and that was fine. The trouble started at Passport Control.*

My papers and Hue's were fine, but when the border policeman took Mai's the ink ran! It must have warmed up in my pocket, and he got suspicious. He held it up to the light and then massaged the paper between his thumb and forefinger, and more ink ran. He started yelling at us in Vietnamese, much faster than I could keep track of. Hue translated that he was accusing us of smuggling a baby and that he would have us arrested and thrown in jail. Uncle Quan tried to calm things down, but I think the guy was looking for a bribe, and we had no money left! There was a growing line of people behind us, and everyone was looking at us in a hostile way and starting to mutter, the people in the front telling others behind them that we were trying to smuggle a baby out. I was really worried that we'd be pulled out of line and lynched!

In desperation, Hue asked Uncle Quan and Aunt Trang if they would keep Mai, take her home with them, and we would come back for her as soon as we had enough money. They weren't very happy with the idea, I can tell you, but what could we do? Imagine what it must have taken for Hue to offer to give up Mai, even temporarily. It was like the story of the baby and King Solomon. What mother would do that if there was another choice? I think Aunt Trang, who never had children, was the one who decided to do it. She's quiet but intense. When Hue asked her – in Vietnamese, so I didn't understand it at first – she became very still, put her hand to her heart. Then she nodded, just once. I guess there are some things, even in Vietnam, where it's the woman who chooses. Trang is normally so distant and – with me – even hostile, but Hue is her only niece and the only living connection to her sister. This broke through with her, and she just silently reached out her arms for Mai, tears streaming down her face, Hue bawling, me sputtering. Uncle Quan didn't get a vote, and he knew it, but to his credit he went along with it, more or less graciously.

The border cop had already stamped my and Hue's visas, and I had my American passport, so there was nothing more he could do to us, especially with the line behind us growing restive. He tossed Mai's papers back to me and waved us on contemptuously.

So the long and short of it is that we got on the plane without our daughter. It's just awful. Hue sat stunned through the first half of the flight, sometimes crying quietly, sometimes just staring straight ahead. I can only imagine how awful she feels – I feel it too. I just keep holding her hand and telling her that we'll get Mai back. As soon as we can raise the money, we'll fly back to Vietnam.

We landed in San Francisco a few hours ago, and now we're at the Greyhound station on 7th Street waiting for the bus to Boston. It's almost $100 each, but that's a lot less than flying, or that new Amtrak service that's such a mess. I used Dad's Diner's Club to pay for it (it'll be Christmas before he sees the bill, and I hope the spirit of the season will prevail).

"Oh, my God, that's awful," Maggie said. "How dreadful for Hue. And Dad too, of course, but to be forced to give up her baby on the spot? Not knowing when or if she'd see her again…in a country at war, and with family members she doesn't really seem close to. It's a nightmare."

Benny had been rummaging through the box of photos as Maggie was reading aloud. Now he showed her a small black and white photograph, about three by four inches. It was a smiling Asian infant with a ribbon in her black spikey hair, serious expression, and dark eyes that stared at the camera. "Here is our sister, Maggie," he said. She took the photo wordlessly, staring at it.

Benny sat down heavily. "I think that explains some of how Henry was later. Protective, but also distant. Never fully sharing what he felt, or thought. I only really remember things clearly from after my mother died, but that must have been another blow to him. I have some memories of them together before she died, but she must have already been pretty sick with kidney failure. I remember them holding hands and stuff, but I don't remember a lot of laughter or joy. And we still don't know what happened to Mai, except that neither you nor I ever heard of her before this week. We have to talk to Uncle George."

"Yes, well, we do, but not until we've done our homework. There's a lot more here to go through. I can't believe they kept this from both of us. That Dad did, and everyone else was, well, complicit. I mean, you knew Grandma and Grandpa as a teenager. Even if I was too young to talk to about this, they could have mentioned it to you. Dad must have forbidden it."

"No, they never said anything to me," Benny said.

Benny's phone pinged, and he looked down at a text. "It's Tony, wondering when I'm coming back. I guess I should head home, it's after nine and he must be anxious."

"Sure, I can run you back," Maggie said.

"That's okay, I can get an Uber," Benny answered. "No need for you to go back and forth."

"Actually, I want to see Tony again, see if he remembered anything more," Maggie smiled. "It's not always about you, you know."

Benny rolled his eyes. "Fine. You cooked very well, or someone did, anyway." Maggie did an exaggerated curtsey as they brought their plates and utensils to the dishwasher, packed up leftovers (not much), and tossed containers in the recycle bin.

Their bike-riding tail was waiting in the shadows of Athens Street, actually just an alley behind Maggie's building, and he followed them back to Cambridge. With less traffic at this time of night, the car was faster, but the bicyclist – riding without a headlamp – kept them in sight all the way to Benny's building.

*   *   *

Tony was waiting for them when Benny unlocked the front door of the apartment. He was holding a baseball bat with both hands, looking like he was ready to put a line drive through an intruder's head. When he saw it was them, he exhaled audibly, letting the bat fall to his side.

"I'm glad it was you," he said. "I've been nervous all day."

"Understandably so," Maggie reassured him, "but it's all quiet out there. Did you eat something?"

"Yes, I made an omelet and salad, with some of Benny's wine," Tony smiled.

"Good," Benny said. "Glad you helped yourself! Now we can have a nightcap." He tapped his phone a few times and the Sonos speakers started playing, sixties classic rock at a low volume. Walking over to a multicolored Jonathan Adler bar in the living room, he opened it and turned to them. "What will it be? Cognac? Amarula? Malt scotch?"

Tony chose a cordial glass of Amarula, while Maggie passed. Benny poured himself a snifter of Remy Martin VSOP. John Fogarty and Creedence were singing 'Bad Moon Rising' in the background.

"We were wondering if you've thought more about your last discussion with Lilly," Maggie said. "Anything at all that you can remember? It doesn't have to seem important to be useful, you know."

Tony shook his head slowly. "I've been wracking my brain all day, but no, not really. The last thing she said to me was half to herself, 'I must see the draft'."

On the stereo behind Tony, John Fogarty was singing, or mumbling loudly:

Well don't go around tonight
Well it's bound to take your life
There's a bad moon on the rise

Maggie looked at the speaker in the corner of the room. "There's a bathroom on the right?" she asked. "What *is* this song?"

Benny laughed. "That's a mondegreen, Maggie. One of the classics, actually. He's singing, 'there's a bad moon on the rise'." He enunciated each syllable.

"What's a mondegreen?" Tony asked.

"It's when a song lyric is mis-heard and converted into another lyric. Like what you just thought you heard. Or Jimi Hendrix singing 'excuse me while I kiss the sky' and people hearing 'excuse me while I kiss this guy'. It's from an old Scottish ballad about how they 'slayed the Earl of Murray and laid him on the green', but someone heard 'they slayed the Earl of Murray and Lady Mondegreen', and it stuck."

"Tony, what's wrong?" asked Maggie, concerned. Tony was staring ahead, his glass frozen part-way to his lips, mouth open. "Are you okay?"

Tony shook his head as if to clear it. "Of course! Lilly didn't say 'I have to see the draft.' She said, 'I have to see van Haft'! Oh, my God. Suddenly it's obvious. I don't know why I didn't realize it. It was you and your damn mondegreen, Benny – it made me think about it differently."

Maggie and Benny looked at each other. "Well, he's the head guy, right? Wouldn't she want to let him know?" asked Maggie.

"Yes, sure," Tony said. "But if she told him, that was just a day or two before she disappeared. If she talked to Dimitris, he might have told Thomas also, right? Have you guys talked to Dimitris already?"

Benny started to say something, but Maggie cut him off. "Yes, we have, but I don't think we know everything yet." Compartmentalizing information was getting more complicated, she thought.

"Anyway," she continued, yawning, "it's getting late, and I've got to get some sleep. I'll see you guys tomorrow. And I'll ask one of the troopers to talk to Thomas."

As she drove away in the direction of the Mass Ave bridge and Boston, the bicyclist who had followed her car rode away in the other direction, toward Harvard Square.

Chapter Fourteen, Friday, June 2

Maggie got an early start on what promised to be a beautiful early summer morning. No more brown sky at last – the winds seem to have shifted the smoke away from New England. She drove up to Woburn with plenty of time for a Dunkin Donuts stop before the 9 a.m. daily meeting in Homicide & Unsolved.

Although Maggie was excused from the weekly coffee and donut rotation by virtue of her undercover assignment, she still brought a box of donut holes for the team, along with her own iced coffee. She walked into the conference room and found a seat as the place filled up – the double homicide investigation had pumped up the size of the team and there was a high-energy buzz in the room. She counted seventeen chairs around the table and another dozen along the wall, and all were filled with troopers, detectives, an Assistant District Attorney, and supervisors. Eddie, Jimmy, Heather, and Ted were all seated near her. She saw Shirley Kung come in and lean against the back wall. She sighed – with this larger crew, they would have to repeat a lot of the discussion from yesterday.

Mike Davis stepped to the front of the room and signaled for silence. The buzz died down. "Welcome, everybody. We have some new team members here now, so we'll go over things as best we understand them, and get everyone on the same page. As you all know, we now have a second murder, with a different M.O. but a similar location to the first victim. Meaning, both of them were found in urban parklands, killed at night, and left at the scene. The first victim, Lilly Zhao, was killed by a blow to the head. The second, Dimitris Pappas, by what I can only describe as lethal injection. The first victim was hidden, but the second one just left in the water. What do we take away from this?"

Adelle Watkins, the ADA assigned to the case, spoke up first. "I think we're assuming we have one perp, right? Otherwise things get very weird."

Davis nodded. "Yes, I think so. Both victims worked at the same biotech, both were involved in what looks like faked data from a report that could have major repercussions for the financial health of the company, and for the wealth of the people working there. For the moment, I'm not prepared to say that different weapons are enough to require different killers."

There was a general murmur of assent around the table. Davis looked to the back of the room. "Dr. Kung, why don't you bring us up to date on the forensics?" he said.

Shirley pushed off from the wall where she had been leaning. "On Lilly Zhao, the first victim, we've finished the DNA search, and found nothing. The killer was very clean – no hairs, no blood, no semen, no DNA that we could find on her body or clothing. The body was wrapped in blue laboratory film, you remember, and that retarded decomposition. If it weren't for the Canadian forest fires bringing the Ranger out to close the park, my guess is that the perp would have come back and removed the body, and we'd never have known what happened to her. It was almost a perfect crime."

"No such thing," Eddie muttered to the table at large.

Shirley smiled. "No, but that's because we got lucky, or rather the perp got unlucky. Proves once again, that it's better to be lucky than smart."

"And the second victim?" Davis asked, cutting through another buzz of sidebar conversations.

"He was found in the Muddy River, as you know, probably shortly after he was killed. It was after 11 at night, but it's a much more populated area than the Middlesex Fells, and someone is always out on that path by the river. Bodies outdoors are generally found by kids or people walking dogs. In this case, it was a dog-walker. The victim,

Dimitris Pappas, was much larger and stronger than Lilly Zhao, and he was killed with a large dose of succinylcholine given intramuscularly. That works in a couple of minutes, and it incapacitates before it kills. It can be administered on the run, without much contact time with the victim. Very effective, really quite brilliant, and extremely cruel. The victim asphyxiates because of paralysis of the respiratory muscles while remaining fully aware until hypoxia causes loss of consciousness. It's a very long, awful four minutes."

There was silence in the room. Other than Maggie, the others had not heard the details of how Dimitris had died. She had had a day to come to terms with the horror of it, at least in part, but she saw it starting to sink in for the others. A grim, determined look was the commonest reaction she saw, mixed with disgust and loathing. She'd seen it before, on other State Police teams. The cold fury of seeing a crime carried out willfully, indifferent to the suffering it causes, and determination to get the person capable of such an act. Get them and put them away – either in prison or in the ground, it didn't much matter. Looking around the table, Maggie sensed that the group had just become something more – a team, with a single goal and the motivation to reach it. If it were a single entity, it would have growled.

As the room quieted, Shirley continued: "But since the body went into the water, we have no chance at DNA or other biological evidence that could identify the killer. Whether that was his intent or not, it was just as effective as the precautions he had taken for the first crime. There's nothing in the crime scene that can link a suspect to the murder."

"Okay," Davis nodded. "Now you know what we're up against. Now, motive. Maggie?"

"A few days before she died, Lilly had written down the ID number of a research report, a document that Quercus needed to submit to the FDA to get approval to start human trials of their lead drug candidate. I found it in the files in her desk. It was just a report number, but it didn't match any report in Quercus's on-line file system. There was another report in the system, however, that was off by one digit from what Lilly had written. It's supposed to show that the way Quercus measures its drug concentration in the body is by using a valid assay. But the second document that's in the files is a fake, substituted for the original report number that Lilly noted. This second report had supposedly been signed by someone who had previously left the company, a scientist named Richard Sinsky, and supposedly uploaded by Lilly herself, but she knew that neither of these things was true. She was probably the only person in the company who would have noticed this discrepancy, and there was no particular reason for her to go look at this report. Except that in a monkey experiment she was running, the assay wasn't behaving properly. So it was this confluence of unlikely events – the assay doesn't work, it doesn't work in a study that Lilly Zhao is overseeing, and Lilly is the only person who could have known that she hadn't uploaded that report. That trio of events led her to say something to someone, who realized she was a threat, and killed her."

Jimmy looked up. "I spoke to Sinsky yesterday. He said he left the company on good terms at the end of last December, for a bigger job with another company. That kind of thing happens all the time in biotech. But of course his access to systems was disabled and he never heard of this report. He couldn't have signed a report in February of this year even if he'd wanted to."

Maggie nodded. "Not surprisingly, Lilly was upset by this report that's attributed to her incorrectly, and now she was running a key animal experiment that relied on the method in this report. The results she was seeing in her experiment didn't jibe with what the file said. The file said the assay works, but in Lilly's experiment she couldn't detect any drug in the monkeys' bloodstream when she knew it should have been there. Without this experiment, the company can't file its IPO, and they can't move the drug to the clinic and test it in humans. Without the IPO, the company is out of money and could go bankrupt. Plus, the employees, who are all promised stock when the IPO goes public, would be out millions."

"Did she talk to anyone about her suspicions?" Adelle asked.

"Yes, she sat down with Tony Dupree, the head of manufacturing at Quercus, on the Friday before she disappeared, which was on the following Monday evening. She also told Tony she was going to talk to the second victim, the IT guy Dimitris Pappas, and to her boss, Thomas van Haft, the Chief Scientific Officer, but we don't know if she did or not."

"Why talk to Dupree first, specifically?" asked Adelle.

"Because he was also relying on the results of the assay that was in the faked report," Maggie said. "She needed it for animal tests, and he needed it for measuring how much drug was in each batch. He told her the assay worked for him. It also worked in mice. It just didn't work in monkeys, which FDA requires before going into humans, and that's what Lilly's final experiment was about. Plus there's a high risk that if it doesn't work in monkeys, it won't work in humans either, according to my source at Quercus."

"And then when Lilly was found dead, Tony disappeared," Heather spoke up. "He was afraid he'd be next. But we were able to track him down in northern Maine, and he agreed to come back with us. That's how we know what Lilly found out before she disappeared."

"Okay, but why kill Papas?" asked Adelle. "How does he connect to this report business, or to Zhao?"

Ted spoke up. "Dimitris was pretty much the whole IT department at Quercus. If someone removed a file from a regulatory system, either Dimitris did it or he'd almost certainly know about, as he's the system administrator. Based on what I could find, it's very likely that he did it himself, and tried to cover it up by using a fictitious employee

ID. He would also be a natural first person for Lilly to go to, and we have some indication from Tony Dupree that Lilly was intending to talk to Dimitris after she found out about the fake report."

"How many employees in the company?" asked Adelle.

"About forty," Maggie answered.

"So we have forty suspects?" someone down the table asked.

"Probably not that many. The stocks aren't divided equally – the higher-ups get more, much more. Jimmy, can you fill them in?"

Jimmy nodded. "Some of us have gone over this already, but the bottom line is there are five people who make tens of millions from the IPO, and the rest make about a year's extra salary. So we're focusing on the top leadership – they're also the people who would be in a position to know about the report, and are probably who Lilly would have spoken to about it. They are Art Keogh, the CEO; Thomas van Haft, the Chief Scientific Officer; Jorge Perez, the head of Research; Anita Mercer, head of HR; and Scott White, the in-house lawyer and patent expert."

"What do we know about each of them?" Davis prompted.

"We know at least two of them have something to hide," Maggie answered. "Keogh was involved in an illegal scheme at a previous employer in Florida, but turned whistleblower and made a pile of money ratting out his former partners. He lay low for a few years, but then changed his name and came to Quercus. I don't think he'd enjoy having that information come out before the IPO. Perez is having an affair with one of his employees, a woman named Lisa Clark. He's married but she's not. Obviously, if that came out they'd both be in trouble, maybe out of a job, plus his marriage sounds like it's already teetering. On top of that, Jorge is the one that the system should have automatically notified of the faked report, because after

Richard Sinsky left the company, the report would have automatically been routed to Jorge for signature when it was created. The others are clean, as far as we know."

"Wait a minute," Ted said. "Whoever was able to fake Sinsky's ownership of the February report in the system could have also bypassed Jorge and faked his signature, just signing it as Jorge himself. The same person who created the report, obviously. Dimitris could have done that in his sleep."

"So the fake report is only one possible motive, and Jorge may or may not have known about it," Davis said. "We have to keep in mind that there are additional motives, at least for Keogh and Perez. Maybe Lilly or Dimitris found out about their secrets and were blackmailing them. And that could bring us back to two killers, in theory."

"We also know something else. Last night Tony Dupree realized, or thinks he did, that at the end of his meeting with Lilly, she said she had to go talk to Thomas van Haft. That could mean nothing – he's the CSO and that makes him the natural person for her to report an irregularity to – but it definitely makes him a suspect."

"We already talked to these guys, and mostly what we got was a bunch of speeches about how biotech is going to save humanity, and how hard it is to make a drug. I get that, but I don't want to hear it again if we don't have any new leverage, any new evidence we can use," said Jimmy. It was a long oration for Jimmy, normally a man of few words, and it summarized the frustration in the room.

"I agree, we don't have any new leverage yet," Davis said. "But we can do some things. One, we can track their phones and see if anyone was by the Muddy River on Wednesday. Two, we need to talk to van Haft about whether he spoke to Lilly or not. Regardless of what he says, we need to get him on the record. Three, we need to double down on looking for physical evidence. This perp is smart – wrapping Lilly's body in the laboratory film, pushing Dimitris into the river – both of these minimize the likelihood of finding any DNA or hairs or fingerprints. Four, we still haven't found Lilly's work computer – it wasn't at her home or car. Ted, take another look at her email accounts – did she send any files to herself, or to someone else, that could have the original research report? Even if someone deleted it, could you still find a trace?"

Ted looked up, "I already looked at the servers for both her work and personal emails – nothing suspicious there. Any chance I have of finding something she had kept against the rules would need the hard drive in front of me. If we can find it."

Maggie leaned forward, "If Lilly had the computer in her car, and the perp drove it down the road to the parking lot where we found it, he would probably have taken the computer out of the car and taken it with him. He has to dump it somewhere, right? He can't keep it because it's incriminating, but he also doesn't want it found. He also doesn't want it back at his home, like a smoking gun. So he hides it somewhere, preferably nearby so he doesn't risk being stopped with it on his way home. Not under a bush, where anyone might find it. And he's walking back from Lilly's car to – presumably – his own car or bike. Draw a circle a mile in diameter from Boston Regional Medical Center – what's the likeliest place?"

"Well, Spot Pond, I would say," Eddie answered. "But it's like 300 acres. How can we search all that?"

"We don't need to, Eddie," Maggie said. "Our perp is in a hurry, he's just driven a dead woman's car on a public road to an abandoned parking lot. Nobody's around and he must feel pretty damned conspicuous walking around an empty lot, even if it's dark and drizzly. Now he's on foot and carrying a hot computer that could land him in prison for life. If you're right and he biked up there, he could have put his bike in the trunk of the car, or he could have left it in the Fells and would have to go back for it. He needs to get rid of it pronto. And it's not like he's got a motorboat handy to go fishing in Spot Pond at six in the evening."

Davis nodded to Ted, who was pecking at his laptop. "Can you project a map of Middlesex Fells and surrounding area?"

Ted didn't bother to answer, he just clicked a little faster and louder. In a moment, everyone in the room was staring at a wall-sized map of Spot Pond. It was shaped like a leaf, about two miles long from north to south and one mile across, with the smaller Quarter Mile Pond acting as a stem at the south end. The former hospital and parking lot were on the east side of the leaf, about one-third of the way up from the stem.

"Put in the location of the parking lot, and then set the direction to Spot Pond. What does that look like?" Maggie told Ted.

A trail of blue dots appeared on the screen, from the former hospital's parking lot, formed a question mark shape along the access road, and then pointed north to the entrance to Botume House Visitor Center. Ted peered at his screen:

"Four tenths of a mile. Eight minutes to walk it, 3 minutes to bike to the shoreline. There's a boating dock there, though the boat rental closes at 5 p.m.."

"I've been fishing there for years," Jimmy said. "At the end of the pier, the water is about ten feet deep, and the bottom is mud and silt. If you stood there and threw the computer as far as you could, it would sink in maybe fifteen or twenty feet of murky water and never be seen again. You're not allowed to swim in the pond, since it's a drinking water reservoir, and I doubt anyone in a boat would see a black computer on the bottom."

"What do you say, L-T?" Maggie asked, turning to Davis. "Can we call in the Dive Team?"

* * *

Two hours later, Maggie and Eddie were back at the Botume House Visitor's Center parking lot with a couple of uniformed troopers, when the Dive Unit's custom 34-foot-long black RV pulled into the lot. Jimmy had gone back to Cambridge to look for Jorge Perez.

It was an overcast but warm day now, gray skies hinting at rain to come, the air heavy with humidity, and temperature in the 80's. Through the trees, Spot Pond looked a sullen dark green, not the inviting blue of sunny days.

The Dive Team consisted of Sergeant Dale Turner, whom Maggie knew from their days at the Academy together, and three troopers who were experienced divers. Dale was driving the RV. Maggie waved and directed the team to park as close to the boat dock as they could get. Once the RV was parked and the team assembled, she explained what they were looking for.

"Right," Dale said. "A needle in a haystack, underwater, and with three feet visibility, is that it?"

"Um, pretty much, yeah," Maggie agreed.

"Okay. We'll let you know," he smiled. "Might bring you back pieces of eight, while we're at it." With that, the men pulled out tanks, masks, hoses, scuba fins, ropes, buoys, and weights, and clumped down toward the dock *in seriam* until the end of the dock was covered with equipment. They came back and pulled a 12-foot Zodiac off cleats on the side of the RV and brought it down to the dock's side. Dale then made another trip and came back with a black Pelican rolling case about the size of a large carry-on suitcase. He knelt on the dock to open it, speaking over his shoulder.

"You'll have to close the boat rentals for a while, I'm afraid," Dale told the Homicide team. "Could you guys handle that?"

"Sure, no problem," Eddie said, going to speak to the troopers.

Dale opened the Pelican case and pulled out a gray and black device about the size and shape of a garden hose reel, but with two propellors on the back, LED lights on the sides, and a video camera inside a spherical Plexiglas cover in the middle. He pulled out a reel of electrical cable, opened its stabilizing legs, and then connected the plug at the end of cable to a matching one on the back of the device. He connected the other end of the wire to a control panel that looked like an overgrown Gameboy. Turning everything on, he flipped toggles and joysticks to test propellers, lights, and camera movement.

Seeing Maggie's curious expression, he explained, "This is Rover, our ROV – a remotely operated vehicle. It has side scanning sonar plus video capability, and it's connected to a GPS system so it can lay down a search grid. We're going to set two jackstay lines to act as borders for our search, and then let Rover do the first search. Anything it finds that looks interesting, one of the divers will go down and inspect. If it's what we're looking for, the chain of evidence starts then and there, with Rover documenting the exact location."

He lifted the ROV by the wire and lowered it gently into the water at the edge of the dock. In the meantime, the divers had put their tanks and masks in the Zodiac, and followed their equipment into the boat. One of them made a blue rope fast to the end of the deck, and they all put on their gear. Dale motioned Maggie to come to the end of the dock.

"Okay, so your perp is standing here and he wants to ditch this laptop, right?" he asked.

"Yes," Maggie said. "From here he throws it out as far as he can. Or at least, that's what I hope he did."

"Assume he wants to get it as deep as possible. If he knows anything about this pond, or even if he doesn't, you gotta assume he throws it as far out straight ahead, more or less, as he can. It wouldn't make any sense to drop it here, or to throw it into the shallows on either side."

Maggie nodded. Dale spoke to the divers in the boat. "Okay, let's start with a 60 degree search pattern from here forward. Set the ropes on a 30 degree angle to either side, and let's go out as far as that rock over there." He pointed to a black outcropping about 400 feet away.

"You think someone could throw a laptop that far?" Maggie asked.

"No," Dale answered, "I'm sure I couldn't. Maybe an NFL quarterback, but not the average guy. Still, going out that far should give us enough margin of safety, plus it's a landmark you could use in court if we find something. If we don't find it, I don't want to worry that we didn't go far enough. That rock is a natural aiming point, even at twilight, so I want to take that into account."

Pulling a lensatic compass out of one of the side pockets of his camouflage cargo pants, he opened the cover and aimed at the rock, and then 30 degrees to each side of it. Once he had his bearings, he called them down to the divers in the boat, who started feeding out nylon line to create jackstays as perimeter lines in a 60-degree arc from the dock, with the rocky outcropping as the midpoint of the arc. The ropes were tied to the dock at one end, to bright yellow floats at the far end by the rock, and clipped to vertical ropes at 50 foot intervals that had down weights on the lake bed and more bright yellow flotation buoys on the surface of the water. Thus, in a few minutes they had their search area laid out in a triangle with its apex at the dock and its base an imaginary line through the rocky outcropping.

As the Zodiac chugged away to the outside of the rope perimeter, Dale activated the Rover control pad, and set the machine on an automated grid search pattern with the two ropes as limit markers. He turned to Maggie.

"OK, now we let Rover here do the work. Anything that looks interesting will get tagged on the screen, and then the guys can go look at it. This will take about an hour. I'll stay here. You guys want to organize some lunch?"

Maggie smiled. "Sure, pizza okay? Melrose has some good pizza joints."

Dale nodded, not taking his eyes off the screen. "Sounds great, thank you."

Maggie went to confer with Eddie, who volunteered to be the gofer. An hour later, the pizzas were mostly eaten and Rover was done with its grid. Dale looked at the search map on his screen. The bottom of the lake was liberally sprinkled with various small objects.

"There are lots of UBO's here – unidentified bright objects – but most are probably beer cans or shoes or whatever. There are only three rectangular objects that look like they're at least a foot across. I've tagged them, and now the divers will look at those coordinates," he said.

"Aren't you supposed to wait an hour after you eat before swimming?" Maggie asked.

"I think in 14 feet of water we can risk it. No one's gonna get the bends here. Plus, the divers didn't eat that much. That's why you still have some pizza left – save it for after. They'll be like a swarm of locusts after their workout."

The divers got back in the Zodiac and puttered out to the first of the three locations that Dale had tagged. One of the divers went over the side and came back up a few moments later with a white object in his hand. It was the cover to a Coleman cooler. Strike one.

At the second spot, they went through the same procedure. This time the diver came back with a piece of plywood, about 18 inches square. Whatever it had been used for, it was not a computer. Strike two.

At the third spot, however, they got a hit. The diver came up holding a matte black object that was, indeed, a Lenovo X1 laptop.

"Yes!" Eddie whooped, while Maggie and Dale exchanged high-fives.

"Amazing!" Maggie said to Dale. "This is incredible! You guys made it look easy."

Dale grinned broadly, waving the divers back in. Maggie met them at the dock with a large evidence bag for the computer, which she dried with a towel and then tagged and sealed. Eddie was on the phone with Ted, instructing him to drive over from Woburn and take possession of the evidence. The divers, meanwhile, started pulling in the buoys, ropes, and weights they had put down on the lake floor, and Dale pulled the Rover out of the water, powered it down, and stowed it away.

Ted arrived about twenty minutes later, looking like a mother who had just been called to a schoolyard shooting and sees her kid coming toward her. For a big man, he could move quickly when the notion took him. Without saying a word, he grabbed the laptop in its evidence bag from Maggie and ran back to his car.

"Hey, how long?" she yelled after him.

He answered over his shoulder, "I don't know yet. Days? Weeks? Never? Depends on the damage. We'll only get one chance at this, and it has to be dry first. Ask me on Monday." With that he maneuvered his bulk behind the wheel of his unmarked Explorer and screeched out of the parking lot.

Chapter Fifteen, Friday Evening June 2nd

Maggie and Eddie drove back up to Woburn and put in a few hours doing reports and paperwork, checking in with Mike Davis and the team, who had drafted a press release disclosing Dimitris's identity as the second victim connected to Quercus Therapeutics. They were getting ready for a press conference, which was certainly going to be a circus. Jimmy was already there, reporting that Jorge had no idea about any report in February.

"Did you believe him?" Maggie asked.

"He was really squirrely," Jimmy said. "More nervous and agitated than when we first interviewed him, and even then he was pretty wired. Doesn't look like he's been sleeping well, he was a bit disheveled. Like we discussed, we don't have any leverage to push him with, but I think we should consider bringing him in for a formal interview. Even if he lawyers up, he is turning into my favorite suspect right now."

"OK, I think we can let him stew over the weekend, and then bring him in on Monday. If he's jittery now, he'll be even more so after sweating it out for a few days," Lieutenant Davis decided. He headed to the DA's office to fend off the local press corps.

Around four o'clock Maggie bid the team goodbye and headed to her car, grateful that her undercover status spared her from joining the Lieutenant. As she was walking through the parking lot, her phone buzzed with a text.

Brad: *"Hi, Maggie. Sorry I haven't been in touch – crazy deadlines all week, now done. If I'm not in the doghouse, are you free for a drink or dinner tonight?"*

Maggie considered. She was tired, but going home to an empty apartment and carry-out dinner held limited attractions.

Maggie: *"You're forgiven this time. Drinks sound good, and dinner if I stay awake? Where?"*

Brad: "*Great! How about that Italian place in Fort Point? Congress and A Streets. Five-thirty at the bar?"*

Maggie: *"OK, see you there."*

Heading south on I-93 was against the rush hour traffic, so Maggie made good time while watching the standstill traffic going north. She called Emily as she was driving and filled her in on what had happened since the Memorial Day party.

"Oh my God, you might have a sister? In Vietnam?" Emily's voice rose an octave when she was excited. "Wow, that's amazing! How will you find out?"

"Well, we still have more sleuthing to do through Dad's diaries," Maggie said. "But Benny and I will get together tomorrow, and we'll do some more time travel. At some point, we have to go talk to Uncle George."

"Holy cow, is he still alive?" Emily asked.

"Oh yes, very much so. He lives down the Cape, in Eastham. I talk to him every month or so, and I guess Benny does too. Another example of the family *omerta* – he never said boo about this. He might as well be from Charlestown."

"Meanwhile," she continued, "Brad texted, and we're meeting for drinks in about an hour. What do I wear?"

The ensuing discussion, as technical as anything heard in a biotech conference room, lasted till Maggie got home.

* * *

Maggie walked into the restaurant a few minutes after 5:30 p.m., wearing a sporty light blue top with a cross-over front that flattered her, black leggings, and a white linen blazer that was silk-lined and concealed her holstered S&W. On the way she had ignored two texts and a call from Dan Beardsley ("Chan4Dan", according to his text handle).

Finally she had texted him back that she would call him tomorrow.

Fort Point, along with the Waterfront, had been redeveloped over the previous decade from a seedy docklands warehouse area into one of the city's hottest trendy neighborhoods. Even at this relatively early hour, since it was Friday, the restaurant's bar was humming, and about half the tables were taken. Brad had staked out a couple of stools at the sinuous bar with views out the large windows onto Congress Street. He had a drink in front of him and a glass of water and menu at the adjacent seat he was saving.

"Hey there," Maggie said, kissing him on the cheek, "what're you having?"

"Old Fashioned with Pikesville rye," he said, beckoning to the bartender. "How about you?"

"Sounds good, make it two," she answered, slinging her purse on the back of her stool. Her hair was brushed loosely back over her collar, just long enough to cover it. She knew she looked good, and Brad's appreciative once-over confirmed it.

Over the drinks, they talked about their respective weeks. Maggie couldn't say much about the case, and she was shyly reluctant to tell Brad about her father's diaries, so he did most of the talking. He could make even a struggle over supply chains and manufacturing snafus sound funny rather than frustrating. Emily had been right that he was handsome, but he also had an easygoing manner that Maggie liked. Unlike her last boyfriend Chris, an intense brooding type who brought out the competitive perfectionist in Maggie, Brad had a way of de-escalating her that was welcome. Especially on a soft, warm, June evening after a long, tense week.

After the drinks they decided to stay at the bar for dinner, which lived up to expectations. Maggie chose the lobster gnocchi, and Brad decided on Spanish octopus with Nduja. They shared a salad to start and split a bottle of 2016

Barolo Cannubi Riserva that was worth the price. They skipped dessert but had espressos before heading out, arm in arm.

They walked down Congress Street and crossed toward A Street. It was after nine in the evening now, but the sky was still light, and the streets were full of people strolling. They turned to each other at the same time, Maggie starting to say, "Do you…" and Brad kissed her softly on the lips. She smiled into the kiss, and it became fiercer, more passionate, urgent.

"Yes," he said. "I do."

"We're not that far along yet," she answered, smiling more. "But do you want to come to my place?"

"Yes," he said. "I do."

"Man of few words, I see," she sighed. "Okay, good."

They walked arm in arm down A Street toward South Boston. As usual, there was a line of twenty-somethings outside Lucky's Lounge, waiting for their turn at eardrum damage. They walked companionably under the Summer Street viaduct, with its blinding under-bridge lighting throwing the folk art on the walls of the underpass into bright, colorful relief. Once past the lights, the sidewalk was shrouded in comparatively greater darkness. Here, the crowds were gone, leaving only an occasional pedestrian or couple, and a few cars or bikes on the roadway.

A block further down, the buildings on either side of the street gave way to empty parking lots, meant for employees at the nearby central Post Office or manufacturing plants. They crossed Necco Street, a remnant of when the New England Confectionary Company made candy downtown. The area was desolate. They were walking on the west side of the street, where the sidewalk was too narrow to allow them to walk side by side. They were on a two-foot-wide stretch of sidewalk bordered on one side by a chain-link fence enclosing a large, empty parking lot, and on the other side by the roadway. Brad stepped back so that

Maggie could go first. The trees that shaded the sidewalk gave way, and there were no parking meters, leaving the sidewalk open to the street.

Behind them, a car engine started and revved up, followed by the sound of screeching tires. Maggie was suddenly aware that it was accelerating loudly, at a far greater speed than the legal limit. She pivoted to her left, seeing headlights coming at them and silhouetting Brad as he turned to see what was going on. Acting on instinct, she pushed Brad against the parking lot fence with her left arm as she reached under her jacket for her pistol with the right.

A car, obscured behind its lights that were on the high-beam setting, was careening down A Street and now climbed the curb, clearly aiming for them. It was still accelerating, now frighteningly close, only twenty feet away. There was nowhere to run – they were sitting ducks between the car coming right at them and the chain-link fence behind them. The noise of the over-revved engine was overwhelming, more like a jet landing than like a car driving past. Between the noise and the blinding lights, coming closer and getting brighter, it was impossible to speak or think, much less evade what would surely be a lethal impact.

Maggie finished pivoting and fired three shots in quick succession, clustered on where the driver's head should be. She didn't have time to move out of the way. Events happened too quickly for her to register fear, but she sensed Brad reaching to pull her back toward the fence. At the last second, the car veered back off the sidewalk, slewed around across A street, and slammed into a telephone pole on the opposite side. The pole was pushed backwards at a 45-degree angle, but the car stopped moving. Steam was rising from the hood, visible under the streetlamp. The car's horn blared continuously, adding to the surreal nature of the scene.

"Are you okay?" she yelled at Brad, looking over her shoulder at him.

"Yes," he called back. "Are you?"

She nodded and said, "Call 9-1-1".

Dropping into a tactical crouch, pistol clamped in both hands in a firing position, she ran across A Street to the disabled car. Absently she noted it was a grey Honda Pilot SUV. Coming to the driver's side diagonally from behind, she yelled, "Police! Put your hands on the steering wheel where I can see them!"

There was no answer from the car. Maggie could see the airbag had deployed from the steering wheel, and that the driver's head was resting on the partially deflated pillow. There was blood on the white nylon – quite a lot of blood, actually. Behind her she heard Brad talking to the emergency services operator.

Moving to the door handle, Maggie held the Smith & Wesson in her right hand and lifted the latch with her left. The door was unlocked. She swung it open and stepped back and against the side of the Honda, keeping her gun on the driver's head. He didn't move. She stepped forward and away from the car in an arc to her left so she could see the driver more clearly.

The driver was leaning on the steering wheel, his head turned toward the door, an expression of surprise on his face. Except for a missing piece in the center of his forehead, where a bullet had entered, he could have been asleep. As it was, he would never wake up again. Maggie recognized him. His name was Jorge Perez.

* * *

It seemed to Maggie like Groundhog Day. Again, the crime scene tape, the Medical Examiner's truck, the police cars, both Boston and State. Hard to believe, she thought, it's less than 48 hours since the finding of Dimitris's body, and here was a third victim from Quercus Biotechnology. Though this time, it was her fault. Or at least her action that had led to his death. She gave a rapid head shake. Better him than me, I suppose, she thought.

What was Jorge doing here? Why had he tried to run them down? How did he even know where she was? He must have been tailing her. Had he suspected she was a cop? If so, what had given her away? Was he also the one who killed Lilly and Dimitris? It would certainly be convenient if he were, but if so, her lead suspect had just died without a confession or any evidence linking him to the other murders. Maggie's contrarian instincts rebelled – this was nothing like the other murders, which were diabolical, methodical, and thoroughly scrubbed of any incriminating evidence. This seemed like an act of passion by an upset or unbalanced mind.

Lieutenant Davis, along with Eddie and Jimmy, had come to the scene even though it was Friday night and definitely family time. Jimmy had been there first, coming in hot with siren and lights. He had jumped out of his car, picked up Maggie as if she were a child, and enveloped her in a bear hug.

"I heard on the police scanner that there was an officer-involved shooting down in the Seaport, and of course I thought of you. I called in and heard it *was* you, and Jorge, too," Jimmy said, his voice choked with emotion. "I am so sorry – I should have leaned on him more, or brought him in…"

Maggie shook her head. "It's okay, Jimmy. Really. On what charge? Being squirrely? There's nothing to blame yourself for. I'm okay – I got lucky. All's well that ends well, you know?" She heard the tremor in her voice but hoped it wasn't too obvious.

Lieutenant Davis stepped between them, an arm on each of their shoulders. "Look, I'm the one who told you to let Jorge stew over the weekend, Jimmy. If it's anyone's fault it's mine. Just add it to the list," he sighed, "the one that reminds us we're not perfect."

Maggie introduced Brad, ignoring Eddie's smirk and Jimmy's lifted eyebrow; Davis didn't say anything but there was a twinkle in his eye. Brad told the story of what happened while Eddie took notes, and Davis went over to liaise with the Boston Police watch commander who had joined them.

Jimmy had been walking the area, and now came back with a satisfied smile. "Two video cameras," he said, pointing above their heads. There was one camera on the wall of the adjoining office building, and another across the street over the parking lot to the side of the Gillette 'World Shaving Headquarters'. "I'll ask BPD to contact the owners of the video cameras and get us the footage." He walked after Davis and the BPD commander.

When Davis came back Maggie turned to him. "I think we need to get to Jorge's wife, make sure she's okay, and notify her of what's happened. And someone else needs to interview Lisa Clark ASAP."

"Yes," agreed Davis. "But the big question is, was Perez our perp for both murders? That would sure be nice, and I bet we'll be getting some not-so-subtle body language from above to make it so. Or is this something else?"

"We'd better get moving if we want to find out," Maggie said. "If I'm still going to be undercover at Quercus next week, I shouldn't talk to Lisa. How about Eddie and I go to Jorge's house, and you and Jimmy interview her?"

Davis said, "You've just been in an officer-involved shooting, which means I have to activate FIRST. Officially, you are on administrative leave for up to five working days."

FIRST was the Force Investigation Response and Support Team, which was assigned to investigate any officer-involved shootings. The State Police manual went on in considerable detail about how this was to be handled, interpreting the Code of Massachusetts Regulations into actionable language that was only slightly less legalistic.

"Oh, come on, L-T. You know this was a good shoot. There'll be video from the cameras. Jimmy's organizing with BPD about getting the footage now. We've got two unsolved homicides and our lead suspect is dead.

We've got to move now, before people disappear if they know something."

Davis sighed. "Yes, I knew you were going to say that." He drew himself up to his full height and looked at her in his best avuncular manner, with a voice reminiscent of how he would have read her the Miranda warning. "I have just ordered you to present yourself for an interview Monday morning with the DIS investigator and myself at GHQ. As I am your supervisor, you may hand over your weapon to me now, and I will submit it to Firearms ID Section. Tomorrow morning, even though it's a Saturday, and before your interview, you will fill out the SP-376 Use of Force Report, and submit it to me. I'll know who the lead investigator is by then, and I'll forward it to them. You may also fill out an ADM-20 form to request a temporary weapon. You are strongly encouraged to contact EAU as well." EAU was the Employee Assistance Unit, which offered psychological support and counseling. Maggie shook her head. Going into the State Police General Headquarters in Framingham to undergo a Division of Investigative Services interview was annoying enough, she didn't need to talk to a shrink as well.

Davis continued, "You are to take the rest of the night off. If you happen to accompany another trooper in their appointed rounds, I guess I don't need to know about it until after the fact." He walked away.

She found Jimmy, who got Jorge's home address from his wallet as it was going into an evidence bag. Seeing Jorge's cell phone in the bag, she said to Jimmy, "Is that phone on?"

Jimmy tapped the phone screen through the clear plastic bag, and it came to life, showing a picture of a smiling dark-haired woman, who Maggie assumed was Jorge's wife, Carmen. At least it wasn't a picture of Lisa Clark, she thought.

"I suggest you bag that separately, and get it to Ted first thing in the morning. Have him trace where Jorge's been over the past week. Something must have set him off

– he didn't seem *that* crazy – homicidally so, I mean – at work."

"When was the last time you saw him?" Jimmy asked.

Maggie thought back. "It must have been Wednesday morning, he was in the coffee area on the second floor, but we didn't speak."

Jimmy said, "Having your cell phone on you and powered up during a crime is dumb. It would obviously place you at the scene of the crime if you're a suspect. None of our potential suspects had a phone on around the Fells when Lilly was killed – we checked, remember? I don't think Ted's checked on the time and place of Dimitris's death yet, but I'll bet you dollars to donuts we won't find any hits."

Maggie nodded. "Exactly, it's another thing that doesn't fit, along with the means of attack and the location. Plus, if he thinks I'm a secretary, what danger do I pose? And if he knows I'm a cop, what's the upside to attacking me? Unless it was emotional – more likely about the affair with Lisa than about the Quercus IPO." Jimmy walked away to get another evidence bag and talk to the Medical Examiner techs about moving the body to the morgue.

Maggie turned to Brad. "You'll be contacted by someone from the Detectives Unit to describe what happened," she said. "Just tell them exactly what you saw. And, I'm sorry tonight ended like this."

He smiled. "Hey, me too, but I prefer it to the alternative, the one where his plan worked. Thank you for thinking – and acting – so quickly. You saved us both."

Maggie felt the heat rising in her cheeks. Christ, I'm blushing, she thought. Shaking that thought, she leaned forward and kissed Brad on the lips, neither quickly nor slowly. He put his arms around her and they held each other for a moment.

"I've got to go," she said. "Can we catch up tomorrow?"

"Yes, sure," he said, squeezing her hand. "Go get 'em."

Chapter Sixteen, Saturday Morning, June 3rd

The Perez's address was on Willow Lane, in Wellesley, a toney suburb full of doctors and academic types, just outside Interstate 95. It was a ranch style house with a one-car garage on a small quarter-acre lot, modest by Wellesley standards, too near the traffic noise of both I-95 and Route 9, and pretty far from the elegant parts of town around the College and town center.

On the drive over from South Boston, Maggie had looked up the house records on the mobile data terminal in Eddie's car. The house was owned by Jorge and Carmen Perez, ages 37 and 32, who had bought it about a year earlier for $969,000, assuming a mortgage for $500,000. That matched what Benny had told her – it seemed so long ago – that Jorge had been in the US about two years. It also seemed to be within their means, Maggie calculated. Jorge's salary was in the mid-350's, but he got annual stock awards that would easily double that amount if they ever vested. Carmen worked as a Spanish teacher in the Wellesley Public Schools, making about $56,000 pre-tax. Clearly Jorge was the main breadwinner. They did not have any children.

"Hey, Sarge, you doing okay?" Eddie asked softly, keeping his eyes on the road.

"Thanks, Eddie. Yes, I think so. It hasn't really sunk in yet."

"Have you shot anybody before?"

"No. I drew my weapon a few times when I was in uniform, but that was just precautionary. Have you?"

Eddie nodded, still looking at the road. "Yeah, about five years ago. I was stationed out in Springfield, and we raided a crack house. There were three guys in there. Two ran, but one decided to fight it out. He reached for the pocket of his sweatshirt. I saw something shiny in his hand, and I fired as he raised his gun. Afterwards I was tortured –

what if it hadn't been a gun? How could I wait to know for sure? I'm just glad it wasn't a can of Coors Light."

Maggie looked at Eddie's profile. He was a bit pale, and his lips were compressed into a thin line. The usual clowning Eddie was nowhere in sight. "I'm sorry," she said, putting a hand on his arm. "How did you get right with it?"

"Actually, I talked to the EAU shrink. She was very helpful. It took a few months, but I found a way to live with it. You have to, if you want to do this job, and do it as right as you can. I know you weren't interested in EAU now, but don't be a hardass. They can help. Wait and see how you feel."

This was a long speech without a joke for Eddie, Maggie thought. "Thanks, Eddie," she said. "I will do that."

* * *

Eddie and Maggie arrived at the Perez house after midnight, without lights or siren. The night was moonless, still relatively warm in the upper 60's, and stars were visible even through the light pollution of the nearby I-95/Route 9 interchange. The driveway was unilluminated, but lights shone through the front window and through the glass of the front door, throwing quadrilaterals of yellow light on the lawn and walkway. Eddie parked in the driveway and they walked to the door, which had three small rectangular clear glass viewports rising diagonally from left to right at chest height.

At the door, Eddie rang the bell and Maggie called out, "Mrs. Perez? Troopers Bushell and Thompson of the Massachusetts State Police. Can we speak to you please?"

There was silence. After a moment, they could see movement through the front door viewports, and a dark-haired woman came to the door. She answered them without opening it.

"Can I see some identification, please?"

She had a low, warm voice with a Spanish accent that slurred the word endings into a soft legato. Eddie and Maggie put their shields up to the door viewports, Eddie's lower down, Maggie's above. After a moment, they heard the deadbolt slide back and the door opened.

Carmen Perez was slim, about 5'3", with a mass of raven hair and large, almost-black eyes. These were accessorized by a shiner under her left eye that was swollen, red and black, almost closing the eye. She wore black sweatpants and a white T-shirt, without any jewelry aside from a plain gold wedding band on her left ring finger. She stepped back from the door and led the way wordlessly into the living room, which corresponded to the large window they had seen from the driveway.

"I…I don't want to press charges," she said, sitting on a white nubbly sofa under the window.

"Mrs. Perez…" Maggie began, but Carmen interrupted her, clearly trying to speak and not cry at the same time.

"Was he drunk? Is he under arrest? He didn't hurt anyone did he? He's a good man, you know…it's just been a difficult time."

"It would really help if you can tell us what happened. I believe you've been having some, uh, marital difficulties lately?"

"How…well, yes. I flew back to Argentina to see my parents last week, since we had the long weekend off for Memorial Day. But things have been wrong for months. I suspected he was having an affair, and when I came back on Wednesday night I asked him straight out. He…he wouldn't answer, but he said that we had been growing apart, and that he thought we should get a divorce. I know he was lying – I am sure he is seeing someone at his work."

Maggie nodded sympathetically, knowing the value of silence in a listener with a willing speaker. Carmen had a lot to get off her chest.

"I…I'm a good Catholic. I don't believe in divorce. I know that sounds crazy in America, but in Argentina it's not. I spent the week at home crying. I still think – I hope – that we can work this out. That he'll – how do you say? – come to his senses. And now – what's happened to him? What has he done, that you are here?"

Maggie glanced at Eddie, who took the hint. "Mrs. Perez," he said, leaning forward, "I am very sorry, but Jorge is dead. He tried to run some people down with his car, in Boston, and he was shot."

It was a dodge, but it meant Maggie didn't have to lie directly to Carmen about who Jorge was after. Somehow, she thought, that matters, even if I'm caviling. She watched Carmen closely, seeing the blood drain from her face, turning her skin sallow under the bruise and cloud of black hair. She swayed, with Maggie reaching over to catch her by the shoulders. Carmen had not known about Jorge's plans in advance, she thought, or else she had an alternative career as an Oscar-winning actress.

Eddie stepped into the kitchen to get Carmen a glass of water, while Maggie settled her back in the sofa. After Carmen drank a bit her pallor eased, and Maggie asked, "If you had this fight on Wednesday, what happened yesterday and today? Did he stay here? Did he pack up and leave?"

"Wednesday and Thursday he slept in the spare bedroom, that we use as an office. It has a couch. I was so exhausted Wednesday, after the long flight, and the argument, that I was numb, and I just took a sleeping pill and went to bed. When I woke up on Thursday he was gone, I assume to work. He bikes to work, and his bicycle was gone. We only have one car, and he normally leaves it for me. But I had taken the whole week off, so I didn't go anywhere. I just stayed here and tried to think about what to do."

"Did he come back Thursday night?"

"Yes, but very late. After eleven. I was already in bed, with the door locked, and I didn't go see him. He…he didn't try to see me either. Then Friday morning when I woke up, he was gone again. But this time he had taken the car, so I couldn't go anywhere anyway. I've been waiting for him all day." She broke down in tears now, the last sentence bringing it home that she would always be waiting for Jorge in vain.

Maggie and Eddie waited patiently, letting her cry. Eddie got up and brought a box of Kleenex from the kitchen.

"When did he hit you?" Maggie asked softly.

"That was Wednesday night. I said to him…I said that I knew he was having an affair with that woman at work. I didn't know, really, but I know him – he's always looking at other women. And he's always at work – where else would she be? But he went crazy, yelling at me to tell him how I knew? Who told me? Was it someone he worked with? He named a bunch of names. I only know some of them – Art, and Thomas, and Tony of course – I've met them all at company events. Others I never heard of – someone named Brian, and Benny, and I don't remember who else…Of course I couldn't say who – I just guessed about the affair, but now I know I was right. That's when he hit me. It sobered him, you know? He turned around and went to the spare bedroom and slammed the door."

Maggie nodded, imagining the fight. She could see the connection to tonight's attack. Jorge was already paranoid about being found out, knowing that he'd lose his job if the affair with Lisa was revealed. Then he stayed late at Quercus on Thursday and he somehow found out about me and Benny snooping around, setting up a camera on the 2nd floor. Of course, he must have thought we were trying to trap him and Lisa. And then Jimmy came back on Friday and pressured him about the report. And on top of that, Jorge was the one that the forged report supposedly signed by Richard Sinsky would have gone to, and after talking to Jimmy he must have known we suspected him of being involved. Either way, he must have gotten so unhinged that he turned to a murderous attack. How did he know where to find me? He must have followed me home. When Ted tracks his cell phone locations, maybe we'll know more.

It was time to come clean. "Carmen," Maggie said, "there's been a lot of trouble at Quercus while you've been away. Two employees have been murdered, and tonight Jorge tried to kill me and a man I was with by running us down with his car. I've been working undercover at Quercus to try and find the killer, but I don't think it was Jorge. I think this is something private because of the affair he was having. You were right about that – we have evidence of it. I'm very sorry, but as we were investigating the murders we found out about Jorge's affair, and we confronted him about it. I think it must have made him paranoid. Then when you came home and accused him of the same thing, he flipped out."

Carmen looked at her wordlessly, her hand to her mouth. She shook her head, as if in disbelief, as fresh tears rolled down her cheeks.

"Is there someone we can call, someone who can stay with you?" Maggie asked. "You shouldn't be here by yourself now. Can your mother come from Argentina?"

"Yes, I can call my friend Maria. We work together at the school. She lives pretty close, in Newton. I'll ask her to come over. I'll call my mother in the morning. Thank you," Carmen said, blowing her nose and drying her eyes.

Maggie and Eddie waited until Maria arrived, about half an hour later. Even though it was far after midnight now, Maria was brisk, calm, and immediately took Carmen into her arms in a big hug. Feeling like at least she wasn't leaving Carmen to face a terrible situation by herself, Maggie nodded to Eddie and they left.

Half an hour later, Eddie dropped Maggie off at her condo building and headed home. Back in her apartment, Maggie poured two fingers of Macallan into a glass, added a splash of water, and sat back to think about the past few hours. She knew she'd not get to sleep until she at least started processing all that had happened. Then she'd let her subconscious work on it while she was sleeping. At least she didn't need to set the alarm at 6 a.m..

Chapter Seventeen, Saturday, June 3rd

When she woke up a little after ten, Maggie savored a quiet moment before the events of last night came rushing back. Groaning, she swung her bare legs out of bed and pulled the oversized T-shirt down past her hips. It was a faded red Washington Redskins shirt, a relic of her now ex-boyfriend Chris, the team's name nicely matching him for insensitivity. I should get rid of the shirt to match the guy, she thought. Brad was definitely an upgrade, and so would a Patriots shirt be.

She had to write up her SP-376 Use of Force Report, and get it to Mike Davis. At least she could also submit the ADM-20 and get a temporary weapon. Then she would make the case for staying undercover, instead of going on desk duty for 5 days as required by the State Police manual. Given how many dead bodies this case was generating, she thought she had a pretty good shot at it. So to speak.

But first, she wanted to know about Jimmy's interview of Lisa Clark. She called his cell phone, finding him at his sons' softball game. "What happened with Lisa?" she asked after getting a report of the score, the game conditions, and the batting order.

"For someone getting rousted out of bed by a cop at midnight, she was pretty calm, not flustered at first, just like we saw in the office," Jimmy said. "She was clearly shocked that Jorge was dead, and she got very pale, shed a few tears but didn't exactly break down. She denied that he had said anything to her in the past few days about you, or about the death of Lilly. Still, I got the feeling she wasn't totally surprised that Jorge might go off the deep end. She said he had a 'hot Latin temper', that he was a very ardent lover, and that she was devastated. I think that in her own schizotypal way, she probably is."

"Wow," Maggie said. "Schizotypal? Where'd you get that?"

She could almost hear him smile on the phone. "Married to a social worker." He hung up.

Rather than schlepping all the way up to Woburn, she decided to fill out the report at the Boston Barracks by the Museum of Science. It was closer, and then she could catch up with Benny and Tony first, and then maybe see Brad for dinner. She knew the South Boston shooting would be all over the news by now, but she hoped that names weren't being released yet. Scrolling through her phone, that seemed to be the case. She turned to the Boston Globe website to see the headline: 'Attempted Murder in South Boston ends in Shooting.' She also had two voicemails from Dan Beardsley asking her to call back. After all, she had promised she would. At least the second message also asked how she was.

She texted Benny about coming over in the early afternoon, and received a "Sure, I'm around" reply. Then she called Brad, who picked up on the first ring.

"Hi," she said. "How are you doing?"

"I'm ok, thanks," he answered. "More importantly, how are you?"

"I'm alright, I think. Look, what happened last night was terrible, but it's not our fault. I'm sorry Jorge is dead, but it looks to me like it was him or us, and he chose to do this, for whatever reason. Maybe I'm supposed to, but the reality is that I don't have a problem with what I did." She paused. "I hope you don't, either."

"No, absolutely not," Brad replied without hesitation. She was relieved to hear the determination in his answer. Eddie's comments from last night were still ringing in her ears, and she knew he had a point. But Brad did too. "Like I said last night, I'm glad you reacted so fast. I told you when we met, my dad was a cop, and I think I understand how real-life reactions have to take place in a split second. You did great. I hope you don't get into any trouble for it. Saved my ass, after all," he laughed.

She smiled to the air. "Well, the manual frowns on shooting at moving cars. Too many things can go wrong – you can hit an innocent bystander, or there may be a passenger or hostage in the car who gets hit, and it's unlikely you can stop a car with a pistol anyway. That's just in the movies, where you can shoot out a tire or the gas tank and the whole car goes up in the air."

"So what happens now?" he asked.

"Well, today I fill out some paperwork. A lot of it. And then I'm going to see Benny and Tony and fill them in on what happened. Maybe Tony can tell us something about Jorge's state of mind. Then after that you can buy me dinner."

"Now that's the best plan I've heard in a long time," he said. "I'll look at reservations and text you."

"Good use of your project management skills, don't you think?" she said with a smile. "See you later."

* * *

It took Maggie about an hour to fill out the SP-376, carefully editing it to include enough information about what was going on at Quercus to make the story sensible, but without divulging anything more than necessary. The last thing she needed was to give some theoretical defense attorney a loophole to acquit a theoretical defendant, once caught. She emailed the final version to Mike Davis, and then emailed an ADM-20 to the Armorer in Framingham, copying Davis on it as well. She then emailed Davis separately to request continued undercover duty in lieu of administrative leave as required by General Order UOF-02, and for accelerated review by the State Police Surgeon to facilitate this. The Quercus guys might complain about the regulatory machinery of the FDA, but the State Police bureaucracy could give them pointers, she decided.

She sighed, seeing Dan Beardsley's voicemail still unanswered on her phone, and toggled the call-back option. He picked up on the first ring.

"Maggie, I heard about the shooting in South Boston! Are you okay?" he asked, sounding fairly sincere.

"I'm fine, Dan, thanks. What have you heard?"

"Well, I heard someone tried to run you down, and that you shot the driver as he was coming at you. Yikes – sounds scary as hell!"

"Well, it was definitely nerve-wracking," she said.

"Can you tell me who the driver was?" Dan asked. "All I got from the department so far is that they're informing the family."

"Yes, and that's all I can say too, Dan, as you well know. We'll have more information on Monday. I'm sure there'll be a press conference."

"Well, what about the body in the Muddy River? You've been up to your elbows in dead people recently, Maggie!"

"Yes, you saw the statement last night identifying him as Dimitris Pappas. I guess it's no secret by now that he was employed at the same biotech firm as Lilly Zhao. Obviously, we're still investigating what's going on there."

"Yes, we figured that out, it's how we led the morning news this morning."

"Oh, I was still sleeping, Dan, I must have missed it."

"Is there a link between these two murders and the shooting last night?"

Maggie took a deep breath and blew it out through puffed cheeks. To tell or not to tell? Well, now that Carmen had been notified, they really couldn't keep Jorge's name out of it for much longer. That would make Monday's press conference a bit of an anti-climax, but she owed Dan.

"Yes, I'm afraid so. The driver was also a researcher at Quercus Therapeutics, name of Jorge Perez. P-E-R-E-Z.

That's all I can tell you, Dan. And it's more than anyone else has right now, so that's your scoop for the day."

After hanging up with a half-hearted promise to give Dan a heads-up if something else came up, Maggie headed out of the Boston Barracks and drove to Cambridge. She got lucky with street parking and buzzed Benny's apartment to be let in.

Upstairs, she found Tony packing, whistling 'Don't Worry, Be Happy'.

"I'm heading down to my sister's in New York for a few days," he said. "I'll work remotely from there. Much as I appreciate Benny's hospitality, I don't want to overstay my welcome."

"Now, Tony…" Benny started to respond, but Tony laughed.

"Look, Benny, Ben Franklin was right about the guests and fish smelling after three days. And thank you for letting me stay here, and just get my head together. I was really freaked out when I got here, but now I feel much more like myself. And besides, I've got two nieces to spoil! That's revenge on my big sister being a pain when we were growing up."

Maggie smiled. Indeed, Tony, resilient soul that he was, did seem much calmer and more centered.

"I guess you heard about the shooting in South Boston last night?" she asked them.

"Only the headline in the Globe this morning," Benny said. "I didn't read it yet, though."

"Me neither," said Tony.

She filled them in on the events of the previous night, leaving out the question of the affair between Jorge and Lisa, instead asking about Jorge's state of mind at the end. Both Benny and Tony were shocked and horrified by the news.

"Oh, my God, Jorge?? Jorge's always been a high-strung sort," Tony said. "He's…um, it was easy to get him excited, both in a good way, about new data, or in a bad way, if something didn't turn out well."

Benny nodded, "Yes, he and I just had a bit of a clash about Lisa Clark's backup program. He was pushing hard for it, but it was clearly not ready for going into the clinic. I didn't really like the guy, but I certainly never thought of him as violent."

"Me neither," Tony repeated. "Jorge and Thomas are kind of at the opposite ends of the excitability spectrum, you know? Jorge was a very passionate supporter of the researchers, but could go up like a rocket about anything, while Thomas is always cool, calm, and collected. They made a good team that way, for the research folks."

"Thanks, guys. That's helpful. I'm sure we'll learn more about what was going on with Jorge in the next few days. Meanwhile, how are you getting to New York, Tony?" she asked.

"On the train from Back Bay Station. I can catch the 3:20 and be in Penn Station by dinner time."

"Well, that's easy. How about a police escort to the station?" Maggie said. "Unmarked car, no siren or lights, okay?"

"Oh, that's nice of you, Maggie, but I can just take an Uber," Tony said.

"Well, Benny and I," she looked at Benny, "have some work to do at my place anyway. You'd be right on our way to South Boston."

Benny opened his mouth to say something, then changed his mind, and nodded. Tony took that as assent, and said, "Well in that case, sure, thank you. I'll be ready in 5 minutes."

Twenty minutes later Maggie dropped Tony off at the Clarendon Street entrance to the concrete vault that was Back Bay Station. He waved and disappeared inside. The concourse wasn't jammed with people, but there were plenty of travelers inside, enough to let Maggie feel okay about dropping him off alone.

As she pointed the Ford toward her apartment, she said, "I thought we could do a little more on the family history stuff, if you have time. I've got a date later, so maybe just a couple of hours. What do you say?"

"Sure," Benny replied. "But do you think Jorge killed Lilly? And Dimitris?"

"I don't think so, Benny," she said. "It's so different, what he did last night, from the first two murders. Those were clearly premeditated, carefully done in cold blood, and left no physical evidence. This one was different – for one thing, he had his cell phone on him and active, which means he could be tracked to the crime scene. Nothing like that with the first two murders. Even if he had hit us and gotten away, that car would have left an evidence trail a mile wide. There were two video cameras that filmed the whole thing, while the first two killings were out of sight of anyone. Last night looked like the act of a man out of control."

"Are you okay?" he asked her. "You sure don't seem very upset considering that someone just tried to kill you, and you killed him! That's kind of a big deal!"

"I know it is, Benny," Maggie answered quietly. "I know it is. But I find that this works for me. I compartmentalize it for the first day or two, like I put it in a corner and don't look at it. Then I let it come into focus again, and I can be a little more calm about it. It's something Dad taught me, and it's worked for me since school days. It's why I want to go back to Dad's journals and stuff that happened fifty years ago. Don't worry, I won't snap or anything."

"Well, you can always talk to me, you know," Benny said awkwardly. "Um...I hope we trust each other that much now."

She pulled into a parking spot in her garage and turned off the engine before answering. "Yes," she said slowly, stretching the word out. "Yes, I think that's true. I wouldn't have said that a couple of weeks ago, but working on this case with you has been...been good, you know? Oh,

I realize it's been horrible with all these deaths and no obvious clue to the perp, but getting to know each other? That's been a plus."

"I guess it's a good thing we have another case," said Benny with a twist of his lips. "The Case of the Missing Sister, from fifty years ago. Sounds like an Agatha Christie or something."

"Well, maybe you can be Hercule Poirot, but I'm not ready to be Miss Marple yet," Maggie said as they walked to the elevator.

In Maggie's apartment, she offered Benny drinks, and he chose coffee. It was one culinary art that Maggie took seriously. She ground freshly roasted beans, poured filtered water into a Moccamaster, and set out steaming mugs as soon as the coffee was done.

"Here's where we left off," Maggie said, sitting at the living room table where Henry's diaries were still spread out. They huddled over the musty notebooks, Benny leafing ahead. He read out loud:

> *November 21, 1971: Happy Thanksgiving, more or less. A lot has happened in the last week, and this is the first time I have a chance to write anything down. It's almost noon on Thursday now. We finally got to Vermont on Monday afternoon, after what seemed like a lifetime on the bus. Three and half days to Boston, then we slept at the Greyhound station until we could get a bus up to Vermont. I felt as grimy as back at Ripcord, but at least nobody was shooting at us. Still pretty gross. Makes you realize what a huge country this is, when you drive across it.*
>
> *Hue was a good sport about it all. I think she's still in shock about Mai, but at least she's not crying all the time. Somewhere in the Badlands she started to pay more attention to her surroundings, and wanted to practice her English with me before she met*

my parents. Very sweet of her – and her English is fine!

Mom and Dad were happy to see us, though it was awkward. Hue was very polite and formal, and when Mom learned about the baby she gave her a big hug. Dad was his usual standoffish Yankee self, I guess. We'll see if he warms up after a while. We went to bed early on Monday night, and slept most of Tuesday in delicious languor. I think the 'rents are a little shocked that we're staying in the same room, and same bed, but I don't care and I don't think Hue has noticed.

Yesterday we spent most of the day helping Mom in the kitchen, getting ready for Thanksgiving dinner for 14. George arrived in the middle of the afternoon from Burlington. He's got hair down to his shoulders, and wears some sort of headband like Abbie Hoffman. Even with all his anti-war posturing, it was great to see him. We hugged like brothers – well, why not? – before we started arguing, at least! He was very sweet to Hue, however, which I am very grateful for. He was the only warm person in the house, except for occasionally Mom.

It's been snowing since some time last night, and there's already a foot of snow on the ground. George and I are taking turns shoveling the walk and driveway. Hue's never seen snow, so she's very excited – we showed her how to make a snowman and how to throw snowballs. Given a little training, she could pitch for the Red Sox! Dinner is at 2 p.m., crazy early like always. I guess it's nice that some things don't change. All four grandparents will be here, plus the Davidsons and the Cunninghams from next door on either side. George is going to collect the old folks – at least they're not far away. Mom invited old Mr. Barwood from across the street too, which is nice, but

I think she only did that so we wouldn't be 13 at dinner.

"Sounds like Grandpa was a tough audience," Maggie said. "I can see how he and Dad didn't get along."

"Yes," Benny said. "I know that Grandpa wanted Henry to follow in his footsteps, to become a college professor. But Henry wanted to do more practical stuff, not to be sequestered on some campus somewhere. He kind of split the difference, in the end. He went to back to school to get his teaching certificate and master's degree in education, and then as we both know, he taught high school for forty years."

Maggie was reading on. "Well, I see this didn't go so well," she said.

> *November 26, 1971: Well, I'm glad we got through Thanksgiving, but it wasn't easy. George got the old folks here all right, but then the snow was so deep by evening that they couldn't get home. We talked about the weather, and about football, and everyone was tiptoeing on eggshells around not talking about the War, but of course that's on everyone's mind.*
>
> *We did talk about the war eventually, of course. Mostly about the draw-down of US forces. I told them what I heard from the guys over there before we left, that the 101st will be leaving by January, and by next year there'll be fewer than 60,000 US troops left. When Hue heard that she said very softly, "Then the Communists will win. The ARVN won't fight."*
>
> *"But we've been training them for years," Dad said, "and we've given them so much equipment. Aren't they ready to take over?"*
>
> *"There is a lot of equipment," Hue said slowly. "But there is no will. Now when they hear*

that there is going to be an attack, they just withdraw, and wait for the American helicopters to come. How will it be when the Americans are gone?"

She surprised everyone with her calm, quiet, certitude. "And when the Americans are gone, their money goes with them. That money feeds hundreds of thousands of my countrymen – and especially women." Here she blushed (so prettily). "Even bar girls have to make a living, you know," she said. I could tell that my friends and family hadn't really thought about the realities of this war – it was just this abstract 'thing' that they were either for or against. They could no more conceive of the situation than they could of the overwhelming humidity, or the monsoon rains that go on for weeks. It's nothing like Vermont – could anywhere be more diametrically opposite? Now they could see that it isn't a 'thing' – it's a lot of real people, with real suffering. I guess I shouldn't be too judgmental – I didn't know either, till I went over there.

George said he thought the Communists would win anyway, and that we had lost almost 50,000 dead without much to show for it. He quoted John Kerry, 'who wants to be the last man to die for a mistake?' Dad and Grandpa were for staying there till we got a Korea-like settlement, and how we had to stop the Commies from taking over all of Asia – dominoes, etc. I tried to explain that the jungles and rice paddies of Vietnam are very different from the terrain in Korea – that big armies and tanks and planes don't make that much difference. Then Mr. Cunningham weighed in that we should just bomb the North back to the stone age. Hue burst into tears, saying that this would kill her baby because the bombs just kill everyone. Then she ran upstairs and that was kind of the end of the dinner. It was agonizing.

After she calmed down, I went back downstairs. It was dark by then, but the snow was still coming down. It was clear that no one could drive. Since Hue and I had my room, and George had his, the Cunninghams invited Dad's parents to stay with them, and the Davidsons took in Mom's parents. So George and I went out and shoveled the paths to their doors, plus Mr. Barwood's, and then they left.

Hue has been writing a letter to her aunt and uncle almost every day. We mailed three of them on Wednesday, before the snow started. Hopefully by tomorrow we'll be able to get into town again to the post office. I hope we'll hear something back in a couple of weeks.

December 5, 1971: Again, hard to find time to write a bit, but here goes. It's been a winter wonderland around here since the 'Thanksgiving Blizzard', as they're calling it on TV. Like Jimmy Stewart running down the street in Bedford Falls, but in color. Hue is still full of wonder at snow. We had to get her a 'real' winter coat – her first one! Yesterday we had a 'real' date – I took the old man's car, and we went over to Hanover, where I showed her around Dartmouth College and the town. We went to the Nugget Theater for a movie – 'Play Misty for Me' – and then dinner. It was really nice.

We came home to find a letter from Aunt Trang! Finally. Seems like Mai is doing fine, she's eating and sleeping and doing all the stuff babies are supposed to do. There was even a photo of Mai in Trang's arms, and she had grown so much already! Hue was both relieved and sad, crying from both happiness and longing. Same for me, really – just seeing the baby's face was a real jolt.

We've been making plans. I can get GI Bill benefits to work on getting my education certificate and a Master's in Ed. I'm pretty sure I want to teach high school history. I think the best place for me is Boston University, and that would also get Hue and me out of here. She could also take enough nursing classes to get licensed in the US. If I apply right away, it's possible I can start next semester, in January. Once Hue and I are officially married (in the US, I mean), the GI Bill benefits go up to $205 a month – maybe enough to live on and pay tuition with some loans. It won't be plush, but we'll be together. This kind of pushes us to get married right away, which is what we want to do anyway. Once we're married here, Hue can apply for US citizenship, and we can go back to Vietnam and officially get Mai back.

I'm writing to Dave, and Dan, and as many of the guys as I can get hold of from the old outfit. I hope they can get here for the wedding. We'll just go to the Justice of the Peace at Town Hall. Dad is set against this plan – all of it. He says I should get an engineering master's degree and go to work after one year, not as he says 'waste' time on a teaching certificate that's not worth much. And he said that he and Mom won't attend the wedding. But I think teaching kids really matters, and that's what I want to be part of. And I'm not giving up Hue. All that's another reason to leave soon – the tension around here, you can cut it with a knife.

"Well, that explains how they got to Boston, anyway," Benny said.

"And why Grandma and Grandpa weren't at the wedding," Maggie said. "How sad. Can you imagine a parent being so rigid and judgmental? Say what you will about Dad, he was never that way."

"No. No, he wasn't. But he did turn his back on me, so maybe it's not so different," Benny said, holding up a hand. "Now don't say it – I bet you think he was trying to juggle me and you and Jessica." He shrugged. "I got the short end of the stick."

Maggie stared at him. "You were also a lot more independent at sixteen than my Mom is now at age 55."

"Maybe," Benny said stiffly. "At least on the outside."

Maggie turned back to Henry's journals.

December 17, 1971: It's been a busy time. Hue was so happy with the letter from Aunt Trang, but there hasn't been another one since, and I can see her getting more anxious by the day. It doesn't help that we're stuck here with the parental disapproval. George went back to finish his semester at UVM after Thanksgiving, and he won't be back till Christmas Eve, which means we don't have his 'lubricating' presence. Never thought he'd be so helpful, but he actually is – even if he and I don't agree, at least he talks to everyone!

I got my transcript from Norwich – luckily there was someone in the Dean's Office when I drove up there – and sent it with an application letter to BU School of Ed. It's a long shot, I know, but I've got to try. We'll be much happier if we're living on our own.

I drove to Concord this week to talk to Larry Berman about writing something for the end of the year about what's really going on in Vietnam. He liked the idea. Told me to do a three-part series, to publish between Christmas and New Year's. He'll pay $100 per article, at 1000 words each. Hey, it's not much but it's something, and it's not coming from Dad. So what I've been writing since *then is the first draft of these articles. I have to turn them in on Monday next week.*

The wedding is set for Saturday, January 8th at the American Legion post. It won't be fancy. A bunch of the guys are coming, from school and from here in town and from the Army. George will be best man. It's sad that Hue doesn't really know anyone here, but the priority now is to get married so she's able to get US citizenship. George's girlfriend, Ginny, sort of volunteered (according to George) to be the maid of honor, so that's settled at least. Hue found a wedding dress at the Thrift Shop in Hanover, and she's been busy altering it to fit. Girl knows her way around a needle and thread!

"Well, they wasted no time," Benny said.

"Can't blame them," Maggie answered. She put down the 1971 journal and picked up 1972. This notebook was thicker, and obviously had old newspaper clippings attached to many of the pages.

January 9, 1972: Well, we did it!! We're married! It was a great party, anyway. Everyone showed up – friends from high school, from college, from the Army – and got along! Hue was the toast of the town! I think she had a good time too – she was able to forget some of her troubles for one night, at least.

The articles for the Monitor were well received, if I do say so myself. I wrote one about the drawdown, one about mixed-race children, and one about coming home. Got lots of autobiography for this, but I tried to keep it a little more objective. Anyway, it will pay the rent in Boston for a small apartment to get us started. We're leaving as soon as we can.

January 21, 1972: Wow, it's been a whirlwind. We got to Boston ten days ago, without an apartment or a job or any idea how we were going to live here. The first night we crashed at Dave's place in the South End. It's kind of a pit, but it's cheap. The whole neighborhood is pretty decrepit, I must say. The next day we found an apartment – well, it's like a big room – 260 square feet! – but it's got a little kitchen and a tiny bathroom; there's a Murphy bed that folds out of the wall next to the kitchen counter. And it's only $58 a month – so we can afford the first few months' rent. And it's upstairs above Marty's Deli, so we can at least get pizza easily.

Then I went over to BU to the Graduate Education department, and there I had a bit of luck. I met Dr. Evans, who I'd written to from Vermont. There was someone who was supposed to start on their master's degree last semester but he pulled out – decided to go to Hawaii instead. So they have an open slot with a scholarship! With my GI Bill qualification, I can take this position, and they won't have to give back the scholarship money. So it's a win-win. I think Evans was as relieved as I was, to tell the truth. The scholarship is $150 a month, and the GI Bill pays $205, so all of a sudden we're rich! Yippee!

Classes are already starting this week, so I have to scramble to get registered and hopefully get into the swing pretty quickly. I'll have a lot of classes this semester and next, and then I hope I can find a thesis project. Hue is going to take a more advanced English class and then see if she can get a nursing job. She can't be an RN yet, but maybe an LPN. We're both so relieved to be out on our own and away from the parents that we're just happy to be together. It's amazing, but things are breaking our way!

Tomorrow on my way to BU, I'll take her to the main Boston Public Library in Copley Square, and get her a library card. It's scary what counts as fun these days!

Maggie looked up from the page. "Well, zippy-di-doo-dah, they're on their way." She leafed through the pages slowly, scanning the crabbed handwriting that had become so familiar again.

Benny looked over her shoulder. "Looks like the next few months are all about school and exploring Boston, going to movies and some concerts…look at this – J. Geils Band, Aerosmith. They were just local bands back then," he said.

Maggie turned more pages. "Hue writes to Trang, eventually gets a letter back…Mai is doing well…Quan and Trang want to leave Saigon, say it's getting dangerous – they're planning to go to Quan's family in a town called An Lộc…Dad is trying to catch up on material from the previous semester while also keeping up with the new material…Hue is taking English classes."

She kept turning pages.

"February, March, it looks like more of the same. April…oh crap."

"What?" asked Benny.

"This place, An Lộc? That's where Trang and Quan were planning to take Mai. It looks like the North Vietnamese attacked it during the Easter Offensive of 1972."

Benny sighed. "The Easter Offensive was the beginning of the end for South Vietnam. The North attacked with tanks and artillery and infantry, both from the north across the DMZ and from the west, from Cambodia. They wound up taking a lot of territory. There were only about 70,000 US troops left in the country, and most of the fighting was by the Vietnamese. Eventually, the North was beaten back thanks to American air power – B52's and helicopters and everything in between – but the ARVN never recovered. Even though they fought bravely enough in many places, by the end of the year the peace negotiations let the North keep a lot of what they had captured."

"He's got a clipping in here from the New York Times," Maggie said. "Listen: 'April 6, 1972. A force of several hundred men had cut Highway 13 between An Lộc and Saigon only 37 miles north of the capital last night.' And there's another clipping with a map – four arrows for four invasion routes, and one of them is pointing right at An Lộc. And then on April 13, another clipping: 'Foe Said to Open an Armored Drive on Besieged An Lộc.'"

"This can't be good for civilians in the area," Benny said. "Is there anything about Quan and Trang and Mai?"

Maggie was paging ahead. "Oh, my God, this goes on and on. An Lộc was besieged until June. Artillery and tanks from North Vietnam, aerial resupply and bombing from the US. The whole city was reduced to rubble. There's a picture here he cut out of the Times on June 15 – there's nothing visible but rubble and a blown-up tank. Instead of writing much, he seems to be clipping out everything he can find about An Lộc from the newspaper. Finally, he wrote a short note. Listen:"

> *June 16, 1972: Hue is beside herself. We haven't heard any news from An Lộc, of course – it's been under siege for months. People are comparing it to Stalingrad. It's hard to imagine any civilians could survive this. Our poor Mai – what a horror…*

> *August 13, 1972: They say the battle for An Lộc ended in June, but the road (Highway 13) is still cut off by the PAVN. There's no way to learn if anyone survived. It's so frustrating…there are no US ground combat troops in the country*

anymore, only air support and advisors…no one to try and contact. Maybe if the road is opened we could find out something, but how??

September 7, 1972: They're still fighting around An Lộc. They say the battle ended June 18, and the place is still cut off. So what does it mean, the battle ended? I can see how we lost this war – nothing but bullshit body counts and useless destruction. I can't believe I used to support this war…this government. AAAARRRRGGGHHH!

October 2, 1972: Hue wrote to a doctor friend from Saigon in August to see if he could find out anything about the family in An Lộc. Finally heard back today. He attached a brief report from the ARVN commandant of the area, saying that they could not find any evidence of survivors matching Quan, Trang, and Mai. 'Missing and presumed dead.' But who really knows?

Poor Hue. She's distraught about losing Mai, but at the same time, not knowing for sure is tearing her up. Sad, sad, sad…maybe someday we can get back there and investigate, but right now it's just not possible.

Maggie looked up, tears rolling down her cheeks. Benny was sitting very still, looking into the middle distance. He sighed.

"You know," he said softly, "our generation doesn't know much about Vietnam, it seems so long ago and far away. But for Henry's it was an overwhelming, immediate, in-your-face thing. Those acronyms you asked me about before? Back then, everyone our age knew what they meant.

And even when Henry and Hue thought they were safe, back in the USA, the war reached out and tore them to pieces."

He got up and walked to the door. Without another word, he left Maggie in her apartment, surrounded by the pages of a tragedy she barely recognized.

Chapter Eighteen, Saturday Evening, June 3rd – Sunday, June 4th

Brad texted Maggie an hour or so later: "How about dinner at my place? I'm making my Aunt Abby's Famous Bouillabaisse, if you're up for it."

She texted back: "Sure. What should I bring, where and when?"

He replied: "Wine. 7:30. 16 Fairfield, Apt 3. "

Still a man of few words, she thought. Another one. She sent back a thumb's up emoji and went to shower.

The reaction hit her in the shower. The scene on A Street flashed in front of her as she closed her eyes under the hot water. A sob escaped her, then another and another, the hot tears mixing with the shower water. No matter that he was trying to kill her, she had taken another life. The weight of it pressed down on her so she could barely breathe. It was all very well to know that in theory she was justified in self-defense, but the reality was still hard, if one is not a sociopath.

She waited, turning slowly as the water ran down her body, taking slower and deeper breaths until she was no longer wracked by sobs. When her breathing was under control, she took the shampoo and worked it into her hair, massaging her scalp, remembering her father singing to her, "I'm gonna wash that man right out of my hair…". She grimaced, but kept on washing, feeling sad but calmer now. With a deep sigh, she turned off the water and got out of the shower, reaching for the bath towel.

She chose a simple midnight-blue dress that reached above the knees, with a scoop neck that emphasized her figure, and chunky patent-leather Doc Marten boots. As an afterthought, she opened the safe in her bedroom closet and took out a Sig Sauer P320 XCompact. She dropped the magazine to confirm that it held a full load, replaced it, and put it in a Gucci Marmont shoulder bag along with her wallet and keys. It had been her gift to herself when she was promoted to sergeant, practical as well as pretty.

An hour later she went downstairs and around the corner to Social Wines, and with help from the manager picked out a rosé from the Bandol region of Provence. Might as well get the wine that matches where the recipe for dinner is from, she thought.

She decided to walk to Brad's place. It's only about 2 miles, she thought, and I need to get some air. And no worries about parking. Forty minutes later, she was outside his door. It was 7:20. *Überpünktlich*, she thought, remembering the word a Swiss friend had taught her, as she walked around the corner to window-shop on Newbury Street. Means get there too early, then walk around the block till you arrive right on time. Very Swiss. Definitely un-American.

*　　　*　　　*

Brad's apartment was two flights up in a remodeled brownstone that must have cost millions. He buzzed her in and left the apartment door open, yelling "Come on in" when she knocked. The apartment had hardwood floors the color of good maple syrup, light gray walls with white wood molding and trim, and white built-in shelves. There was a fireplace with blue and white Delft tiles and a Doric-columned mantlepiece. The living room opened on to the kitchen with an island separating them. Behind the two-seat sofa a large three-part oriel window offered a 180-degree view of the street below.

Brad was at the cooktop in the kitchen, stirring something with a wooden spoon in an orange Le Creuset stockpot. There was a cutting board next to him strewn with garlic, parsley, leeks, and tomatoes. An open can of tomato paste, orange rinds, unwrapped white butcher paper and various spice containers were on the counter. The place smelled heavenly.

He came to greet her with a kiss.

"You have tomato paste on your earlobe," she laughed. "It's a good look for you."

"Sure, it's my Susie Homemaker look," he answered. He was barefoot, wearing an old Red Sox shirt and shorts made of gray sweat-pants jersey. "You, on the other hand," he said, twirling her around, "look beautiful."

"Keep talking," she said, handing him the wine bottle. "What's in the bouillabaisse?"

"Ah, secret family recipe. It varies by what's available. Red snapper, halibut, scallops, and shrimp today. The secret is in the orange rind, fennel, and saffron."

"Smells wonderful," Maggie said, realizing suddenly she was very hungry.

"It'll be ready in a few minutes," Brad said, reaching for a corkscrew. "Salad is on the table, bread's in the oven, but we can start whenever you like."

"This is a beautiful apartment," she said. "Not exactly a bachelor pad, is it?"

"Ah, well, the truth is I'm subletting it from someone who's taken a job in London for the year. They have good taste."

A round glass dining table in one corner of the living room was set for two, with candles and crystal. Maggie was impressed – Brad had really made an effort, that was nice.

"Well, I'm starving," she said. "Let's not wait too long."

*   *   *

The food tasted as good as it smelled. Maggie offered up a toast to Aunt Abby, and complimented the chef more than once. They chatted amiably, avoiding discussing their close call until after dinner.

"I'm afraid dessert is pretty basic," he said. "Ice cream – vanilla or chocolate?"

"Hah," she said. "Can't you guess?"

"Of course. You're a chocolate girl, aren't you?"

She nodded. He scooped ice cream into two bowls – vanilla for himself – and brought them to the table along with a small carafe of thick dark liquid. "Balsamic vinegar – the really good stuff – is great on ice cream. It's a secret that only 70 million Italians know, though, so keep it quiet." He drizzled some of the vinegar, which was nearly the consistency of honey, on the ice cream for both of them. Skeptical, she tried it, but he was right – it was terrific.

Finishing the dessert, they took their wine glasses over to the sofa.

"About what happened yesterday," he said. "It was terrible. I've been thinking it over and over ever since. But you were great, like I said before. You reacted so fast, and you did what you had to do to save us. I just want you to know, like I said before, that I am very happy you did."

"You know, the training we do, like any training, it works if you work at it," she answered. "It's not like last night I stopped, and thought, and planned what to do. The whole point of training is to let you react correctly without all the slow cerebral work – the reaction is happening at a much faster, more primitive part of your brain. It's the same for concert pianists, or for surgeons, as it is for first responders. You have your tools, or your instruments, and you work with them so much that they become extensions of your hand and subconscious. So what I did yesterday was based on decisions I made nine or ten years ago, not last night."

"Well, that may be so, but I'm still grateful that you did," he said. "I'm sure it's hard on you, thinking about this stuff, isn't it?"

She nodded, blinking, suddenly unable to speak or look at him. He reached for her, put his arms around her and gave her a fierce hug. She closed her eyes. Funny, she thought. He's talking about me saving him, but he's the one making me feel safe here.

He pulled back and kissed her gently on the lips, then on each eyelid. She opened her eyes and kissed him back, gently first and then more urgently. He cupped her cheek with his hand as their tongues sought each other out. Silently he pulled her up to standing, and led her to the bedroom in the back of the apartment.

Later, she didn't remember how they got their clothes off, just that they were in bed with a passion and ardor that she had never felt before. He was a considerate and gentle lover, but his urgency matched hers. He kissed her all the way down her body, stopping at all the right places, until he made her come the first time with his mouth. Then he entered her gently, building with her to a greater height, a deeper orgasm, than before. She heard him make male sounds of satisfaction as he climaxed with her, her legs around his and their lips entwined. Distantly she heard her own moan of satiety. He moved to one side and held her as they both returned to the present.

"Sex," she said. "The antidote to death."

"Is that what this is about?" he asked.

"Only partly, friend, only partly. It's also about us. Or about what we could be." She kissed him lightly on the lips.

He kissed her back, harder. "I think we should find out," he said.

*　　　*　　　*

They stayed in bed the rest of the night, talking, making love, sleeping. The next morning Brad made coffee, poached eggs, and toasted bagels to have with lox and cream cheese. During the night, she had told him about her father's and Hue's odyssey in Vietnam and after, and some more about the Quercus case. After all, she figured, he had almost been killed for Quercus, he should know something about it.

Talking around a mouthful of bagel at the dining table, Brad said, "Something Tony said is bothering me. If he didn't see anything wrong with the report, then he must be using the assay at the manufacturing site for the test batches they must be doing now ahead of the clinical trial starting. Those are usually analyzed very quickly – they need data before they can tweak the manufacturing process, so they're using that assay every day. How well can those be working?"

Maggie looked up from her almost-gone eggs. "What do you mean?"

"Look, Lilly found the assay didn't work in primate serum. Okay, that's what we call a matrix problem. The chemicals used in the test react with the stuff being tested, and it's different if it's blood, or saliva, or urine, or whatever the matrix happens to be. So you have to show that the test works in each new type of sample. Turns out, it's not uncommon to find inconsistencies like this, and it can usually be solved with time. They have to fix it before they go into people anyway, and if there's a problem with monkeys there's often a problem with human serum as well. Whoever killed Lilly would have to be working on a real solution to the assay problem, he or she just can't get it done in time for the IPO. So for the sake of millions of dollars, they're willing to kill – kill twice now, as a matter of fact. Right?"

Maggie nodded.

"But Tony said the assay *did* work in cell culture and in rodents, or they wouldn't have a drug to manufacture. So presuming that assay actually IS working for Tony – that he's not in on the whole scam/murder thing – I would still expect a lot of variability with the assay. At the very least, your villain would have to be out there monitoring the assay results very closely, to make sure there isn't anyone else who figures it out, the way Lilly did."

"So our perp would have to be traveling back and forth to the manufacturing site?" Maggie asked.

"Yes, definitely. Do you know where Quercus make their drug batches?"

Maggie looked blank. "No, we've never talked about it."

Brad smiled. "Most start-ups can't afford to make their own product, so they contract it out to a CMO – a contract manufacturing organization. They could be anywhere in the world, a lot of them are in China and India. But for a complex product like Quercus's – it's a strand of RNA inside an LNP, right?"

"Um, I think so. Remind me what LNP is again?"

"Lipid nanoparticle. It's like a slightly more rigid soap bubble, on a microscopic scale, that can float the RNA payload to the target cell before disintegrating. This is really cutting-edge stuff – it's been done, but only a few times, and all pretty recently. Think about the Covid-19 vaccines – the ones made using RNA, from Moderna and Pfizer/BioNTech – that's how they're made and delivered. I think there're only a few other approved drugs that work this way. That puts Quercus right up there in terms of innovation."

"Okay, so…?"

"So they're much more likely to use a CMO that's around here, so they can go there easily and check on progress. There are half a dozen. Or maybe, since they were pretty well-funded when they started, with the famous founders they have, they could have done the manufacturing themselves. But I doubt it, that would be a big chunk of money even for an established company, much less a start-up."

"I'll call Benny," Maggie said, putting down her bagel and reaching for her phone.

Benny picked up on the second ring and heard her out. She put him on speaker so Brad could hear too.

"Well, it's kind of a mix," he said. "Art Keogh is pretty paranoid about controlling our manufacturing process. When he joined the company he pushed them to create a subsidiary that would do the manufacturing. We use CRO's for the toxicology and stuff, of course, but actually not for the manufacturing. That's part of why there's so much pressure on the IPO – they spent something like $10 million on getting a facility and setting it up for sterile production and manufacturing. So the company ran out of money faster than they originally expected, and that's why the IPO has to happen now."

"That makes sense," Maggie said as Brad nodded. "Where is it?"

"They had to build it as cheaply as possible, but still accessible for regular visits from the main office, so it's out in central Massachusetts. In a little town called Westminster – it's off Route 2, about an hour from here. It's very creatively named, Quercus Biomanufacturing. I was only out there once – it's basically a building in an industrial park. Easy street name to remember, though – Simplex Drive."

"So who's in charge of it?" asked Maggie. "Who is the link between Cambridge and Westminster?"

"Technically it's Tony, but he's mostly been working on developing the processes in Cambridge, and then going out to Westminster when they're ready to transfer the technology for scale-up and compliance with Good Manufacturing Practice – that's the GMP part. Thomas and Anita have also been going out there some, hiring people there and setting them up, so that Tony can concentrate on the technical issues. But Thomas also has a lot of expertise in the LNP side of the drug – that's the lipid nanoparticles that protect the RNA from being chewed up by white blood cells. I'd say they're all three of them are there at least once a week."

"Thanks, Benny. Do you think we can go out there and see it?" Maggie asked.

"Well, not on a Sunday, it'll be locked up, and I don't have access. But we could go tomorrow if you like."

"Yes, let's plan on that. I'll text you a time and come get you."

Hanging up, she looked at Brad. "I wonder if we let Tony leave town too soon. He was the first one Lilly confided in, and now it seems like he was hip-deep in using this assay, but he really never mentioned it to us in all our talks."

"Maybe you'll know more after you see the place in Westminster," Brad said.

"And maybe Ted will get something off the laptop tomorrow, too. That's probably a better shot than a wild goose chase to central Mass."

Brad smiled. "Well, that gives us the rest of today to…um…entertain ourselves."

Chapter Nineteen, Monday, June 5th

There was a distinct buzz in the air at the Homicide & Unsolved office in Woburn when Maggie got there. It was just before 9 a.m. and the 'large' team, as she thought of it, was gathering in the conference room to start the week. Ted was sitting at the front of the long conference table, with his laptop open and projecting onto the screen. But what caught Maggie's eye was the computer next to his. It was also a black Lenovo laptop, but disassembled, the screen to one side, the keyboard removed, and the motherboard and solid-state drive visible, like a high-tech autopsy.

She took a seat as Mike Davis brought the meeting to order. He turned it over to Ted, who spoke to his computer rather than the room. Maggie knew he got nervous speaking to groups, and he compensated by dropping into cop-speak. And mumbling. But with his lung capacity, everyone could hear what he said anyway.

"I received Lilly Zhao's computer on Friday afternoon. It had been immersed in Spot Pond water for approximately 12 days. Fortunately, it had been turned off before immersion, probably by the victim, so it didn't actually short out when it hit the water. The issue was mainly one of drying it out before turning it on, and hoping it wouldn't arc – I mean short out – when it got power again. I opened the case and dried it as much as possible on Friday with paper towels, and then left it under warm transitive air flow…"

"What's that?" asked Davis.

"I set up a hair dryer on a tripod with a hose clamp, and left it on low aimed at the computer over the weekend," Ted answered without raising his head.

"Aha," Davis said. "Very high tech. Thanks."

"Last night at 6 p.m. I returned to the lab and checked the computer, which appeared to be dry. I then turned it on and observed that it powered up successfully…"

Maggie tried to imagine Ted's bated-breath anxiety when he decided to power Lilly's computer up. Ted was not ever going to make it as a used car salesman or an entertainer, she decided. But definitely worth his considerable weight in gold as a forensic scientist.

"…and was able to access the drive using Lilly Zhao's user credentials, as obtained from the Quercus Administrator database. I then searched her email account for the five days preceding her death, looking for any emails that were still on the local drive but not on the backup. I did not find any emails that had not been visible to us through the administrative account at Quercus."

There was a *sotto voce* hum of disappointment, a sort of exhalation that swept the room. Maggie held her breath. She hoped Ted had more to say.

"However…" the room silenced at once. "…I did find the following Teams chat between the victim and another Quercus employee that the vic had archived as a PDF on her desktop. It's dated Monday, May 22, at 9:32 a.m. I'm projecting it now…"

> *Lilly: Hi, Thomas, do you have a minute?*
>
> *Thomas: Yes, sure, Lilly, what's up?*
>
> *Lilly: I am having some trouble with the PK assay for '101. I'm getting a lot of null values in the monkey tox study.*
>
> *Thomas: OK, happy to review with you. I'm in meetings till 2. How about then? Come see me?*
>
> *Lilly: Sounds great, thanks. See you then.*

There was a deep silence in the room. Maggie looked at Jimmy. "When you interviewed Thomas, he told you he had not spoken to Lilly about the assay issues, right?"

Jimmy nodded. "Yes, he flat-out denied it."

Davis looked at them. "Bingo," he said. "There's your leverage."

Maggie smiled. "This is why the perp had to get rid of this laptop. He could – or Dimitris could – delete the Teams chat on the server. But he was afraid that Lilly might have saved a copy, as she obviously did."

Adelle Watkins, the ADA, spoke up. "I suggest we get an arrest warrant and pick up Thomas van Haft as soon as possible."

Maggie shook her head. "I've got one more line of investigation to follow, something that came up yesterday. It seems that Quercus has a manufacturing facility out in Central Massachusetts, where they actually make the drug batches. The assay that we've been concentrating on would have been used there as well. Both Thomas van Haft and Antoine Dupree have been going back and forth between there and Cambridge, and both of them clearly knew about Lilly's discovery before she was killed. While I *think* Dupree – Tony – is a good guy, we really don't have any evidence to support that. A good defense lawyer could make up a story that could generate reasonable doubt if we focus on van Haft alone."

"So what do you suggest?" Adelle asked.

"Jimmy and Eddie go to Quercus, and bring van Haft in for questioning. I'll go to the site in Westminster with Benny and look around. See if we can find evidence that implicates van Haft, and either implicates or exonerates Dupree. We'll come back here and join you for the interrogation. If you give us a couple of hours' head start, the timing should work out."

Davis nodded. "We can make that work, can't we, Adelle?"

Adelle inclined her head. "Yes, that can work. If he lawyers up, we also bring in Antoine Dupree and play them off against each other."

"OK, great," Davis said. "Next, let's hear from Heather about the surveillance video that Maggie set up inside Quercus. Heather?"

Corporal Martin plugged the projector cable into her laptop and toggled up a video screen. It showed the second floor of Quercus, with the drug refrigerator and freezer in the center, in a wide-angle shot that included most of the west side of the floor.

"Note the time indicator in the upper right-hand corner," she said. "We start a bit before 7 p.m. last Thursday. You can see Maggie and Benny walking away to the right of the screen. About 20 seconds later, we see another person emerging from behind the fume hood on the left side. He approaches the fridge, looks at the clipboard, and then follows them out to the right. His face is away from the camera until he's almost off-screen, but then we can see him in profile…here." She froze the video and enlarged the head of the figure.

"It's Jorge Perez," Maggie sighed. "We…I…missed him hiding in the back of the room. We were basically whispering the whole time, so I think Jorge couldn't hear what we said – the room is like a hundred feet long – but he could see that we were interested in the cold storage area. Damn, I wish I'd searched the room first."

"It would have been more awkward if you found him," Eddie said. "What would you have said?"

Maggie shrugged. "At least he doesn't open the fridge and get more sux, though if he was the one who killed Dimitris, he still had enough, just like Benny said. But we didn't find any sux in Jorge's house or car, and his behavior was much more erratic than you'd expect from someone who killed Lilly and Dimitris so efficiently and cold-bloodedly. I know it would be very nice and neat if Perez were our killer and he wound up dead, but I really don't think we can prove that. And I don't believe it."

Meanwhile, Heather had teed up another video. "I also looked at available surveillance from security cameras outside Quercus. Starting from a little before 7 p.m., we can see Maggie and Benny leaving the building and getting into Maggie's car. They sit in the car for about four minutes…"

"Yes, I was ordering food for us to pick up on the way home to work on, um, another project," Maggie said.

Davis shot her a look but said nothing. Heather continued to scroll the video forward. "But if you look in the background on the left, you see that there is a man on a bicycle coming around the side of the building. He waits in the shadows until Maggie's car pulls out, and then he follows the car."

She froze the screen as the bicyclist passed under the sodium-yellow streetlamp, casting his face in high relief. "Once again," Heather said, "it looks like Jorge Perez. Looks like he followed you home, Maggie. That's how he knew where to look for you the next day. He must have been watching when you left your apartment to go meet Brad."

Davis cleared his throat. "Well, that puts a few pieces together. Thank you, Heather. Nice work." He turned back to Ted. "Any update on the phone location of our top suspects?"

Ted shook his head. "No one near the Middlesex Fells or the Fenway around the time of the murders. If one of them did it, they had their phones either turned off or safely at home."

Maggie turned to him. "Can you check on which of them have been out to Quercus's manufacturing site? It's in Westminster, Mass, out Route 2." She turned to the room in general. "Knowing the timing and pattern of their travel might help."

Ted nodded. "On it," he said. "I'll let you know."

Mike Davis stood up again to address the room. "All right, let's get our act together. Jimmy and Eddie, you get an arrest warrant for Thomas van Haft, and go to Cambridge and pick him up, either at Quercus or at his home. Maggie, you take Benny and go out to Westminster and check out this other Quercus site, see if anyone there knows anything about the faulty assay. Once you're done there, liaise with Jimmy and Eddie and if they have van Haft, meet back here for the interrogation. Adelle will be here to back you up, and we'll see if he lawyers up or not. Ted, you keep looking at Lilly's laptop for any more info, and check the cell phone locations. Heather, you call Antoine Dupree and check in on him, tell him we'll want him back in town for more assistance by tomorrow."

He looked at his watch. "All right, people, it's coming on 10 o'clock now. Let's get moving, I'd like to get this case wrapped up today! We're starting our third week on this thing, and we still don't have an answer. What we do have is three dead bodies, and I don't want any more. *Capisce?*"

As the meeting broke up, Davis beckoned to Maggie.

"You have an appointment with DIS at 4 p.m. today in Framingham to review the shooting. The investigator is Lieutenant Abrams – good guy, he'll be thorough but sensible." Maggie made a face, but Davis ignored her. "Also, I have the indoor speed record for a response to your ADM-20, Maggie," he said. "Approved. You can draw a temporary weapon from the Armorer. If you don't have time to get to Framingham today, you can borrow my backup."

"Thanks, L-T, that would be great. I'd like to get out to Westminster as soon as possible, so if yours is handy, I'll borrow it now and go to Framingham for the interview after I get back. Is that okay?"

Davis nodded, and led the way to his desk. He unlocked a drawer and took out a Smith & Wesson M&P45, identical to the one that Maggie had handed over on Saturday. She took the proffered weapon and a spare magazine, checked the load and replaced the magazine. Back at her desk, she pulled her empty shoulder holster from her backpack, inserted the handgun, took off her blue blazer, and put it on again over the holster and gun. Pulling her Gucci Marmont shoulder bag out of the backpack, she slung it over her other shoulder and headed for the door, texting Benny as she went.

Chapter Twenty, Monday June 5th

It was close to noon when Maggie and Benny pulled off State Route 2 at the Westminster exit. Driving through rolling farmland with comfortable-looking houses along the two-lane country road, Maggie followed the GPS directions to Simplex Drive, an industrial park incongruously set in such a pastoral landscape. During the drive, she had filled Benny in on what Ted had found, but she hadn't heard back from Ted yet about the cell phone locations.

They passed a trucking company, a cardboard manufacturer, and plastics fabricator, all in matching functional one-story gray and beige industrial buildings. Quercus Manufacturing was on the far end of the building that housed the plastics company. Maggie saw an empty loading dock with a closed gray overhead door. Next to it were concrete steps bounded by metal side rails that were bright yellow above and mostly rust below; the rust had seeped into the concrete, staining it the color of dried blood. These led to another gray door, this one human-sized, with a wire-mesh and frosted glass window and a sign that proclaimed 'Quercus Biomanufacturing – Authorized Personnel Only' in block letters.

Benny led the way up the stairs and used his badge to unlock the door.

"I thought you didn't have access, Benny," Maggie said, trying to keep any hint of suspicion out of her voice.

"I can get through the front door, but not the inner one. You'll see. Since this is a GMP facility, everything – every entry, exit, action, reaction – is logged somewhere. FDA can come in here unannounced on an audit, and in theory we can account for every person and activity carried out here. Failure to do that could prevent – or at least delay – getting a drug approved, or even get it suspended after approval. Happens all the time, actually."

Inside was a small waiting room, with an unoccupied receptionist's desk, a few chairs, and a shelf unit holding boxes of masks, blue disposable shoe and hair covers, and white polypropylene 'moonsuits'. A sign pointed to a button on the wall and instructed visitors to push it for service. Benny did so, and presently someone fully dressed in protective gear opened a door in the wall opposite the front entrance.

Benny identified himself and introduced Maggie as his colleague.

"Oh, hi, I'm Jerry Stein," said the figure. "I met you last time you were out here."

"Uh, yes, right, of course," Benny said. "We've been trying to sort out some issues with the release assay for the IND submission. I guess you guys use it more than anybody. Who could we talk to about that?"

"Well, me for one. I've been using it regularly. Tony and Thomas have been out here too, working on improving the process throughput. I think we're closing in on 80% encapsulation at 50-mL scale! Not bad, huh?"

"Not bad at all," Benny said appreciatively as Maggie looked on blankly. "At what pressure?"

"500 bar at 4 degrees C," Jerry answered. "That should be scalable up to commercial production levels if we get good clinical response. Anyway, why don't you guys gown up and we can go inside."

Maggie and Benny nodded, looking briefly at each other. Benny handed her a moonsuit, followed by shoe covers, hair cover, and mask. She put her purse strap over her head so it crossed her chest, with the purse on one hip, leaving the top of it unzipped. She put her phone in the bag, activating the voice recorder app unobtrusively as she did so. Once they were dressed, Jerry led them through the door into a hallway that appeared to run down the whole length of the building. Everything here was an antiseptic bright white – floor, ceiling, walls, doors. The light was the pitiless cold white of operating rooms and airport gates.

Jerry led them to a door about half-way down the hall. Through the glass top half of the door, Maggie could see a half a dozen ceiling-high stainless steel tanks in a row down the middle of the room, connected to each other by a maze of stainless steel pipes and tubes that wrapped around the wall and ceiling. Some of the pipes led to several stainless steel consoles, with blue metal control panels and occasional red or green hoses connecting to some of the innumerable valves that jutted off the pipes at various points. On the far wall was a lab bench, sink, and several tall battleship-gray chests that even Maggie recognized as minus-70-degree freezers. The whole place looked like a brewery on the Starship Enterprise.

The room was empty except for another moonsuited figure seated at a desk – white of course – set in one corner, tapping at a computer keyboard. He looked up as they came in, and Maggie recognized Thomas van Haft from his ice-blue eyes and rimless glasses.

"Benny? Er, Maggie? What are you doing here?" Thomas asked, his Dutch accent a little more pronounced than usual.

"We came to learn a bit more about the release assay from Jerry," Benny said. "It's become something of an issue for the IND submission. Seems there's a problem with the research report, and I'm worried it will hold up the filing."

He turned to Jerry. "Can you bring the lab notebooks for the past few batches? Let's see how much variability there is."

Jerry nodded, and turned to the door, evidently headed to an adjacent room. Maggie was acutely aware that she couldn't easily reach her gun inside the moonsuit. She felt the hair on the back of her neck rise, and edged slowly away from Benny and Thomas.

"I don't think that's necessary, Benny," Thomas said quietly, though somehow his voice was full of menace. "The assay has been working very well here. I understand from the police that Lilly thought there was a problem with the assay in the chronic tox study, but I told her it was probably just poor sample handling at the CRO."

"That's funny, Thomas," Maggie said. "I thought you told the police you didn't know anything about an assay problem at all."

"I might have said something like that," Thomas answered. "But how would you know that, Maggie?"

"Oh, I heard them talking when they came out of your room a few weeks ago," Maggie said as nonchalantly as she could.

"Thomas, we can't submit an IND with a questionable PD and release assay," Benny said impatiently. "We need to get to the bottom of this."

"I'm sure we can sort out the technical issues in parallel with the submission, Benny," Thomas said coldly. "This is not unusual, that we have a second generation assay that we replace the original with later. No need to endanger our, ah, *timelines*, you know?" From the emphasis on 'timelines', Maggie knew he was referring to the IPO, not the IND. So many acronyms in this business, she thought incongruously.

Jerry came back into the room with an open black laptop in his hand. "Here you go, guys," he said, "here are results from the last 3 batches. I can…"

"Jerry, why don't you check on that HPLC run, it should be ready by now. I can take Benny through these data," Thomas interrupted him smoothly. Whatever else he is, Maggie thought, Thomas is a cool customer. Turning nonchalantly toward Jerry as he spoke, with her back now to Thomas, she quietly unzipped the top of her moonsuit so she could reach her gun in its shoulder holster.

"Sure, Thomas," Jerry said, putting down the laptop on Thomas's desk and heading out a door at the back of the room that was barely visible between the stainless steel tanks and pipes.

Benny started moving toward the laptop, just as Thomas swiveled in his chair and opened the top drawer of his desk. The hairs on the back of Maggie's neck were in five-alarm mode now, and she had learned to trust them. She reached into her moonsuit for the gun and said, "Wait a minute, Benny. Stay where you are."

Benny paused, surprised, and looked at her.

Shit, in for a penny, in for a pound, Maggie thought. Adelle better have gotten that arrest warrant by now. She pulled her gun out, but kept it at her side. "Thomas van Haft, I'm Sergeant Maggie Thompson of the Massachusetts State Police. You are under arrest for the murder of Lilly Zhao and Dimitris Pappas. Turn around and put your hands on your head."

There was silence in the room, except for various hissing and gurgling sounds from the stainless steel spaghetti of tubing above their heads.

"Now wait a minute, Maggie," Thomas said, "you've got this all wrong. I didn't kill anybody."

He still hadn't raised his hands, Maggie thought. He's stalling. What's he up to?

She raised her pistol, though still keeping it in one hand. "Hands up now, Thomas, then we can discuss everything in good time."

Thomas looked at Benny. "Benny, surely you believe me? This is a ridiculous accusation, and you know it."

Benny shook his head. "Thomas, they found Lilly's laptop, and they have texts between you and her. If you know something about all of this, then please tell Maggie. She just wants to get to the truth."

Thomas turned pale, then laughed bitterly. "I wish I had your faith in the American justice system, Benny. But I'm afraid I don't."

Maggie was impatient now. "Okay, Thomas, that's enough stalling. Hands on your head *now*."

"Not so fast, Maggie," a voice said behind her. Maggie heard the metallic click of a pistol being cocked. "Put your gun down on the floor slowly. That's good. Now kick it away, toward Thomas. No sudden moves."

Maggie recognized the voice, but couldn't believe it. Benny was staring over Maggie's shoulder as if he was seeing a ghost.

"Anita?" he said. "What…?"

Anita, for it was indeed her, walked around Maggie to stand next to Thomas's chair. She held a small pistol in her hand. Maggie automatically identified it by its oversized trigger guard as a Baretta Bobcat. Only 0.25 caliber, but deadly enough at this range. Thomas picked up Maggie's Smith & Wesson, looked distastefully at it and put it on the desk.

"Thomas," Anita said, "why don't you go ask Jerry to get us lunch? Send him over to the Westminster Café. Tell him I want a turkey BLT. Too bad we'll be gone by the time he comes back, and I won't have a chance to eat it. Their food is good."

Thomas nodded meekly and went out the door at the rear of the room.

Maggie was still trying to wrap her head around this. "Anita? You're involved in all this?"

Anita laughed, waiving the Baretta a little bit in a way that made Maggie wonder about her sanity.

"You might say so, Maggie. This has been my idea from the beginning. As soon as Thomas told me that the assay was for shit, I knew we had to cover it up until we got the IPO done. Then we – I mean Thomas and Tony and the other scientists – could fix it, given enough time and money. Thomas said so. That we could fix it, I mean – it's all just a technical problem, isn't it? But if we run out of money first, and then we have to publicly tell the world that that we have a delay, that could kill the company. But the drug, it works, Maggie. Doesn't it Benny? It works in mice, and rats, and cells. It could really help people with ALS, couldn't it?"

Benny didn't answer.

"But I thought Thomas…" Maggie said.

"Oh, Thomas did the dirty work, of course. He loves me, you see. More than my selfish jerk of a husband. And together we'll get about thirty million dollars from the IPO. Of course you've ruined all that now, haven't you? Now we have to disappear. Well, I've been preparing for this eventuality too, you know. Last week, when that big cop called me about Tony's place in the mountains and direct deposit account? That's when I knew we'd better be ready to run. But no one suspects the little old H.R. lady, do they?" She giggled.

"But how? Did Dimitris work for you also? Why kill him?" Maggie asked, trying to keep her talking. Benny was standing frozen, staring at Anita.

"Oh, well, Dimitris certainly did work for me. More than anything, Dimitris wanted a green card, and of course he could only get it with Quercus sponsoring him, couldn't he? But poor Dimitris, he has – or had – a past. He's not exactly Greek, it seems, and his real name isn't actually Dimitris. He's from somewhere further east, Belarus or Turkmenistan or something. Someplace where the US Government is not kindly disposed to let people in. He came here on an H-1B visa under his assumed name, you know, and then when he joined Quercus we sponsored him to stay here. I found out about his not-so-real papers, and from then on it was easy to control him. Until it wasn't. After Lilly's body was discovered, he freaked out. Then when Tony disappeared, he ran. He became a liability. Fortunately, Thomas dealt with him."

"So you had Lilly killed too?" Maggie asked with as little expression as she could muster, trying not to think about how Dimitris had died. "Did Thomas do that as well?"

"Oh, yes. He followed her to the Fells when she went jogging. Thomas is an excellent bicyclist – you know how the Dutch love their bikes. And the traffic was slow enough that he could easily keep up with her car. He got her alone – it's so foolish for a woman to go jogging alone in the dark, don't you think?" Anita giggled again.

Maggie's neck hairs were standing up and claiming overtime now – Anita was a serious sociopath, she thought

– wow, how did I miss that? On top of missing Jorge following me all over town. And letting Tony leave the state – if he's involved in this after all, he could be anywhere by now. Maybe I should become an admin for real, instead of playing cop.

Anita went on. "And he had a perfect plan for hiding the body. Normally, no one goes into that old barn where he left her – it's so spooky, and the doors and windows are all normally locked. We were going to come back with a car the next day and then dump her body in the ocean, but we never got the chance. All because of that damn Canadian forest fire."

Maggie had to keep her talking. "What about Jorge? Did you know he was going to try and kill me?"

Anita tilted her head slightly, eyes narrowing. "No, I didn't. Is that right? I'm afraid I can't take credit for that one. It would have saved me a lot of trouble now. How did he do it?"

"He tried to run me down in South Boston."

"Jorge was always a little, um, unstable. And his affair with Lisa was stressing him out. Of course, as the HR Lady, I offered to counsel him when he came crying to me about his wife threatening to leave him. But of course I had to warn him that he could be violating our policies and procedures by having a relationship with a direct report." She giggled again. "I didn't mention that Thomas and I were carrying on too."

Thomas came back into the room. "Jerry's going now," he said. Anita nodded.

"Good, as soon as he's gone we can also go. Tie these two up. I'm afraid this facility will have to have an unfortunate accident. An explosion and fire, and their bodies will be discovered in the ashes. Use duct tape – it should burn away. We have enough toluene here to blow this place up, and they'll only be identified from the dental records."

Anita sounded as though she were discussing the weather for all the emotion she displayed, Maggie thought. Benny made a gagging sound, but didn't say anything.

Thomas went to a cupboard next to the sink and pulled out a large roll of gray duct tape. He unlocked another cabinet and pulled out several large brown glass bottles. Maggie could see the labels, which read 'Toluene – Lab Grade – 4 Liters'. When he was done there were five of the bottles – all full – on the floor by the desk. Thomas unscrewed the black plastic caps and tossed them aside; the sickly-sweet chemical smell of the toluene hit her nostrils almost immediately.

"Jesus," Benny said, "that's enough to bring down the whole building."

"Yes, it is," Anita said happily. "Now Thomas, start by taping Maggie's hands together behind her back." She pointed her pistol at Maggie. "And no funny stuff," she said.

Maggie knew this was her last, best chance. As Thomas came up behind her, she waited until she could hear his breathing in her ear. Half expecting to feel a shot go through her, she pivoted, grabbed Thomas by the front of his moonsuit, and executed a perfect *seoi nage* shoulder throw, dropping to her knee and rolling to her side as she reached for her purse. Maggie knew she wouldn't have time to avoid a bullet from Anita, she just prayed that Anita was a lousy shot, and that she would be enough of a moving target to be hard to hit.

She hadn't counted on Benny. As Anita lifted her gun to aim at Maggie, Benny launched himself in a surprisingly agile dive, directly at Anita. The gun went off as Maggie reached for the open zipper of her purse. Her hand closed around the Sig Sauer that was still there from Saturday night, and she fired it through the side wall of the Gucci purse.

Anita's shot hit Benny in the chest, and he crumpled to the floor. Maggie's first shot missed Anita but the second one caught her at diaphragm level, mid-chest, forcing her backwards against the desk and then into a seated position on the floor in front of it. Maggie turned to Thomas and found he was lying prone on the floor, out cold.

She scrambled over to Benny. He was breathing, but barely. She cradled his head in her hands, saying, "Benny, Benny, don't you leave me."

He looked at her and smiled briefly. Then something shifted in his face, the luster left his eyes, and with a long exhale, he was gone.

Chapter Twenty-One, Monday June 5th

Maggie was sitting on the stairs outside the Quercus Manufacturing door when the first State Police cruiser and an ambulance came screeching into the parking lot. Her phone was next to her on the steps, showing a text message from Ted: 'Westminster visitors today are Thomas and Anita. Be careful.' A little late for that, she thought.

She had left Thomas on the floor, still unconscious but handcuffed to the desk leg. If he woke up, he would have two corpses to keep him company. Serve him right, she thought. She did screw the tops back on the toluene bottles; no need to find out how explosive the stuff actually is.

She had found a pack of cigarettes in the receptionist's desk in the Quercus anteroom, while phoning 911 for backup and angrily ripping off the moonsuit. She hadn't smoked since college, but this seemed to be a good way to keep her hands busy, and not shaking so much. Remembering the toluene inside, she walked out to the concrete stairs with their blood-red rust stains. She had the cigarette in one hand and her State Police shield in the other as she watched the first trooper approach her with gun drawn. He wasn't someone she knew.

"Sergeant Maggie Thompson," she said to the trooper, whose name tag said 'Blaszeck'. "Situation is under control, but we need a Medical Examiner and Crime Scene Services here. Two deceased and one unconscious suspect cuffed inside, who needs medical attention. As far as I know, there's no one else here."

She waited, still numb. A white Ford Fiesta pulled into the parking lot and Jerry got out, carrying a white paper sack presumably with the sandwiches, but she diverted him to Trooper Blaszeck. After what seemed like a long while, Mike Davis arrived with Jimmy and Eddie. She heard them speaking as if from a great distance, or under water. She knew she was answering questions, but wasn't sure what they were, or what she said. Thomas was wheeled out on a stretcher, handcuffed, and loaded into the ambulance, which left followed by a police car.

Later on, she saw news vans, reporters, more cops, State and local, who were keeping the press behind yellow and black police tape. She saw Dan Beardsley in the crowd of TV cameras and reporters, but didn't respond to his wave. The Medical Examiner van arrived, and then two body bags were wheeled out on gurneys. She followed the black bags with her eyes, knowing Benny was in one of them. There seemed to be a hissing in her ears, and her color perception seemed off somehow, the blue sky too blue, the gray asphalt, black body bags, and the building behind them seemingly shot in black-and-white film while the rest of the world, far away, was in color.

Finally, Mike Davis took her gently by the arm and said, "Come on, Maggie, let's go."

Docilely, she stood up and went with him. For the second time since the shooting in South Boston, she felt Jimmy stop her by enveloping her in a bear hug, dwarfing her 5'10" frame inside his far burlier six-foot-four. With that, the dam broke. She sobbed, her shoulders shaking, crying, heaving, gasping for the brother she had almost had and lost again.

Now her hearing came back, she felt Jimmy rubbing her back and murmuring "There, there, it's okay. You let it out," over and over again.

Cried out, she pushed back from him. Accepting a fistful of Kleenex from Eddie, she blew her nose, dried her eyes, shook her head from side to side, like a horse shooing a particularly irritating insect.

"Okay," she said. "I'm okay. Enough to get through the procedures now, at least."

Davis looked at her. "Are you sure?"

"Yes," she said. "Let's get it over with, then I need a nap."

He shook his head. "Fine. Let's go to the Leominster barracks and get your statement. Once again, I need your weapon for investigation. At this rate, you're going to have to move to Framingham to keep up with the rate at which you lose hardware."

She took the Sig Sauer out of her purse, looking ruefully at the hole it had made in the side of the once elegant leather, and handed it to him. Davis shook his head, and signaled to a crime scene technician, who came up with an evidence bag and took the proffered gun.

*　　　*　　　*

The State Police barracks in Leominster was a two story building about 10 miles east on Route 2, grey concrete on the first floor, red brick on the second. Lieutenant Davis commandeered an interview room and they waited for Adelle Watkins to arrive from Woburn. Then Maggie led them through the whole sequence of events since the discovery of Lilly's body, while Adelle took notes to supplement the recording being made by Eddie. Sixteen days, five deaths, a company in ruins, the hopes of thousands of patients with ALS dashed yet again, her brother gone – just telling it left Maggie feeling even more exhausted. Finally, she played the voice recording from her phone, capturing Anita, somewhat muffled but still audible enough, explaining how she and Thomas had planned the whole thing.

"Is that going to be admissible?" Mike Davis asked Adelle.

Adelle shook her head. "No, in Massachusetts you have to get consent to record – obviously not practical here – or a warrant specifically requesting permission to wiretap. Our best bet here is to either get a confession from van Haft, or to get evidence of the affair with Anita Mercer, which would impeach his credibility vis-à-vis Maggie. If they've been seeing each other for a while, I bet we can find that kind of evidence. Credit card receipts for hotels, restaurants, stuff like that. Somebody must have seen them together somewhere where they shouldn't have been. Van Haft might not get the full murder rap, but we should have enough for accessory and conspiracy to commit, with Maggie's testimony. That might not get him life in prison, but it should do for 20 years at least."

"Okay, we'll start digging," Davis said, his lips set in a thin line. "Anything else you need, Adelle, or can we let Maggie go home and get some rest?"

"Nothing else, just this," Adelle said, getting up and giving Maggie a hug. It was turning into a banner day for hugs. "Thank you, Maggie. You and the whole team have done an amazing job on this case, and with what you've found, I'm sure we'll get justice for Lilly and Dimitris and their families yet."

* * *

It was after five p.m. when Maggie got home. She was surprised to find Brad waiting in the lobby of her building. He stood up and came toward her as she walked in. They both spoke at once.

"Are you okay?" he asked.

"What are you doing here?" she asked.

He tried to smile, but she noticed his lips tremble. "I heard about the shooting at Quercus Manufacturing on the news while I was at work. I figured if I camped out here, you'd have to come home eventually. I thought you could use a friendly face, but if you want to be alone, I can go."

She shook her head, smiling sadly. "No, I'm glad you're here. It's been a tough day." He hugged her gently, and kissed her softly on the lips. They walked to the elevator.

"Come on," he said. "You can tell me all about it. According to the news, you're a hero."

"I don't know about that, Brad. Benny's dead, and it's my fault that he was there in the first place. I was mad at him for years, and then with this case, somehow we found a new start. He died to save me – he literally took a bullet for me. How do I live with that?"

"Well, obviously I didn't know him," Brad said, "but at the same time, just as obviously, he cared for you very much. In his own way, I guess. From what you've told me, he's not – he was not – someone very comfortable showing his emotions. There's nothing you or anyone can do to change what's happened."

"I know, I know," Maggie said, crying noiselessly now, the tears rolling down her cheeks. "I've lost my dad, and my half-brother, and evidently also a half-sister I never even knew about until last week…how can I lose so many people I never even had?"

"Well, I know it's not much of a consolation, but you've gained me, if you want me," he said, blushing.

She smiled through the tears. "Well, that's the first good thing that's happened today, I guess. Shut up and make drinks. I need a shower. Then you can kiss me."

Chapter Twenty-Two, Friday, August 18th

Maggie pulled the blue Ford Explorer up to the curb of a rambling two-story shingle-style house on top of a cliff overlooking Cape Cod Bay in Eastham, Massachusetts. Her Uncle George had lived here ever since Maggie could remember, and she had spent countless summer days here, or at the foot of the cliff in the Bay. At low tide, even a toddler could walk out for half a mile and only be in water up to her knees. She took a deep breath of salty air and bittersweet memory.

Uncle George had come to the door as she crunched up the crushed seashell and pea stone driveway. He swung the screen door wide and hugged her tightly. At 72, with a gray ponytail and white beard that contrasted nicely with skin tanned the color of old mahogany, he was as lean and fit as ever.

"How's my favorite niece?" he asked.

"I'm your only niece, Uncle," she answered. It had been their standard greeting ever since she could remember. But now she wondered – was there another niece in Vietnam?

"Don't be so sure," he grinned. That, too, was part of their standard hello.

"I'm not, actually," Maggie said, walking through the large living room-kitchen area – pale blue walls, white trim, white wicker furniture – to the wall of glass doors overlooking the bay. The tide was out and the sand glistened under a few inches of seawater for miles around. It was spectacular, as always. The walls were decorated with gold records and awards from George's career as a sound engineer.

She had last seen George at Benny's funeral, in early June. There had been a huge turnout – she was a little surprised to see that her introverted, privacy-seeking brother had such a large number of friends, but not at all surprised that he was held in high esteem by so many at the intersection of the worlds of biotech, pharmaceuticals, medicine, and academia. The whole thing had been a blur, with Brad at her side, her mother flying in, and her overwhelming feeling of loss and that it was somehow her fault. She had barely had a chance to speak with George before he fled back to his seaside lair.

They walked out to the wooden deck overlooking Cape Cod Bay. "I know we said this a hundred times," George said, "but though I'm endlessly sad about Benny, I'm glad you and he had a chance to get to know each other again, at least a little bit, as adults."

"Yes, I still can't believe how heroic he was. He didn't even hesitate. And it's my fault that he's dead."

George shook his head. "I'm not so surprised. When you were a baby, he was always watching out for you. I'm sure you don't remember this, and I don't know if anyone ever told you, but when you were about a year and a half old or so, just a toddler, you were injured while he was watching you. Do you know about this?"

Maggie stared at him. "No, I don't. This family never talks without the third degree, you know?"

"Well, you guys were at the park, and there was a sliding board. You were scared to go by yourself, so he went up with you, put you in his lap, and you went down together. Somehow the sole of your sneaker got caught on the side of the slide, and your leg was forced backwards. Long story short, you broke your fibula, the small bone between the knee and the ankle. You didn't seem to be in any pain, no one thought anything of it. We only noticed it the next day, when suddenly you were crawling again instead of walking. Henry took you to the pediatrician, they did an x-ray, and you wound up with a bright blue cast for three weeks."

Maggie made a face. "Really? Something else nobody ever said a word about."

"Well, Jessica made a big deal about how Benny had been careless, and couldn't be trusted to watch you, blah blah blah. Henry, of course, just waved it away as trivial and went back to grading papers. But Benny really internalized it, as he did with everything. He felt like he'd let you down. He and I talked about it, later, much later. So no, I'm not surprised he took a bullet for you. Benny wasn't great at expressing his emotions, but he certainly did feel things. Maybe more strongly than someone who could vent more, you know?"

She shook her head, feeling tears at the edge of her eyelids. "Oh, Benny," was all she said. They stood in silence for a moment.

"It's never just one thing, is it?" said Maggie.

"What is – or isn't?" George asked.

"People say, 'life is good.' *La vita è bella.* Or, they say, 'life is nasty, brutish, and short.' Life's a bitch and then you die. But it's both of these things."

"Yes. Sometimes both at once, sometimes sequentially."

They were silent for a few more minutes, staring at the sea.

"I heard more about that case you had up in Cambridge," George said. "That was some interview you had on Channel 4 with Dan Beardsley. Sounds like a bad scene, but you seem to have saved the day. Well done! Is it over now?"

Without waiting for an answer, he walked back inside to a large stainless-steel refrigerator, pulled out diet tonic water and a lime from the top and ice and gin from the freezer. He busied himself building drinks as she told him about the Quercus case. They walked back out to the deck an sat in matching white Adirondack chairs.

"So Thomas is in jail without bail," Maggie concluded. "We think we have enough to convict him on conspiracy, accessory before the fact, aggravated assault, and interfering with a police investigation, and maybe on murder one. It was certainly premeditated, and the second one was definitely with extreme cruelty."

"What about the biotech company?" George asked. "Quercus, is it? Funny name."

Maggie nodded. "Yes, this is one oak that won't grow mighty. They were supposed to go on their 'road show'" – she did air quotes – "starting on Monday, June 5th, the day that Benny died and everything went down at the site in Westminster. Obviously, that didn't go forward. The company is in bankruptcy protection now. Art Keogh is out, and the investors have a temporary CEO who's trying to rescue what's left of the QT-101 program. Who knows, it might even work someday."

George shook his head. "What a mess," he said. "It would be a damn shame if the world lost a treatment for ALS because of these greedy bastards."

"Exactly," Maggie said. "I imagine someone will buy the remains and take the drug into people. The biotech world is very efficient." They drank some, looking at the tide moving out slowly. "But what I really wanted to ask you about now relates to Dad's time in Vietnam, and his marriage with Hue. When I was undercover at Quercus, Benny and I started reading through Dad's journals from back then. We never found their marriage certificate. Mom doesn't know where it is. She cleaned out their safety deposit box when she left for California, and it wasn't there. Do you know?"

"Yes, I have it here," George said. "Henry gave it to me for safekeeping before he married Jessica. I'm not sure why. I just put it away."

"So you knew about Mai all these years, and you never thought it worth mentioning to Benny that he had a sister? Or that I had a half-sister?" Maggie could feel her face getting redder. "Seriously? More of this non-communication crap that our family specializes in?"

She took a deep breath. Calm down, she thought. It wasn't his secret to tell, was it? "We found out about Hue, and Mai, and the whole mess in Vietnam. But the diaries don't say what happened to Mai and Quan and Trang. They just disappeared in An Lộc. Did he ever go back there to find out?"

George looked out at the ocean. He sipped his drink. The ice cubes made a soft clinking sound as the liquid level fell in the glass. He sighed. Maggie had a lot of experience waiting out people who were psyching themselves up to talk about something painful, so she waited, unmoving. If I were a dog, I'd have my ears forward and one paw off the ground, she thought.

Finally, George turned back to her. "It's complicated," he said. "Henry tried to find out about Mai. Nothing was possible for the first twenty years after the fall of Saigon, you know? They normalized relations between the US and Vietnam in 1995, but even then it was another few years before there was regular travel from here to there. Henry tried to go back in, oh, I think it was 1997, but there was still a lot of anger and distrust of Americans. He came back very dejected, saying he'd hit a stone wall of silence."

"But he kept at it. He went back again around 2006 or 2007, I think it was. That time he hired a local guide to help him, and he went back to An Lộc and then worked with people at the National Archives in Vietnam. He went to both Saigon – I guess it was Ho Chi Minh City by then – and Hanoi. He was there for weeks. When he came back, he wouldn't say much about it. Just said that Mai had survived the war, but that she was 'gone now'. Those are the words he used. 'Gone now.' He wouldn't tell me what he meant by that. And you know your father – if he didn't want to talk about something, he just wouldn't."

Maggie nodded. "Oh, yes, I remember him stonewalling me about many things. And there's nothing in his journals either. He stopped writing after Hue died, in 1983. Or if he did keep writing a journal, I don't have it. All I have is what mom kept. Do you know of any others?"

"No," George said. "You know, we weren't that close in those years. He was teaching full time, and I was traveling all over doing concerts and albums…"

Maggie grinned, "And you were in your stoner phase, weren't you?"

"Well, that too, officer, but I'm clean now."

"Lucky for you, recreational marijuana is legal in this state."

"Damn skippy it is," George said. "And so is gin."

"Gin they had on the Mayflower. Just stay off the hard stuff."

"Anyway," George said, "Henry never said another word about Mai, or Quan or Trang for that matter. I always wondered what happened to them, and if Mai is still out there somewhere. Probably never know, now."

Maggie sat up, putting her drink down on the table. "Well, let's not get too pessimistic. I'm a trained investigator, you know. And I've got a lot of leave coming to me after this Quercus thing, since I'm on Temporary Modified Duty thanks to Employee Assistance. Thomas van Haft's trial won't start till October, and that's when I'll have to be here to testify. Until then, I think I need a vacation. I hear Vietnam is very nice this time of year. Wanna come with me?"

The End

Acknowledgements

I would like to thank my friends and family who indulged me through the writing of this story, and who read and reviewed and commented to make it better. Special thanks to Joan Fowler, my former English teacher who taught me to love American Lit. And to Coos Hamburger, my brother by another mother, whose insights on many, many topics have guided me for decades. I am also very grateful to all my colleagues in biotech and pharma who have contributed – knowingly or not – to the development of the characters in this book. Any resemblance to actual people, living or deceased, is unintended; the characters in this story are all blended from people I have known or worked with over the years, although no one I have actually met has been a murderer, to the best of my knowledge.

My thanks to the staff of the Massachusetts State Police Museum and Learning Center in Northbridge, MA, for patiently answering my questions. I am also grateful to Nguyen Phan Que Mai for her excellent book, *Dust Child*, and its poignant description of Amerasian children in Viet Nam and America.

About the Author

Ronenn Roubenoff trained in internal medicine, epidemiology, and rheumatology at Johns Hopkins, and did postdoctoral training in inflammation and nutrition at Tufts University. He was Global Head of Translational Medicine Discovery and Profiling at Novartis Institutes for Biomedical Research, in Cambridge, MA, USA and Basel, Switzerland until he retired in 2023. He is also Adjunct Professor of Medicine at Tufts. He is an internationally recognized authority on sarcopenia, obesity, osteoarthritis, translational medicine, and the use of biomarkers in drug development. He has published over 280 papers in the medical literature, as well as writing for lay audiences. He has won multiple awards, including membership in the Alpha Omega Alpha and Delta Omega honor societies; Fellow of the American College of Physicians and the American College of Rheumatology; and the Robert H. Herman Memorial Award of the American Society for Nutrition. He lives in Brookline, MA.

www.ingramcontent.com/pod-product-compliance
Lightning Source LLC
Chambersburg PA
CBHW070613310726
48982CB00001B/71

* 9 7 9 8 9 9 9 6 6 1 9 2 0 *